Paranormal Romance by Kate Douglas

DemonFire
HellFire
"Crystal Dreams" in *Nocturnal*
StarFire

Erotic Romance by Kate Douglas

Wolf Tales
"Chanku Rising" in *Sexy Beast*
Wolf Tales II
"Camille's Dawn" in *Wild Nights*
Wolf Tales III
"Chanku Fallen" in *Sexy Beast II*
Wolf Tales IV
"Chanku Journey" in *Sexy Beast III*
Wolf Tales V
"Chanku Destiny" in *Sexy Beast IV*
Wolf Tales VI
"Chanku Wild" in *Sexy Beast V*
Wolf Tales VII
"Chanku Honor" in *Sexy Beast VI*
Wolf Tales VIII
"Chanku Challenge" in *Sexy Beast VII*
Wolf Tales 9
"Chanku Spirit" in *Sexy Beast VIII*
Wolf Tales 10
Wolf Tales 11
Wolf Tales 12

Published by Kensington Publishing Corporation

starfire
The DemonSlayers

KATE DOUGLAS

ZEBRA BOOKS
KENSINGTON PUBLISHING CORP.

http://www.kensingtonbooks.com

ZEBRA BOOKS are published by

Kensington Publishing Corp.
119 West 40th Street
New York, NY 10018

All Kensington titles, imprints, and distributed lines are available at special quantity discounts for bulk purchases for sales promotion, premiums, fund-raising, educational, or institutional use.

Special book excerpts or customized printings can also be created to fit specific needs. For details, write or phone the office of the Kensington Special Sales Manager: Attn. Special Sales Department. Kensington Publishing Corp., 119 West 40th Street, New York, NY 10018. Phone: 1-800-221-2647.

Zebra and the Z logo Reg. U.S. Pat. & TM Off.

ISBN-13: 978-1-4201-1001-2
ISBN-10: 1-4201-1001-2

First Printing: April 2011

10 9 8 7 6 5 4 3 2 1

Printed in the United States of America

*This one's for Rufus,
the fuzzy, neurotic little mutt who
keeps me company in my office,
loves me no matter what, and
reminds me that even writers need to get up and
take walks on occasion*

ACKNOWLEDGMENTS

There's nothing quite like brutal honesty to keep an author humble—and also eternally grateful. My sincere—and humble—thanks to my brutally honest, absolutely terrific beta readers who somehow manage to find time in their own hectic schedules to critically read my completed manuscripts and let me know in no uncertain terms when the story needs work. On this project, Karen Woods, Jan Takane, Sheri Ross Fogarty, Rhonda Wilson, Rose Toubbeh, and Margaret Riley, aka Shelby Morgen, definitely went above and beyond the call of duty. Many thanks to all of you.

My sincere thanks to my editor Audrey LaFehr for her insightful comments and revision suggestions, to assistant editor Martin Biro, who somehow manages to hold it all together, and to my agent Jessica Faust, BookEnds LLC, for always knowing the right thing to say and exactly when I need to hear it.

Thanks also to Kensington's amazing art department for once again coming through with an absolute killer cover. You guys are fantastic!

And last but not least, I want to give a heartfelt "thank you" to my copy editor on this book—Debra Roth Kane—for not only finding the obvious errors, but also for noticing those subtle glitches that can make or break a story. I am in awe of your eagle eye!

Chapter One

The crystal mines beneath Lemuria

The steady *drip, drip, drip* and the soft hum of overtaxed air purifiers were the only sounds Selyn heard as she cautiously pushed herself away from the cavern wall and moved silently through darkness to the sleeping quarters.

With any luck she might be able to catch a couple hours of rest before her shift started, but she'd missed the evening meal in order to make her clandestine meeting with Roland of Kronus. It would be a long time before she had another opportunity to break fast.

A hulking shadow suddenly filled the narrow passageway. Light glinted off pale eyes set in a massive frame a full foot and a half taller and three times wider than her own.

Nine hells. As usual, her luck sucked. Selyn straightened to her full height, raised her chin, and looked the guard in the eye. That alone should be enough to piss him off. The vicious wardens who kept the Forgotten Ones imprisoned here in the mines were quick to anger. If she could truly infuriate him, he might even forget to ask why she was wandering along a passage so far from the slaves' quarters.

"Ah, Birk. Fancy meeting you here." She folded her arms across her chest and hoped he couldn't see how she trembled. Showing fear was the same as giving up.

Selyn never showed fear. Never would she give up.

The huge guard didn't say a word. His fist came out of nowhere. The crushing blow to her cheekbone left her lying dazed and barely conscious on the ground.

He planted his hands on his hips and leaned over her. "So, bitch. You want to tell me what you're doing out here?"

Blinking back the shooting lights blinding her, Selyn slowly shook her head.

He grabbed her hair in a meaty fist and jerked her to her feet.

"Ouch! Nine hells!" She twisted away. He grabbed her breast through the thin cloth of her robe and squeezed. Thick fingers dug into soft flesh.

"Ah!" Excruciating pain blinded her. Frantically, Selyn bucked and writhed, but his grasp only tightened on her breast and in her hair. She lashed out with her bare foot, and connected just below his right knee.

Birk cursed. His leg buckled, and he lost his grip on her breast. Selyn jerked her head up as he fell. She slammed him hard under the chin, but her long hair was still tangled in his fist. He pulled her down with him.

Scrambling beneath his massive weight, she broke free, kicked again, and caught him soundly between the legs. Birk roared in pain and clutched his balls, but her hair was still tangled in his thick fingers. He jerked her head sharply down and caught her between his thighs.

Twisting, turning, Selyn struggled for freedom. Birk flipped her beneath him, clamping down on her head and shoulders with his powerful legs. Enraged, he tore his hand free of her hair and punched her with both fists, landing powerful blows across her chest, along her ribs.

She felt one rib crack, and then another. Gasping, unable to move or catch her breath, her vision clouded. She couldn't breathe, couldn't fight, could not give up. Not this close. Not with freedom only days away.

Blow after blow slammed into her ribs. Frantically, Selyn sucked in a breath of life-giving air and tasted blood. Darkness broken by fitful flashes of sparking lights closed in on all sides, but the terrible pounding continued. Then, somehow, she floated free, apart from the hammering fists, as if she hovered in a separate space, beyond pain, beyond fear.

Maybe freedom would finally come as her mother's had—in death. Did it really matter anymore? Selyn no longer felt the blows, even as Birk continued to pummel her unresisting body.

A beautiful, achingly familiar face swam hauntingly just beyond her reach. With split and bleeding lips Selyn whispered her mother's name.

"Elda?"

There was no answer, no sign of recognition, but it was all right. Her mother, once a proud warrior who long ago fought demons beside battle-hardened Lemurian men, had found peace in death. Only days ago Elda had come to Selyn in her dreams. She'd told her daughter she'd been reborn to fight again—reborn in a crystal sword called DemonSlayer.

Was that to be Selyn's path out of this hellhole? Through death? No matter. Not anymore. Giving in to the darkness, Selyn gratefully embraced the only freedom she had ever known.

At last.

Freedom, and darkness, and death.

* * *

Finally. After mere days of frantic discussions, they were moving against the Council of Nine tonight. Though Roland had been part of Alton of Artigos's plans since the beginning, he still feared what their actions against the ruling body would mean should they fail.

Failure is not an option. The fate of Lemuria—of all worlds—depends on us.

Alton's words still rang in Roland's ears as he reached Selyn's level in the caverns. He cast out his thoughts. Though he'd only known the young woman for a few days—since first venturing into the mines in search of proof of the terrible rumors of slave-keeping—she'd always responded immediately, even if he awakened her from sleep.

This time, he heard nothing. A great void where her active mind should be. He glanced along the shadowed tunnel and prayed to the gods he'd not be discovered. He had no business at this level. None at all, but Selyn should have answered by now.

He grasped his crystal sword and walked purposefully down the dark passageway. The lighting was dim and did little to dispel the shadows. Calling silently for Selyn, he rounded a slight curve and stopped dead.

A body lay in the middle of the corridor. A woman's body. From the long tangled mass of her coal black hair and the coppery color of her skin, it could only be Selyn. Roland glanced both ways, saw no one, and raced to her side.

"Ah, child . . . what in nine hells have the bastards done to you?" Kneeling beside her, he pressed his fingertips to the big artery in her throat and felt for her pulse. Erratic, unsteady, it fluttered beneath his fingertips. Her eyes were closed, her face battered and swollen, her rough-spun robe badly torn. Bloody saliva foamed at the corner of her lips.

Roland couldn't risk a call for help. The only ones strong enough to have hurt Selyn this badly were the wardens who guarded the Forgotten Ones. Selyn's latest trip to meet him at the upper level must have been discovered, but how could anyone have done such a horrible thing?

He glanced about, saw and heard nothing but his own harsh breathing, and accepted his duty. Though Alton had sent him below to warn the Forgotten Ones of tonight's coup, he had to get Selyn out of here, and hope like the nine hells she lived long enough for him to find a healer.

Carefully, Roland slipped his hands beneath her slim body and lifted her as gently as he could. He cradled the broken young woman against his chest and carried her down the dark tunnel, passing through portals and eventually reaching the first set of steps without anyone spotting him. Then he began the long climb to the surface. But where could he take her? Not to anyone in Lemuria. Members of the aristocracy claimed ignorance of slavery's existence.

Roland hadn't wanted to believe Lemuria kept its own citizens as slaves, but fear the rumors were true had driven his search. What he'd found was worse than anything he could possibly have imagined. All those poor young women, daughters of Lemuria's brave warrior women who'd been secretly purged from society, condemned to lives of slavery in the crystal mines.

Condemned, it appeared, by Alton's father, the head of the Council of Nine.

No, he'd not find help for Selyn in Lemuria. It would have to be someone in Earth's dimension.

She was still alive, but barely, when Roland finally reached the upper levels and made telepathic contact with Alton. The young aristocrat didn't hesitate. He set his earlier plans for tonight's coup aside and told Roland where they could safely meet.

Less than an hour later, Roland passed through the Lemurian portal that led directly into the energy vortex in Bell Rock, a large formation outside of Sedona, Arizona. Alton waited in the dark chamber with his woman, Ginny Jones, close beside him.

The Lemurian heir to the council took one look at the battered woman in Roland's arms and cursed, shaking his head in dismay. "Ah, Roland, my friend. How could this be?"

Roland was shocked to see Alton's eyes sparkling with compassionate tears—tears that reaffirmed Roland's decision to follow the young aristocrat no matter where he might lead. This was not a man interested in power. No— Alton's only goal was a strong and vital Lemuria, and equality for all its citizens.

Ginny gasped and stepped close. "Oh, my God." She lightly touched the pulse point on Selyn's throat and looked up at Roland. "She's still alive, but her pulse is so weak. Who did this to her?"

Roland shook his head. Anger, frustration, and his fear for the girl's life had him blurting out, "One of the gods-be-damned guards, I imagine. I hear they treat the women most cruelly, but I've never seen anyone so viciously beaten."

"Will she live?" Alton's soft question calmed him.

He sighed. "I don't know. I'm sure she's got broken ribs, internal injuries. She's a tough one, though. At least she's still breathing."

Alton wrapped his arm protectively around Ginny. "I had no idea when you contacted me that she was so badly injured." He glanced at Ginny. "Do you think Dawson can help her? He's a veterinarian, after all, not a doctor for humans."

Ginny stared at Selyn so intently, Roland felt as if she

were trying to force the injured woman to heal by the strength of her will alone.

"He's going to have to," she said. "Alton, we have to see if Dax and Eddy can bring BumperWillow. Willow might be able to help, but we need to hurry. Roland? Can you come with us?"

He'd not spent much time in Earth's dimension, and never here in Sedona. It was forbidden, after all, but a young woman's life was, literally, in his hands. "Yes," he said, gazing at the battered girl he held as gently as he could. "I can."

Chara would understand. His wife was used to the long hours he kept, though she had no idea the danger he faced. It was just as well. What was the point of alarming her?

Alton led the way through another, smaller portal. They stepped out into a cavern almost identical to the first. "We just moved from one side of Sedona to the other using the vortex," he said. He pointed to a shimmering gateway on one wall. "That's a secret portal we've discovered that leads directly to the chambers of the Council of Nine, but do not use it to return. The risk of being caught by a member of the council makes it too dangerous. We'll go this way." He nodded toward another glowing portal. "We're meeting a friend of ours here who should be able to help the girl."

Lightly he touched Roland's shoulder. "I can take her if you're getting tired. He'll have his vehicle waiting nearby."

Roland nodded. "I'm okay. Let's hurry." Even though his arms ached from carrying her, Roland didn't want to risk further injury to Selyn by shifting her to Alton's grasp. She hadn't stirred, but she drew soft, shallow breaths, proof she still lived. Thank the gods she was unconscious and, hopefully, unaware of pain.

They stepped out into a star-filled night. Roland had

seen stars once before, when he'd fought demons a few days earlier on the flanks of Mount Shasta, but he knew he'd never get the chance to see them enough. Damn it all, but his people had lost too much when their continent sank beneath the sea.

They had survived these many millennia, but at what cost?

Life without stars, without the warmth of the sun. Anger gave Roland strength for the short hike down the dark path. He was still grumbling to himself when they rounded a curve in the trail. Alton flashed his handheld light at a large vehicle waiting in the shadows. A dark-haired man—tall for a human—climbed out and quickly opened the back door. Roland nodded without speaking and carefully slid into the wide seat with Selyn still in his arms.

"Who in the hell did this to her?" Dawson Buck leaned in the open door and pressed his fingers to the girl's throat. He was surprised by the strong pulse he found.

The big Lemurian holding her nodded tersely. "One of the guards must have caught her after our meeting. Her name is Selyn—one of the Forgotten Ones. Can you help her?"

Dawson nodded and raced around the SUV to the driver's seat. His hands shook as he turned the key in the ignition, though he had no idea if it was from fear of the job ahead or rage at what had been done to an innocent young woman.

Her face was battered beyond recognition, eyes swollen shut, lips badly split. Her gown was drenched in blood. From the bloody froth at her lips, he figured she probably had a punctured lung, which meant broken ribs.

He was still shaking when they reached his house just a couple of miles away. Dawson got out, walked quickly to the house, unlocked the front door, and held it open.

The Lemurian guard held the girl as if she were the most fragile of china. He walked briskly down the long hallway to Dawson's small home clinic at the back of the house. Carefully he laid his bruised and bleeding burden down on the examining table.

Then, with an exhausted sigh, he turned and focused on Dawson. "You will save her life, healer. You must. She is much too fine a young woman to die like this."

Before Dawson could reply, Alton grabbed the guard's arm. "Come, Roland. We'll leave the healer to his work. You need food and rest."

Nodding silently, the big man followed Alton out of the room. Dawson raised his head and stared at Ginny.

"I'll help," she said. "Just tell me what I need to do."

He breathed a huge sigh of relief. "Thank you."

He could do this. He had to.

Clearing his mind of everything but helping this young woman survive, Dawson went to work.

Finishing up after a long day at his clinic in town, Dawson had been prepared for another quiet night at home when his cell phone rang. He'd certainly never expected to hear Alton's voice. When he'd recently offered to help his new friends in their battle against a demon invasion, Dawson honestly hadn't thought anyone would actually call.

He was, after all, merely human. What good could a mortal do among creatures who were not only virtually immortal but capable of things he'd only read of in his favorite science fiction novels?

But when Alton told him one of their kind was badly injured and in need of medical attention, Dawson hadn't hesitated. He'd quickly finished up the nightly feeding of his canine and feline patients, locked the doors to his clinic, and raced to the parking lot at Red Rock Crossing near the energy vortex at Cathedral Rock.

And there he'd waited. He'd had plenty of time to think about the changes in his life since that morning, a little over a week ago, when he'd arrived a bit late at his veterinary clinic and discovered the place was already filled with dozens of animal patients—all exhibiting the same unbelievable behavior.

He knew his staff thought he was slightly nuts when he'd suggested the pets were all possessed by demons. Of course, he was well aware that his capable young assistant as well as the women who worked for him looked at his offbeat diagnosis as part of his charm.

They loved to tease him about his easy acceptance of the mystical stories about the land around Sedona and the energy vortexes. Most folks thought of the stories as nothing more than fodder for the tourist trade.

His Aunt Fiona had been the only one who truly understood him. When he was little and talked to his imaginary friends, she'd called him fey. As he'd grown older and lost himself in books with tales of the unusual and unexplained, she'd merely nodded and said he was learning to understand things that a lot of his real-life friends would never be able to see.

The imaginary friends had eventually faded away, cast out by a teenaged boy's need to act like everyone else, but Aunt Fiona had understood. She'd told him that when he was ready, they'd come back.

Now, as Dawson stared at his wristwatch and realized he'd spent an entire night treating a woman who couldn't possibly exist, he sent a silent thank you to his long departed aunt. He could almost swear he heard her chuckling laughter and the soft, Gaelic lilt to her voice whispering, "I told you so, me boyo. I told you so."

Smiling through the memories of someone so dear, Dawson stretched his arms over his head and heard the pop and snap of tired joints. It was almost five A.M.—the time when he normally crawled out of bed to start his day—but he'd stayed with Selyn throughout the night. By now, he figured Alton and Roland, the big Lemurian guard, were probably sacked out on the couches in the main quarters of his house.

He checked his patient's pulse. It was steady now, and she was breathing easier. He'd worried about carrying her from the clinic to the spare room, but he knew she'd be more comfortable here in a regular bed, rather than on the hard examining table where he'd worked on her bruised and battered body.

He hoped Ginny had gotten some sleep. She'd assisted him for hours, playing the unaccustomed role of nurse. By the time he'd finished all of his stitching and doctoring, Ginny'd looked exhausted and a little bit numb from all the blood. Daws had sent her off a couple of hours ago while he finished cleaning up and bandaging the worst of the young woman's injuries.

They'd been extensive and well beyond his training. He'd suctioned blood out of chest cavities for dogs and cats that'd been hit by cars, but he'd never done it for a woman with a punctured lung—at least, not until last night.

Dawson gazed down at the young woman now resting as comfortably as could be expected, and hoped he'd done the right thing. He was a veterinarian, for crying out loud! He dealt with dogs and cats, birds, rabbits, and the occasional hamster or guinea pig—not young, beautiful women barely clinging to life.

What if he'd screwed up? What if she died?

What choice did he have?

None at all, according to Alton. They couldn't take

Selyn to a human doctor, and they couldn't take her to one of their own healers. It had been Dawson Buck or no one. Her lung had been the most serious injury, along with bruising to her spleen and liver. Her cracked and broken ribs would hurt like hell for a while, but they'd heal. He'd stitched a couple of spots on her side where heavy blows had actually split her skin, but most of her injuries were bloody scrapes, bruises, and contusions.

The darkly defined fingerprints on her right breast sickened him. More than once during the long night he'd thought of killing the one who had done this to her. That was so unlike him. Dawson had never been the violent sort. He abhorred conflict of any kind, which was why he'd chosen animals as his patients. Dogs and cats were more the *what you see is what you get* kinds of patients. They rarely came with baggage, and they didn't hold grudges.

Even now, he wasn't sure what he'd expected when Alton had called him, but it certainly hadn't been a beautiful young woman who'd been beaten nearly to death.

He rested his fingers on her shoulder, one of the few spots without the mottled black and blue and red from bruises. Though he wasn't a religious man, his prayer was heartfelt.

Dear God. Let her live. Please, let her live.

Taking a deep breath, Dawson tried to ignore the rapid pounding of his heart. For a brief moment, he thought of all the laws he'd broken by treating a female victim of an obvious assault. Any other medical doctor would have followed the law and reported this to the police. Another veterinarian would have made sure she was treated properly, in a hospital for humans.

Then he bit back a nervous laugh. Who was he trying to kid? She wasn't human. Maybe he hadn't broken any laws after all, but after he'd looked at all her injuries and realized how terribly she'd been hurt, Dawson had known there was no question at all as to whether or not he'd do whatever he could for her.

Now he could only hope his efforts had helped and not harmed her. He gently touched a dark bruise on her cheek. Thank goodness the facial bone was merely bruised, not broken. Her bruises would fade; the ribs would heal.

But what of her state of mind? A beating this horrific had to leave more than bruises on the body. He'd learned that these Lemurians healed much faster than humans. They were obviously a lot tougher, too. Her injuries would have killed a human woman.

Plus, injuries such as these would definitely leave emotional scars with a human. He had no idea how a Lemurian might react to such terrible treatment.

Alton said she was a slave.

Then he'd really confused the issue when he told Dawson that Lemurians were a free society, that they didn't believe in slavery. He, Alton of Artigos, the son of Lemuria's chancellor, had not even known of the slaves' existence.

Not until Roland, the sergeant of the Lemurian Guard, had taken it upon himself to follow up on rumors and search for the women who called themselves the Forgotten Ones. Roland had met Selyn and learned of their terrible history. He'd offered Alton's promise to help the women, and in turn, Selyn had agreed they would help Alton with his plot to overthrow his father.

She'd been willing to risk everything for freedom.

Now, this.

Dawson sighed. He wished she were awake and could tell him she would be okay, wished he knew for sure he'd done the right thing by not taking her to a hospital. What a mess.

Obviously, there were things going on in Lemuria that were every bit as convoluted as human politics.

And this young woman was unquestionably a hero.

A breathtakingly beautiful hero.

Dawson carefully pushed her tangled hair away from her face and tucked the soft blanket around her badly beaten body. He couldn't bear to look at her, to see such perfection so terribly disfigured by someone's cruelty, and it wasn't just the fact that her injuries made him so angry.

No, it was even more unsettling. Her beauty and bravery affected him on a most unexpected—and unprofessional—level.

He'd done all he could as a doctor with the detachment his position required. Now that he'd finished, he realized he saw her as any man would see a beautiful woman. Those dark bruises and bloody contusions were a travesty, a horrible insult to such perfection. He'd never seen anyone as perfect as Selyn. Even battered and bruised, she was lovely.

Lovely and very brave—and right now, Dawson Buck was a terribly conflicted doctor.

Never once in his life had he lusted after a patient.

Shaking his head with the convoluted stupidity of his thoughts, Dawson quickly turned away from her bed. He left the room, mumbling under his breath.

"Of course you've never lusted after a patient, you idiot. All the others have four legs."

Chapter Two

Selyn drifted awake in a world of pain. Eyes closed, she took a moment to catalog the various parts of her body. She must have survived Birk's horrible beating, though she wondered if she'd be whole, even if her injuries healed.

Others had died beneath the wardens' heavy fists. She knew she was alive. She hurt too much to be dead.

Carefully, Selyn wriggled her toes, then her fingers. They worked. That was good. Slowly, cautiously, she licked her dry, cracked lips with the tip of her tongue. Her chest ached, and it hurt to breathe, but at least she could draw sufficient air, as long as she did it carefully.

Taking another breath, she noticed that the stench she'd long associated with her world was missing. Instead, the air lacked any discernible scent at all. Squinting through swollen lids, she saw cream-colored walls and shelves neatly filled with books and jars and unfamiliar stuff. There were cabinets with closed doors and light streaming in through a window.

Window? She knew what windows were, but in the mines they looked out onto dark caverns and poorly lit passageways. Blinking, curious enough now to risk drawing attention, Selyn tried to sit up. "Nine hells!" . . . *and then some.* Gasping, she lay back against the pillow and tried to catch her breath.

The door flew open, and a tall, lean man stepped into the room. "Don't move. Please. Be still, or you'll hurt yourself."

Fear left her speechless, but only for a moment. Then she took a deep, calming breath—or as deep a breath as she could with lungs that hurt and ribs that ached. "I discovered that on my own, thank you." Aware she wore nothing beneath the blanket, Selyn tugged the soft folds higher, almost to her chin. "Who are you? Where am I?"

He smiled and his dark blue eyes actually seemed to sparkle as the corners of his mouth, almost hidden in facial hair, turned upward. "I'm Dawson Buck," he said. He moved closer, slowly and carefully as if he knew his presence frightened her. "You're in my house, in Sedona. It's in Earth's dimension. Roland of Kronus brought you here last night. You were badly injured and unconscious." He shook his head and smiled even wider. "I wasn't sure you'd awaken this soon. You must be healing faster than I expected."

There were dimples in both his cheeks, partially hidden by his neatly trimmed facial hair. Selyn frowned as she studied him. She'd never seen hair on a man's face before. She'd been told that Lemurian men had body hair in places besides the tops of their heads, though she'd never seen a naked man. She knew absolutely nothing about human men, but the dark hair framing this one's lips and covering his chin was absolutely fascinating.

Besides, it was easier to concentrate on the odd growth of hair and those delightful dimples than to think of what he'd just said.

She was on Earth? But how? Lemurians were forbidden to leave their world, though she knew from snips of gossip

that Alton of Artigos had crossed through the portal. It was
said his woman—one who carried sentient crystal—actually
came from this world, but Roland? How would he know to
bring her here? And why?

"It was last night?" She wanted to sit up. She wanted
her clothing, and she wanted to get away while she had the
chance. Earth! She'd dreamed of one day seeing Earth.
Maybe she could disappear into one of the cities she'd
heard tales about.

Disappear and never return.

Never have to face Birk or any of the other guards
again.

*Never hold the crystal sword Taron is replicating for me
even now.*

Selyn thought of her mother's spirit, bravely fighting
demons once again as the sentience in a sword called
DemonSlayer. Who would inhabit the sword Taron might
have already finished making for her? What woman warrior would be her partner in battle? If Selyn left Lemuria
now, she'd never know.

She'd be forever a fugitive, trying to exist in a world
where she didn't belong. No, she couldn't leave. As one of
the Forgotten Ones, as the daughter of a woman warrior,
Selyn knew she was honor bound to stay. She sighed.
Always a slave, but a slave to honor as much as to the mines.

She focused once again on the man.

"Yes," he was saying. "Roland brought you here late
last night." He stepped closer.

She flinched. She hadn't meant to, but he was big and
male and what she knew about men wasn't very comforting.

He stopped. Held his hands out in front of him, as if he
meant to show her he was safe. He had big hands, but not
like Birk's. No, his had long, slim fingers and neatly
trimmed nails. His hands fell to his sides. "I won't hurt

you," he said. His voice was deep but very soft. Gentle. "Please. I just wanted to check your eyes. Make sure they're tracking correctly. You have a head injury." He sighed. "Among so many others."

Swallowing, Selyn nibbled on her swollen lip and nodded. He sat on the edge of the bed and used a small tube to shine a bright light into her eyes. He moved it back and forth, and she followed the light as he asked. He clicked it off and stuck the thing in his pocket. Then he lifted her hair away from the side of her face and gently touched her cheekbone.

"Oh!" She grabbed his wrist.

"I'm sorry." He jerked his hands away from her. "I didn't mean to hurt you."

She stared, even as she felt the flush spreading across her face. How could she possibly tell him it hadn't hurt at all? She wasn't quite certain what she'd felt when he'd touched her so gently, but it certainly hadn't been pain.

Before she had time to wonder further, there was a loud noise and the sound of something sliding across the floor. The door to the room flew open, and a curly-haired creature with four legs and huge teeth bounded into the room. It skidded across the floor and stopped beside the bed, wriggling all over.

"Hey, Bumper!" Dawson Buck leaned over and patted the creature's head.

A voice sounded in Selyn's mind. A voice filled with laughter. *You must be the one Eddy told me about. Are you Selyn?*

Selyn's gaze flashed toward Dawson and back to the beast. "What creature is this? It speaks to me!"

Dawson grinned at her. "This is BumperWillow, though you're actually speaking to Willow. Bumper is the dog— the animal you see—and Willow is the spirit of a tiny sprite, like a fairy, whose body was destroyed by demons. Her consciousness found safety inside the dog, so they sort of live in there together."

Selyn wanted to touch the beast, but her arms ached too badly to reach for the softly curling coat.

"Hey, Dawson. Good morning! BumperWillow, you were supposed to wait." A beautiful woman stepped into the room. She looked directly at Selyn and smiled. "You must be Selyn. I'm Eddy Marks. Alton thought Willow might be able to help you heal faster. Willow? Can you help?"

I can. Will you lift me up on the bed, Dawson? I don't want to jump up there and maybe bump Selyn's bruises.

Dawson picked up the solid little beast and set her on the bed beside Selyn. Selyn looked into intelligent brown eyes surrounded by silly blond curls. She'd never seen a dog before, though Lemurian history mentioned their existence.

That was long before her time. Before Lemuria sank beneath the sea, before the brave women warriors were purged and exiled from an ungrateful Lemurian society.

Before her mother's untimely death. Then, before she could follow that terrible line of thought any deeper, Selyn felt a soothing warmth spread over her body. It was easier to breathe, easier to move, but so relaxing that she settled back against her pillow and lay still while the silly dog stared at her with the eyes of a healer.

Who would ever believe? She had to go back to the mines, if only to tell her sisters of the wonders of this world. Drifting, she wondered what the next days would bring. Would Taron, a man she'd never even met, have the swords ready, one for each of the women? Would they really be free after a lifetime of slavery?

He was risking so much to help women he didn't even know, staying deep below the mines in the hidden crystal caves, with only one sword to replicate a full one hundred more.

One for each of the forgotten daughters.

She hoped her mother would somehow know that her daughter was helping the cause for freedom. Elda would be so proud to know Selyn hadn't forgotten her teachings.

"How do you feel?"

Dawson's voice snapped Selyn back to reality. Freedom was still a long way off. Holding the blankets tightly against her chest, she tried to sit up. His big hands helped, as he gently supported her back and slipped one hand beneath the covers to lift her legs, to help her scoot back against the headboard.

The feel of his warm palm against her bare thighs was unsettling. Not unpleasant, yet definitely disconcerting. Just as confusing as the equally warm, strong hand supporting her naked back.

Once she was upright, he pulled his hands away and tucked the blankets around her. Selyn had been so aware of his touch, she hadn't noticed the absence of pain. Where were the bruises, the painful ribs? She ran her tongue over smooth lips that had been badly split and swollen. Dawson handed her a mirror, and she gazed at her reflection. There were no marks at all, no sign of her injuries. "Amazing." She stared at the dog. "You did this?"

I did. You are too beautiful to be covered with ugly bruises. I'm glad I could help, though Dawson had already repaired the truly serious injuries.

Thank you, Willow. Selyn ran her fingers through the dog's saucy curls. "And thank you, Bumper. I feel well. As if I'd not been hurt at all."

Eddy grinned at her. "That's terrific. We need you healthy. I think the next few days are going to be crazy. I sure hope Taron is . . ." Her words drifted to a stop, as if she listened to someone Selyn couldn't see or hear. Then Eddy's eyes went wide. She reached over her shoulder and withdrew her sword.

Selyn had never seen a crystal sword up close. The guards in the mines all carried steel, and Roland had kept his crystal blade sheathed. This was the most beautiful thing she'd ever seen. Eddy lay the long blade on the bed beside Selyn and gazed at her for a moment with what could only be compassion.

Selyn frowned. Eddy grabbed her hand and placed Selyn's fingers atop the shimmering crystal. It was warm to the touch.

"Selyn, this is my crystal blade," she said. "She is sentient. The first time she spoke to me, she told me her name was DemonSlayer. But I believe you know the spirit that gives life to my sword. Was the warrior Elda your mother?"

Taron of Libernus rose from his thin pallet and set another glow stick in the sconce on the wall near the altar he'd discovered so far beneath the world he'd once thought he knew. As he replaced the fading stick from the night before, a stark, blue-white light burst forth and reflected from crystal walls that seemed to stretch forever, illuminating the huge cavern as if from a million different lamps.

Who would have guessed such beauty lay beneath his world? How many of Lemuria had ever ventured to such depths before?

Someone, obviously, if the crystal altar meant anything. It appeared to have been carved from a single blood-red ruby, the only colored crystal in the entire cavern. A cavern his sword had led him to.

His silent sword. He chuckled ruefully, recalling how

thrilled he'd been when first learning of this mission he'd been charged with—to use his own sword to replicate more crystal swords for the Forgotten Ones.

Forgotten? More like unknown. It was hard to believe that there had been slaves working the mines of Lemuria for thousands of years—women unknown to the rest of Lemurian society.

Once he'd learned what would be required of him, he'd sworn to do everything in his power to end the abuse of the remaining women. He'd actually *felt* the vow he'd sworn to Alton and the others—like a physical mark branded upon his heart. He, Taron of Libernus, would help to free these women. It was his duty as a free man of Lemuria to see that no one endured a life enslaved.

Slavery was wrong. It went against everything Lemurians stood for, and he embraced this challenge, heart and soul. He'd felt it so strongly, experienced the sense of his oath so powerfully, that he'd been certain it meant his own sword would finally speak to him.

If nothing else, wouldn't the blasted thing have to tell him how to find the place where the swords would be created?

Obviously not, because he'd found this cavern without any trouble at all. Somehow he'd known where to go. He stared at the sword lying across the altar. "It didn't work that way, my old friend, did it? Maybe you've just been too busy to talk." He reached out, grasped the jeweled hilt, and lifted his sword from the altar. Lying beneath it, row after row of perfect crystal blades shimmered in the reflected light, each one identical to his beautiful—albeit silent—weapon.

He turned the blade, swinging it in careful strokes before setting it back on the altar. "One day I'll prove myself worthy. I promise you that."

Then he carefully stacked the swords that had appeared

during the hours he'd slept and added them to the growing pile. There were close to a hundred. He should have the last of them before this week ended.

Whenever that might be. He'd lost track of days and nights since his arrival, though he'd not been bored.

No, while his sword had birthed more crystal, by whatever magical means it happened, he'd explored the other crystal caverns beneath the world of Lemuria. Room after room, ranging in color from deepest amethyst to ruby red to the pure blue of sapphire, from deep yellow citrine to brilliant green emerald.

It had been like walking through multi-colored geodes, each room expanding to the one beyond, shimmering with huge crystals—precious gems curving overhead in crystalline perfection.

He'd found clear streams of pure water and tiny creatures that obviously had never seen the light of day. Having lived so long in a world without animal life, he'd been fascinated by the blind frogs and eyeless salamanders, and he'd wondered what they found for food so deep within the Lemurian dimension.

Or, was he still in Lemuria? He'd gone well beyond the level of the mines, those horrible caves where he'd heard the sound of women's voices and the creak and groan of heavy machinery. The sounds of women toiling and men shouting out orders had been all the proof he'd needed to know that Roland's tale of the Forgotten Ones was true.

And so damned wrong. Alton's father and the rest of the council had much to explain, and more for which to atone.

Taron knelt near an icy stream that ran through the cavern and quickly bathed. Then he combed out his hair and braided the crimson strands, fastening the end with one of those neat little rubber band things Alton had given him.

One day he would spend time in Earth's dimension and

see the wonders Alton spoke of. Some day he would experience the sun on his face, see the stars at night, watch the beauty of storm clouds gathering.

All those things Alton had seen and shared with Taron—all experiences denied the citizens of Lemuria.

Denied Taron. He stood and tossed his long braid over his shoulder. A shiver ran across his spine—the strange sense there was someone else nearby. Slowly, with his breath trapped in his throat, Taron turned and glanced about the huge cavern.

Nothing moved. Nothing seemed to have changed. There was no shift in air currents, no sound beyond the gentle trickle of water over a bed of diamonds. The silence had been more a comfort than anything for the past few days—a gentle silence that was rarely interrupted by the occasional scuff of his own sandals against the floor.

Now, the silence had a sense of portent about it, as if even the cavern waited for something. Light continued to shimmer in multifaceted shards of blue, but something . . .

Something was different.

His eyes were drawn to the ruby altar. All week it had glimmered faintly with refracted light bouncing from the diamond-studded walls. Now it glowed with an inner fire, pulsing rhythmically with the beat of life. He felt the living pulse in the altar within his own body, timed to the rush of blood through his veins, the slow and steady thud of his heart.

Silent, yet powerful and alive, the altar drew him close.

Taron felt no fear, no sense of worry. Wonder filled his soul. Was this a sign the final sword had formed? Was his mission complete? He'd not counted the swords this morning, had no idea if he'd reached the mark of one hundred, though he knew he must be close.

Drawing near, caught in the sonorous beat that thrummed beneath an audible level—pulsed in time with the ebb and flow of ruby light shining within the altar—he spotted something new lying beneath his sword.

Something glowing the same blood-red color as the altar.

Carefully he lifted his sword and set it aside. Beneath it lay another, but this was unlike any of the rest. Glowing with the same brilliant red as the altar it lay upon, the entire sword was longer, the blade thicker at the base, the crystal formed from faceted ruby rather than diamond.

The hilt was gold, set with a single huge diamond in the pommel. Without even thinking of the consequences, Taron reached for the handle and wrapped his fingers around it.

Heat raced through his palm like a bolt of fire and shot the length of his arm. He turned the hilt loose before he'd even had a chance to move it.

The blade glowed, shimmering so brilliantly, Taron stepped back and covered his eyes. Blinking, he took a steadying breath and stared once again at the ruby sword. It flashed a deeper red, then flashed again. This time he could swear flames danced along the blade.

And then it spoke, in a voice ringing with authority. A powerful, masculine voice.

"You will take me to Artigos the Just."

Artigos the Just? Alton's grandfather had died sometime during the move from their sinking continent. No one had seen him after the DemonWars ended, after their world was destroyed by earthquakes and cataclysm. Taron shook his head in fear as much as denial. "I can't. Artigos the Just is dead. His son rules now. His grandson is my friend."

The red glow flashed brightly enough to stain the surrounding walls blood red. "He lives. I would not exist without him. I sense his life force, and it is as strong and vital as when he last carried his sword. Take me to Artigos the Just, but do not tell his son that either I or his father exist."

Taron stepped closer. "Tell me where to find him. How do I take you to him when I don't know where he is?"

Once more the sword flashed blood red. "You will find Artigos the Just, and you will deliver me into his hands."

As suddenly as it had flared, the fire died, and the crystal lost its glow. Taron let out a whoosh of air and a heartfelt curse. "Nine hells! Just go find a guy who's been dead for a few thousand years. Sure. I can do that. No problem."

The sword flashed, almost blinding him. He jerked out of the way and choked back a laugh. "Really. Don't worry. If he's out there, I'll find him."

He did a quick count of swords. There were seventy-nine stacked beside the ruby altar. As much as he hated the idea, he'd have to leave his own sword behind to finish the job of replicating the full one hundred weapons while he took this new one to either Roland or Alton. He sure as hell didn't know how to go about finding a dead ruler on his own.

Carefully, without touching either the hilt or the blade with his hands, Taron wrapped the ruby sword in his blanket and tucked it under his arm. He couldn't risk anyone seeing it, but until he got to the upper levels, there was no way to contact anyone who might be able to help.

He'd been away for days now. He wondered what had happened during his absence, if Roland and Alton and the others were still safe. Was Alton's father still head of the council? So many things might have changed while he'd been entirely out of touch in the caverns beneath the mines.

A ruby sword asking for a dead leader was probably the least of his problems.

Chapter Three

Selyn stared at the blade shimmering softly against the bed coverings and fought back the sting of tears. She refused to cry, not when she felt such overwhelming joy. Slowly stroking the warm crystal, she whispered, "Mother? DemonSlayer? Are you . . . ?" The blade glowed and pulsed, and Selyn knew it lived.

Then she heard her mother's familiar voice.

"I am here, daughter. Yes, I am Elda, her spirit and her heart, the one who carried you, who gave you life. I fight now with a woman you shall call sister, for Eddy Marks is a brave and powerful warrior. As are you, my daughter."

Wide-eyed, Selyn shot a glance at Eddy, and then stared once again at the sword. She took a deep breath. "I am ready to fight. We all are. The others didn't want to believe me, but when I told them there would be swords for each of them, it gave them hope. These people—and this curly-haired beast—have healed my injuries. I'm ready."

"It is good. I was with you when you fought the warden. I feared for you then, though I was sure you would prevail. You are stronger than you realize, more powerful than you know, and I celebrate your healing. A word of caution, beloved daughter—those you count as your enemies may not be guilty of their many sins. All is not always as it appears." The sword glowed once more and then faded.

Eddy waited for a moment while Selyn rested her fingers against the blade. Then she quietly sheathed her weapon and rested her fingers on Selyn's wrist. "She does that a lot, says things I don't entirely understand. But DemonSlayer always tells the truth. That 'all is not always as it appears' will make sense eventually. And Selyn, anytime you feel you need to talk to your mom, just let me know, okay?"

Selyn raised her head and smiled at Eddy. "I dreamed she was the sentience of a crystal sword, but to hear her voice . . ." She brushed a hand over her eyes. "It's as if she lives again."

Eddy took Selyn's hand and squeezed her fingers. "She does. She is very much alive within my blade. Your mother has become my friend as well as my companion in the battle against demonkind. I don't know how much you hear of the world, working in the mines, but demonkind threatens all of us again. DemonSlayer has already saved my life and the lives of my friends on more than one occasion. Selyn, I'm so glad you're all right, and I'm really glad we found you, that you got to talk to your mom. Anytime you feel the need, please . . . anytime."

Eddy sighed and sat on the edge of the bed. "I would give anything to hear my mother's voice. She died when I was little."

Selyn looked into Eddy's dark brown eyes, felt her sadness, saw the compassion in their chocolate depths and, without further thought, wrapped her arms around her new sister and hugged her close. "I'm sorry for your loss, but I am so happy you carry the sword with my mother's spirit."

She leaned back far enough to see the tears tracking

down Eddy's face and knew they probably matched her own. Smiling now, she said, "This means I no longer have to worry about her. Where she is, how she fares in the afterlife. Knowing she is once again in the midst of battle . . ." Selyn sniffed and then laughed. "It must make her very happy. She was a brave warrior. A good and loving mother, but my mother was first a warrior."

"Thank you." Eddy sniffed, and then they both giggled. "I wonder who'll be the sentience in your sword?"

Selyn thought about that a moment. Then she shook her head. "I have no idea. There were so many brave women who fought in the DemonWars. All of them are gone now."

Dawson stepped closer. She'd been almost preternaturally aware of his presence, as if she sensed him on levels she didn't truly comprehend. Even though she hadn't seen him, she'd felt him standing silently by, watching the interaction between her and Eddy, so it was no surprise when he moved closer and lightly touched her shoulder.

She was proud of herself for not flinching this time, but she'd expected his soft touch even before his fingers rested on her shoulder. Surprisingly, the gentle connection steadied her.

"That's something I don't understand," he said. His soft voice rolled over her like a physical presence. Soothing, comforting. "I thought Lemurians were immortal. What happened to all the women warriors? Why did they die?"

Selyn shrugged. She'd often wondered the same thing, though in her heart she knew the truth. For the first time ever, she spoke her mother's tragedy aloud.

"After they were exiled from Lemurian society rather than treated as the heroes they were, when they realized they couldn't escape their jailers, they gave up hope." She tilted her head so that she could see Dawson, watch the emotions that flickered so openly across his expressive face. Already she'd learned to read him, in spite of the dark beard he wore.

"After so many years toiling in the mines—victimized by the cruelty of the guards, with no hope of freedom for themselves or their daughters—they began to choose death. Within a couple of years, all of the women warriors had passed beyond the veil."

"Were they pregnant when they were sent into slavery?"

Eddy's question hung there—a question Selyn knew she must answer. She shook her head. "No. The guards used rape as a form of intimidation, a way to control the women, to subjugate them. They were warriors—women used to fighting demonkind—and they fought the wardens with every bit as much passion as they'd fought during the DemonWars, but they had no weapons. Their swords had been taken away and destroyed. They were physically smaller than the males guarding them, and, without weapons, powerless against them. Sexual assault was demeaning and terrifying, but they might have continued to fight, except almost all of them became pregnant. That was unexpected, and it changed the dynamic of their existence."

She shivered, remembering the terrible stories of the wardens' cruelty. Remembering her mother's mixed emotions—the love she felt for her unexpected daughter; the absolute hatred for the man who had forced the pregnancy on her through a brutal act of rape.

Selyn swallowed past the bile that rose in her throat at the telling. "The Lemurian fertility rate is historically very low, and yet, one by one, most of the women conceived, and most of the babies were daughters. The few boys who were born were taken away by the guards, never to be seen again. But pregnancy meant the women had new life to consider. The option of fighting the guards no longer existed, because it meant putting their unborn babies at risk.

They gave up the fight and turned their energies to raising daughters who would one day avenge them."

She raised her head and realized she was telling her story to Dawson. The others listened just as attentively, but her words were directed at him. "We are those daughters," she said. "We who call ourselves the Forgotten Ones."

Dawson nodded. "Forgotten no longer, Selyn. All of Lemuria will soon know about you, about your mothers and the role they played in your world's history."

"I hope so. That is my wish. My prayer. My mother's prayer as well."

"They don't still rape, do they? Not their own daughters?" Eddy's gaze flicked to Dawson, then back to Selyn.

"No. The sexual abuse stopped as soon as most of the women had conceived. They'd achieved their purpose by changing the dynamic, by making it impossible for the women to fight. At first it was to protect their unborn children, and then it was to keep the children safe. In a way, it was as if the pregnancies were part of the punishment, though our mothers loved us and were always good to us. Pregnancy made it easier for the guards to control the women warriors. The beatings, though . . . the beatings continue, and there have been some deaths among us. We number one hundred, now. There once were almost a dozen more."

Eddy glanced once again at Dawson. Then she squeezed Selyn's hand. "We'll find answers, Selyn. And we'll get all of the Forgotten Ones out of the mines. I promise you. Once the swords are ready and Alton has control of the council, we'll put an end to slavery and find the answers all of you need."

Selyn almost laughed. "It sounds wonderful, but how do you plan to accomplish all these things?"

A soft knock on the door interrupted Eddy's answer.

Selyn glanced up as the door opened and a beautiful, dark-skinned woman stepped into the room. She was followed by a tall, strikingly handsome Lemurian with long, blond hair. He smiled directly at Selyn, as if he knew her.

"Selyn," he said. "It's good to see you looking so well this morning. I'm Alton, and this is Ginny. She assisted Dr. Buck last night when you were brought in. Your recovery is amazing."

Ginny laughed. "No shit. I hate to say it, but you were a mess when Roland showed up with you." She slung her arm over the healer's shoulders and gave him a familiar hug and a kiss on the cheek.

Selyn smiled, but she wasn't sure how she felt about another woman hugging and kissing the man who'd healed her. Nor was she sure how she should feel about this Lemurian. She knew his name, that he was son and heir to Chancellor Artigos.

Until she knew more of what was happening, she figured she'd keep her worries to herself. "Thank you. I don't remember much at all after Birk hit me." She shook her head, realized her hands were trembling, and clasped them together in her lap. The curly dog leaned close against her side, as if offering comfort.

For some reason, BumperWillow's solid presence really did seem to make things better. She glanced around the room. "Is Roland still here? I need to thank him. I imagine I would have died without his help."

Alton shook his head. "No. He returned almost immediately to Lemuria after bringing you here. He didn't want his absence noted, and he was worried about his wife and child."

"He's a brave man," Selyn said. "He risks much."

Another man stepped into the room, which seemed to shrink with the presence of yet another large male,

some reason she couldn't explain. Was it gratitude for his healing her, or was it something else?

He watched her with a most fascinating intensity in his brilliant blue eyes. Why had he, a human, agreed to take part in this dangerous exercise? What was he thinking right now, as he watched her so carefully?

She realized the answer to that question was the one she wanted to know the most. Because, more than anything and for some strange and as yet unexplainable reason, she wanted to know what he thought of her, not as a victim, but as a woman.

Alton reached over his shoulder and lightly touched the pommel on his sword.

I am here, Alton. And I am ready.

Good. HellFire, I wish I felt as confident as you sound.

Alton heard soft laughter in his mind, and then Hell-Fire's strong voice. *We will prevail. Do not doubt yourself, and do not doubt me. Your goal is mine, and it is just.*

Alton almost laughed. No snark from his usually snarky sword? He hoped that was a good sign. Glancing from Ginny to Eddy and Dax, he asked, "Are you ready?"

At their affirmative answers, he turned to Dawson and Selyn. Selyn looked absolutely regal, even though she wore nothing more than a faded bathrobe that must have belonged to Dawson. She stood close beside the vet in the front room, tall and proud and every bit his equal. The two of them already looked like a team.

It was impossible to ignore Dawson's interest in his exotic patient, but Alton wondered what would happen, once Dawson realized his mortality made anything permanent between them impossible.

Well, it was their problem, not his, though he knew how

it could complicate things. Even so, Alton had more than enough to worry about without adding another couple's hypothetical relationship to his list of problems. "You'll have the room ready for my father?"

"We will." Dawson glanced at Selyn. "If he tries to use compulsion, Selyn knows how to handle him. He might be able to control me, but she should be immune to him, right?"

Alton shrugged. "She should be. Compulsion doesn't work on other Lemurians. It's something we appear to have developed to use against humans." He winked at Ginny. "I should have known something was up when it wouldn't work on Ginny."

Not that he hadn't tried, because he had, on more than one occasion. He should have guessed, but discovering she was descended from Lemurian royalty had been a shock. It still gave him chills. Knowing she'd been gifted with immortality, that they would always be together, completed him. He'd never imagined what it would be like to love a perfect woman, and know she loved him in return.

"We'll be ready for your father." Dawson glanced at Selyn and then gazed seriously at Alton. "Be careful. All of you."

Alton thought of Dawson's words barely an hour later as he and the others followed Roland through hidden passageways used primarily by Lemurian guards to move about within their world. The tunnels were narrow and dark, but there was little chance of discovery as they quickly circumvented the great plaza and made their way to the residential area.

Roland paused just beyond the rooms where Artigos now resided. He touched Alton's shoulder to get his attention, and whispered, "Will your mother be a problem?"

Alton shook his head and answered just as quietly. "I recently learned she and my father no longer share their living space. Her apartment is connected to his, yet they live separately, each with their own portal to the main passages for access. Because they've always been such private people, very few citizens realize they're no longer living as man and wife."

"That should make it easier for you." Roland paused. Then he frowned at something only he could hear, and whispered, "Taron's trying to contact me. He doesn't say why, and his voice isn't very clear, but I've not heard from him for days. Maybe he's got the swords ready. I'd best head below and find out what he needs. Good luck."

Alton watched as the big sergeant slipped quietly down yet another passage. Then he drew HellFire. "Is the way clear?"

His sword pulsed with a blue glow. "Your father is alone. The way is clear, and the time is right. We must go now."

Alton adjusted the pack strapped tightly to his back beside his scabbard. He and Dax nodded to one another, and then Dax and Eddy moved to either side of the glowing portal that opened into his father's rooms, taking the positions they'd agreed upon.

Alton paused as Ginny unsheathed her sword. Together, holding their glowing blades high, they stepped through the portal. Alton's father sat alone at a small table, but the moment they entered, he leapt to his feet and glared at his son.

"What right do you have, entering my quarters unbidden?"

Before Artigos could mentally call on anyone for help, Alton pointed HellFire at him. Ginny did the same with DarkFire. Blue fire shot from the tip of Alton's sword while dark purple shimmered forth from Ginny's amethyst blade.

Trapped in the blended glow of light, Artigos went

rigid. Eyes wide, lips parted in mid-curse, he was held immobile by the combined power of the two crystal blades.

"What now, DarkFire?"

Ginny's soft question startled Alton. He'd focused so intently on his father's angry face, he'd lost track of time.

"He will know nothing for the next few hours." DarkFire's glowing light shimmered, softened, and faded. Artigos sat heavily in his chair and stared straight ahead, entranced.

"Quickly," Alton said. "Call Dax and Eddy." He couldn't allow himself to think of what they had just set in motion as he slipped his shoulder pack to the ground and pulled out a tightly folded duffle. His hands shook so badly he could barely hang on to the damned thing. He concentrated on unfolding the bag, on getting the zipper open. He couldn't look at his father sitting there in the chair, staring into space like a plastic mannequin, a parody of the vital, forceful man Alton had always known—a man who had publicly disowned his only son.

By the time Dax and Eddy entered the room, Alton had his emotions under control and the bag open, and he was stretching it out on the floor. Even his voice sounded steady as he sat back on his heels. "Help me get him inside."

Dax nodded and carefully grabbed Artigos beneath his shoulders while Alton turned around and lifted his father's legs. Artigos offered no resistance at all, though his eyes were open. He appeared at least vaguely aware of something going on.

Artigos closed his eyes, though, as Dax and Alton stretched him out beside the duffle and, with Eddy and Ginny's help, got him tucked inside. At the last minute, Alton grabbed his father's crystal blade. He caught Ginny's curious gaze. "I can't take everything away from him. Not this, too."

Ginny smiled softly as he slipped the blade and scabbard

into the bag beside Artigos, and closed the zipper. "I won't allow him near it when he's conscious." Alton ran his fingers along the zipper and sighed. "We just need to keep it close. Just in case . . ." The fabric was light enough to allow his father to breathe, but strong enough to carry him using the sturdy handles along the top.

Dax grabbed the handle above the chancellor's head and shoulders while Eddy lifted the one at his feet. Alton glanced at Ginny. She should have grabbed part of the weight, but instead she stood off to one side with her arms folded over her chest.

"Ginny? Aren't you going to help Eddy?"

"No." She stepped closer, wrapped her fingers around his forearm and shook her head. "They can handle him. My place is with you, Alton. I'm staying." She glanced toward Eddy. "You're sure you don't need my help? You'll be able to carry him as far as the portal?"

"No problem. Now, Alton I might have trouble with, but his father's not quite as big." Eddy flashed a quick grin. "Don't worry—either of you. You deal with Alton's mom, and we'll take care of dear old dad."

"Thank you." What else could he say? Obviously Ginny and Eddy had worked this out ahead, but he turned to her anyway, and grabbed both her hands in his. "Are you sure, Ginny? It could get ugly. This is treason, no matter how you look at it. It's a capital offense in Lemuria. We could end up in jail again. Or worse."

She laughed. Only Ginny . . .

"I'm sure. Now stop it. You've got bigger things to worry about." She stood on her toes and kissed him. "Wherever you go, I'm there. Jail. Lemuria. Earth. You're stuck with me."

"Good. I think." *Thank the gods!* Relief didn't come close to describing how her words made him feel, but he held tightly to Ginny's hand and watched until the portal closed behind Eddy and Dax. He wasn't going to think of the risk they were taking. He couldn't. "I hope they'll be okay."

Ginny squeezed his hand. "I hope you'll be okay. I can feel your anxiety. It's pouring off of you in waves." She kissed his cheek. "C'mon, big guy. We need to talk to your mother."

"I know." He dragged his gaze away from the empty portal. "First I want to give Dax and Eddy time to get him through the gold veil and away from Lemuria. Dax will let me know once they're ready to leave this dimension." He wrapped an arm around Ginny's waist and held her close. When she grinned at him, he leaned over and kissed her perfect mouth, losing himself, if only for a moment, in her heat and her taste, and her soft, full lips.

Ginny's love surrounded him. With HellFire strapped to his back and Ginny beside him, Alton felt as if he could accomplish anything. "How did I survive so many years without you?"

She laughed and kissed him hard and fast, then backed away and said, "You didn't. Your life didn't begin until you met me."

She had no idea how truthful her words actually were. No idea at all.

Chapter Four

As soon as everyone left, Dawson dug around in the storage closet in the hallway until he found a set of his old surgical scrubs for Selyn. They'd faded nearly white from so many launderings, but they were clean and soft. He figured they'd cover her enough that she wouldn't feel threatened.

He'd noticed her clutching at the gaping neck on his old bathrobe. She was holding it closed now.

"Try these," he said, handing her the folded pants and shirt. "They'll be more comfortable than that old robe. They should fit you. You're almost as tall as me, and I was a lot skinnier when I was in vet school."

"Vet school?" She gazed up at him and frowned as she took the scrubs.

"UC Davis, where I studied to be a veterinarian. I wasn't trained to treat people. Only animals."

"You healed me." Smiling, she shook her head. "I'm not an animal."

He let out a big breath of air. "You can say that again, Selyn." He walked the few steps to her room, reached around her and opened the door. "Try those on. See if they'll fit."

Without a word, she left him standing in the hallway, and shut the door behind her. He'd known clothing was going to be an issue for her from the moment she awoke and immediately tugged the blanket all the way to her chin.

She was probably used to her full, flowing robe, but the one she'd worn last night was totally ruined. The rips and tears could be mended, but bloodstains had already set in the soft fabric. The last thing Dawson wanted was to put Selyn back into clothing that would be a constant reminder of that terrible beating.

Clothing that covered her completely and yet was still comfortable to move in should help her relax a little, especially since she'd be staying here in his home. She'd tried to hide her reaction to his nearness, but he'd sensed her anxiety whenever he got close to her. That was the last thing he wanted—for this beautiful young woman to fear him.

He waited outside the bedroom, leaning against the wall in the hallway with his arms folded across his chest. After a few minutes, Selyn slowly opened the door. He wasn't certain, but she seemed relieved that he'd waited for her.

At least she smiled when she saw him.

"Does this look okay?" She ran her hands down the front of the worn cotton. "It feels so strange to wear pants. I've never worn anything other than my robe."

Her toes peeked out from beneath the wide pants leg. She lifted up one bare foot and laughed. "The pants look so silly."

"I don't think so." He pushed himself away from the wall, though it was hard to stop staring at her. He paused for one more look. "I think you could wear rags and make them look beautiful." Her eyes flashed wide in surprise, and he could have bitten his tongue for making such a personal comment. Awkwardly, he turned away and headed toward the kitchen. "C'mon. Let's get something to eat. Are you hungry?"

She nodded, padding quietly behind him on bare feet. Shoes were something else she'd need. She hadn't had anything on her feet when Roland brought her in the night before. She'd worn nothing but that torn and bloodied robe that was beyond repair.

Until they had time to shop for clothing, the scrubs were the best he could do. They'd sure never looked like that on him!

The soft fabric clung to her tall, slender frame, and the deep V-neck offered a glimpse of the hollowed shadows between her breasts. He'd seen those perfect breasts last night, when he'd used a syringe to drain blood and fluid from her punctured lung.

He'd not thought of her as a woman then. No, she'd been a badly injured patient, someone he shouldn't even have treated. He was an animal doctor, damn it! What if he'd harmed her in some way? What if he'd not had the skills to help her?

Shit. She was fine this morning. He had to quit worrying about what was done and think about what was coming. Alton's father would be here soon, and before long, if what Alton said was true, they'd be more deeply immersed in the fight against demonkind. Thank goodness Selyn had recovered so quickly. Her body was healthy, her injuries healed from a combination of his medicine, her Lemurian healing ability, and Willow's magic.

He almost stumbled when all those thoughts collided at once. Damn, but if he didn't know this was all really happening, he'd think he was losing his mind. Demons and Lemurians and talking swords and a talking dog! Aunt

Fiona's spirit must be loving every minute of this. She'd warned him, hadn't she?

Chuckling softly, he held open the door at the end of the hall. Selyn glanced at him and stepped through. She had to be starving, but she'd not said a word. BumperWillow jumped off the living room couch and trotted alongside, blond curls bouncing and tail wagging. Eddy'd been smart to leave her behind.

The dog seemed to make Selyn more comfortable with him, though Daws couldn't blame her for being nervous around a strange man. Even though he'd been the one to treat her injuries, she'd been unconscious the entire time. He wondered what it must be like, to awaken after such a nightmare and discover you were in another world among complete strangers.

He regretted that Roland had decided to leave before Selyn regained consciousness. At least she knew him, if only slightly. She didn't know Dawson at all, though he had every intention of changing that. Just not quite yet.

Carefully, he refrained from touching her as he guided her to a stool at the breakfast bar in the kitchen. The last thing he wanted to do was make her more nervous than she already was. It had to be hard for her, knowing that, other than the dog, she was alone with a man in his home. Except, she didn't seem as nervous, now, sitting comfortably on the tall stool, looking wide-eyed at Dawson's bright kitchen filled with morning sunlight streaming through the big windows.

Like a flash it came to him—what she was seeing, what she was experiencing for the first time. "You've never seen sunlight before, have you?" He paused beside her, fascinated by her expression, by the sheen of tears in her sapphire-blue eyes.

She shook her head, transfixed. "Never. I've heard of it.

My mother used to speak of it with such longing. She told me of the sunlight glistening off the water on the bay near her home, before Lemuria sank beneath the sea. How the blue sea sparkled like diamonds. She loved to swim with the dolphins." Selyn turned away from the sunlit window with its view of Sedona's famous red rock formations, and smiled at him.

It was the first true smile of hers Dawson had seen, and if he hadn't been holding on to the edge of the granite bar, he'd have had to grab it to keep from stumbling. Her smile blazed a path right through him.

"Do you know dolphins?" she asked.

He had to clear his throat to get his voice to work. "I've seen them." He wished the ocean was close enough to take her there right now. He wanted to give her anything she desired, whatever she dreamed of. "We're a long way from the ocean here in Sedona, but one time, years ago, I watched dolphins swim beside a boat in the Pacific. Beautiful, fascinating creatures."

She had a dreamy expression on her face when she nodded. "I would like to see dolphins one day. And the sea. I definitely want to walk along the shore and stick my toes in the waters of the sea. Those are the stories I remember the best. The ones my mother told of her life before the DemonWars, before the purge that sent her to the mines and a life of slavery."

Without thinking, Dawson reached for Selyn and wrapped his fingers around her hand. She didn't pull away, but her head snapped up. She stared at him from wide, almost frightened eyes.

He didn't turn her loose. He kept his grip light, as non-threatening as he could, but he had to touch her. Needed this connection now, at this precise moment. "I promise you, Selyn. When this is over, when the demons are gone and all this crap is done, I'll take you to the ocean, and we'll walk along the shore. You can hunt for seashells and dip your toes in the water. Your entire body, if you want."

He stared at her as she watched him. Her lips curved up in that delicious smile once again, and he was almost certain his heart stuttered in his chest.

"I would like that. I would like that very much." And then she tugged her fingers free of his.

This time he let them go.

He took a step back, moving out of temptation, if there were such a place while she was here, in his home. In his world.

"It's almost lunchtime, but I'm going to make us some breakfast. Eggs and bacon okay? Or do you prefer cereal?"

She actually laughed at his question. "I always feel lucky if we're allowed bread and a piece of cheese when we break fast. Surprise me. I have no idea what kind of foods you eat."

"I guess it's all pretty strange to you, isn't it?" He glanced over his shoulder, talking to her while he pulled a couple of pans out of the cupboard, and then raided the refrigerator.

"Even Lemuria is strange to me. I'd never been outside the mines until I met Roland, and then only to the level above the one where we live and work. I had to be very careful not to be caught when I met him." She sighed. "Obviously, this last time, I wasn't careful enough. I've heard of so many places, but I've never seen any of them. Not even pictures. We had a few books to learn to read, but none with pictures."

He started the bacon frying and grabbed clean flatware and a couple of plates. "How is it you know as much as you do?" He smiled at her, hoping to put her at ease. The things she'd never experienced had to make this simple breakfast in a kitchen in Earth's dimension utterly mind-boggling. "You're comfortable with our language. That's something I've never thought to ask. How is it all of you speak English?"

She grinned. "Ah, that's where my Lemurian heritage helps. We speak and understand all languages. No matter what you speak, we hear and understand the words, all the nuances of the language. You might be speaking English, but I am hearing Lemurian."

He set a glass of orange juice in front of her. Her eyes lit up. "What is this?"

"Orange juice. From a type of fruit, a citrus. Try it."

She sipped. Her eyes widened, and she took a huge swallow. Then she set the glass down and slowly licked her lips. Dawson almost groaned when the pink tip of her tongue swept over the fullness of her upper lip and then brushed the lower.

Staring at the glass, now only half full, she said, "This is wonderful. We have water and tea in the mines, but nothing like this." She took another swallow. Again she licked an errant drop from her top lip.

He couldn't stand it. Turning away, Dawson poured himself a cup of coffee, took a swallow, and burned his tongue.

Shit. He'd never felt so awkward around a woman in his life, nor enjoyed himself more. He loved the fact he could show her new things, give her new experiences. Orange juice was safe, but that wasn't where his imagination wanted to lead him.

The image of her perfect body, covered in bruises and contusions, flashed into his mind. She'd been through too much. More than any woman should have to bear. *Damn. Stick to new memories, Daws. Good memories.* Something besides slavery and brutality and a life where the sun never touched her smile.

The snap of bacon frying drew him back to the stove. Selyn took another sip of orange juice and closed her eyes, as if lost in the sensual pleasure of the cold drink. Dawson tore his gaze away from her before his damned testosterone-fueled brain went off on other sensual pleasures, other things he'd like to show her. "Did you go to school?"

That was a safe question, wasn't it?

She shrugged. "Not really. Our mothers taught us what they could. There was nothing organized for us. We're slaves, after all. Not worthy of an education. I can read and write, and I know my numbers and the basic history of our world. I know some history of Earth, but not as much as I should."

She smiled as she ran her fingertip through the condensation on the side of the glass. "I know how to fight. How to protect myself." Then she sighed. "At least, I thought I did. Birk's attack taught me I'm not as strong as I thought."

Dawson put the strips of bacon on a paper towel to drain, and stuck some bread in the toaster. Then he cracked and beat half a dozen eggs, poured off most of the bacon fat, and dumped the eggs into the pan. Concentrating on the eggs, he asked her the question he'd avoided so far. "How did it happen? What did you do, that you were beaten so badly?"

She stared at her hands clasped around the base of her glass of juice and shook her head. Her long, dark hair rippled in midnight waves over her shoulders. "I don't really know. Birk caught me coming back from a meeting with Roland. Normally, catching one of us in the passageways where we don't belong would warrant a slap, maybe the loss of what few privileges we have, but he surprised me with a solid punch to my jaw. I wasn't expecting it. I never recovered from that first punch, not enough to fight back. He was too strong, too fast. . . ."

Her voice trailed off as she gazed once more at the sunny window. "I'm afraid to go back to the mines. I know I have to, but I've never been so close to death before. It was terrifying."

"You were badly hurt. Your injuries might have killed a human woman . . . or man." He shoved the eggs around the pan, concentrating on the lift and swirl of brilliant yellow, watching them solidify as they cooked. When they were almost done, he raised his head and caught her sapphire gaze in his own. "When you go back," he said, "I'll go with you. I don't want you to have to face that bastard alone. Never again."

She laughed. It was a harsh sound without mirth. "He would kill you. He's a large man. Bigger even than Alton. Taller. Broader. He's grown more cruel each year, as if something drives him to terrorize us as much as possible."

Dawson didn't respond. She might be right, and maybe he wouldn't win a fair fight with the man who'd beat her, but as far as he was concerned, fairness didn't enter the contest when a man did to a woman what that bastard had done to Selyn.

Calmly, Daws scooped eggs onto a plate, then buttered a piece of toast and set it next to the eggs with a couple of strips of bacon. He put the plate in front of Selyn along with a small jar of jam. Then he put a serving of eggs into a shallow bowl with a strip of bacon crumbled across the top, and set it on the floor for BumperWillow, next to the water he'd put out earlier.

Thank you, Dawson. It looks wonderful.
You're welcome.

He would never, not ever, get used to conversing with a

dog. Smiling, Daws filled his own plate and sat across from Selyn.

She stared at the food.

"Is something wrong?"

She shook her head. "No. It's too right. This is amazing." When she raised her head, she was smiling again. "It's too pretty to eat."

He laughed and put thoughts of killing Birk out of his mind, at least for now. "No, it's not," he said, taking a forkful of eggs. "You're the only thing at this table too pretty to eat, except that's all I can think of doing with you."

Oh, crap. I didn't really say something that stupid . . . did I?

She paused with the fork halfway to her mouth, cocked her head to one side, and stared at him. "What is it you want to do?"

He felt the blush all the way to the top of his head. She was probably as innocent as a young woman could be, no matter her actual age in years. He shook his head. "Nothing," he mumbled. "Eat your breakfast."

She stared at him a moment longer, and then dug into her food. From the hurried yet efficient manner in which she ate, he figured mealtimes in the slave quarters weren't necessarily a social occasion.

Sadness flowed over and through him, a sense of time lost, of innocence crushed. At the same time, he knew wonder, and the powerful awareness that his life would never be the same again.

Sticking to the shadows, Taron managed to get through the mining level without stumbling over one of those massive guards. From there he climbed more stairs to the main level, and then went straight to his quarters with the ruby sword.

Within a few minutes he'd found his grandfather's white leather scabbard in the back of his closet. The leather was still supple, the buckles and straps soft and well used, though not badly worn, considering the fact that his grandfather had fought in the DemonWars before Lemuria sank beneath the sea. Though the ruby blade was larger than the average crystal, it fit perfectly into the scabbard. The leather didn't hide the gold pommel, but at least the unusual crystal was out of sight.

Taron quickly shoved the ruby sword beneath the bed and sent out a message for Roland.

Taron! Where are you?

Roland. Thank goodness! I'm in my quarters. I have something here you have got to see. I need your help.

I'm on my way, Taron. Stay put. Things are beginning to happen. Artigos has been taken. He is on his way to Earth, and Alton is preparing to take over the council. You might not be safe if word gets out about the crystal swords before he's got complete control.

Taron glanced at his bed and thought of the ruby sword lying beneath it. *Roland, I think the crystal swords might be the least of our problems.*

Alton paused outside the portal that led to his mother's lodgings. Enough time had passed that Dax and Eddy were well away from Lemuria, possibly at Dawson's by now. At least Artigos couldn't make contact with anyone, should the trance wear off. Alton knew he'd run out of excuses to delay any longer.

"Alton?"

Ginny's soft fingers wrapped around his wrist.

"I know." He took a deep breath. "I'm ready." He really did not want to have this conversation with his mother. How did one approach a woman who had lived a lie for most of her life? Though her rooms connected to the residence his father kept, that door was kept locked, and his parents had maintained separate entryways to their own rooms since the great move.

Even Alton hadn't realized the truth—that their marriage was truly a sham.

He thought of how much he loved Ginny, how complete she made him feel, and sadness for his mother's lonely life almost felled him. What he intended to tell his mother now could very well be the final blow. How much disappointment could a person bear?

Ginny gazed up at him, cupped his face in her hands, and kissed him. "I love you, Alton. You can do this." Then she took his hand in hers and lightly tugged him toward the doorway.

"You're sure?" He looked down at their fingers, so tightly linked. Of course she was sure. Ginny never doubted herself—or him. Her faith set a high standard for Alton.

She made him a better man than he ever could have been on his own.

"I'm sure," she said, tugging him closer. Her soft laughter melted away much of the anxiety that had been building since Dax and Eddy took Artigos away.

"C'mon. It's time to talk to your mom." Ginny kept her hold on his hand. Alton sighed and pressed a small button beside the door. Soft tones echoed on the other side of the portal.

The shimmering light brightened, and Ginny followed Alton through, into Gaia's lodgings. His mother waited on the other side with her hands folded tightly beneath her chin. When she saw them, she bowed her head, formally acknowledging the two of them. Then she raised her chin. Tears streamed from her eyes.

"What have you done?" Her harsh whisper condemned them both. "He called to me. He begged for my help, but now I can't reach him. What have you done to him?"

Ginny shot Alton a quick glance.

Alton froze, obviously stunned by his mother's accusation. Ginny took one look at his ashen face and stepped forward. "Gaia, Artigos is safe. Everything we're doing is to save him, not harm him. Remember what you said when we met, that your husband had changed, that he lost his soul many years ago?"

Gaia's eyes went wide. She shook her head, denying Ginny's words and her own. "No. No, it was only a figure of speech. I didn't mean it literally." She laughed, still shaking her head, but it was a harsh and broken sound. "He has a soul. I know he does. He must!"

Ginny took another step closer and wrapped her arms around Alton's mother. Gaia felt rigid, almost brittle within her embrace. "We fear it might have been taken from him," she said, using soft, soothing tones. "Not by his choice. By demon possession. He's in a safe place, where we can help him. So we can help Lemuria. And you, Gaia. We want to help you, too."

Gaia's eyes flashed from Ginny to Alton and back to Ginny. Nervously she licked her lips. "I don't know." She practically moaned the words. "I heard him cry Alton's name in anger, but then he was gone. His thoughts are always with me, even though he doesn't want to share them. Ever since we wed, he's been with me. What have you done to him?" she demanded.

"A trance, Mother." Alton ran his hand over her hair, soothing her as if she were a child. "That's all. Merely a form of compulsion that will keep him from being afraid until we can help him. You know he's not the same man he was. You see the difference, don't you?"

Gaia closed her eyes and turned away. "Many, many years ago when we were still young, we were so much in love. He was a good and kind man, a loving father." She turned to Alton, raised a hand as if to touch his face, then dropped it heavily to her side. "You remember him that way, don't you?"

Alton looked absolutely stricken. "No, Mother. Not since I was a small child. Maybe then, but not for most of my life."

Gaia didn't appear to hear him. She stared at something. At nothing. "Something changed." Slowly, she shook her head, still denying the obvious truth. "I thought it was me, that I wasn't a good wife, that the stress of our world sinking beneath the sea, the move, his father's disappearance . . . I blamed so many things for the changes in Artigos. Changes I couldn't explain."

Alton rested his hand on her shoulder. "Let's sit down, Mother. We have a lot to discuss. I know this is quite a shock."

"Yes." Trembling from head to toe, she nodded and turned away. "Where are my manners. What would you like to drink? May I bring food?"

"No, Mother. We're fine. Sit. Please." He waited until she perched nervously on the edge of a long, low sofa. He sat beside her and took her trembling hands in both of his.

Ginny sat on Gaia's other side. She smiled at Alton, encouraging him. This had to be so hard for him.

"What happened to Grandfather? I don't remember him very well."

Gaia shook her head. "He disappeared during the big move, when the DemonWars were just ending. It all happened so quickly then. Our world was being destroyed. There were earthquakes and terrible upheavals. Huge waves drowned entire cities, and buildings collapsed and fell into great rifts in the earth or were washed away by the seas. Artigos the Just was overseeing the transfer of many ancient records, but he was supposed to meet us here, in our new home. He never arrived. Your father bravely stepped into his place and took on the heavy task of governing our world. Everything was chaos. So many of our people were lost during the chaos of the move, from the horrendous cataclysm, from the war. Terrible times. Just terrible."

"Is that when Father changed?"

Gaia slowly nodded her head. "I blamed the pressures of the move, the massive responsibility, but it was something more. He stopped coming to my bed. He no longer wanted anything to do with you, his only son." She raised her head, and her eyes were wide. "He banished the warrior women, the ones who'd fought demonkind so bravely. No one knew what became of them, but I knew. I wasn't supposed to hear, but I knew when he had their swords destroyed. When he sent them below to work the mines. For all I know, they're still down there, like a dirty secret. Those brave, brave women." Her voice broke, and she bowed her head.

Ginny caught Alton's gaze and almost wept. Gaia had known. She'd known the truth all these years and had never said a word.

"Why didn't you say anything, Mother? Why didn't you speak out? What he did was terrible. It was wrong."

She stared at the floor. "Because I loved him. I still love him. I keep hoping the man I married is in there, that he's not lost to me, but it's been so long. So very, very long."

Gaia pulled her fingers free of Alton's grasp and clasped her hands together. She straightened her spine and was once again the wife of Chancellor Artigos of the Council of Nine. "Where is he? What have you done with him? What do you intend to do next?"

"We've taken him to a safe house where he'll be cared for. We believe he was possessed by a demon many years ago, one that has influenced his choices throughout his years as leader of the Council of Nine. One of our group will try to remove the demon from his heart and mind. With any luck and a lot of skill, we hope to get him back, healthy and able once again to rule Lemuria, but we need your help."

She stared suspiciously at her son. Ginny could only imagine how it pained Alton to have his mother's anger and distrust focused on him. "My help? How? What can I possibly do?"

"You can officially introduce me to the people. They know you as his wife, know you've stood by him all these years. They trust you. Tell them I will be temporarily holding his position—the position I've been groomed for all my life—until he is cured of an unknown illness. Tell them he's with healers now. We don't want people to know we suspect demon possession. That would cause too much fear. An illness would be easier for the citizens of Lemuria to accept."

"You'll bring him home when he's well? When his soul is restored?"

Alton glanced at Ginny. She shrugged. They didn't know what was going to happen. There were no guarantees, but Alton looked at his mother and said, "We will do everything we can to bring him home. You have my promise."

She smiled, and it was as if the sun were actually shining here in the depths of Lemuria. "Whatever you want, my son. I will do what I can. Just bring your father home to me."

Ginny gazed at Alton and opened her thoughts. *I'll stay with your mother. Go and do what you need to do, but be careful. I love you, and I'm going to be really angry if you don't come back to me in one piece.*

Gotcha. "Mother, Ginny will stay with you. I'm going to meet with the council and let them know what's going on. Then I'll check on Father before I return." He leaned over and kissed Ginny, patted his mother's hand, and then he was gone.

Ginny sat there beside Gaia and wondered just how much they could count on a woman who'd allowed so many brave women warriors to die as slaves.

Chapter Five

Dawson closed the door behind him and walked out toward the main room where Selyn waited. The quarters—originally the site of his veterinary clinic—where he intended to house Artigos, were ready. Now all Dawson and Selyn could do was wait until Eddy and Dax delivered Alton's father into their hands for safekeeping.

The fact he was entangled in the kidnapping of a world leader—one not of his own world, at that—wasn't lost on Dawson. Neither was the presence of the young woman waiting impatiently in the next room.

He made a quick left into his home office and grabbed the phone. It took only a matter of minutes to make arrangements for his assistant, who had covered for him today, to take over the clinic for the rest of the week. Esteban Romero—called Romeo by the staff of young women who worked for Daws—was young, handsome as sin, and good with both animals and their people. He'd been more than happy to take charge of the clinic.

With his more mundane worries covered, Daws headed to the main room—and Selyn. She sat in front of the big screen TV with BumperWillow sprawled on the couch beside her. The dog—and, most likely, her symbiotic guest—slept, but Selyn was totally engrossed in a program on the Discovery Channel. Tiny red frogs enlarged to fit a fifty-inch flat screen crawled across thick foliage in some far off jungle. Equally engrossed, Dawson leaned against the doorjamb and crossed his arms over his chest, watching Selyn.

She leaned forward, sitting on the edge of his old leather sofa, elbows planted on her knees, long fingers cupping her face. Her hair fell in ebony waves over her shoulders, down her slim back, to curl softly against the leather cushions.

The loose neck of her cotton scrubs shirt had shifted to one side, baring her left shoulder and the fine line of her collarbone. With the late afternoon sunlight slanting through the window, her skin took on an almost reddish hue against the faded fabric.

Her concentration on the program was absolute, and he wondered what she thought. All of this was so new to her. It must feel both terrifying and exciting, to be faced with an entirely new world, all new experiences . . . new people.

She was so lovely she made him ache. So achingly innocent she terrified him. He felt drawn to her on too many levels—wanting to protect her, to teach her, to take her and make her his.

And that is something I cannot do.

She was his to protect. No more. She was an immortal, a woman who had known—for more lifetimes than he would ever live—nothing but slavery. A woman who, while accepting the friendship of those who were helping her, still burned for revenge.

He'd watched her watch Alton, had felt her rage when they spoke of Artigos and their desire to save him. She blamed the chancellor for her mother's death and her own horrible life.

With damned good reason, Daws thought, though if Alton's father were truly demon-possessed, the man himself might be as much a victim as Selyn. Not guilty at all. What a mess.

Selyn tilted her head, almost as if she'd sensed his presence. She turned away from the big screen and watched him with an unsettling stare. He wished he knew what she was thinking, what she thought of him.

Blinking slowly, she asked, "Will that room be strong enough to hold the chancellor? I would hate to think he could break free after the risk Alton and Ginny are taking to get him out of Lemuria."

At least Daws knew he was on safe ground here. "He can't get out. That was my veterinary clinic when I first opened my business. Since I kept restricted drugs here for treating the animals, I had the windows reinforced and barred, and a good lock put on the door. There's a bathroom in there, and he'll have access to an intercom when he's ready to contact us, but it's definitely secure." He gestured at the television. "He's even got a TV in there, though it's not as big as this one."

"He can compel you to do as he says. All Lemurians have that ability. What if he forces you to unlock the door and set him free?"

Dawson shook his head. They'd discussed that issue already. "It won't matter," he said, "because you're here. He can't force another Lemurian. You're my ace in the hole, Selyn. You'll be the one in charge of the key to the room, not me."

Selyn nodded. Then she stood up and walked to the window. Dawson had always loved the view from here.

The dark red, wind-shaped stone of Cathedral Rock soared majestically against the blue desert sky. Juniper, Mediterranean cypress, and a couple of scraggly ponderosa pine trees framed the formation. A row of silvery century plants marked the edge of the drive to his home. Cacti dotted the deceptively desolate landscape, and dark gravel defined the driveway from the main road to the garage.

"Would you like to go outside?"

Selyn's head snapped around, and she stared at him. "We can do that? Go out in the sunlight? Shouldn't we be here to wait for them to bring," she paused and flipped her hand in a careless gesture, "him. That one?"

"The chancellor?" Daws shook his head. "We're just going out in the front. No farther than the patio. We'll see them coming long before they arrive."

He held out his hand, not really expecting her to take it, but when Selyn slipped her warm fingers into his, he tightened his grip almost possessively. At the last minute, he tucked his cell phone in his pocket, and then led her toward the door that led out to the covered patio area in front of his house.

The dog snored and stretched out on her back. Her feet twitched as if she chased rabbits in her sleep. Dawson wondered if the sprite slept when her host did, or if she was in there, metaphorically tapping her tiny foot, impatiently waiting for action. Smiling, Dawson shut the screen door. BumperWillow would let him know if she wanted out.

When Selyn would have continued on to the rocky path, he tugged lightly on her hand. "We need to get some shoes for you before you try walking in the desert. See those?" He pointed at a prickly pear cactus growing beside the pathway. Needles stuck out in all directions. A few old pads lay on the ground, covered with sharp spines. "You don't want to step on any of them."

"I can see that." She laughed, but there was a sense of sadness to the sound. "So different from what I'm used to. All of the plants grow in containers in our world. Pathways are kept clean. There's nothing like this, so wild and unkempt." She slanted him a bright glance. "I like this. It's so big, and there is so much color. And sunlight."

She spread her arms wide and lifted her face to the sky. Daws watched her, enthralled by the sensual pleasure she took in the warm, afternoon sunlight and fresh, dry, desert air. It was almost painful to drag his gaze away from her, but he had to.

It was either divert his attention or pull her into his arms, and that wouldn't do. Not at all. Angry with the direction his thoughts kept straying, he stared out across the desert, at the sparse trees and scrubby brush, the soaring rocks scoured by wind and rain, and he thought of all that Selyn had never seen, the things she'd never felt. Sunlight on her skin, the cold splash of rain, the chill from a winter's wind.

A man's hands, not raised in anger.

The thought of what that bastard had done to her had his entire body tensing up. He clenched his hands into tight fists, fully aware he really wanted to kill the one who had hurt her. He'd never felt such anger toward another man in his entire life, especially a man he didn't know, but it was real, and it burned hot and heavy inside him.

A loud "char, char, char," rising in volume caught Selyn's attention. She turned to Dawson, frowning. "What's that?"

He pointed to a brown bird streaked with white, perched amid the sharp spears of a desert yucca. "Cactus wren."

"And that?" She pointed at a small fluff of brown fur on the rocky ground below the bird.

"That's a cottontail. They're rabbits. See that?" He pointed to a man-made pond on the far side of the yard. At one time it had been full of goldfish, but they'd not done well with the desert heat. Now he kept water for the wildlife that needed a safe place for a drink, and mosquito fish to keep the bugs under control. "The pond draws lots of wildlife. Look in the shade of the shrub. Do you see them? Over there."

He hadn't noticed them at first, but a small group of javelinas had found a cool spot beside the garage. "There are five little guys that have been coming in for water. It looks like they decided to hang around today."

"What are they?" Slowly Selyn moved across the concrete patio until she was only about a dozen feet from the sleeping creatures. "Yuck! They smell horrible."

"That they do." He chuckled softly as he studied the odd looking creatures. "They're actually collared peccaries, but here we call them javelinas. Most people think they're related to pigs, but they're not. They're just another of the weird creatures that live in the desert."

Selyn turned away with laughter on her lips and sparkles in her blue eyes. "So many wonders. It would take forever to see so many things. All this, and we've not even left your house!"

He stared at her bare feet peeking out from beneath the ragged hems of his old scrubs. "And we're not going to be able to leave the house until we get some shoes for you." His sandals wouldn't work on her smaller, narrow feet. But Ginny's might.

He wondered how Ginny and Alton were doing, if they'd managed to capture Artigos. The day was almost gone. Selyn would have been missed by now, so there was no way she could return to the mines—not until it was time to hand out the swords to the Forgotten Ones.

For now, they'd just have to wait, and hope that things were going according to plan.

Dawson had gone in to start something for their dinner, and she really should have gone with him and at least offered to help, but Selyn couldn't bring herself to go back inside the dark, cool dwelling.

Not when the sun was setting behind the amazing masses of red rock, bathing the desert sand in shades of red and purple and dark, dark blue. She'd never imagined such beauty, much less actually seen it with her own eyes.

This day had been one surprise after another, from the moment she'd awakened in that strange room, to the gentle care she'd received from a man. She probably shouldn't trust any of them—not Dawson or Alton or especially Dax. He'd started out as a demon, according to Dawson. A demon from Abyss, sent to this world to fight his own kind. How could one trust a demon?

Her mind wouldn't stop spinning. So much to absorb, to try to understand. New information, new feelings, new everything.

Her feelings were the most confusing, the way she couldn't stop thinking about Dawson and how he affected her. The way her body seemed to respond to his. Men were not to be trusted.

Hadn't Birk proved that?

But what of Roland? He'd risked his own safety to rescue her. And what of Dawson? Even now he protected her. He'd used his skills to heal her. And Alton, promising swords to the Forgotten Ones, and his friend Taron, sequestered at the deepest levels of the crystal caves, replicating those swords.

All men, all risking their own safety, their status, by

doing good things to help her and her forgotten sisters. It went against everything she'd always known, always believed, and it was so very difficult to trust.

BumperWillow whined. She'd come outside a while ago to keep Selyn company. Now she sat up, and her curly tail slapped against the concrete patio. She gazed out across the desert, as if awaiting something—or someone.

Selyn heard a strange noise and glanced up to see a large vehicle coming down the pathway to the house. Terrified, she thought to run inside, but then BumperWillow barked and wiggled her sturdy, curly-haired body as if she were dancing with joy.

At the same time, Selyn recognized Eddy's face through the clear windows and Dax sitting beside her. BumperWillow leapt to her feet, and her curly tail wagged so hard it whapped Selyn's leg like a drumstick beating out a rhythm.

Selyn stood beside the excited dog and waited until the dust settled and the doors on the vehicle opened. The dog didn't wait. She took off with a leap into the air and then proceeded to run around the vehicle in mad, skidding circles.

A door opened, and Eddy got out. "Hey, girl. Slow down. You're going to hurt yourself!" She leaned over to pet the beast and got her face licked in return. Finally she stood up and grinned at Selyn. "Hi, Selyn. Is Dawson around?" Eddy looped her scabbard with DemonSlayer over her shoulder and shut the door of the vehicle.

BumperWillow bounced and yipped and whined as if they'd been separated for months, not merely a few hours.

"He is. I'll get him." She turned toward the dwelling, but Dawson was already opening the door and stepping outside.

"Have you got him?"

"We do," Eddy said. "He's still pretty groggy, but he's able to walk. Where do you want him?"

"Selyn can show you. I'll go in and open the room."

Dax helped an older gentleman out of the back of the vehicle. The man stumbled, and Dax caught him with a sturdy arm around his waist. Eddy took his other side, and between the two of them they guided the chancellor into the house. He walked as if he'd had too much to drink, but Eddy and Dax managed to keep him on course.

BumperWillow trotted along beside them with her tail wagging and tongue hanging out. Selyn led them through the main room and down the hall to the quarters Dawson had prepared.

She kept glancing back, shocked to see that the one who had destroyed so many lives was nothing more than a tall, gray-haired man who didn't appear at all big and strong or even particularly dangerous.

No, he just looked like a slightly inebriated older man in a wrinkled robe who needed to fix his messy hair. She stepped aside when they reached the room. Dax and Eddy walked Artigos inside and then helped him lie down on the big bed. Eddy carefully removed his sandals, while Dax helped center him so he wouldn't fall off.

Even knowing what evil he had done, they treated him with respect. Confused, Selyn stayed back, out of their way.

Dawson left a cup of water beside the bed and checked to make sure there was cool air circulating from an overhead fan. He stopped Dax with the light touch of his hand. "Do you think he'll be okay?"

Dax nodded. "He should be. The longer he's out, the better. He'll need to be well rested before we try removing the demon from him."

Dawson paused and stared intently at Dax. "You're positive he's possessed?"

Dax shrugged, staring at the chancellor. "I can definitely sense demonkind in him. It's difficult to tell how powerful it is. Its presence is subtle, as if it consciously hides itself, which makes it inherently more dangerous. I fear it has become more deeply entrenched—a part of him, like a parasite feeding off his soul. Rather than fighting for absolute control of a man's mind, some demons are capable of melding entirely to the host's consciousness. They control in a more passive manner, but over time, they control completely."

Dawson glanced at Selyn, then again at Dax. His eyes looked haunted. "That doesn't sound good. Does Alton know?"

"Not yet. He's supposed to call later. I'll tell him then. It wasn't until I'd spent time with his father that I could be certain." Dax opened the door, but he gave Artigos one final look. Then he stepped out of the room with Eddy behind him.

"How long do you expect him to be out like this?" Dawson carefully locked the door. He handed the key to Selyn, folding her fingers around it, before following Eddy and Dax down the hallway. Selyn stared at the key for a moment, surprised at the trust Dawson placed in her. He'd said she would control the key, but she really hadn't expected him to follow through.

He hadn't even hesitated. Bemused, she stuck the key in her pocket and walked with him.

Eddy glanced over her shoulder. "Alton wasn't sure, but he expects his father'll be pretty loopy, at least until tomorrow."

"Loopy?" Selyn glanced at Dawson.

"In a trance," he said, laughing softly. "Must be one of those untranslatable words."

She returned his smile without even thinking about it,

and then she realized she couldn't recall ever smiling as much as she had today. Not in her entire life.

Definitely a day of firsts, and so far, especially now that the chancellor was out of Lemuria and no longer in control of the council, all of them good.

By the time he'd organized a meeting of the council for later in the evening and gone back to Bell Rock where he could use his cell phone to call Dax and check on his father, Alton was beginning to think the coup was actually going to work as planned.

The phone call had settled one of the big issues—Dax confirmed demon possession in Artigos. After speaking with him, Alton agreed that Dax and Eddy should wait before attempting to remove the entity until Ginny could come with DarkFire. Her sword had already displayed more specialized skills. Hopefully, removing demons was one of them.

For now, Artigos was locked safely away at Dawson Buck's with both Dawson and Selyn watching over him.

It was time to face the citizens of Lemuria. Alton returned to his mother's quarters. She and Ginny were sitting in the small kitchen area, sipping tea and chatting like old friends. He kissed his mother's cheek and then leaned close and kissed Ginny's soft lips. He wanted to grab her up in his arms and take her away from all this, but all he could do was kiss her again. "Is everything okay?"

She smiled at him, and her eyes were twinkling. "Everything is fine. Your mom and I've been talking. I know all your secrets."

"Oh, crap." He smiled at his mother. "All of them?"

She leaned her head against his side, and looked up at

him playfully, the way he remembered from his youth, as if she were just another playmate and not actually his mother. "Well, I didn't tell her about the blanket you hauled everywhere with you until we had to burn the filthy thing."

"Gee, thanks." He blinked suspiciously. "You burned it?"

Gaia winked. Then her expression sobered. "What did you learn of Artigos?"

"There is definitely a demon lodged within his soul. It won't be easy, but we think we can remove it."

"And I will have my husband again." She closed her eyes, almost as if she prayed. Then she stood and shot a sharp glance at each of them. "It's time. We will install you in your father's place, and then we can see about making things right."

Those were the words that kept Alton going through the long night ahead. That, and Ginny's steady presence beside him. The council members questioned his abilities when they met with them first in private, but he answered their concerns and faced up to their disbelief. When they referred to their leader's public declaration that Alton was no longer his son, his mother stood proudly and blamed it on her husband's strange, unexplainable illness. She bravely countered anyone who questioned her son's ability to lead.

And steadfastly, Ginny stayed beside him. Tall and lean in her black jeans and boots with the purple hoodie that barely covered her slim belly, she stood proudly with DarkFire clasped in both hands. It was impossible to deny Alton's ability to lead when he carried a sentient sword. Impossible when the woman beside him carried one with the spirit of the Crone, a crystal blade presented to Ginny in a most public yet personal fashion.

The people of Lemuria still spoke of that amazing

event, and probably would for many years to come. Ginny's instant popularity and her dark crystal blade reflected well on Alton.

Long hours later, he took his place as temporary chancellor of the Council of Nine and faced the citizens of Lemuria from the same dais where Ginny had received DarkFire just a few days ago. Though some of the council members disputed Alton's right, they were overruled by their peers and the overwhelming public approval both Gaia's and Ginny's presence had ensured.

The crowd dispersed. Alton and Ginny walked his mother back to her quarters and left her there. She assured them she was fine by herself—essentially she'd lived alone most of her life.

Finally, well into the early morning hours of the day to come, they headed through the maze of tunnels to Alton's private quarters and a chance for some much-needed sleep.

Roland's voice slipped into Alton's mind.

I've spoken to Taron. The rest of the swords should be ready by tomorrow, but he has an unusual sword with an even more unusual demand.

The sword has spoken? Alton clutched Ginny's hand tightly and stopped in his tracks.

It has, and it's made a specific request. It said, "You will take me to Artigos the Just."

My grandfather? He's been dead for thousands of years. Ever since the move to Mount Shasta.

Roland's soft laughter was impossible to ignore. *Not according to the very large sword I now have in my possession. The one with the golden hilt and the ruby crystal blade.*

Alton glanced at Ginny. She was practically stumbling

from exhaustion, but time was growing short. *Where can we meet?*

I'll be at your quarters in two minutes. I'm headed that way now.

So am I, Roland. He squeezed Ginny's shoulders as she leaned against him. *So am I.*

Chapter Six

"Ginny, putting the swords together was a brilliant idea."

Ginny stood back, watching as Alton carefully sheathed the strange ruby and gold sword in Taron's old scabbard. He didn't touch any part of the weapon, instead holding it with an edge of the blanket Roland had used to hide it. Once it was firmly sheathed, he carefully wrapped the scabbard and sword in the blanket until it was entirely hidden within the soft folds. There was power in this sword—a great and terrible power. They'd all felt it—no one wanted to risk actually touching the thing.

Finally, Alton tucked the wrapped blade under his arm and kissed Ginny much too quickly. "I had no idea they'd actually be able to talk to each other. That was amazing. C'mon."

Ginny adjusted the sheath holding DarkFire and followed Alton through the portal leading from his quarters. At least now they had an idea where to begin on their search for Artigos the Just. Ginny looped her fingers around Alton's arm. "I wasn't sure if it would work, but I figured it couldn't hurt to try. Now we know where to start asking questions."

"We start with Selyn. I wonder what she can tell us?" He kissed Ginny again. "Hurry. Before citizens fill the passages." Alton took off down the wide tunnel with his usual long strides. Ginny stretched her legs to keep up with him, but she didn't try to slow him down. There was so much to be done, and so very little time to do it before all hell broke loose.

Literally.

But what an amazing morning. They'd stared at that damned ruby sword the night before until Roland had finally headed back to his quarters and Ginny'd fallen asleep. It had been a startlingly clear dream that had her lining up all three crystal blades on the bed in the early morning hours.

When HellFire and DarkFire had not only acknowledged the ruby sword, but had pledged allegiance, both she and Alton had been totally blown away. The ruby sword had remained mute, though the crystal glowed like fire.

Whatever the swords said afterward, though, had remained private. The blades had glowed and then faded. DarkFire had been the one to utter the name of the woman Roland had rescued.

At least they knew exactly how to find Selyn, which made her the perfect point to begin their search.

Suddenly, Alton grabbed Ginny's arm and pulled her into a dark alcove. A moment later, a group of guardsmen marched by. Their footsteps echoed against the cavern walls until the measured sound finally faded into the distance. Alton poked his head out of the opening, looked both ways, and then grabbed Ginny's hand and tugged her along with him.

He glanced over his shoulder, but he didn't slow his stride a bit. "That's really weird. I didn't recognize any of those men. We've a fairly small population. I know most of the guards, at least by sight if not by name."

Ginny scrambled to keep up. "They're Lemurian though, aren't they?" They were big men, though. Really big. Taller and heavier even than Roland or the other guards she'd met.

"They are, but where have they served before now? Why don't I know them?" He tightened his grasp on Ginny's hand and picked up the pace. She glanced at him, but he was frowning and staring ahead, along the passage, so she raced beside him, running now for all she was worth. Quietly, without further interruptions, they raced toward the vortex.

Ginny wasn't all that sure of her way around within Lemuria, but she didn't think they were all that far from the energy veil that separated this world from the portals in the vortex. At this pace, they should be there really soon. But why were they running? Why was Alton so concerned about discovery? "You're the new chancellor," Ginny whispered. "Why'd we hide?"

He wasn't even breathing hard when he answered her. "Roland said not everyone accepts the change of leadership. We don't have time to convince some hardheaded guard I'm no longer a wanted man for breaking Dax and Eddy out of jail."

"Good point." She glanced at the tall, strikingly beautiful man running purposefully beside her and decided that anyone who didn't admire and respect Alton of Artigos was an absolute idiot. But he was so terribly conflicted right now. She knew how badly he wanted to help his father, to regain the man he barely remembered—the one who had loved the child Alton had once been.

Even stronger was his desire to protect both his world and hers from demonkind. There were so many forces against them, so many things that could go wrong. She hoped like hell they'd all find the happy ending that seemed so impossible at this point.

Ginny was breathing hard and fighting a stitch in her side when the golden veil marking Lemuria's boundary came into view. Alton wasn't even winded. She looked at him, and a sense of destiny swept over her, a feeling that maybe, if they could pull everything together, this whole convoluted plan might work.

Though right now, a lot hinged on Selyn's willingness to help. Ginny hoped the woman didn't harbor too much anger and too great a need for revenge. Selyn had suffered terribly because of Artigos. Why would she ever want to help them find the man's father?

Selyn sipped her cup of coffee and tried to decide whether or not she liked the strange brew. Eddy had added some sugar and a squirt of foamy white cream out of a can, and the flavor had been much improved, but now Eddy was gone, and somehow the coffee and cream no longer tasted as good.

Everything seemed different since Eddy and Dax had left, though they'd only been gone a short time. Selyn wondered if it was the fact that her mother's spirit was no longer here. Not that she'd spoken to Elda again since that one time, but just knowing she was nearby and happy had given Selyn peace.

That, and having another woman around. Now it was just Selyn, Dawson, and Artigos. And BumperWillow, of course, though Selyn found it difficult to count her as an actual woman—not when she barked and chased her tail and liked to stalk rabbits in the yard.

She sipped her cooling cup of coffee and thought of

how it had been this morning, waking up in Dawson's home, seeing him with his eyes sleepy and his hair mussed. She'd felt strange sleeping alone in a big bed in a room by herself, having her own bathing room and private facilities after a lifetime of living in the slaves' barracks—a hundred women sharing everything.

All of this felt strange. This world, her life. Everything.

She glanced at Dawson. He'd been on the phone, talking to someone at his clinic, whatever that was. She knew he dealt with the health of animals like BumperWillow, but she wasn't at all certain exactly what he did.

Whatever it was, it seemed to make him smile. Of course, a lot of things made Dawson smile. Often, when she looked up and caught him watching her, he was smiling . . . or frowning. He frowned, too. He was a confusing man, but maybe all men were confusing. She had so little knowledge of the gender, and none at all of the men of Earth.

This particular man was more fascinating than any she'd ever met. She wished she knew what he was thinking. Why he watched her with so many different expressions.

Earlier, he'd taken Eddy and Dax to the vortex at a place called Red Rock Crossing so they could go back to Eddy's home in Evergreen. Eddy had decided to leave Bumper-Willow behind, and that had actually made Dawson laugh out loud. He'd said something about taking his talking dog to the clinic and surprising his staff.

Of course, Selyn knew he wouldn't actually do anything like that. He wasn't about to give away the existence of demons or Lemurians or talking dogs. He'd tried to explain it all to her last night, the fact that, as far as his world knew, she didn't exist. Demons didn't exist, and dogs hosting talkative spirits were absolutely impossible.

Just like the man locked in the back room. He couldn't

exist either, at least by human beliefs. Selyn knew better. Her hatred refused to allow her to forget his existence. He was awake this morning. She sensed his anger, his desire to escape his prison. He'd kicked the door a couple of times, but now he appeared to be sulking.

She sensed it. All of it: his anger, his frustration—and his demon. There was no denying the fact the man harbored a demon. Dax wasn't the only one able to feel the evil surrounding Artigos, the deposed Lemurian Chancellor of the Council of Nine.

He was evil all the way through. And he was the one who had condemned her mother to death, the one who had decreed that the Forgotten Ones should never be free of enslavement in the mines.

He really needed to die, and she, quite literally, held the key to his prison. Dawson had no idea what power he'd handed to her when he put Selyn in charge of the key. When he trusted her.

Selyn took another sip of her coffee and studied Dawson over the rim of the cup. Of course, it wasn't like she could just march back there and kill the chancellor. Not when Dawson had sworn to protect the bastard. Selyn owed Dawson her life.

Somehow, she needed to work through this conflict without compromising Dawson's honor—or her own.

But how? She had sworn to avenge her mother's life of slavery and her untimely death. Not only for herself, but for all the other Forgotten Ones who toiled below. But how could she kill Artigos without putting Dawson's honor at risk?

Something nudged her leg. Selyn glanced down, into the deep brown eyes of that silly looking dog. It was impossible to plot a murderer's death when a creature like this one was staring at you. "Did you want something, BumperWillow?"

The dog blinked. Then she sighed. *I feel your anger, Selyn. And I must apologize, but I couldn't help but hear your thoughts. You are conflicted, and rightly so. Artigos has done terrible things, but he does not command himself. Truly, he is not to blame. He is ruled by a demon that has controlled him for many years. The death of Artigos would not avenge the Forgotten Ones, nor would it avenge your mother. It would only hurt Alton and Dawson—two good men who have risked much to help you—and it would destroy the life of a man who is as much a victim as any of the warrior women who died, as much as the women who toil in the mines. Please, think of that when you plot your revenge.*

Selyn didn't answer. She couldn't. What could she say? Was the spirit within the dog right? Was that old man merely one more victim of demonkind?

She'd have to think about that. Better to be sure before taking a life, especially one everybody seemed so worried about saving. She stared into her cup of cold coffee and realized the person she hated to hurt the most was the man standing across the room.

"Ginny just called."

Surprised by his nearness, Selyn blinked and spun around on the tall stool. Dawson was no longer across the room. He was right beside her. She hadn't even realized he was there.

He was so close she had to blink and refocus her eyes to see him, yet she felt no need to back away. He smiled with just the corners of his lips as he stuck his phone in his pocket, and she had the odd feeling he was laughing at himself.

That made no sense. No more than the fact he'd reached for her and now lightly ran his fingers down a long curl of the black hair hanging loosely over her shoulder. His gaze shifted from her eyes to his fingers. He seemed mesmerized by the lock of hair he now curled around his hand and slowly rubbed between his thumb and forefinger.

"What did she want?"

He blinked and raised his head. "What? Who?"

Selyn covered his fingers with hers. Wrapped her hand around his. "Ginny. You said she called. What does she want?"

"Oh." He laughed, and his face flushed. It appeared humans blushed exactly the same way Lemurians did. *Interesting.*

"She called to tell me they're at the portal and need a ride here. Alton has something he wants to show you." He shrugged. "No idea what. She didn't say. The thing is, I'm not comfortable leaving Artigos here alone, even locked away, and while I hate to leave you again, I'd feel better if you were here to keep an eye on things. Do you mind guarding the fort for a few minutes?"

She shook her head, still bemused by his blush. What could it mean? "I was fine when you took Eddy and Dax," she said. She turned his hand loose. His fingers dropped away from her hair.

"You were hardly gone long at all," she added. "I've got BumperWillow to keep me company."

He laughed and ran his hand over the dog's curly head. "That you do. I'm glad she decided to stay."

"Together we will guard your fort." She watched the way his long fingers slipped through the dog's curls and felt a strange yearning inside. So much she didn't understand. So many odd feelings, so much about this man.

He glanced up and stared at her for a long moment. Then, almost as if he were as bespelled as the old man in the other room, he slowly straightened, reached out, and cupped her jaw in his hand.

His touch surprised her. The other had been almost

accidental, as if he'd touched her hair without thinking, but this time, the intimacy of his hand cupping her face so carefully was a more conscious act. He was very gentle for a man. Surprisingly gentle, though she'd known that from the beginning. Still, she wondered if she would ever be totally comfortable when a man touched her, knowing what violence they were capable of.

But Dawson appeared to have no violence in him. His palm was warm; his fingers warmer still. Selyn held very still, unsure what he wanted . . . what he intended.

Unsure of how she felt about his touch. It wasn't unpleasant. Not at all like anything she'd ever experienced with a man. Nor was it like the comforting touch from one of the sisters of her soul. This was unique—almost a caress—and the more she thought about it, the more she decided she liked it.

She leaned against his palm, stared into his blue eyes, and wondered what he saw when he looked at her.

Suddenly he blinked, and his hand fell away from her face. The quickness of his movement startled her; the loss of contact surprised her. She missed the warmth, the sense of connection she'd felt when he held her face so carefully.

Definitely something she'd have to think about.

He stepped back and cleared his throat. "I'll be away for just a few minutes. Don't let anyone in, okay? Bumper-Willow, guard the house and protect Selyn."

The dog yipped. The sprite was silent. So was Selyn as Dawson turned quickly away and left the house.

Shit. He'd almost kissed her. What the hell was he thinking? Poor kid had been beaten half to death just the night before last, and the last thing she needed was some idiot pawing her. So what did he do? Played with her hair, put his hand on her face without even thinking how it must appear to her.

He should apologize, at the very least. He would apologize, as soon as he got Alton and Ginny.

What the hell was he going to do about Selyn?

Nothing. You're not going to do a damned thing. She's off limits. Get over it.

Yeah. Right. He laughed out loud as he pulled into the parking space at Red Rock Crossing where Alton and Ginny waited. Selyn was currently living in his home, sleeping across the hallway, eating at his table, and watching him with those beautiful blue eyes. Getting over Selyn was probably not going to happen anytime soon.

"Hey, Daws. How's it going?"

Ginny leaned in through the open window and kissed his cheek. Then she crawled into the backseat while Alton rode shotgun.

"Going good. What's that, Alton? Got a baby wrapped in that blanket?" He really needed to get his head screwed on straight. Ginny and Alton were the ones to help him do exactly that.

"Not quite." Alton lifted a corner of the woven blanket back just enough for Dawson to see what looked like a solid gold hilt to a sword that was sheathed in a white leather scabbard.

"What the hell is that?" He glanced in the rearview mirror at Ginny's big smile, and backed out of the parking space.

"It's a crystal sword that spoke to Taron and said it belongs to Alton's grandfather." Ginny was practically bouncing in the backseat. "Isn't that just cool?"

"Only he's been dead for ten thousand or so years, which means we've got a bit of a conundrum." Alton covered the sword once again. "How's everyone doing?"

Dawson headed back toward his house. "Selyn's great, your dad's pissed, and Eddy and Dax have gone home to Evergreen to check on the portals there and make certain the ones to Abyss are still sealed. We've got Bumper-Willow. She thought she might be able to help drive the demon from your father."

"Good." Alton turned and glanced at Ginny in the backseat. She leaned forward and clasped his shoulder.

Dawson couldn't help but notice the way they communicated without words. He knew Lemurians used telepathy, and even he could understand Willow, but there was more than that working between Ginny and Alton. They obviously understood one another on so many levels.

He wondered what it would be like to be so in tune with another person that her fears became yours, her desires, her needs, her interests—all shared because you were so tightly connected.

And he thought of Selyn, of the way she'd looked when he'd touched her hair and she'd reached for his hand, when he'd cupped her cheek in his palm. He wasn't sure, but he thought she might have actually leaned into what could only be described as a caress. He didn't think she'd pulled away, but that might be his wishful thinking.

She had definitely wrapped her fingers around his when he'd stroked her silky hair. Maybe she'd done that to stop him from doing more.

He pulled into the driveway and turned off the engine. Selyn and BumperWillow stood in the doorway. "Everything okay?"

She nodded and stepped outside with the dog on her heels. Even in the old pair of his surgical scrubs, Selyn was absolutely breathtaking. She'd braided her hair while he'd been gone, pulling all of it back from her face into a single long braid that looped over her shoulder.

The tightly bound hair made her eyes look bigger, her cheekbones more pronounced, her lips fuller. He missed the soft curl of dark hair falling all the way to her hips. It softened her, somehow. Made her look more approachable.

She looked stronger with it tied back, though. More self-contained. Every inch the warrior woman. No way in hell could he see her as a slave when she looked this way. No, this woman was not a slave to any man.

His body didn't seem to care. He was hard as a post and hoping like hell no one noticed. He cleared his throat and made a point of focusing on those deep blue eyes of hers. "How's Artigos?"

Selyn smiled and rubbed the dog's curly head. "I just peeked through the window on the door and checked on him. He sleeps, but his breakfast tray is empty. I think he likes your bacon and eggs." She flashed a big grin at Ginny and Alton. "Hello. It's good to see you. I'm glad to hear everything went so well." She nodded and stepped aside.

"Hey, Selyn. I brought you something." Ginny held up one of the cloth bags she carried. "Sandals. I think they're your size. Dawson said you needed shoes."

Selyn's eyes lit up like a little kid's at Christmas. "For me?" She took the bag from Ginny, tugged the drawstring to loosen it, and pulled out a beautiful pair of leather sandals.

Dawson stepped closer to see. "Wow. Those are gorgeous. Will they fit?"

Her eyes sparkled as she knelt to put them on. Dawson almost laughed aloud. Obviously shoes appealed to all women.

Selyn finished buckling the sandals and stood. "They're perfect. I've never had anything like them. Thank you."

"Wonderful." Ginny leaned into Alton. "When you meet Gaia, Alton's mom, you can thank her. She sent them."

"Your mother?" Selyn's eyes went big. "I thought they

looked like something one of the aristocracy would wear. Are you sure it's all right for me to . . ."

Alton seemed to understand what she was thinking. "Of course it's all right. They're a gift from my mother. She wanted you to have them. She sent a robe for you, too."

Ginny held up the other bag, but she elbowed Alton.

Laughing, he added, "but Ginny thought you'd prefer pants."

"I guess." Selyn brushed her hand down her cotton-covered legs. "Like these?"

"No. Like these." Ginny laughed and held up one jeans-clad leg. "I've got some extras in our room, and we're about the same size. C'mon."

Dawson watched the women go inside his house and couldn't quit grinning. When he'd bought this big place, it had originally been his intention to set up his clinic here, but he'd quickly discovered his patients wanted the convenience of a veterinarian in town rather than out in the country. Then he'd dreamed of filling it one day with a wife and children.

Never, not in his wildest dreams, had he imagined filling it with Lemurians and talking dogs. Luckily, it hadn't been difficult at all to convince Ginny and Alton to give up their expensive casita. They'd been staying at that ritzy lodge north of town, but it felt right having everyone here, and he had more than enough room in the sprawling ranch-style house.

"Ginny and her clothes." Alton was laughing softly as he followed Daws back inside. "She's easily sidetracked! Let me show you the reason we're here, besides trying to rid my father of his demon." He carried the rolled up blanket into the kitchen and set the bundle on the counter. Carefully, without touching the contents, Alton unwrapped and then unsheathed an amazing ruby sword. Larger than the crystal blade he carried, it had what appeared to be a solid gold pommel. The crystalline blade glowed a deep blood red.

"Holy shit. Where'd that come from?" Dawson clenched his hands into fists to keep from touching the thing. Obviously, with the care Alton was showing, fondling someone else's crystal sword wasn't a good idea.

Alton sighed. "It's one of the replicated swords. The others are all clear crystal, like mine. This one shocked the nine hells out of Taron, especially when it asked to be taken to my grandfather, who supposedly died when we made the move from Lemuria to Mount Shasta. This morning, HellFire and DarkFire both pledged allegiance to the sword, but it didn't say anything. There was a lot of glowing and an aura of true power, so we both sensed they were communicating. Then DarkFire said one word: 'Selyn.'"

"Selyn?" Dawson stared at the blade as if he might actually find answers there. Somehow. "Why would she say Selyn's name?"

"I imagine as a place to begin our search for Artigos the Just. Wow! Selyn, you look hot!"

Dawson spun around.

Ginny laughed out loud. "Hot? Alton, when did you start sounding like me?"

Alton just laughed. Dawson didn't really give a damn. The big guy was right. Selyn wore a pair of Ginny's tight black jeans that looked like they'd been glued to her legs, with a bright blue halter top that sort of flowed around her waist and yet still managed to cling to all the right places. Dawson couldn't have said a word if his life depended on it, but yeah, Selyn was definitely hot.

Hot enough to make his temperature rise a few notches.

"Do I look like a human woman in these pants? They

feel so strange." Selyn laughed and sort of held her arms out, as if she wanted to show off her outfit.

Dawson wanted to lock her in a dark room. Yeah, he'd seen her naked when she was all beat up and he'd been trying to heal her wounds, but for some reason she looked more naked to him now, covered in denim and silk, than she had without a stitch on. He shook his head, feeling absolutely dazed. "Selyn, I hate to tell you, but you don't look human at all. There's no human alive as beautiful as you."

He caught a quick look at Ginny's wide eyes and heard Alton chuckle, but he didn't care what they thought. Not at all. All he cared about was the woman standing in his kitchen. Selyn was a combination of shy innocence and sex incarnate. She stared at him with a whole raft of expressions flitting across her face. He couldn't read any of them, though she didn't seem at all put off by his comment.

He hoped she didn't mind that he thought she was too gorgeous to be human. Hoped she didn't think it was an insult. He stepped closer, but a brilliant flash of red caught his eye.

He turned to look as Selyn stepped around him and stood in front of the counter. She stared, transfixed, at the ruby sword. It glowed as if someone had turned on a light switch. Dawson reached for Selyn and caught her hand before she could touch the crystal blade.

She shook her head. "No. Can't you hear it? It wants me to touch it."

He didn't hear a thing. Daws glanced at Alton, who gave him a short, sharp negative shake of his head. He hadn't heard it, either.

Selyn licked her lips and tentatively laid her fingers on the glowing blade. It pulsed blood red beneath her fingertips. Dawson, Alton, and Ginny all stayed back.

The sword wanted Selyn.

Another bright flash lit the room. A deep voice raised chills along Dawson's spine. BumperWillow whimpered.

"You know of the one I seek, Selyn of Elda's line, daughter of the DemonSlayer. Take me to Artigos the Just."

The glow faded. Selyn stepped back and bowed her head, her respect obviously bordering on awe. When she turned, her excitement practically radiated from her shining eyes. While she looked at the three of them, Dawson was certain she spoke only to him. "I know where he is. We have to go back to the mines. He's there. A prisoner locked away for millennia, kept apart from all of us, approached with fear by all the guards. I never knew his name. Now I do."

She turned her attention to Alton. "Your grandfather Artigos the Just, the father of your father, is imprisoned deep within the mines of Lemuria."

Chapter Seven

Alton didn't say anything while he carefully wrapped the blanket around the sword and scabbard. Finally, when it was covered once again, he turned and leaned against the counter. Exhaustion was evident in every move he made, in the deep lines etched beside his mouth and the dark circles under his eyes.

Rubbing his forehead with one hand, he sighed. "Okay. Here's where we stand. Roland said Taron's almost got the swords ready to go. We need to meet with him down in the lower caves at some point so we can help deliver them to the Forgotten Ones. Once that's done, I have to return as soon as I can and take up my position on the council. I've got to have a firm grasp of things before the Forgotten Ones make their presence known."

He shook his head. "I've got the chancellor's role for now, but my hold is tenuous. Today Ginny and I spotted a group of Lemurian guardsmen I've never seen before, which tells me that some of the council are up to something. I doubt it's anything good."

Ginny handed him a tall glass of water. Alton took a few swallows and set it aside. "Thing is, I can't afford to be away for long, or what little hold I have on the chancellor's seat will be lost. While we're here, though, Ginny and I have to try to remove the demon from my father."

He focused on Dawson. "I know you're not familiar with Lemuria, but I may have to ask you to go into the mines with Selyn. Would you be willing to take this sword with you, to take it to the prisoner Selyn speaks of? That needs to be done as soon as possible. If my grandfather is still alive, his presence could change everything—in a good way."

Dawson almost laughed out loud. Go to Lemuria? Was Alton kidding? He'd give anything for the chance to see that fabled world. "I'll do whatever you need, Alton. You know that."

Alton wrapped his arm around Ginny and tugged her close against his side, but his focus was on Dawson. "You've already done so much. You hardly know us, and yet you've opened your home and your heart to a cause that's not even yours."

Dawson shrugged. "But it is mine. Every bit as much as it's yours, don't you think? If demons threaten Earth, it had damned well better be my cause. I've got as big a stake in the outcome as any of you."

"He's right, you know." Ginny smiled at Alton and snuggled close against his side. "This battle affects every single one of us." Then, in a melodramatic whisper, she added, "Don't scare the man off. He's helping. We need him. He's giving us a free place to stay with a really comfortable bed." She kissed Alton's cheek. "And he cooks. C'mon. Let's go check on your father before you fold up on me and fall asleep on the floor."

Alton yawned. Then he nodded to Dawson. "Don't let her kid you. We really do appreciate everything you're doing for us. I don't know where we'd be without your help."

"I think you'd be doing fine, but I mean what I say. Anything I can do, whatever I've got you can use; it's yours."

Without another word Alton pushed himself away from the counter as if it took every last bit of his strength. Dawson snapped his fingers, and BumperWillow followed them back to the suite of rooms where Artigos was being held.

Dawson glanced through the window on the door and saw Alton's father stalking back and forth across the room like an angry lion. "You might want to have your swords out," he said. "Your father's pacing like he's ready to kill someone."

Alton shrugged. "He probably is. Probably a good thing we're keeping his sword well away. I imagine he and his demon are less than thrilled with their situation about now."

Dawson took the key from Selyn and unlocked the door as both Ginny and Alton drew their swords. Artigos stopped in mid-stride and glared at all of them as they entered the large room.

"Is my assassination next on your schedule, my beloved son?" Artigos wrapped his arms across his broad chest and sneered at Alton. "Are you so afraid of your father that you must approach him with your weapon drawn?"

"It's pity more than fear I feel, Father. If I appear cautious, it's not because of you. It's the demon who rules your heart and mind that concerns me most. That and, whether you choose to believe me or not, your well-being."

Artigos laughed. "Demon? Controlling me? I think not." Without warning, he lunged at Alton, but Alton and Ginny were ready. Dawson grabbed the dog's collar as BumperWillow leapt to their defense, but her enthusiastic barking let him know she was more than willing to fight.

As one, Ginny and Alton pointed their crystal blades at Artigos. Dark purple fire burst from Ginny's blade. A brilliant blue glow shot from Alton's and intersected with Ginny's, catching Artigos in the crossfire of light.

He lurched to an immediate halt, held mid-step in the shimmering fire. Eyes wide and angry, Artigos struggled within the beam, but he couldn't break free of the force holding him almost a foot off the ground.

BumperWillow stopped barking. Dawson let go of her collar, and she stepped away from him and stood in front of Artigos. She glanced back once at the small group, and then she concentrated on Artigos.

The man's mouth was moving, and he was obviously cursing, but no sound escaped the shimmering field of swirling blue and purple light. With her head cocked to one side, the curly dog studied him for long moments, while Ginny and Alton held Artigos immobile with the power of their crystal blades.

After a good five minutes, BumperWillow stepped away and stood beside Dawson. He tangled his fingers in her curly hair. The dog sighed. Willow's voice slipped into Dawson's head, and he knew she spoke to all of them.

The demon's possession is almost total. I fear it is beyond my ability to remove. What do DarkFire and Hell-Fire think?

When DarkFire answered, Dawson wondered if he'd ever grow used to a talking sword. "The demon is too deeply entrenched. We could remove it, but Artigos the man would not survive. Killing the demon will end his life."

Alton shook his head. "That's not acceptable." He lowered his sword, as did Ginny. Artigos crumpled to the ground, dazed but still conscious. Alton gently sheathed his sword and lifted his father in his arms as if the large man were a child. Carefully, he laid him on the bed.

Artigos stared up at his son. His forehead was wrinkled in a confused frown, and he blinked his eyes slowly. After a moment, his expression relaxed; he closed his eyes and drifted gently into sleep.

Alton rubbed the back of his neck and yawned. He looked absolutely discouraged. "We'll need to try something else. I just wish I knew what."

Ginny took hold of Alton's hand. "Maybe your mother can help. I think it's worth a try. Love is a powerful motivator."

Alton's tired smile spoke volumes. "You've proved that to me more than once."

Ginny kissed him quickly. "I got some sleep last night. You didn't get any. I want you to go and lie down while I go back to Lemuria for your mother."

Alton rested both hands on her shoulders and shook his head. He was smiling, but it was more than obvious he didn't like Ginny's idea one bit. "I don't want you going alone. It's too dangerous."

"I'll be fine." She glanced over her shoulder and caught Dawson's eye. Hopefully, she said, "I'll take Dawson. You and Selyn stay here with BumperWillow and keep an eye on your dad. You okay with that, Daws?"

He nodded. "Of course," he said, but he was thinking, now? Just up and go to Lemuria, sort of like running down to the corner store? *Hell, yes!*

The fact that Alton agreed so readily was proof just how exhausted the man was, but before he had the time to change his mind, Ginny had hustled them all out of Artigos's room. She grabbed Alton's hand and dragged him toward the guest room they'd moved into just down the hall, with BumperWillow trotting along behind.

"I'll be ready in just a few minutes, Daws." Laughing, she added, "I'm going to put my baby to bed, first." Grumbling, Alton followed, but he looked as if he could barely put one foot in front of the next.

Dawson and Selyn were left standing outside Artigos's locked room. Selyn pocketed the key and studied Daws with a soft smile on her lips. "You will get to see my world, just as I'm seeing yours."

"Looks like it." He grabbed her hand and tugged her toward the kitchen. "Will you be okay here while I'm gone? You know how to work the remote, and there's plenty on TV."

She laughed. "I will be fine. I love watching that screen. Will you be okay, entering a strange world?"

He grinned. He couldn't help himself. What they all treated as commonplace was something beyond his wildest dreams. "You're kidding, right? I can't wait!"

"It's dangerous. Humans are not allowed in Lemuria, and if you are captured . . ."

He stopped and turned to face her. She really did look worried. He thought that was pretty cool, that she cared enough to at least worry a little. "I'll be with Ginny, and she's already achieving rock star status in Lemuria, according to Roland. The Lemurians love the fact she's descended from royalty."

He heard Ginny coming down the hallway with BumperWillow. "I need to go. You're sure you'll be okay?"

Selyn nodded. Then she surprised him by touching his beard with her fingertips. "Be very careful, Dawson Buck. I don't want anything to happen to you."

He stared at her lips, heard the words, and yet it still took him a moment to absorb what she'd said. Once he managed to wrap his stunned brain around the content, there was only one way he could respond. Cupping Selyn's face in both hands, he leaned close and gently kissed her lips. She didn't pull away, though she didn't kiss him back.

When he ended what was much too chaste a kiss for his

own peace of mind, Dawson stared first at Selyn's slightly parted, damp lips, and then at her sapphire blue eyes.

Ginny stepped into the kitchen. "I brought this for you, just in case. Ready to go, Daws. . . . Oops. Sorry."

He glanced over at Ginny, slowly dropped his hands from Selyn's face, and grinned. "Yeah, I'm ready. What have you got?"

"Pepper spray." With a quick, curious glance at Selyn, she handed him a small can attached to a key chain. "Granted, it's not a crystal sword, but if we need to get away from anyone in a hurry, it should help slow 'em down."

"I'll take it." He clipped it to his belt loop. Like Ginny said, it wasn't much, but it was better than nothing. "How long do you think we'll be?"

Ginny shrugged, grabbed the car keys to her rented Yukon off the table, and tossed them to Dawson. "Couple of hours, maybe. Hopefully less, definitely no longer. Selyn, if anyone comes, wake Alton, okay? It's probably best that you not answer the door. BumperWillow will stay with you. Trust her instincts."

Selyn nodded, but her gaze was locked on Dawson. It made it difficult for him to turn away, but he followed Ginny out to the car, torn by his desire to remain with Selyn, something he wanted as much as he wanted to see Lemuria for the first time. When he glanced at the house, Selyn stood in the doorway with BumperWillow beside her.

She waved. So did he, and then he got in the car with Ginny, and the two of them headed for the portal.

He'd watched as others disappeared into the solid rock wall at Red Rock Crossing, but he'd never imagined doing it himself. Now that he knew what to look for, how it felt, he realized he could use this passage at any time.

It was all dependent upon the way you saw the rock. Perception, in this case, created reality.

The concept totally boggled the mind. They passed through what appeared to be solid rock and entered a small cavern. Ginny stopped Dawson with a light touch to his arm.

"This vortex only powers two portals. The one we usually take moves us across Sedona to Bell Rock where there's a large portal that opens directly into the main entry to Lemuria. This one." She pointed to a glowing swirl of light on one wall.

Dawson stared at the portal, almost mesmerized by the sense of energy emanating from the light. Finally he forced himself to look away. "Why do I hear a 'but' in that statement?"

Ginny laughed. "Because you're obviously paying attention. We're going to take this one." She pointed at a smaller swirling mass of light. Not as bright, not as filled with energy. "Alton and I were told it led directly to the council chambers for the Council of Nine. Once he was made temporary chancellor, we discovered this portal's Lemurian gateway is actually in his father's private office. It's dangerous, because someone could be in there who doesn't belong, but so is trying to sneak through the tunnels in Lemuria without getting caught. We can't count on Roland to get us through. His schedule has been a mess lately."

"Do you think anyone suspects he might be helping us?"

"I don't know." Ginny shook her head. "I hope that's not it. He's got a wife and child to worry about, and we need him if we're going to carry this off. Anyway, this trip, we're going to take the portal directly into Artigos's office." She unsheathed her sword and held DarkFire ready. "C'mon."

Sword raised, Ginny slipped through the portal. Dawson followed, pepper spray in hand.

The man inside the office jumped away from the desk he was searching and raised his hands in the air. The glowing point of Ginny's sword ensured he wouldn't attack. Dawson held on to the can of pepper spray, just in case.

"What are you doing, besides searching through the chancellor's private papers?" Ginny stepped closer until DarkFire practically touched the man's chest.

He stammered and shook his head. "I . . . I . . . I was told to retrieve records."

"Told by whom? What records?"

He focused on the point of the sword. His eyes went wide as the blade flashed with dark purple light.

"Maxl and Drago. They requested proof of succession." He swallowed loudly. "They want to make certain your man"—his eyes flashed from Ginny to Dawson and back to the sword—"that Alton has a right to succession after being disowned by his father."

"He was approved by the citizens. His mother, Artigos's lifetime mate, championed his position so that her husband might be healed without fearing for the safety of Lemuria. You have no need of any papers from Artigos's desk. This office is for the use of the chancellor, and it shall remain private."

Shaking from head to foot, obviously terrified, the man bowed his head. "Should I relay that information to Maxl and Drago?"

Ginny smiled, but it wasn't a particularly friendly expression. Dawson doubted it would give the thief much confidence. "You do that," she said. "Chancellor Alton is resting for the moment. He'll meet with members of the council later this evening."

"Yes. Of course. I will relay that information to the others." He gave one last, fearful glance at the shimmering crystal blade and then turned away and slipped out through the portal on the far side of the room.

"DarkFire? Can you secure the portal to keep others out?"

The sword glowed, and a beam of dark light shot across the room, flowed over the portal, and then dissipated. "Only those of you in the fight against demonkind will be able to pass through the portal."

"Thank you." Ginny sheathed the sword. "Okay, Daws. Let's hope he was more terrified of DarkFire than curious about you. Lock up the pepper spray, and let's go get Gaia. You're going to like Alton's mom. She's pretty nice, considering she's had to put up with Artigos for all these years." She paused for a moment as if considering what she should and couldn't say.

Finally, she sighed and fiddled with the buckle on her scabbard. "Daws, there's one thing you should know, though. Gaia's been aware of the Forgotten Ones all along. She knew when Artigos arranged for the women warriors to be enslaved, and yet she did nothing about it."

Dawson's chest actually ached thinking of anyone living with that kind of knowledge. "Probably not a good idea to tell Selyn that."

Ginny nodded. "I imagine you're right, but I wanted you to know. You need to know what you're involved in."

"A whole shitload of trouble?"

Ginny laughed. "Exactly," she said. Then she slipped through the portal.

Dawson followed right behind her, stepping through the swirling light as if he'd done it a hundred times before. They moved quickly along a tunnel that appeared to be lighted from within the rock. Before too long, they passed by a large arch that opened onto a huge underground plaza. The walls were lined with what looked like solid gold, decorated with gems and precious stones of all kinds.

Dawson stopped, mesmerized by the vast size of the cavern, the glitter of gold and gems, until Ginny had to grab him by the arm and tug him along behind her. He could have stared at the amazing room forever.

"That's the great hall," she said. "Some call it the central or great plaza. It's where all the citizens of Lemuria gather for important events. It's empty now because it's still early in the day, but it's where I got my sword, where Daria the Crone gave me immortality."

"Wow." What else could he say? Every new thing they passed by was more mind-blowing than the last. Head spinning as he tried to see everything, Dawson followed Ginny through a series of narrow passages until she paused in front of another portal.

"Gaia says to come in."

He frowned. "How does she know we're here?"

Grinning, Ginny stepped through the portal. "Telepathy. C'mon."

The woman in the room they entered waited with her hands clasped and an expression of hope on her face. "Ginny? What word of Artigos?" Then she blinked in surprise. "Who is this man?" She focused on Dawson.

"Gaia, Dawson Buck is the human who's helping us. He's given Alton and me a place to stay, and he's keeping Artigos safe at his house. We're hoping you can come with us, maybe help keep Artigos calm while we try to remove this blasted demon. It's been part of him for a long time, and it doesn't want to leave. Alton and I are convinced you can help us, but it means coming to Earth."

"Anywhere. I'll do whatever you need." She turned

to Dawson. "Thank you, Dawson Buck. I imagine my husband is not the easiest guest to have."

Daws wasn't sure what prompted him, but he took Gaia's hand and lightly squeezed her fingers. "We'll do whatever we can to help your husband. Thank you for sending the sandals and robe for Selyn. They're a perfect fit. She was really excited to have such a nice gift from you."

Gaia's smile lit up the room. "I'm pleased," she said, but then she sobered. "I owe the Forgotten Ones more than sandals. More than a simple robe. When this is over, I'll do whatever I can to help them join our society as full and free citizens."

"We need to hurry," Ginny glanced around the spacious room. "What do you need to take for a few days away from Lemuria?"

Gaia stared at her. "I have no idea." She laughed. "I've not left for ten thousand years. I have an extra robe, my personal items, but . . ."

"Good. I'll help you pack." Taking control, Ginny led Gaia out of the room. "Roland just contacted me," she said to Dawson. "He should show up any minute now."

Dawson stared around him at what could have been any home on Earth, except for the lack of windows. The thought kept flitting through his mind, that he'd been left standing alone in a Lemurian living room, awaiting a member of the Lemurian Guard after fending off a thief in the chancellor's office. It all left him feeling as if he'd just dropped down the rabbit's hole.

Then Roland of Kronus popped through the portal. "Hey, Dawson! How is Selyn doing?" He clapped Daws on the shoulder as if they were old friends.

And damned if it didn't feel as if they were. "She's doing well. BumperWillow completed her healing. The bruises are gone; the bones entirely healed. You Lemurians are tough."

Roland chuckled. "That we are. We have to be, to survive so many millennia of absolute boredom." Drily, he added, "Of course, that's all drastically changed. Is Ginny here?"

"She's helping Gaia pack. We're taking her back to Sedona to see if her presence helps Artigos."

"Having trouble removing the demon?"

Dawson nodded. "Even BumperWillow couldn't shake it loose."

Ginny walked back into the room. "Roland. Good to see you. How's Taron coming with the swords?"

"He should be finished this afternoon. Any luck with the ruby sword?"

"Selyn believes she knows where the owner is."

Dawson noticed Ginny didn't mention the name of the missing leader.

"The one we thought lost?" Roland's smile disappeared beneath the focused stare of a warrior.

"The very one. That's why I've asked you to meet us here." Ginny glanced over her shoulder, as if to make certain Gaia was still busy packing. "We're changing plans by the minute. Can you get Dawson and Selyn into the slaves' level without detection? The person we're looking for is held prisoner below."

Roland nodded and turned to Dawson. "When do you want to meet, and where?"

"Ginny? Will the portal allow Roland entrance into the chancellor's office? That's the only place I know how to find."

"DarkFire?" Ginny withdrew the sword.

The blade shimmered. "Roland is a DemonSlayer. He will be granted access."

Dawson shook his head. The sense of the rabbit hole was growing stronger. "Roland?" he asked. "Can Selyn communicate with you telepathically?" When Roland nodded in the affirmative, he added, "Then why don't we wait and contact you when we get to the chancellor's office? Would that work?"

"It would. I'm going to be off duty in another hour. Contact me, and we'll use the security route to get below."

Just then, Gaia walked back into the room, carrying a small satchel. "Roland of Kronus." She nodded formally. "It's good to see you. I thank you for standing beside my son during these difficult times."

Roland bowed from the waist. "Gaia of Artigos. I wish you well, and health to your husband."

Tears sparkled in Gaia's eyes. "Thank you, Roland. I just wish I could be certain we can remove the demon from his soul. It's a very frightening time for both of us."

"Yes, Gaia. It is. For all of us." Roland frowned. Then he folded his arms across his chest. "Much has happened since I brought Selyn to Earth's dimension. The gateway to Abyss from the vortex here in Mount Shasta continues to reopen. I've shut it now more than a dozen times, but whenever I must be away, it opens again. Even now, I imagine it's being repaired. I'm beginning to think it's someone here, inside Lemuria, who is responsible."

"Crap." Ginny glanced at Dawson. "I'm thinking Maxl and Drago. What do you think?"

Dawson nodded, thinking of the two who'd ordered the search of Artigos's office. "Do you think they're demon-possessed as well, sort of like Artigos?"

"It stands to reason." Roland sighed. "Our problems appear to be growing faster than we can control them, but I have a bit of good news. I've heard of a woman who might be able to help remove the demon from Artigos.

Three of my men were involved in a fierce battle with demons at a shop called Crystal Dreams in the Earth town of Evergreen. A young woman there, Mari . . ."

Ginny interrupted. "Mari Schwartz? I know Mari, and I know the shop. Her mom owns it. What's going on?"

"It appears Mari has been running her mother's shop while her father is ill. One of my soldiers—Darius, who was one of the young men who received his crystal sword from DarkFire—followed demons into town. For some reason they were targeting the shop. Darius ended up staying on to protect Mari. There was a terrible battle, one that only ended when Mari invoked powerful magic and cast a spell that stopped the demons. Darius said that Mari was killed in the battle, but his sword not only helped restore her life, but also granted her immortality."

"Mari Schwartz? Wow! She's okay now, though, right?" Ginny laughed. "I love it! Mari's an investment banker— she's been working in San Francisco since college. She hated the fact her mom claimed to be a witch. The whole time we were growing up, she was in total denial. I can't wait to see her. Mari as an immortal witch will take some getting used to."

Roland chuckled. "According to Darius, she appears to be a powerful witch with abilities she is only now beginning to understand. And yes, her mother is also a witch. I'm wondering if their magic might help Artigos."

Gaia reached for Roland and wrapped her fingers around his arm. "I'm willing to try anything," she said, "whatever we have to do to save my husband's life and his soul." She turned to Ginny. "Take me to Artigos now, please. I don't care if it takes a witch or a talking dog, or the spirit within your amazing sword. I want my husband back."

Chapter Eight

Selyn sat outside by the front door in a chair that was made entirely out of little branches all tied together. It fit perfectly with the style of Dawson's house, and was surprisingly comfortable, considering it was nothing more than bundles of twigs. Willow said it was made of willow branches, which might have made more sense if Selyn had the vaguest idea what a willow branch was.

They obviously had nothing to do with a fairy stuck inside a dog. So many unfamiliar things to understand! Selyn knew willow branches had to come from some kind of plant, but she couldn't see anything like these bundled sticks growing around Dawson's house. This land was dry and rocky, with strange, spiky plants and huge, weathered rock formations all about.

It was beautiful and desolate all at the same time, and so big. Big and open and bright, and filled with unusual sounds. She smiled, listening to the cactus wren chattering and chirping nearby. So far, it was the only bird she knew how to identify, which made her feel as if the silly creature sang for her alone. She occasionally heard other birds, but she'd have to ask Daws what they were.

The sky was a brilliant blue—so bright it reminded her of Dawson's eyes—and the sunlight made her squint. Already Selyn loved the feel of the warmth on her skin. She'd never again be happy without it, not now, and it was almost impossible to believe she'd lived her entire life without sunlight. Knowing her people had consciously accepted artificial light over sunlight when they'd chosen exile inside the mountain to save themselves made her unaccountably angry.

How could intelligent Lemurians, people known for their ability to think things through, have allowed themselves to be trapped within a separate dimension inside that dark and foreboding mountain? What were they thinking when they made the move to Mount Shasta, rather than to another part of the planet Earth where they could still live outside in the light of day?

Unless what she'd been told was actually true—that the move was somehow forced on her people by leaders who were controlled by demonkind. Demons needed darkness. They thrived away from sunlight, which would explain the Lemurians' exodus to a world beneath ground. It made terrifying sense, if demons truly ruled them.

Even so, she'd still think it was all a foolish lie, if she hadn't witnessed Artigos when he'd been trapped in the beams of the two crystal swords.

Not that she hadn't already accepted the fact that demons were real. She knew they were, but she honestly hadn't accepted the power they had, not really. Not the fact they could get inside a person and actually control their actions.

Well, she was a believer now. Something about the strange light from the crystal blades—a thing she'd never before witnessed—had revealed more than the eye actually saw. She'd sensed another entity, somehow intertwined with the man she'd learned to hate. She hadn't actually seen a demon—not with her eyes—but she'd recognized its existence with some other sense she'd never used before. She'd known the demon was there.

No one could deny the sense of evil about Artigos. That had been obvious from the first moment she saw him. Nor could anyone deny the fact he was somehow possessed. But what she'd witnessed this morning went beyond any prior concept of possession she'd ever had.

It was an unusual evil, a presence separate from the man himself and yet very much a part of him. It felt horribly wrong, and yet exactly the way she now imagined a demon's possession of a person would manifest itself.

The implications were terrifying and sad. If Artigos were really an innocent victim, then that made all of them victims. It meant that the DemonWars had never ended, that Lemurians had not won that war. Either it meant they were still fighting the same war today, so many thousands of years after everyone believed the terrible scourge had ended, or it meant they'd already lost.

Had they lost? Was it too late even to try anymore? She wasn't ready to accept that. Wasn't prepared to admit her mother and the other women warriors had fought in vain, that they'd died in vain. Selyn wasn't prepared to admit defeat. Not while there was still breath in her body. Not while she had it within her to fight demonkind.

Not that she'd ever experienced demons. At least not that she knew of.

But what of Birk? What of the other guards?

Were they possessed as well? Was demonkind that thoroughly entrenched within Lemurian society that even those who were supposed to guard and protect the people had somehow become compromised?

Not Roland. No, Roland of Kronus was one of the good guys. Knowing men like him existed—men of free will—

gave her hope. He'd risked much to find her, to discover the truth behind the rumors of the existence of the Forgotten Ones. He'd risked his standing as a member of the Lemurian Guard to meet with Selyn, and he'd risked his life to come into the mines and save her.

She could only hope there were more like him.

Now Alton wanted Selyn to return. He wanted her to go back to the mines with a human man and a sword she couldn't wield, to risk her life once again to help a society that had enslaved her for millennia.

A society responsible for the death of her mother.

Except, if they were controlled by demonkind, they were victims as much as she was, as much as her mother had been.

Nine hells, but thinking this through was making her head hurt! She wished Dawson would come home. She missed him. But how could that be? She hardly knew the man, yet she wanted to talk to him about everything that had happened over the past couple of days. She wanted a better feel for the mission they were being asked to accomplish.

She wanted Dawson.

Now where the nine hells did that thought come from? What could she possibly want with him? He was human. He wasn't a warrior; he was a healer. He couldn't protect her, and there was no way he could go up against a brute like Birk. Dawson wasn't much taller than she was, and he certainly wasn't as big and muscular or as strong as Dax, or even Alton. He was just an average human male with eyes the color of a desert sky and gentle hands that made her want.

Want what?

BumperWillow whined and rested her chin on Selyn's knee. Once again the little spirit must be eavesdropping.

Selyn idly scratched the dog's curly head. She stretched

her legs out, arched her back, and sighed. Though she was completely healed, her muscles felt tight. Probably from not working her regular shift in the mines. She'd never in her life spent so many hours without hard labor.

She'd changed back into the comfortable cotton clothing Dawson had given to her. The baggy pants and loose top were cooler and more comfortable than Ginny's jeans. It was going to take a while to get used to such tight, restrictive clothing after a lifetime in formless robes. The jeans might attract Dawson's eye, but the fabric wasn't as forgiving as this outfit he called "scrubs."

What a silly name for clothing. She smoothed the soft fabric over her thighs and then once again ran her fingers through the dog's curly hair. She half expected Willow to pop into her mind and tell her she was thinking unfair thoughts about the citizens of Lemuria.

Why would I do that? Everything you've wondered about is true.

Selyn laughed and scratched under the dog's chin. "I wondered if you were eavesdropping on me again. Is it all really as confusing as I keep thinking it is?"

It's worse. The dog sighed and laid her ears back against her broad skull, but it was Willow's mental voice that Selyn heard.

I don't know what to do about Artigos, she said. *He has a very persistent demon that's almost entirely melded to his soul, but he is Alton's father. I don't want to harm him, but we must remove the demon, even though it's a terrible risk we take. I don't know what we can do, or who can help.*

"Maybe the one we're taking the ruby sword to will be able to help him."

If he doesn't want to kill him. If that is truly Artigos the Just who has been held prisoner all these years, he's only

*there because his son ordered it. He might not be feeling
too kindly toward Artigos number two.*

"I hadn't thought of that."

I have. BumperWillow sighed. *It's all I can think of.*

Dawson sat back in the wooden chair at his big kitchen
table. Gaia was in the back, sitting with Artigos, and Alton
still slept. Selyn had been terribly quiet since he and Ginny
had returned with Alton's mom, but he couldn't worry
about her right now.

He couldn't let himself think about her at all, or thoughts
of her would consume him. Instead, he focused on Ginny.
"So you and Alton will take his mom and dad to the portal
in Mount Shasta, and Eddy and Dax will take over from
there?" Dawson shook his head, wondering over the confused logistics. "How will they get him to Evergreen?"

Ginny folded her hands in front of her on the kitchen
table. "We'll have to take him through the portal that opens
to the flank of Mount Shasta and hike down the mountain
to the end of the road. If Eddy and Dax can meet us there
with Eddy's dad's Jeep, and if we put a strong enough
trance on Artigos, they should be able to get him to town
without too much trouble."

"He has promised to behave as long as I'm with him."
Gaia stepped into the room. She managed to look absolutely regal in spite of the trauma of the past hours—her
life had been totally upended in such a short span of time.
"We're ready to go whenever you are."

Ginny pulled out the chair next to her. "As soon as
Alton awakens . . ."

"Alton's awake." The big Lemurian stepped into the
kitchen. His eyes looked sleepy, and he yawned, but he
threw his arm around his mother's shoulders, leaned close,

and kissed her cheek. "It's good to have you here, Mother. I just checked on Father. He seems somewhat calmer, now that you're with him."

Gaia leaned into her son's embrace. Her smile was for Alton, not the situation. "That's because he expects me to help him escape your evil clutches, my son. He doesn't realize I'm on your side."

Alton shook his head. "No, Mother. There are no sides here. There is only the right thing to do, and in this case, that's removing the demon that has corrupted a good man."

"Thank you." Gaia's soft reply was followed by an even softer sigh. "Then we need to go, and go quickly. You, my son, must return to Lemuria as soon as possible and take up your position as chancellor before anyone has time to mount a serious challenge to your claim."

Alton nodded. "I fear that's already begun. I'm still concerned about the unfamiliar guardsmen we saw. Where they come from, who they are." He kneaded the back of his neck. Ginny grabbed his hand, stuck him in a chair, and began to rub at the stiff muscles.

Alton sighed, but he tilted his head and focused on Daws. "Dawson, you and Selyn should be ready to leave immediately for Lemuria as soon as Ginny and I return from delivering my parents to Eddy and Dax. We'll go straight to my father's office through the small portal, then you can connect with Roland for your journey into the mines." He paused for a moment, and focused his gaze on Selyn. "Are you sure you're up to this, Selyn? We're asking a lot of you."

She glanced toward Dawson. He winked at her, and she smiled. "No more than the Forgotten Ones will soon be asking of you," she said. "I'm ready."

* * *

Dawson stood in the doorway long after the SUV carrying Ginny, Alton, Gaia, Artigos, and even the dog and Artigos's carefully wrapped crystal sword had gone, and thought of all the changes in his life since the day he'd treated a whole clinic filled with demon-possessed pets.

He wouldn't trade these past few days for anything, unless he could have kept Selyn from being hurt. He sensed her behind him. Slowly, almost with a sense of disbelief, he turned away from the bright afternoon sun.

His eyes took a moment to adjust to the shadows inside the house. She stood just a few feet away, with her hands clasped in front of her and that long black braid hanging over her shoulder. Her beautiful blue eyes were as dark and deep as an ocean, and every bit as filled with mystery.

Would he ever get past the feeling of awe, of clumsy, inept reverence that swept over him whenever he saw her? The hopeless, helpless awkwardness she inspired? He'd never been all that much of a player, though he'd had comfortable relationships with women over the years. Friendships, a few light romances.

There was nothing comfortable about Selyn.

None of the women he'd known had ever affected him this way, but then he'd never known a woman who was anything remotely like Selyn.

He blinked, but she was still there. He kept expecting her to disappear. Such perfection couldn't be real, could it? He cleared his throat to make sure his voice would work, and realized he had no idea what to say.

She left him speechless. He decided to stick with the mundane, though he figured that would just convince her—if she needed more convincing—that he was an idiot.

"Do you want something to eat before we have to leave?"

She smiled, every bit as unaffected by him as he was

driven nuts around her. "Alton said they might be gone a couple of hours. Later, maybe. I'm not really hungry yet."

"Oh. Okay."

"I thought maybe we could go outside, now that I have these." Smiling, she lifted one foot and showed off a sandal.

He nodded. Okay. Outside worked. Then, without thinking, he took her hand, and he was absolutely shocked when she not only slipped hers into his grasp, but clasped his tightly. The connection, the feel of her warm but callused palm was almost his undoing.

He'd never wanted to touch a woman so desperately, never reacted to one on so many levels, but Selyn had him tied in knots. She had his heart speeding up and then slowing down, his chest feeling almost too tight to draw breath, his muscles locked with a tension he couldn't describe.

All from holding her hand. He almost laughed. No doubt, the woman was going to be the death of him. He gently squeezed her fingers and opened the screen door. Selyn followed him outside. The sunlight, even this late in the fall, was almost blinding.

"Just a minute." He stepped back inside and grabbed a floppy straw hat off the rack by the door. Carried it outside and gently placed it on Selyn's head. She touched the brim and smiled. "Thank you. I'm not used to the sunlight."

Now there was an understatement if ever he'd heard one. He smiled at her, adjusted the angle of the hat to better protect her eyes. Then he took her hand in his once more.

They walked across the yard to the small fish pond. The javalinas were gone, but the pond was home to frogs and turtles and hundreds of tiny gray mosquito fish. A couple of tired water lilies still bloomed, but they were well off their peak.

"What is that?" She pointed at a turtle sunning itself on a flat rock.

"A painted turtle," he said, pointing to another one floating at the surface with just its nostrils showing. "There's another. They live in the pond, along with some frogs and, on occasion, a small water snake or two."

They watched the turtles for a moment, and then continued walking around the house to a point where the Verde Valley spread out below them and the red rocks around Sedona shimmered in the distance.

"So many wonders." She sighed. "So many things we who live below never imagined even existed. How could my people choose to give this up?"

"Maybe they didn't choose. Maybe demonkind chose for them."

Selyn turned and looked at him through eyes filled with tears. Frustration and anger seemed almost a part of her, but there was more he sensed. Sadness. Soul-deep and heartfelt sadness. Despair and a terrible sense of grief, of loss.

Dawson wasn't sure how it happened, what gave him the courage to act. Empathy, a desire to take away her pain? For whatever reason, before he had time to think this through, he had his arms around her and she was close, so damned close he breathed in her scent and felt the warmth of sunlight on her long, black hair.

Her arms wrapped tightly around his back, and she leaned into his embrace. It seemed perfectly natural to lift her chin with his fingertips and kiss her. The floppy straw hat tilted away and dropped to the sand at her heels, but Dawson didn't care. Not when he was doing something he'd barely dreamed of.

And, surprise of surprises, it wasn't nearly as frightening as it should have been for a man who felt woefully inept around women. Dogs and cats were so much easier to figure out, but Selyn didn't seem to mind that he lacked the finesse of most men when he tasted the full curve of her lips, when his tongue traced the seam between them and gently begged entrance.

She parted for him, tilting her head just right in order to make their mouths fit even more perfectly. Dawson fought the powerful urge to press his body closer, to kiss harder, to slip his hands beneath her loose shirt and explore the woman under the soft, cotton scrubs.

Her breasts were soft against his chest, her fingers digging into his back as she clung to him, holding on as if he were somehow anchoring her, holding her in safety.

She had no idea what his body was driving him to do. No idea how difficult it was to fight his baser instincts. He didn't want to frighten her, and he forced himself to move slowly, to proceed carefully, but the thought of never taking this beyond a kiss terrified him. Somehow, before too long, he needed to know what her body felt like, how well it would align to his. How perfectly he could fill her, make love to her, make her his own.

Her tongue slipped into his mouth in a timid exploration that sent Dawson's heart stuttering in his chest. Her taste was unique, the soft pressure of her lips against his—of her tongue exploring the edges of his teeth and the sensitive curve of his mouth—an almost uncontrollable aphrodisiac.

He clasped her head in his palms, holding her so that he could taste and nibble and make love to her mouth. He wanted more, so damned much more, but this was neither the time nor the place, and it was all much too soon.

He felt the soft wind on his face and the tentative touch of her warm fingers sliding beneath his shirt. He groaned against her mouth. His body surged to readiness, and the desire racing through him practically drove him to his knees.

She had no idea what her innocent touch did to him, no concept of a man's reaction to a woman he wanted. It meant that, no matter how much Dawson wanted to take this to its perfect conclusion, he had to end this kiss now, before he was totally incapable of ending anything without finishing it first.

Slowly, gently, and very reluctantly, he pulled away from her lips. Sucking in one, slow, deep breath after another, he rested his forehead against Selyn's and did his best to drag in enough air to keep himself conscious.

Long moments later, when he felt as if he'd gained control over his wayward body, he lifted his head and gazed into Selyn's sapphire blue eyes. They sparkled with more than mischief. In fact, they practically glowed with the same arousal rocketing through his veins, with the same powerful sense of need that still tightened his body. He hardened even more, knowing she shared the same desire to take this amazing kiss, this budding yet impossible relationship, to its natural conclusion.

She ran the tip of her tongue over her top lip and then across the bottom, staring at a point on his throat instead of into his eyes. Finally she glanced up, smiling, and touched his beard with her fingertips. "It tickles when you kiss me."

"I'll shave it off."

She laughed. "Don't you dare." She stood on her toes and kissed his chin. "I like it. Just as I like your kisses, though they leave me feeling . . ." She paused and shook her head. "They leave me feeling very unsettled."

"Should I stop kissing you?"

This time she kissed his lips, too quickly for him to kiss her back. "Never. Well, for now, maybe, but I want to do it again. When we have more time. I want to know what comes next."

He sighed and stepped back. "So do I, Selyn. But not until you're very, very sure."

She raised her chin, and there was an unspoken question in her eyes. Maybe she didn't even know what to ask.

He answered her anyway. "There are some things, once done, that can never be undone. Some things too important to rush. This. You and me? This is one of those things."

She worried her bottom lip with her teeth, and then she nodded. He grabbed her hand and tugged. She followed, and they headed back to the house. There were sandwiches to make to take with them into Lemuria, and a few things to pack. A new chancellor to seat on the Lemurian Council of Nine, a sword to return to its rightful owner, and a hundred new crystal swords to deliver to women too long forgotten.

That was all. Nothing more than a war against demonkind to be won before Dawson figured they'd have time to find out what came next.

It was only a couple of hours later when Roland met all of them in the chancellor's office deep within Lemuria. Dawson figured that by now, Artigos and Gaia should be at Eddy's house in Evergreen. Darius and Mari, the Lemurian guardsman and the human witch, were planning to meet with them tonight.

Alton had gone immediately to his father's desk, where he was now checking schedules and preparing to call a meeting of the Council of Nine. Ginny would stand beside him as the chancellor's consort, which left it entirely up to Dawson and Selyn to return the ruby sword to its rightful owner.

If the man Selyn had heard of really was Artigos the Just.

Dawson tucked the carefully wrapped sword and scabbard under his arm and clapped Alton on the shoulder. "Good luck, Alton. Don't worry if you don't hear from us until tomorrow. It may take us a while to actually reach the prisoner."

"I know. Plus, you'll need to remain, at least long enough to help Taron get the swords to their rightful owners. So damned much to do." Alton stood close beside Ginny. The strain of the past few days was beginning to show on his face, but the two of them looked more than ready to face the council. "Be safe. Try not to take any chances, and listen to Roland."

Roland chuckled. "That'll be a first. I don't think anyone listens to me. C'mon."

Dawson and Selyn followed him through the portal as soon as the sergeant was certain the way was clear. Selyn had donned the white robe Gaia had given her so that she'd blend in better, should they be discovered. She looked like an exotic princess with her long hair unbound and flowing in soft, ebony waves down her back. Gaia had also given her a gold circlet to hold the hair back from her eyes. It glowed against her bronze skin and only emphasized her beauty. This woman most definitely was not a slave.

Never again. And how anyone as gorgeous as Selyn expected to blend into anything was beyond him.

Roland unsheathed his sword and marched Dawson and Selyn along the tunnel as if he were taking them to the cells below the main level. He glanced over his shoulder and grinned at Dawson as they descended to the next level. "I still think you should have worn one of those blue guardsmen's robes. Then you wouldn't have to act the part of a prisoner."

Dawson shook his head and glanced at Selyn walking beside him. "Sorry, Roland, but all I could think of was that if things got ugly, I didn't want to try running for cover in a dress."

"Dress? This is not a dress. It's my uniform."

Dawson laughed at his indignant reply. "On Earth it's a dress. Maybe a gown. Not what a real man would wear."

Roland raised his eyebrows in mock outrage. "A real man, eh? Watch what you say to a real man carrying a crystal sword, human."

Dawson grabbed Selyn's hand and shot her a quick grin. He squeezed her fingers. "I'll remember that when your crystal sword gets tangled in your girly skirt. Seriously, Roland. How do you fight wearing a robe? Doesn't it get in the way?"

Roland paused beside a portal that led to an even lower level. "It does," he said. "Guardsmen of old dressed in pants and boots, similar to what you wear. The robe became our official uniform when someone on the council decided we needed to appear as philosophers, not warriors. Alton has already said we can change the uniform as soon as things settle a bit."

"For women, as well." Selyn pulled the full skirt of her robe to one side. "It looks very pretty, but the pants I wore at Dawson's house are much more practical. I think I shall bring that design to the women once we are armed."

Laughing, Dawson followed Roland through the portal with Selyn beside him. Just what Lemuria needed. An entire army of women warriors, all dressed in surgical scrubs.

Neither Roland nor Selyn had a clue what Dawson thought was so funny. Probably just as well.

They passed through more portals and walked down stairs cut into solid stone. Quietly, they followed the secret and well-hidden tunnels Roland had discovered, where dim lighting barely showed the way. Selyn kept listening for the sounds of the Forgotten Ones laboring, but all she heard was the steady breathing from the three of them, and the echoes of their footsteps. It was almost an hour later and many levels down before they reached the mines where the Forgotten Ones were enslaved.

At this point, Selyn took the lead. She had, after all, lived here for her entire life. How could she have forgotten the stench? The air was musty and reeked of sour sweat and something rotten. It was warm in some places, frigid in others, and the sound of heavy machinery rumbled in the background.

She'd forgotten how noisy it could be at all times of the day or night, though there really was no difference here. Day or night—it didn't matter. Not here where their work and sleep schedules followed the deep tone of a bell and the shouts of the wardens telling them to move faster, work harder.

It was hard to stomach—even harder to believe—that they were barely an hour's walk beneath the levels where civilized Lemurians lived in quiet comfort, entirely ignorant of slaves toiling below. Free folk, living lives of ease and total luxury a short hour away.

"Caution," she said, touching Roland's shoulder. "We can't afford to be seen. They will have missed me by now, which means my life is forfeit should I be caught."

She didn't mention that theirs would be forfeit as well. How could she have allowed Dawson to accompany her into this hell? He was an innocent bystander, caught up in this battle through no fault of his own. Involved merely because he was a good man with a desire to see wrong made right.

He leaned close and kissed her quickly on the lips before she realized what he was up to. "Then I guess that means we don't get caught, because no one is going to hurt you again. Not on my watch." He smiled at her. "Where is this prisoner held? Can we get to him now, or should we wait for a better time? Do the guards ever go off duty?"

She glanced at Roland. "What time is it, Roland? Is there a shift change due?"

He shook his head. "I can't say for sure. I've never figured out how they schedule things down here. Your wardens aren't like the regular guard." He tapped his forehead. "We can't even communicate telepathically. It's like they're a different species from the rest of us."

Selyn frowned. He wasn't kidding when he'd made such an absurd comment. Different species? They were men. Big, ugly, mean men. Then she glanced at Dawson, and once again at Roland.

They were men as well, one human, one Lemurian, and both of them were really terrific guys. Maybe Roland knew what he was talking about. Maybe the guards were not true Lemurians.

"Follow me." She edged toward a narrow passage. "This leads us behind the sleeping quarters where the women are kept when we're not working. The prisoner is housed in another chamber beyond. I've never seen him, but I know how to find his cell."

They'd covered only a short distance when the scrape of sandals warned them someone drew near. Dawson grabbed Selyn and pulled her into a shallow alcove on one side of the tunnel. He wrapped his arms around her and held her tight, shielding her with his body. Roland slipped out of sight, hiding in the shadows just across from them.

A huge man was coming their way. Selyn strained to see over Dawson's shoulder, but the man's face was lost in shadow. Even so, Selyn would have recognized his form and his walk anywhere. "That's Birk," she whispered. "The guard who beat me. He's a vicious fighter. Very powerful. We can't let him catch us."

She felt Dawson stiffen beside her. Heard his muffled curse against the bastard who had harmed her. Suddenly, a red glow seeped through the blanket wrapped around the ruby sword. Without considering what drove her, Selyn quietly reached for the hilt protruding from one end of the covering. She wrapped her fingers around the gold pommel and slipped the sword free of the scabbard and surrounding cloth.

"What are you doing?" Dawson's whisper tickled the side of her neck.

"I'm not sure, but I know the sword wants me to hold it." Grasping the golden pommel in both hands, she raised the ruby blade high. Though they were still partially hidden from the oncoming guard, Selyn knew the red glow would give them away the minute he chanced to look in their direction.

The scarlet crystal pulsed red, then redder still. Suddenly a brilliant flash of fire spun from the tip of the blade and lit up the entire tunnel in shimmering red lights.

Before the oncoming guard had time to react, the voice in the sword shouted a single word, "Demonkind!"

Roland leapt from his hiding place with his crystal blade drawn. Birk immediately drew his steel sword, but before he could call for help, Selyn pulled out of Dawson's grasp and planted herself in front of Birk with the ruby sword held high.

The blade was long and when she'd lifted it earlier, the sword had been almost too heavy to raise, but now it fit her grasp as if it had been made for her—perfect balance, the perfect weight—not heavy at all.

Dawson stood beside her with nothing more than a small can in one hand. Roland covered her other side, and his clear crystal blade glowed with a brilliant blue fire.

Birk's eyes flashed as he looked from Dawson to Selyn and then at Roland. His gaze settled on Selyn, and with his massive sword flashing, he shouted a curse, and charged.

Chapter Nine

Dawson felt like an idiot standing beside Selyn with nothing but a tiny can of pepper spray clutched in his fist, while she and Roland faced a raging maniac armed with their glowing crystal swords.

Then it was all about self-preservation when Roland clashed blades with Birk's steel, and Selyn took a swing at the man's unprotected belly. Birk twisted out of reach of the shimmering crystal much faster than Dawson would have expected a guy his size to move. In the midst of his twist, Birk swung his sword.

Dawson ducked. The steel blade split the hair on top of his head. He rolled to his left as Birk slashed the air once more. Birk twisted aside, avoiding both Selyn and Roland and going for Dawson with a single-minded determination. It was obvious he wanted to remove the easiest target first, but once again Dawson ducked beneath the flashing sword.

This time, he came up behind the big guard.

Selyn lunged with her blade. Birk pivoted to the right, out of reach of either Roland or Selyn. Dawson kicked hard, catching the back of the big man's left knee. Birk grunted, and his leg buckled, but he caught himself and spun on his right, slashing at Dawson, recovering quickly, and taking a swing at Roland.

Blowing hard, Birk evaded another thrust of Selyn's borrowed ruby blade. He managed a quick turn that put his back to the wall and had the three of them circling him in front.

Roland made a quick thrust that Birk parried. Steel clashed with crystal. Sparks flew, but the two guards appeared to be of equal strength. Their blades met, held, and then slid apart. Birk feinted left and then lunged at Selyn. She evaded his thrust and twisted aside, but Birk's quick footwork put him right in front of Dawson.

The guard raised his massive arm with the steel blade held high, preparing to strike hard and fast. Dawson pushed the plunger on the lipstick-sized can of pepper spray. He caught Birk directly in the eyes with the blast. Birk screamed. Blindly, he swung his sword. Dawson ducked and rolled out of the way. Roland did the same, and Selyn lunged forward for the killing stroke.

At the last moment, her blade twisted in her hand, as if it shifted of its own free will. Instead of piercing the furious guard's heart, the ruby crystal slapped him flat across the chest.

Birk went rigid. His eyes rolled back in his head, and his steel sword clattered uselessly to the ground from slack fingers. A thick, black, sulfuric mist streamed out of his chest and hovered in the air in a seething, oily mass.

Without a sound, Birk dropped to his knees. He wavered there a moment, and then fell over on his back. Roland lunged and thrust his crystal blade into the center of the mist.

Clear crystal sliced through the dark wraith. Sparks flashed, and a horrific banshee cry echoed off the tunnel walls. The demonic wraith burst into a mass of fiery blue sparks before it dissolved into nothing more than a horrible stench.

Birk lay unmoving, unconscious.

"What the nine hells was that?" Selyn glanced at her blade and then at the huge guard lying at her feet. "That thing that shot out of his chest. What was it?"

Dawson glanced at his little can of pepper spray and carefully clipped it back to his belt loop. Who needed a sword when you had a weapon like this? "That was a demon, Selyn. Birk was possessed. From the way it burst out of him when you touched his chest, I wonder if we shouldn't use that sword to help free Artigos?"

"It might work." Bemused, she stared at the sword in her hand for a long, silent moment. "How strange. It's not really speaking to me, but I somehow know that the demon in Artigos is different than the one in Birk." She raised her head and focused on Dawson. "It won't work on Artigos. This is very strange. I shouldn't be able to wield this sword, much less understand it. I've always heard that it's asking for death to touch the sword of another, yet it called to me. It communicates with me."

Roland stood beside her, but he kept his gaze on Birk. "I've heard that about crystal swords all my life, but it appears it's entirely up to the sword. They seem to consciously know who should or should not handle them. Eddy bested a demon with Alton's sword without injury to herself."

Birk began to stir, though he still lay on his back, eyes unfocused and filled with tears from the pepper spray. Blinking slowly, he rubbed at his streaming eyes with one big fist. Selyn nudged him with her foot. "What do we do with him?"

Dawson knelt beside the man with his hands clenched tightly into fists. "Just give him a minute. I want to see what he remembers. If he knows he was possessed." He glanced at Selyn, and unexplainable anger welled up in him. "I want to know if the bastard remembers hurting you."

"I do." Birk's voice rumbled up out of his chest. He closed his eyes as if in pain. "I am truly cursed." He groaned and rolled his head back and forth against the stone floor. "I remember everything—every terrible thing."

Blinking his eyes, red-rimmed from the irritating spray, he sighed noisily. "It's as if I watched from afar. I know now, as I knew then, I have done terrible things." Slowly he rolled over and pushed himself to his hands and knees. He raised his head and gazed up at Selyn. "But knowing made no difference. I did them anyway and didn't care. That's not who or what I am. I swear it. But why?"

He glanced at Dawson and Roland. Then once more he focused on Selyn. "Why would I hurt you, Selyn? You didn't deserve my anger, but I remember. Not everything, but too much. Dear gods, I remember too much. I am so sorry. So terribly sorry and ashamed."

He pushed himself upright, though he still knelt. Clasped his hands at the small of his back, and bowed his head before Selyn.

Time stood still. None of them moved until Selyn quietly asked, "What does he want?"

Dawson wrapped an arm around her waist. His anger at the man was gone. It had given way to nothing more than pity, almost as if he shared the shame the big guard felt. "I'm not really sure."

Roland shrugged. "I think it's obvious, don't you? He expects you to kill him."

"What?" She shook her head in absolute denial. "But why? What he says is true, and he was not at fault. I saw the demon. It wasn't him doing those terrible things. Not really. Birk? Why do you kneel that way?"

Obviously confused, the big guard raised his head. "I have wronged you, and I've wronged Lemuria. I've broken my vow to serve my people. I await my punishment."

Selyn shrugged and glanced at the ruby sword in her hand, as if she asked the thing for guidance. Then she shook her head. "Birk, wouldn't you rather redeem yourself by fighting demons instead of wasting your life? We could really use your help."

He bowed his head even deeper. "I've served evil long enough, and I've done enough harm. I would be honored, but only if you serve Lemuria."

Indignantly, she rolled her eyes. "Of course we do. All of us are on a mission to save Lemuria from demonkind. You can help us. Killing you isn't going to do anyone any good. Look, Birk, we need to deliver this sword to the prisoner you hold, the man you've kept behind bars for thousands of years. It's his. Will you take us to him?"

The sword pulsed with a deep, red glow. Birk stared at the ruby blade, and then he shook his head. "Impossible. I remember that sword with the ruby blade and the gold hilt. It belonged to Artigos the Just, the one, true leader of Lemuria. It's too late to return it. That Artigos died during the great move."

Roland held out his hand. Birk took it, and Roland drew him to his feet. Though Birk was a bit larger than Roland, the two were almost of equal strength, and both such large men that Dawson felt like a kid beside the huge guards.

Dawson gestured toward the ruby sword clasped in Selyn's hand. "Birk, I've been learning a lot about the crystal swords of Lemuria. If Artigos the Just were dead, his blade would have turned black. It would be obsidian, not ruby. Look at that thing. That's not the crystal blade of a dead man. We have reason to believe Lemuria's true leader has been held prisoner here since the great move, but his identity has been kept secret. You've been possessed, most likely the entire time you've served here in the mines. The demon has probably hidden the man's true identity from you."

Birk stared into Dawson's eyes, as if trying to judge the worth of a mere human. After a moment, he nodded. "Follow me, and I'll take you to him. If the man is who you think he is, the sword will recognize its master."

They skirted the women's quarters and followed a dark passage that seemed to take them even deeper into the caverns. Here the light was not as good. Roland's sword cast an eerie blue glow, barely enough to keep them from stumbling in the dark.

Finally they arrived at a broader passage. Birk checked to make sure it was empty and then led them through a portal into a large cavern. Peering around a partial wall of shimmering stone, they could see a single door, with a barred grill across the top and what appeared to be a regular lock that took a key on the front, set into the stone wall on the far side of the cavern.

Birk stopped them with a soft whisper. "Wait here. I'll relieve the guard on duty."

The three of them pressed against the wall in the shadows just inside the cavern. Birk quietly slipped around the wall and then strode boldly across the open area to a desk where a young man in a guard's uniform sat. He was writing in a large book when Birk stopped in front of the desk. The guard looked up, obviously surprised to see his superior standing there.

Birk planted both hands on the desk, and shook his head as if he was disgusted by the request he had to make. "Aeron. I've got some hells-be-damned paperwork that needs to be done. Why don't you go ahead and take off. I'll relieve you now so I can get to it."

The guard clambered to his feet. He looked flustered by Birk's request. "Of course, sir. If you wish, though I still have half my watch to serve."

"I know. And I'd like to be back in my room sleeping, but you know how that works." He chuckled. "They're serving third meal right now in the guards' mess. There's no point in both of us wasting our evening. Go ahead. I'll take the watch."

Aeron was already gathering up his paperwork and adjusting his sword. "Thank you, sir. If you're certain you don't mind."

Smiling affably, Birk nodded. "I am. You can probably use the break. This is a most boring duty."

The guard nodded, spun around before Birk could change his mind, and left by a portal opposite the one where Dawson and the others waited. They stepped into the light the moment he was gone. Birk was already headed to the locked door carrying a large ring with a pair of keys on it.

He unlocked the door. Selyn had slipped the leather scabbard over her back, but she kept the sword free. Now she came forward with the hilt clutched in her hand and the point of the long blade aimed at the ground. She glanced over her shoulder and looked directly at Dawson. He stepped close and grabbed her left hand in his.

She radiated tension. He tugged just hard enough to bring her to a halt. "Are you okay?" he whispered. "You're trembling."

Selyn nodded. "So much is happening, so very fast. After so long. What if it's not him?"

Daws grinned and squeezed her hand. "Then we keep looking, but if we're making bets, my money's on the sword. And on you. Let's go." He nodded to Birk. The guard tugged on the door and pulled it open. Roland stepped through first with his crystal sword unsheathed. Selyn followed with the ruby sword in her right hand and Dawson hanging on to her left.

Birk closed the door behind him as he entered the cell.

The man seated in a comfortable-looking chair on the far side of the room raised his head from the book he was reading and stared at the four who had entered his quarters.

Dawson's first thought was that this was not the cell of a common prisoner. The space they entered was large with doors that appeared to lead to other rooms. It was furnished in what had to be high-quality tables and chairs, the walls decorated with beautiful paintings of a forgotten world. Scattered about were what looked like personal belongings—small statues, a vase, some carvings. Even a few colorful seashells. Dawson wondered if they'd come from an ancient Lemurian seashore. Lamps glowed brightly, and the shelves were lined with books. He recognized current authors of Earth and familiar titles among them, but some of the spines had titles in other languages and writing that was totally unfamiliar.

It was hard to look away from those fascinating shelves, but the room itself was just as intriguing. Not a miserable cell at all, but still a cell. There was that lock on the door to reinforce the fact that this gentleman was a prisoner, but there was no doubt as to the identity of the man who stood to greet his obviously unexpected visitors.

He was Alton, only he was not. An older, wiser version of Alton, he looked much more like his grandson than he did his own son. As he stood, the resemblance was even more pronounced—he was every bit as tall, as regal-looking as Alton. He carried his age and his dignity like a well-worn cloak, yet he retained the bearing and the look of a man in his prime.

He smiled in greeting, but then he appeared to recognize Birk and frowned when the large guard looked his way.

Then the sword glowed. Dawson turned Selyn's hand free. She stepped forward and knelt on one knee in front of the man—the one who was, without any doubt, the lost leader of the Lemurian people and the master of the crimson crystal blade.

She held his sword out to him, raising it above her bowed head in both hands. Artigos had been ready to speak, but he stopped and stared at the blade. Raised his eyes and looked at the men flanking Selyn, and then once again at the ruby sword.

His voice was scratchy, as if he rarely spoke. Thick with emotion as he finally recognized what Selyn held up to him.

"DemonsBane? Is it really you, my old friend?"

The sword flashed, and fire danced along the faceted blade. Artigos the Just reached for the hilt, but before he could grab it, the sword leapt out of Selyn's hands and into his grasp. He clasped it in both hands and held the ruby sword with its fiery blade upright before him. Selyn sat back on her heels, grinning at the reunion between the man and his sentient crystal sword.

Tears coursed down his cheeks. He seemed transfixed by the weapon in his hands. It was obvious the two communicated, from the pulsing light dancing over the crimson blade, to the myriad expressions crossing Artigos's face.

Long moments later, he lowered the blade and reverently set it on a nearby table. Selyn slipped the scabbard off her shoulder and handed it to him. "It's not the original, Lord

Artigos, but this scabbard belonged to a man who carried his weapon bravely in battle."

"Thank you, my dear. I thank all of you." He took the scabbard and gently slipped the sword inside the beautifully tooled leather. "DemonsBane tells me there are great things afoot. That my grandson has staged a coup and deposed his own father, the one who imprisoned me here."

Roland stepped forward. "That is true. We've discovered that your son has been possessed by a demon. His son, Alton, has temporarily taken over the chancellor's seat on the Council of Nine. He holds it only until the rightful leader of Lemuria can take his place."

One expressive eyebrow arched as Artigos studied Roland for a long moment. Then he smiled and gestured to the various chairs about the room. "Please. Sit." He grabbed the sheathed sword and carried it back to his chair, where he sat down with the look of one expecting to be there for a while.

"Tell me now," he said. "I want to know everything that has happened and why you, Birk, a guard known for his cruelty, are here, now, helping these good people. And, it appears, helping me."

"So that is the way of it, sir." Roland rolled his big shoulders after telling the long and convoluted tale. He turned to Birk. "What of you, Birk? Is there more we should know? Do you have any idea how many of the guards are possessed?"

Birk nodded. "I do. All of them. There are two dozen of us, though a small contingent were recently called to serve above. I'm not sure why."

Roland glanced at Dawson and Selyn. "That explains

the unfamiliar guards I saw earlier, probably called in for backup by the possessed members of the council. They could be a problem for Alton." He let out a huge gust of air. "Go on, Birk."

Birk nodded. "I believe all of us who serve as wardens below have been possessed since the great move. Maybe even before that time. I wish I knew for certain. So many of my memories are just . . . gone." He sighed, staring at the floor. "Yet, at the same time, I recall all too much. I fear I may never regain my honor, when I think of the terrible things we did to those poor women." He raised his head and looked at Selyn. "Is there any chance of forgiveness, from you or from any of the Forgotten Ones?"

How could she answer for all her sisters? Selyn had listened to Roland's story, and she'd told her own. She'd explained how the warrior women originally had been betrayed by Artigos—the son, not the father—who would now and forever be known as the usurper. Betrayed, purged from Lemurian society, and exiled to lives as slaves. How those same women had raised their daughters, how they'd grieved for the sons stolen from them. She'd been unable to look at Birk when she explained how all those babies had been the result of sexual assaults by the guards—they'd been raped by Birk and his fellow soldiers.

It had not been easy to tell the story without betraying her own anger, but she'd done her best. Could she rise above her need for revenge and actually forgive the one who had beaten her almost to death? The same man who might have fathered her sisters in the mines? A man who might even be her own father? She didn't want to go there. Could not allow herself to think those thoughts.

Instead, she must consider whether or not she could

forgive a man who, as both her heart and mind insisted, was as much a victim as any of the Forgotten Ones.

There was no other choice. She looked at the big man, sitting there with his hands dangling helplessly between his knees, and knew exactly what she had to say. "There is nothing to forgive you for, Birk. I saw the demon myself. It was an ugly, black stain upon your soul, and now it's dead. That creature is responsible for the evil things done in your name. Not you."

"Thank you." His deep voice broke on the simple words. "I can only pray the other women will feel the same."

She reached across the space between them and grabbed his hand in hers. That same hand had beaten her bloody, had broken her ribs, bruised her body. She squeezed his fingers and felt him return the pressure. "I can't answer for them, but if you choose to help us I imagine they'll understand and accept that you're on our side. If what you say is true, there are twenty-three more guards we know of who are controlled by demonkind. We'll need your help with them."

There was no hesitation when he answered. "You have it."

She glanced at Dawson. He'd added to their description of events with details of the battle against demonkind on Earth. Even Artigos the Just had laughed at Dawson's tale of sucking up demons with a shop vacuum and freezing them into ice cubes.

"It appears—if all you say is true—that the Demon-Wars never ended. This is what I believe, and while I have no proof, I have had many long years to reach my conclusions, so please, hear me out." Artigos stood up and unsheathed his sword.

"Time means nothing to demonkind. The plan to

conquer Atlantis, Lemuria, and then the rest of Earth was set into motion thousands of years ago, long before Lemuria was destroyed. Atlantis was the first victim. I remember when they chose to encase their civilization in a protective shell and live beneath the sea, apart from all other worlds. We Lemurians were so quick to judge, to trivialize what had happened to a once great and powerful nation."

He paused and gazed off into space, and Selyn wondered what terrible things he saw. Then he straightened his spine and returned his attention to them. "We thought the DemonWars were the final battle between Lemurians and demonkind. We thought we had won, but now I believe the battles were a ruse, nothing more than subterfuge to get us to let down our guard. We were warriors then. Our men were strong, our women every bit as powerful. We carried crystal, and demons could not stop us in battle.

"They could, however, stop us from the inside. Literally. One by one they began to take over members of the ruling class. Possession was subtle at first, and it appears many more possessions must have occurred after I was captured."

"How did that happen?" Roland rose to his feet. "How could our leader simply disappear during the great move and not be missed?"

"My son must have been one of the first to be possessed. There was no reason for anyone to doubt his version of events. He arranged for these quarters in this dimension and organized a secretive group of special Lemurian guardsmen." Artigos nodded at Birk. "You must have been one of the first, Birk. Possessed by demonkind, your every thought controlled by the evil within. Do you recall bringing me here, locking me in this room so many years ago?"

Birk hung his head. "Vaguely. Much from those early years is lost in a haze, as if I wasn't really there."

"I understand. In many ways, you weren't. Birk, the young man who was an honorable soldier, was buried beneath the thoughts and actions of a lesser demon, one who ruled your mind with a subtle use of demonic power. It was a long time before I figured it out myself. In the beginning, I was convinced my son had staged a coup because he was mad for power. I ruled Lemuria more as sovereign, an overlord destined to hold my title for life. I had a council of advisors—a precursor to your current Council of Nine—but I was, for all intents and purposes, the king of Lemuria. At first, I was surprised when my son chose a more democratic form of government.

"Then, over the years, as I saw more here in the mines, and learned of more through gossip of events above, I became convinced of the constant presence of demonkind. The purge of the women warriors was irrevocable proof that evil now ruled my world. What happened to those brave women was a criminal act, one that can never truly be avenged."

He smiled sadly at Selyn and shook his head. "Demons-Bane tells me you fought bravely against Birk, that you have inherited the skills and the aptitude of your mother. I remember Elda. She was one of our finest soldiers in the DemonWars."

"Thank you." Selyn clutched Dawson's hand and fought the tears choking her. Knowing her mother was remembered so well by their ruler was an unexpected gift.

Artigos had been pacing in the space between the chairs. Now he reached over and softly stroked Selyn's hair. "My dear, there are so many wrongs that cannot be righted until demonkind no longer rules our people. I've maintained some mental connections with a few of those above without their knowledge, and stayed informed of some of our world's events. I've come to believe that many of the members of my son's council are possessed, just as my son, Artigos the younger, is possessed. The fact he instituted a democratic council and ruled from the chancellor's position rather than as a king convinced our citizens that he had not overthrown my rule. That I had most likely died during the cataclysm of our dying continent. There was no reason for them not to trust him, but they were wrong to trust. The chancellor and council members are mere figureheads for the true leaders of Lemuria—demons."

He paused and made eye contact with each one of them—Roland standing to one side, Birk, Dawson, and Selyn sitting so quietly, listening to his every word. Selyn knew she was in the presence of true greatness. This man was a born leader.

"Now, with all of you, with my grandson, and with my sword beside me, we have a chance to put our world right. A slim chance, but still a chance."

"What happened to DemonsBane?" Dawson was studying the ruby blade. "This sword was only recently replicated below, and yet you recognize it as the one you had before. How can that be if the original was destroyed?"

Artigos stared at the blade for a moment. "I'm not sure. My weapon was taken from me the day I was captured, and I thought I would never see it again. DemonsBane? Would you care to answer?"

The sword pulsed with red fire. "My physical body was destroyed, the blade crushed, the pommel melted down, my spirit driven out. I have waited patiently in Mother Crystal for all these many years. Waited beside many other warriors who now inhabit the newly replicated swords. Once the crystal blade was formed anew, my spirit returned to it."

Artigos ran his fingers over the faceted blade, stroking it as if it were a lover. "It is good to have you back, my old friend." After a long, contemplative moment, he raised his head. "So, that is what you have, my friends. A world infiltrated by the enemy, a move forced upon an entire civilization by the very ones they thought they had vanquished in battle. Our home, our continent, was destroyed by demonkind. Many lives were lost, and I was betrayed by a demon masquerading as my son."

He folded his hands behind his back and rocked back on his heels. "I am anxious to return to Lemuria, to take my rightful place as leader. But what of my son? Will Artigos fight to retain his seat? And what of his son, Alton? I've not seen him since he was a very young man, still a boy. Will he want to stay on as chancellor? If I am to rule my people once again, I must regain my position without bloodshed. We cannot fight evil by doing evil."

Dawson and Roland exchanged glances. "I'm human," Dawson said, "and therefore not really part of this discussion, but I do have a suggestion."

"Speak. I am always open to fresh ideas." Artigos chuckled. "The fact you are here in my residence, as one of those bent on freeing an old man too long imprisoned, gives you every right to offer as many suggestions as you wish."

Dawson gave Selyn's fingers a squeeze. "Taron of Libernus should have the swords ready to deliver to the Forgotten Ones any time now. I would suggest you remain here, as a decoy. That way the guards won't suspect anything unusual is going on. It's going to take us a while to transport a hundred crystal swords to the women. More time to get them handed out and for the women to get to know them.

If we're lucky, we should be able to accomplish this during the various shifts so that all the Forgotten Ones are fully armed before the guards realize what we've done. We also need to make our move against the demons controlling the guards."

"Ah. This move against the demon-enslaved guards that you're planning." Artigos folded his hands across his chest. "Do you remember what I said about bloodshed?" He cocked an eyebrow at Dawson.

"That I do." Dawson pointed at DemonsBane. "We know your blade will remove demons, just as we know any other crystal blade can destroy them once they're separated from the body they've been inhabiting. I suggest we bring the guards to you one by one." He glanced at Birk. "That's where you can tip the balance for us, Birk. If we can get the guards in here to Artigos one at a time so he can use DemonsBane to remove their demons, we should quickly get control of all of the ones still down here. We'll have to worry about the guards on the upper levels later. Still, you are all sworn to uphold Lemuria. The demons have interfered with your ability to stick to your oath. I imagine the other guards will react much as you have, Birk, once they realize what's been controlling them."

Birk nodded. "I agree. Lord Artigos, if you're all right with that, I can start bringing the guards in at any time."

Artigos nodded. Dawson continued, making his points clearly and without hesitation. "I think they'll want to follow you as the rightful leader of Lemuria. I can't speak for your son or his feelings about giving up his seat as chancellor. Maybe, once his demon is gone, he'll understand the error of his actions. I know that Alton wants no part of the chancellorship. His hold on the position, for now at least, is tenuous. He's only taken the seat for the good of Lemuria. He has no desire to rule."

"That makes me proud. He was an honorable young man. It's good to know his honor continues."

Birk stood. "I need to go back outside and stand guard before the next man shows up to relieve the post. Are you ready for me to bring him to you?"

Artigos nodded. "No time like the present. I just wish I had a backup. I'd hate to allow any to escape."

Roland unsheathed his sword. "I might be able to help."

Birk stared at him. "I thought so! You carry crystal. How is that? I thought only the ruling class carried crystal blades."

"Times have changed, Birk. Hold your sword high."

"I don't want to fight you." Birk frowned, but he pulled his steel sword from the sheath and pointed the blade up. Roland pressed the crystal point of his sword to Birk's. The crystal shimmered and glowed, growing ever brighter until Selyn had to look away. Birk's soft curse had her squinting to see what had happened.

His formerly steel blade shimmered with the clear blue light of crystal. Roland sheathed his sword. Artigos shook his head in utter disbelief. "You're not kidding, sergeant. Times have definitely changed. How did you do that?"

Roland grinned at Birk as the big man twisted and turned his sword, admiring the faceted blade. "Alton's woman, who thought she was purely human but is, in fact, a descendant of Lemurian royalty, has a sword that was presented to her in front of the entire gathering of Lemurian citizens in the great plaza. It was replicated by Alton's white crystal, but Ginny's glows with a dark purple fire. The crystal blade appears to be amethyst. It is known as DarkFire, and the blade's spirit is Daria the Crone."

"The Crone?" Artigos shook his head. "Daria, as I remember her, was a beautiful woman who bravely fought demonkind. She was no crone, though she was not a young woman even then. But what does this have to do with . . . ?"

Laughing, Roland continued. "She personally welcomed Ginny, a human woman, as the daughter of Lemurian royalty, gave her a kiss that offered immortality, and then turned to dust . . . all in front of our citizens. When the sword appeared, replicated by Alton's, DarkFire spoke with Daria's voice. Later, when three of my men and I were in the energy vortex trying to keep demons from entering Lemuria, Ginny's sword turned mine and those of my men to crystal. I sensed Birk's could be changed as well. My sword doesn't yet speak, but she makes her wishes known."

"She? Your blade's spirit is female?" Birk looked at his blade. "Will mine have the spirit of a woman as well?"

Roland shook his head. "I don't know, Birk. But I do know that you now have a power you lacked before with that steel blade of yours. You have a weapon that will become your companion in battle, your advisor, your closest friend. But even better, you now have the weapon you need to battle demonkind, and win."

Chapter Ten

Dawson held tightly to Selyn's hand as they slipped through the last of the common passageways to the hidden tunnels that would lead them even deeper into the bowels of the Lemurian dimension. Roland led the way, his glimmering sword the only light now that they'd moved beyond the regular underground pathways.

"Selyn, have you ever been this far below before?" Dawson kept her hand clenched in his. He felt her tension, the nervous energy that had her breaths coming in short, staccato bursts and her feet occasionally stumbling on the rocky path.

"Never. We were forbidden to leave the levels where we lived and worked. I knew there were passages that led below, but I've never followed them. Roland, how did Taron find this way? From what I have heard, the citizens of Lemuria generally know little of the levels beyond their own, including the one where the Forgotten Ones live."

Roland held his sword high and checked a split in the tunnel ahead. "Taron was led by his crystal sword. I merely follow the markings he left on the walls." He pointed to a long scrape at eye level leading to the passage veering off to the right. "I've only been to the levels beneath yours once before, and never this far or deep. That other time, Taron met me halfway. We passed that point some time back, at that last set of steps. Come. I don't think it's too much farther."

The walls were damp and cold. In some areas, strange, luminescent algae added a soft, yet otherworldly glow to the passage. The constant sounds of water dripping, of their labored breathing, and the clatter of rocks and pebbles underfoot echoed ahead and behind.

There was something timeless about these passages, as if the three of them passed through more than space . . . as if they marched into time itself.

A shiver spiked along Dawson's spine. Time? He had no idea if it was day or night, how long since they'd left Sedona, how many hours since their last meal, since they'd last slept. Adrenaline coursed through his body, and he was high and filled with energy—and totally out of touch with time.

He rarely wore a wristwatch, and he hadn't thought to wear one today. What day was it? How long had they been here, and how much longer before they reached Taron, before they had swords for all the women?

Did it matter? Alton was waiting to hear from them, but he'd been prepared to wait.

This was truly a timeless realm, and Dawson passed here with a sense he walked on ground no human foot had ever trod, not only in a dimension separate from Earth's, but in an area that was basically off-limits to this dimension's inhabitants.

Who had created this labyrinth, what forces determined the tunnels and caverns, the odd forms of life? Though he knew the dimension existed within the volcanic core of Mount Shasta, the caves and passages they hiked through now were not volcanic in appearance. Instead, they reminded him of the limestone caves he'd clambered through when he was young.

Stalactites and stalagmites projected bizarre shadows and twists to the light from Roland's sword, and in some areas, brilliant color ran in bold bands across the walls and over the relatively smooth floor. It was an unworldly experience, almost beyond belief.

He thought of his clinic and the employees there who had no idea where their nerdy vet was spending his time away from work. How he wished he could share this adventure with them, but he had a feeling even the ghost of his Aunt Fiona might have trouble swallowing a story so bizarre.

He gazed at the strange glow shimmering along the walls, at the big man ahead. Felt the warmth of Selyn's fingers linked to his. He realized it wasn't all that easy to believe any of it himself.

Especially Selyn. She was beautiful and exotic and holding his hand. That alone defied belief.

A glow in the passageway ahead was the first hint they might be reaching the end of their journey. Roland glanced over his shoulder. "I'm hearing from Taron. He's got the swords finished, and they're all packed to go." He laughed. "It appears our young aristocrat is more than ready to leave this place. He misses his warm bathing pool!"

He picked up the pace until they were practically trotting down the dark tunnel toward a light that grew brighter the closer they got. It was almost as bright as day when they entered a huge cavern.

Dawson's first thought was that he'd stepped into a massive geode filled with diamonds. The walls curved high overhead and sparkled with clear crystalline facets reflecting an eerie blue light.

Taron stood near the center of the cavern, a man unlike anything Daws had expected. He was the same height as Alton, with a similar build and eyes the same brilliant emerald green, but his hair hung in braids of crimson silk, as fiery and true a red as the ruby sword.

He met them as they entered the cavern, smiling broadly at Roland and looking upon both Selyn and Dawson with obvious curiosity. He stretched his hand out to Dawson first. "So you're the human demon hunter I've heard of." Laughing, he shook Dawson's hand. "When Alton described how you sucked up demons with a shop vacuum and froze them in little bags, he could barely get the words out he laughed so hard. Excellent thinking. Nothing like taking a new approach. It's good to meet you."

Then he turned to Selyn and carefully took her hand. "It is a pleasure to meet you, as well. I've been told of your bravery. Roland says the sword was truly that of Artigos the Just, that our leader still lives. Your knowledge of his whereabouts may just alter the course of this fight in our favor. Thank you."

Dawson couldn't stop the chill that coursed along his spine when Taron held on to Selyn's hand for what seemed much too long. She certainly wasn't trying to pull out of his grasp, though she did send one uneasy glance in Dawson's direction. Then Taron released his hold on her and smiled at all of them.

"For the first time, I have hope we may actually prevail. What first felt like a fool's errand has already borne fruit. The swords are finished and ready, but knowing that Artigos the Just still lives, that I have had a small part in recreating his weapon so that you might return it to him . . ." He shook his head, as if denying all that had passed.

"Amazing, to be part of history in the making," he said. "Absolutely amazing."

Then he showed them the wrapped bundles piled beside a ruby red altar near one crystalline wall of the cavern. Small glow sticks set on sconces on the walls were the source of the brilliant, cold blue light. As insignificant as the sticks were, their multiple reflections off the crystalline walls illuminated the entire cavern. Yet even with the light, as Dawson glanced around, he thought it was a cold and unforgiving place to have spent so many days creating swords for an untried army.

In spite of that unexpected frisson of jealousy, he had to admire Taron and what he'd accomplished. At the same time, he wondered what Selyn thought of the Lemurian aristocrat. She'd hardly known any other decent men. Would she be interested in this guy, one who was more like her? A man of the same people, with an immortal life span to match her own?

Shit. Daws shook his head and pulled his thoughts together. He had no right to be jealous of Taron or anyone else. No right to think along those lines. Selyn belonged to no man, especially not to Dawson Buck. It wasn't up to him to choose a man for Selyn, right or wrong. She was her own woman and would make up her own mind.

But then she reached for his hand, wrapped her fingers in his, and looked at him with such a serious expression on her face, that all his good intentions faded beneath the warmth of her touch and the subtle invitation in her smile.

Even wrapped in rough cloth and bundled together in nice, neat packs, the swords were heavy and difficult to carry. Since they hadn't come with scabbards, the women were going to have to come up with some way to carry them, but just getting a hundred weapons from the lower levels to the slave quarters was turning out to be more difficult than Selyn had imagined.

She had no idea if Birk and Artigos were having any success exorcising demons from the guards, which meant she and Dawson, Taron, and Roland had to slip in and out of this occupied level with every care possible.

She wished she knew what time it was, what the schedule might be, but she'd lost all track. Running on pure adrenaline made it harder to judge how long they'd been going now, but it had taken them longer to reach Taron than she'd expected, and it could be the middle of the night for all she knew.

Whatever. They would just have to trust to luck and hope they weren't entering the passages during a shift change for the guards, or at a time when patrols were moving through.

Once they reached the upper levels, Selyn took the lead. These dark passages and many tunnels had been her home for her entire life. She knew all the hidden pathways, all the places where guards would linger, where sound might carry.

Loaded down with a heavy bundle of crystal swords, she moved as quietly as she could. Even the slightest noises carried in these tunnels. The sound of their passing was only partially muffled by the ever-pervasive rumble of heavy mining equipment and the distant voices of the Forgotten Ones.

These were women who had known nothing beyond slavery. Their lives had been unchanging from the time they were old enough to pick gems from broken rock, mere toddlers sitting in small groups, searching for the shimmer of diamonds and rubies, hunting for emeralds and other precious stones.

As they'd grown, they'd taken on more physical labor. As adult women, they—like Selyn—were strong and broad shouldered, muscular as their mothers had been, and physically stronger than many men. Even so, they still spent part of each day searching for the gems that were so easily lost amid the rubble.

Gems they would never see in their final, cut form. Gems that would go to decorate ladies of the aristocracy, or be sold in trade to an outside world even the free folk never saw.

Selyn couldn't let herself think about the lies, the subterfuge, the horrible lives they'd all been subjected to, all because of demonkind. If what Artigos the Just said was the truth, all of them were victims. All of them subject to the evil plans of demons. Plans that were so far along and so well established and entrenched within Lemurian society, she could only pray they had some hope of changing what had been put in motion so many thousands of years ago.

Selyn stopped at the final portal leading to the more heavily traveled areas. Slowly and quietly she set her bundle on the ground. "I have to be sure the passage is clear. The living quarters are close—only a short walk away—but we can't afford discovery at this point."

Before the men could question her, she slipped through the portal and around a corner. The long tunnel was empty. The only voices she heard were the sounds of women in the nearby living quarters, talking quietly between shifts while others slept. She hurried back to the men. "I'm going to warn them we're coming. I don't want anyone to raise an alarm."

Dawson nodded. Then he shocked her by leaning close

and kissing her. The gentle contact of his mouth on hers made her heart race, but it did something else. Something she hadn't expected.

It gave her the burst of confidence she needed to smile at him and turn away. To slip through the portal, and then to race down the brightly lit passage and walk boldly into the main room where her sisters, the Forgotten Ones, gathered.

There were at least thirty women here. The sense of homecoming almost brought Selyn to her knees. She'd been so afraid she'd never see any of them again.

"Selyn? Where the nine hells have you been? We've been searching for you!"

She hugged her friend Nica, but quickly stepped back. "I will tell you soon, but for now, I bring friends of mine. Wait until you see what they've brought us! Remember when I told you that there were members among the free folk who cared about our fate? That finally, we might have a chance at freedom? Some of you laughed at me; some of you believed."

It was all she could do not to burst into laughter. "This is something beyond our greatest expectations. Wake those who sleep so they may join us. Welcome us quietly. I have crystal blades for every single one of us."

Giving in to laughter, Selyn broke away from an entire room filled with women gasping in surprise, and raced back to the men. "Hurry. The way is still clear." Gathering up her bundle of swords, she led them through the portal and down the tunnel to the main gathering.

At the sight of the strange men, the women backed away, some still rubbing their eyes from their hastily inter-rupted sleep. All of them watched anxiously as Selyn began unwrapping her bundle of swords. She lay five glimmering blades out on a long table and then stood before it.

"These men are here to help us. You've heard me speak of Roland of Kronus, a member of the Lemurian Guard and the first of the free folk, ever, to search for the truth behind the Forgotten Ones. Roland saved my life just a few days ago when I was captured by one of our guards and badly beaten. Roland is a brave and fearless man who has chosen to help us."

Roland bowed his head and then stepped back. Selyn smiled at him before gesturing toward Dawson. "This man is Dawson Buck, a human from Earth's dimension who has unselfishly agreed to help us find freedom. He risks much for a people he didn't even know existed until just a short time ago. We owe him our loyalty and our thanks."

She had to force herself not to allow her gaze to linger on Dawson. Even though he was tired and grimy from their long hours hiking between the levels, she still thought him absolutely gorgeous. Reluctantly, she looked away. "This man is Taron of Libernus, an aristocrat who has joined our cause. Taron has spent the past week replicating the crystal swords—one for each of the Forgotten Ones, that we be forgotten no longer."

She stood aside from the long table now covered with crystal swords. "As our mothers were warriors in the terrible DemonWars, so shall we fight."

Taron stepped forward with his two bundles and set them on the floor at Selyn's feet. "Stay with your sisters, Selyn. Explain what's happening both here and above. We're going after the rest of the swords." He raised his head and smiled at the gathering of women. "Listen to Selyn. She's had a most amazing adventure, one all of you will have the opportunity to join."

Selyn shot him a quick grin. Taron nodded. Then he and

Roland headed for the door. Dawson paused a moment, reached for her, and kissed her full on the mouth, in front of her sisters. "Be careful," he said. And then he was gone, and Selyn faced a very curious group of her oldest friends.

"So," she said, "that is where we stand now. What began as a battle against demons infiltrating Earth's dimension has evolved into an all-out war against demonkind. Already we are learning what actually happened to the women warriors. Our mothers were not betrayed by the Lemurian people. They were betrayed by demons in the guise of their fellow citizens. No wonder it was so hard for them to fight the purge. Their terrible exile wasn't ordered by their peers. It was entirely the fault of demonkind."

"The guards? Are they the ones who fathered us, or were they demons? Who do we kill to avenge the degradation of our mothers?"

Selyn sighed. This was not going to be easy. "The guards are victims of demonkind, just as our mothers were, as we are. That's the truth, Isra. Once the demons have been removed from the guards, you'll see that they are people just as we are. Good people at heart who have been badly used by demonkind. Have you never wondered why we were not sexually assaulted as well? I can only guess that is one sin the guards were able to fight. When you see Birk, you'll believe what I say is true."

"Birk? That bastard." Isra spit on the ground between them. "I'd rather kill him."

Selyn stroked one of the crystal blades. "He asked me to kill him. I chose instead to forgive him and ask him to help us. He is doing that, even now."

Isra glared at her. "You may choose to forgive. That is

your right. When I carry crystal, I will kill him and any other guard. Which of these is mine?"

"I don't know." Selyn picked up another bundle, carefully unwrapped it and lay the swords out on the table beside the first ones. "Each crystal will respond only to its master. The blade will glow. Do not try to pick up a sword that doesn't glow for you."

"Why?" Isra planted her fists on her hips. "What will happen if we choose the one we want?"

Selyn shrugged. "I imagine you could die."

A soft gasp went up about the room. Isra's head snapped back as if she'd been slapped. "You're lying."

It had been a damned long day and an even longer week. She'd never been all that fond of Isra anyway. The woman's temper was always sour, and she loved to harass anyone smaller or weaker than herself.

Selyn really didn't have time for this right now. She folded her arms across her chest and sighed. "Fine, then. Go right ahead. See what happens when you decide to choose your own sword. Just don't say I didn't warn you. Of course, if you're dead, you won't be saying much at all, will you?"

Isra glared at her a moment. Then she planted a hand on Selyn's chest and shoved her aside. Slowly she walked the length of the two long tables, studying each sword. Selyn ignored her and continued to unwrap the bundles. Carefully, touching only the silver hilt, she placed each new weapon beside the last.

They looked identical, but Selyn could feel a slight difference in each one, as if the individual personality of its spirit had somehow changed the balance, the grip, the way the crystal reflected light. None had yet glowed for her. She wasn't worried. She knew there was a sword for her, one with a spirit that would match her perfectly.

Just as her mother's spirit fit Eddy Marks.

Isra stopped and stared at Selyn. "I want this one."

Selyn glanced at the sword. It looked just like all the others. "Does it glow for you?"

"What does that mean?"

"When you pass your hand over the blade, does the blade glow? Shimmer, as if from an inner light."

"That's a myth. They're just swords."

Selyn chuckled. "If you believe that, go right ahead. But I warn you once again, if the sword does not glow for you, it is not yours to claim."

"You lie." Isra grabbed the hilt of her chosen sword. Blue light flashed. She screamed and dropped the blade. The smell of burning flesh filled the room as Isra grabbed her singed hand and glared at Selyn. "I don't know how, but you did that to me, bitch. Watch your back, Selyn. No one attacks me and lives to tell about it. No one."

She spun around and shoved her way through the gathered women. Silently, Selyn watched her go. Then she went back to unpacking the swords, though once she glanced up at the others she wondered what they thought of Isra, if her words had frightened any of them. No matter. This was bigger than one ill-tempered woman.

The others milled about, staring curiously at the swords. No one remarked on Isra or her dramatic exit.

Selyn set another sword out on the table. "If you like, walk past the swords and hold your hand above each one for a moment. If the blade pulses with light, you may pick it up. The sword probably won't speak to you, but the glow will tell you the blade is meant to be yours. But remember. Don't talk about them away from here, and don't let the guards see them. We can't risk discovery. Not when we're this close."

"Which is yours?"

Selyn didn't see who asked the question, but she merely set the next blade on the table. "I have no idea. I imagine one will glow for me as well." At least she hoped that would happen. She opened the final bundle and set the swords out, one by one. None of these had acknowledged her. Not one of them was hers.

Almost thirty blades lay along the tables, half as many blades as there were women in the room. She stood back and watched as her sisters walked slowly along the tables. Hands hovered above swords with blades that reflected the light, but did not shimmer on their own.

"Nine hells! It glows for me."

"Look. Selyn, come and see. Nica's found one."

She choked back the surge of jealousy that slammed into her. This was the reason she was here, why she'd carried swords to this room, to match them to their perfect mates. And if anyone in this room deserved crystal, it was Nica.

She'd long been Selyn's friend, a quiet little thing who was a favorite among all of them with her good heart, yet strong sense of purpose. Nica stood in front of the glowing sword, transfixed by the shimmer and pulse of light along the crystal blade. Almost fearfully, she raised her head and stared at Selyn. "What do I do now?"

Selyn grinned at her. "Pick it up!"

Cautiously, Nica reached for the hilt. Her fingers trembled, her teeth worried her bottom lip, and she looked almost on the verge of tears. Then her fingers wrapped around the pommel, and it slipped perfectly into her grasp.

"Oh."

Her soft whisper was almost lost in the brilliant flash of light from the blade. Nica raised her head, and this time her eyes glowed as brightly as her blade. "I feel it. The sword isn't actually speaking to me, but I can feel a connection. She is meant to be with me."

"That's wonderful." Selyn leaned close and kissed her cheek. "It looks good in your hand, though we'll need to practice once everyone has met their match." She glanced up. "And we'll need a way to carry them. A scabbard or sheath of some kind. Something that will allow you to reach your sword easily in battle."

One more thing to worry about. She glanced toward the door and hoped like the nine hells that none of the guards would come snooping around. They rarely came near the living quarters.

The women were still passing by the blades. More of them had found swords and connected with their match by the time the men returned with the second load of bundles. Dawson knelt and began unwrapping one. "I'm going to stay and help. Roland and Taron can manage the rest of the blades."

"Good. The shift is about to change. We'll have more women here in a moment. So far there are only a dozen or so matches."

Nica joined Selyn and flopped down on the ground next to the bundle of swords Dawson was unwrapping. She cradled her own crystal blade in her lap. "To be exact, Selyn, there are fourteen matches, and one very pissed off Isra. Ignore her threat at your own risk. She is more hateful than ever."

Dawson raised his head. "What threat? Who threatened you?"

"Nica's exaggerating. It was nothing," Selyn said.

"It was Isra," Nica added. "She wanted a sword that had not acknowledged her. When Selyn warned her, she tried to take it anyway, and her fingers were badly burned." Nica shook her head, all the while stroking her crystal blade. "She will be a dangerous enemy, Selyn. I don't want anything to happen to you."

Dawson grinned at her. "Neither do I, Nica. I want Selyn in one piece. Could this Isra be possessed?"

Nica shot a concerned glance at Selyn. "I don't know. How do you tell?"

Dawson pointed to the blade in her lap. "Next time you're near Isra, ask your blade. Some can tell. If she is possessed, we'll know how to deal with her. If she's just a bitch, that's another problem." He laughed. "Look. Two more blades have been claimed."

"We need to get the rest of them up." Selyn grabbed two more and set them out. Dawson helped, and before long the tables were covered in crystal swords.

Dawson looped an arm over her shoulders. "Yours must be in the last batch. Roland and Taron will be back soon. I imagine you're growing anxious."

She didn't answer him. She watched as—one after another—more of her sisters claimed a shimmering crystal blade. The first group of women had either taken their swords and gone back to sleep or they'd left to take their shift in the mines. A few who'd been so quickly awakened hours earlier still waited, though the excitement levels were high enough to keep everyone alert.

The ones who'd just gotten off their shift were now looking over the blades, hearing the story of demon possession and the discovery of Artigos the Just.

Selyn was impressed by their calm acceptance of all that had happened, though she knew it wasn't going to be easy to convince all of them that they would have to work with the same men who had been so cruel to them over the years.

Nor did she want to think of all they had to accomplish before this small army of slaves would be prepared to actually go forth and, if necessary, fight. None of them had ever imagined battling demonkind.

None had dreamed of ever holding crystal.

She had, though. Over the past few days, since meeting Roland and learning of the replicated swords, Selyn had dreamed of holding her very own blade, of finally understanding how her mother had felt as she'd marched into battle, paired with sentient crystal.

Where was her sword? What if it wasn't in the last bundle?

Selyn hung on to Dawson and hoped she'd not be a Forgotten One when all the swords were finally matched to her sisters.

Chapter Eleven

Marigold Moonbeam Schwartz definitely had known better days. Even though she felt like she had to sit on her hands to keep from doing or saying something she'd regret, she managed to stay quietly in the shadows. Her mother was a skilled witch with years' more experience than Mari, but it was so difficult not to make at least a few tiny suggestions.

Gritting her teeth, she breathed deeply of the soothing, vanilla-scented candle her mother had lit and set to one side of the daybed here in her parents' home. With a studied patience she really didn't feel, Mari watched while Spirit sprinkled herbs around the dazed and bound Lemurian chancellor, while Freedom, Mari's dad and Spirit's long-suffering spouse, sat and tapped out a monotonous rhythm on his worn set of bongo drums.

Thank goodness she had Darius here as a reminder that yes, magic did exist, and no, her parents were not nearly as loony as she'd always thought. And, if Mari still doubted, there was that sliver of bespelled crystal lodged forever in her heart, the crystal that—along with Darius's crystal sword—had given her immortality.

Some days, the boring banker's life she'd once led didn't sound all that bad, but today was just flat out terrifying. Life had been simpler when all she'd had to worry about was whether or not she'd still have her job come morning, or who her ex-fiancé was sleeping with now.

Ever since Eddy Marks and her sexy lover Dax, the ex-demon, had brought Chancellor Artigos to her parents' house last night, Mari had been worried. She was barely used to this whole "invasion by demons" thing, much less the fact that Lemurians weren't just a silly legend after all, or that she was a witch with some pretty amazing powers she'd never expected.

Her skills as a witch were so new, however, that she'd immediately deferred to her mother's expertise in the matter of drawing a demon out of the Lemurian leader. And she sure wished Eddy and Dax and even that talking dog of theirs had hung around a bit longer, but they'd gone without sleep for much too long and needed rest. Having Eddy and her amazing crystal sword close by with all this other weird shit going on was a constant reassurance to Mari that she wasn't completely wacko.

There were only so many new things a girl should have to accept at one time, and this week had taken Mari over the top. In just the past few days she'd lost her job, her fiancé, her car, and her heart.

Literally. Not only had she fallen in love with a Lemurian guardsman, she'd battled demons with magic and died.

None of that had been on her schedule when she'd headed home to Evergreen to help her mom run the little crystal shop Spirit had owned for almost forty years.

Neither had exorcising demons.

Now, though, Mari's heart went out to Gaia, the Lemurian chancellor's lovely wife. The woman obviously loved her husband and worried terribly about him. How she managed to sit so calmly with such a regal look about her while a strange witch and an even stranger wizard attempted a dangerous exorcism was beyond Mari. Of course, after this past week, Mari felt like there was a whole lot way beyond her.

Gaia had every right to be worried. Demon possession was a terrifying concept, and if what her old friend Eddy Marks had told her was even half true, demonkind had already staked a powerful foothold in Lemurian society and was currently pushing hard against Earth's totally unprepared defenses.

She'd seen evidence of that push with her own eyes, right here in Evergreen. Thank goodness she had Darius and his amazing crystal sword for protection. Mari was getting better with her demon-killing spells, but she still had a long way to go before she could wield magic the way Darius wielded his crystal blade.

The chancellor let out a long, low groan. His body arched, straining against the ropes that tied him closely to the bed. Gaia leapt to her feet, but Darius was there immediately, catching hold of her arm and steadying her as her husband began to cry out, thrashing back and forth on the bed.

Spirit's voice rose, and her rhyming chant took on a fierce resonance. Freedom pounded the drums harder and faster, until the thundering beat seemed to meld with Spirit's spell.

The growing pressure in the room drew Mari to her feet. She moved closer to her mother as a palpable sense of dread closed in about them. Darius drew his sword while still keeping one arm wrapped tightly around Gaia's slim waist.

He glanced at Mari. *Go to your mother,* he said, speaking to her, mind to mind. *She needs your strength to battle this demon. It feels like a powerful foe, one that intends to fight back.*

Quickly Mari moved to stand beside her mother. Spirit reached for her without pausing in her continuous chant. Her hand latched tightly onto Mari's.

The moment the two women connected, Spirit's voice gained power. Vibrating now with Mari's added strength, her words seemed to take on an actual presence. Freedom's drumming picked up speed as Artigos writhed and twisted against his bonds.

Mari joined her mother's chant. She had no idea how she knew the words to say, where she might have learned this spell, but she had no doubt she owned these words, this powerful magic. She raised her voice as if in song, chanting in counterpoint to her mother's strong voice, adding her own pure contralto as she worked with Spirit to draw the demon out.

This was no common foe. It wasn't anything like the simple creatures of darkness she'd fought with Darius. This *thing* that existed within Artigos, this powerful entity had grown in strength for millennia. Somehow, Mari knew it had sucked much of the life force from its host, existing as a parasite within the Lemurian leader. Feeding from him even as it controlled him.

Mari knew these things just as she knew the words to say. She had no idea how or why, or where her newfound magic powers came from, though she was learning to accept them. To accept the woman she was becoming, just as she accepted that tiny shard of crystal embedded in her heart—a piece of magic that had changed her life forever.

She felt Darius beside her and loved him all the more for his steady presence and honor, for the strength he gave so freely so that she might work this spell. She had accepted him just as easily—evidence of the changes in her life and herself.

Aware of the growing magic—of the power pouring through her body—Mari raised her hands above her head. Vaguely she sensed when her mother stepped back and relinquished the spell to her.

Without truly understanding how or why she knew what to do, Mari let her hands fly in an intricate dance, as if she drew forth a long thread from the chancellor's body. Singing now in an unfamiliar language, her voice rose and fell in an ancient rhyme, in words only the demon would understand.

Hand over hand, she pulled an invisible thread from Artigos's body. She could feel the thread. It was no longer something of her imagination. Now it was an ice cold line with tensile strength, anchored tightly to something within the chancellor, pulling back even as Mari pulled forth with all her might.

Artigos had stopped fighting her and lay still. His eyes were wide open, and he watched her, but she knew the demon saw through the chancellor's eyes. Hatred burned in him and the sense of dread, of evil, grew stronger the harder Mari tugged the invisible line.

The drumming became a heartbeat, a thundering call to the demon that the creature fought with all his ancient power. He denied its seductive lure with every bit of his evil will, but Mari was stronger. Her voice rose and fell in song, and her fingers danced, hand over hand, straining at the heavy weight that somehow anchored the line deep within the Lemurian chancellor.

The thread glowed a dark and fiery red, yet the temperature in the room dropped until Mari's breath puffed from between her lips in frozen clouds of steam. She pulled harder, but the demon actively fought her now, until it felt as if she were trying to land a huge fish on the end of a line. Her hands burned from the horrible cold and the sharp bite of the line she pulled. The tension grew stronger, as if the demon wanted to drag her down with it, down into the hell that had been the chancellor's soul.

Blood flecked her hands where the frozen line cut into her fingers, but she wrapped it around her palms and pulled even harder. Her shoulders ached, and her fingers burned. Her breath came in gasps.

Spirit moved close and stood behind her daughter. She rested her hands on Mari's shoulders, sharing her strength and holding her steady.

Power bloomed in Mari—her mother's power—and she reached down, closer to the chancellor's rigid body, until she grabbed hold of the icy line close up against his chest, wrapped it once again around both her hands in spite of the blood and the pain, and gave a mighty pull.

There was a horrible screeching sound, as if metal dragged against metal. Artigos cried out, and the room filled with the sulfuric stench of demon.

Spirit fell back, and Freedom's hands paused above his drums. Eyes wide, he stared at the black, oily mass that Mari dragged slowly out of Chancellor Artigos. The bound man screamed again, a horrible shriek of unimaginable pain.

Gaia cried out and reached for her husband, but Darius shoved her behind him. He thrust savagely with his crystal blade and caught the demon as it began to take shape mere inches above the chancellor's body—but it wasn't focusing on Artigos.

It was looming over Mari, growing in form and substance, finding its demonic shape, and reaching for her with multiple arms and long, sharp claws.

Darius's sword passed through the oily mass. Sparks

flew, and the creature howled, but Mari still held on to the line connecting her to the fearsome thing.

"Mari!" Darius shouted as he drove his blade into the demon. "Turn it loose. Let it go!"

Mari untangled her hands and dropped the line. She spun out of the way as Darius struck the demon once again. This time his blade cut true. More sparks flashed. There was a loud concussion that felt and sounded like a sonic boom. The demon let out a horrible banshee cry and burst into a roiling ball of fire that blossomed upward, spreading out in a mushroom cloud of smoke and flames against the ceiling.

Freedom grabbed Spirit and rolled her to the floor, protecting her body with his. Darius shielded his eyes with his left arm and swept his crystal blade through the remnants of the dying demon. Then, as the flames and smoke dissipated, he quickly sheathed his blade and reached for Mari.

She'd thrown herself over the chancellor's body to protect him from the burning demon. Now, head down and gasping for air, she trembled from head to foot as she pushed herself away from the man and reached for Darius. He leaned over and gathered her up in his arms. Blood trickled from her hands and ran down her wrists, but she didn't care. Hanging tightly to his neck, she hugged him close as he carried her across the room to an overstuffed couch and sat down with her in his lap.

Gaia ran to her husband's side. "Artigos? My love, are you all right?"

"I need to go to him." Mari tried to crawl out of Darius's arms, but he held her close.

"Not yet," he whispered. "Let Gaia have a moment with her husband. She's the one he should respond to, if he can."

Spirit and Freedom—who moved slowly and painfully from recent surgery—walked unsteadily across the room.

Spirit flopped down on the couch beside Darius and Mari. She handed Mari a towel to wipe the blood from her hands, staring blankly at her daughter and shaking her head in disbelief. Then she let out a big breath of air and said, "What the fuck was that?"

"Mother!" Mari choked back a startled laugh.

Spirit just shook her head. "I'm serious. Really. What was that disgusting thing?"

"That was a demon, Mother. A very large and powerful demon, if I'm right."

Darius kissed the top of Mari's head. "I've seen a lot of demons, but I've never seen anything like that one. It was beginning to take form when I killed it, something they can't easily do in this dimension." He sighed and stared at Gaia and Artigos. "I imagine it's been part of the chancellor for so long that it's gained strength from him, living off his life force."

"Look." Mari gestured toward Gaia and Artigos. Gaia had loosened the ropes that bound her husband and was helping him sit up. He appeared confused, but at least he was alive. This time when Mari tried to stand up, Darius turned her free.

She helped Gaia get the chancellor settled on the edge of the bed. "Are you okay, Chancellor?"

Artigos gazed at Mari with an almost childlike expression. Then he turned to his wife. "Who is she, Gaia, my dear? Who is this woman, and why does she wear such strange garments?"

Mari glanced down at her faded blue jeans and the ribbed sweater she wore. Softly, she said, "I'm Mari, Chancellor. I helped remove a demon that's been living inside you."

He stared at Mari for a long moment. Then he merely

looked away and smiled at his wife. "Will you take me home, my love? I really want to go home now."

Gaia smiled, but her eyes were filled with tears. "Later, Arti. When you've rested. Lie down now, dear, and sleep."

He nodded, still smiling sweetly. Then he obediently turned and lay back down on the bed. Gaia covered him with a soft quilt. Freedom quietly gathered up his drums, and Spirit swept up the herbs she'd scattered. The last thing she did was lean over and blow out the vanilla-scented candle she'd left burning beside the daybed.

Mari and Darius followed the others out of the room. Gaia paused at the door. "I'll stay with him," she said.

Mari took her hand. "Is he okay, Gaia? He sounded almost like a little kid."

Gaia nodded. "I believe the demon has taken much of my husband's spirit, but he is alive, and he remembers me. That's all I can ask for. Go now. Sleep." She sighed and glanced at her sleeping husband. "I have a feeling you're going to need your rest, that things are about to move very quickly."

Mari glanced at Darius. "I'm afraid you might be right. If you need anything, Gaia, I'll be here a while longer. I'm going back to my own apartment in a bit, but my mother and father are just down the hall." Then she and Darius left the room together, while Gaia returned to her husband's side.

Mari's mother waited in the living room. She handed the telephone to Mari. "It's Eddy. She wants to know how he's doing."

"I'll take it." Mari grabbed the phone and tried to figure out how to explain exactly what had just happened. She still wasn't entirely positive. The demon was gone, but what was left of the chancellor? That was not the ruler of an entire civilization sleeping on her mother's daybed. Not anymore.

* * *

Alton ran his finger down the list one more time and sighed. "Six out of the nine—if you include my father—possessed by demonkind. I had no idea it was this serious."

Ginny chewed on her bottom lip and stared at the names. She'd sat beside Alton the night before when he'd called the council members together, and DarkFire had confirmed her suspicions. "That gave them a clear majority when your father was chancellor. Six against three, and those three have no idea what they're up against. Even with you now siding with the three who aren't possessed, demons still have a simple majority."

"I wonder why those three haven't been taken over? What is it that protects some and not others?"

Ginny shook her head. "I'm not sure, though they all appear to be decent, honorable men. Maybe it's the strength of a person's character, his personal honor. Integrity? Who knows?"

Alton smiled sadly. "I have a feeling you're right, though I hate to think that's it. I would rather believe my father's possession was more arbitrary, not that he was so weak that he allowed the possession to occur."

Alton's sword pulsed blue. "Someone comes. DarkFire has removed the lock on the portal. Be prepared."

Ginny didn't say a word. Instead, she slipped behind a curtain hiding a storage closet, where she had a limited view of the room, but wouldn't be visible to anyone coming through the portal. She'd barely gotten out of sight when two men barged into the room without announcing themselves first as was the normal protocol.

She recognized Maxl and Drago, the same ones who had sent a third to snoop through the chancellor's office. Obviously they weren't all that big on proper procedure.

Alton stood up, towering over both men. "Maxl. Drago. What brings you here?"

Drago drew himself up to his full height, which, while above average by human standards, made for a rather small Lemurian. "As chosen representatives of the Council of Nine, we demand to know what you've done with Artigos. We have no proof he's taken ill, no proof you haven't kidnapped him, or even murdered him to usurp his position. Your mother is missing. Have you kidnapped her as well?"

Alton folded his arms across his chest and looked down his nose at both men. "And what did the two of you have in mind, searching for my mother? She has no part to play with the council. Where she is and what she does is no one's business but her own."

"Not if you've harmed her. She's a good woman." Maxl took a step closer, invading Alton's space.

"That she is, Maxl. A very good woman, which is why she chose to be with my father while he is being treated."

"Where?" Drago slapped his palm down on the desk beside Alton. "Where is Artigos and what kind of treatment? He was perfectly okay when we saw him last."

"That's right," Maxl said. He was an even smaller man than Drago, but every bit as pompous. "We know you, Alton. You've been a bane to your father's existence for as long as we can recall. There is no way he would turn his seat over to you and that impersonator who calls herself a Lemurian."

Ginny sensed Alton's anger—his very powerful struggle for control. There was steel in his voice when he answered. She wondered if Maxl and Drago had any idea just how furious Alton was—or how close they both were to ending up in a world of hurt.

"You will leave my woman out of any conversation,

Maxl. Remember that if you wish to survive long enough to remain a member of the council."

"Are you threatening me, Alton? Please, continue. Especially since I have a witness."

Drago shook his head. "There's no need, Maxl. Alton, you've refused to tell us where to find Chancellor Artigos, who is the rightful leader of the council. We have no choice but to call a vote when we next meet. There is a solid majority willing to vote you out of your position. We can't remove you from the council without a two-thirds vote, but we can take you out of the chancellor's seat."

Ginny'd heard all she could take. Gritting her teeth, she stepped into the room. "I'd like to see you try it, Drago. Do you have any idea what's going on here?" She got right in Drago's face. "You and Maxl are possessed. You harbor demons in your black little hearts. Are you aware of that?"

DarkFire glowed in the scabbard and actually vibrated against Ginny's back. She slipped the dark crystal free and held it firmly under Drago's nose. The blade shimmered with its unusual dark light, and tiny purple sparks raced up and down the blade. Both Maxl and Drago moved back a pace.

Drago was the first to regain his composure. "Standing behind a woman, eh, Alton?"

Alton shook his head and grinned at Ginny. "No. Not at all. I stand beside Ginny in all things." He whipped Hell-Fire from his scabbard, but he merely held the weapon as if he were showing it off. "Interesting thing about a sentient sword. Not only does it speak with the voice of an ancient warrior, it has powers we're only now beginning to fully understand."

He turned the blade this way and that, flashing light off the facets in a mesmerizing, hypnotic pattern. Both Maxl and Drago stared unwillingly at the blade, as if their gazes were trapped in the flashing, dancing light.

Though, as aristocrats, the men must have had crystal swords of their own, Ginny figured they were probably stashed in a closet somewhere. They weren't wearing them at the moment, and no way would crystal work for anyone possessed by demonkind. They certainly wouldn't shimmer and sparkle the way HellFire did, but it was obvious to Ginny that Alton's blade was showing off.

Finally, with what had to be a powerful act of will, Drago forced his attention away from the shimmering blade. He blinked owlishly a moment. Then he scowled and focused his anger on Alton. "What kind of powers? What do you speak of?"

Alton smiled. It was the kind of expression that sent chills along Ginny's spine—and they weren't the good kind.

"Well, for instance, HellFire and DarkFire work really well together. Take Maxl here. We discovered last night he was not alone in his body. He's got a parasite living with him. An ugly, dangerous parasite."

Maxl glanced from the crystal blade to Drago and then stared at Alton. "I don't have any parasite in me. What are you talking about?"

"This." Alton pointed HellFire at Maxl. Ginny did the same with DarkFire, and brilliant beams like laser fire shot from both swords. Blue-white light from Alton's. Dark, dark purple from DarkFire.

The blast of light bathed Maxl in cold flame, and he stiffened, caught in the laser-bright power of the crystal. Drago backed away and shielded his eyes, coughing as the room filled with the stench of sulfur. After a full minute, Alton lowered his sword.

Ginny did the same. She glanced up and caught his

shrug as he sheathed HellFire. Drago clutched his partner's arm and steadied him. Then he cursed Alton. "What the nine hells was that all about?"

Alton folded his arms over his chest. "Do you recognize that stench, Drago? It's the scent of demonkind. That's the parasite Ginny was talking about. She was not making a joke when she said both you and Maxl are possessed by demons. So are your cohorts on the council. Have you invited the bastards in, or did they take you unawares? How does it feel, to know that you serve Abyss and demonkind, not Lemuria?"

"You lie, Alton. Everything you say is a lie. Your days are sorely numbered, Alton of No One. What right have you to attack a member of the council?" Looping an arm around the other man's waist, Drago helped Maxl walk drunkenly away from Alton. Then the two of them passed through the portal.

Alton stared at the dark gateway. Then he whispered, "Every right, Drago. Every right as a proud Lemurian and heir to the chancellor's seat. I will not let demonkind prevail."

He sighed, put his arm around Ginny's shoulders, and hugged her close. "We should have killed the demon. A little more power would have forced the creature out."

Ginny shook her head. "If we'd removed the demon, it could have killed Maxl. Even if we wanted to, I don't believe either of our swords would allow it."

"You're probably right. But damn it all, it would sure make our job a lot easier." He leaned down and kissed her. "Or not."

Ginny kissed him back. "We will win, Alton. Somehow. But you need to retain your position. How long can you hold off a vote?"

"A couple of days, max. Drago is right. They've got the

numbers to boot me out of the chancellor's office. I haven't got a chance of pulling any of this off if I'm not the chancellor. What are we going to do, Ginny?"

"Hope like hell your grandfather is still alive, that Taron gets the swords to the Forgotten Ones, and that your father comes through his exorcism okay. Oh, and that the demon king doesn't decide to make a reappearance."

He chuckled and kissed her again. "That's all? What the nine hells could possibly go wrong?"

Exactly. Ginny stared at the portal and refused to let herself think of all the potential for failure, and how little chance of success they really had.

Chapter Twelve

Two swords remained. One was pure, clear crystal. The other a deep, ruby red, just like the blade they'd delivered to Artigos the Just. Selyn sucked in a nervous breath and hoped like the nine hells that the red sword wasn't hers. She wanted clear crystal. A sword exactly like the one her mother had carried.

Not one that frightened her. The red blade radiated power, a sense of force that had all the other women giving it a wide berth.

Its presence hadn't kept any of the others from finding their true matches, though. Every one of her sisters—except Isra, who had yet to return to the room—had claimed crystal.

Every single one except for Selyn. None had responded to her. Not even the slightest glimmer. Now she stood beside the table with her hands clasped tightly against the small of her back. What if neither of these belonged to her? What if, among all the Forgotten Ones, she truly had been forgotten?

She glanced at Dawson. He stood beside her as he had

throughout the long day, reeling from exhaustion just as she was, but celebrating every time a sword had gone to one of the women. The level of excitement within the gathering room had grown as, one by one, woman and blade bonded.

"Aren't you going to see which one is yours?"

She slanted a glance at Dawson without turning away from the swords and whispered, "What if neither one is mine?"

He whispered his reply. "You'll never know if you don't take a chance."

She heard the tired laughter in his voice. Turned and really looked at him. The intensity in his eyes, the soft smile on his lips made his dare so sweet she couldn't ignore it. Taking a deep breath, Selyn cautiously reached out and passed her hand over the ruby blade. Thank the gods. . . . Nothing.

She exhaled, a long, slow release of tension. Then she closed her eyes and held her hand over the clear crystal. She heard Dawson chuckle and opened her eyes. The blade shimmered beneath her hand. She blinked. It pulsed and flashed to life with a brilliant blue glow that warmed her deep inside.

Trembling, speechless, Selyn shot another quick look at Dawson. His huge smile brought tears to her eyes. Disbelief warred with joy as she wrapped her hand around the silver hilt. The sense of connection was instantaneous— the perfect fit, the ideal weight and balance—proof this was truly her very own crystal sword. She lifted it from the table, lost entirely in the shimmering light that rippled along the faceted blade.

Without speaking, she turned to Dawson, holding her sword before her to show him the blade—the one that had chosen her. Dawson's eyes sparkled, but why was he looking at her face?

Couldn't he see that her crystal sword was more beautiful than anything she'd ever held? More precious than any gift she'd ever been given?

"You are so beautiful," he said.

Selyn blinked. Didn't he mean the sword? She frowned at him, and he laughed.

"You are. Don't look at me like that."

"Like what?"

"Like you're going to lop my head off with your new sword." He put his arms around her and kissed her, right there in the gathering room, in front of her sisters.

She lowered the sword, wrapped her free arm around his neck, and kissed him back. It was only going to be a short little kiss, just to celebrate a job well done, but his mouth moved slowly over hers, and Selyn made no attempt to pull away.

What was it about this man? She wanted to be closer to him. Wanted what came after kisses, though her idea of what that might be was pretty unclear. No matter. Kissing was wonderful.

"Is this one mine?"

Isra's rude sneer jerked Selyn back to the present and out of Dawson's loose embrace. She blinked, took a sharp breath, and held more firmly to her own blade. Shrugging, she said, "It's the only one left, but you'd better check to make sure."

Isra scowled and gave her a truly hateful look. Then she passed her hand over the blade. Nothing happened. "What's it supposed to do?"

"It will glow for you, if you're meant to carry it. I told you that already."

"It does nothing."

Selyn sighed. "I don't know what to say, Isra." She gestured toward the other women still gathered in the hall. Most had either gone off to their work or to the barracks where they were sleeping in preparation for the next shift, but the few who remained were all armed with crystal. "All of our sisters did exactly what you just did—they passed their hands over a particular blade, and it would glow. For some, it took many different blades before they found the right sword; for others, the first one glowed for them."

"There are no others for me to try. I want mine."

Dawson cleared his throat and gently nudged Selyn. She nodded slightly. He was more than welcome to explain what might have happened. Selyn had her suspicions—she had a feeling hers were the same as Dawson's.

"Selyn told me you were burned when you tried to pick one up that wasn't yours," he said. "Possibly that action angered the spirit in whatever sword might have been meant for you. There are intelligent, thinking souls inhabiting each of these swords. Maybe, at a later time, if you show yourself worthy . . ."

Probably not the best thing to say. Selyn watched as Isra turned red, and she wasn't at all surprised when the woman let fly with a few choice curses. Dawson didn't back down, nor did he offer an apology. There was no reason to—not when he was probably right.

When he didn't rise to her anger, Isra turned and stalked away. Selyn watched her go with mixed emotions. She knew what it felt like to see everyone else matched with a blade, but she'd been the target of Isra's wrath often enough not to feel all that sorry for her.

She glanced at her own blade and wondered if it would have reacted to Isra if she'd been possessed, if it might have somehow communicated that information to her.

There'd been no sign from her weapon that anything about the woman was at all dangerous or unusual.

"What of this sword?" Dawson glanced at the ruby blade still lying on the table. Then he looked around the hall where small groups of women were gathered.

Selyn followed his gaze. A few of them still worked with Taron as he led them in more intricate battle moves than he'd shown them earlier. Roland had also done some training, but then he'd had to return to the upper levels and his position in the Lemurian Guard.

It appeared the women were learning quickly. Already their form had improved, and their comfort with the crystal blades was obvious. Selyn remembered how it had felt to fight Birk with Artigos the Just's crystal blade—it wasn't even hers, and yet she'd known how to thrust, where to place her feet, how to fight. She'd loved the feeling the sword gave her. Loved the confidence she felt wielding crystal.

Dawson's voice broke into her thoughts. She turned to face him. "I figured it was going to be hers," he said, still looking at the ruby sword. "It's so different from the others. I wonder who it's meant for."

The crimson blade pulsed with light. Dawson frowned and looked closer. "Did you see that?" He reached toward the pommel. The blade shimmered blood red and pulsed again, this time with a rhythmic beat like that of a living heart.

"Daws? Is it yours?"

He stared at the glimmering blade. "I don't know why it would be. I'm not Lemurian."

Selyn shook her head. "No, you're not, but you've joined our battle. Maybe that's all that matters. Pick it up." She tilted her chin and grinned at him. "Aren't you going to at least try?"

He jammed both hands in his pockets and stared first at the sword, then at Selyn. Then at the sword again. "Except for the silver pommel, it looks like the one you gave to Artigos. He's royalty. How can it be mine?"

A few of the women had gathered around. "Did it glow for you?" Nica looked over another's shoulder. "If it glowed, it's yours. You have to take it."

Selyn laughed out loud. "You'll never know if you don't take a chance," she said, repeating what he'd said to her.

Frowning, Dawson shook his head and reached for the silver pommel. It slipped into his palm, and he slowly wrapped his fingers around the hilt. Selyn knew exactly what he was thinking, what he was feeling as he raised the sword and stared into the ruby facets. The look on his face was one of utter bemusement—and complete and total wonder.

The fact he'd not expected a crystal sword had to make this moment all that much sweeter. She watched him as he turned the blade this way and that, catching light off its many facets, getting a feel for the weight in his hand.

The small group of women were smiling right along with Selyn, and her pride in Dawson made her feel almost weak in the knees. He was not afraid to show his joy. Not afraid to let the emotions of this moment shine through on his handsome face and in the sparkle in his brilliant blue eyes.

He was unlike any man she'd ever known, and that knowledge both filled her with great joy and terrified her. For the first time in her long and empty years, she had something to lose, something that mattered, and it wasn't just the crystal sword grasped so tightly in her hand.

There were no words to express Dawson's feelings. None. Daws spun the sword beneath the light and watched the blood-red blade catch fire with each twist and turn of his wrist.

He sensed the life in it, felt it pulse from the blade to the hilt, up his arm, and into his body as if he and the weapon were a single entity. He'd been on the fencing team in college, but those thin rapiers were nothing like this beautiful blade.

"Daws! What the nine hells have you got there?" Taron broke away from the women he'd been working with and strode across the hall with a huge smile on his face.

Dawson held up the blade. "Can you believe it?"

Taron shook his head. "No. I can't." Frowning now, he stared at Dawson. "There were no ruby blades when I bundled the swords together. The only red one went to our gentleman friend."

"It was here," Dawson said. "There were two blades left. One clear and this one. The other glowed for Selyn, and this one flashed as soon as I held my hand above it."

Taron stared for a long moment at the gleaming ruby. "There are many things going on I don't understand. Too many." He sheathed his own sword. "I keep thinking that if my blade would speak, it might fill me in on a few details, but it appears I'll need to discover them on my own."

He glanced around the gathering hall. More women had gone, and it was definitely quieter than it had been. "Look, will you two be all right? I have to return to the upper levels. I've not seen Alton since he deposed his father. I'm concerned about him and about Roland. Roland told me he'd be reporting to me once he returned to his quarters. It was just to let me know how things were progressing, but I've not heard from him. That's got me worried. He always follows through."

"Selyn and I will be fine." Dawson glanced her way. She smiled and nodded in agreement. "We're going to meet with Artigos and see how he's doing with the guards," he said. "The women know enough to train among themselves. There are quite a few who are skilled with leatherwork who have promised to create sheathes for all the swords. Two days max for them to finish the job, but maybe even by tomorrow. The women will need a way to carry their weapons if it comes to actual battle. The main thing is keeping talk of the swords quiet until we have the guards under our control."

"The only one I'm worried about, Taron, is Isra," Selyn said. "She tried to take a sword not meant for her, and her hand was badly singed. Then, when all the swords were given out, there wasn't one left for her. She's a bitter woman to begin with, though I can't imagine her being spiteful enough to say anything to the guards."

Taron folded his arms across his chest and stared at Selyn for a moment. "Is there any chance she's possessed?"

Selyn shook her head. "I don't believe so. My sword isn't speaking yet, but I figured if it knew enough to glow for me, it would know if Isra harbored a demon. I asked it to check, and there was no response. I'm taking that as the blade's answer."

"Let's hope you're right." He glanced at the women working against one wall, participating in mock battles with one another. "How soon can you be ready?"

Selyn nodded. "Tomorrow, maybe. Two days, definitely. We have to be. I doubt we can keep the swords a secret any longer."

"I agree. By then, the women should be comfortable with their blades. Hopefully Birk and Artigos will have most—if not all the guards—free of demons. When I checked with Birk a few hours ago, he said they'd destroyed less than a dozen so far, and there's still that contingent of guards that was pulled to the upper levels. Counting them, we have more than a dozen to go. Selyn, listen for me. I'll report as soon as I'm able so you'll know what's happening above. Be ready to move."

Dawson sighed. "You sound as if you think this group of women will miraculously transform into a trained army."

Taron nodded. "I do. Watch them. They already move naturally with their blades, as if they've done this all their lives. These are daughters of powerful, battle-hardened warriors. And, even though they were conceived through violence, their fathers are wardens. All of them perfect physical specimens—strong men with the natural instincts to fight."

Selyn squeezed Dawson's hand. "He's right, you know. I hadn't thought of that. We are all bred to be warriors."

Taron lifted one expressive eyebrow. It was as red as the hair on his head. "I doubt the demons thought of that either, when their avatars used rape to intimidate the women. I'm beginning to think the warrior spirits in each sword are connecting somehow, passing on their battle knowledge." He clapped Dawson on the shoulder. "Have faith, my friend." Gesturing at Dawson's crystal sword, he added, "You, of all people, should believe in the magical, sentient power of crystal. I will contact you as soon as I'm able and let you know when Alton is set. Be ready."

Dawson glanced at the sword fitting so perfectly into his grasp and had to agree. He watched as the tall Lemurian headed toward the doorway. A number of the women waved to him or spoke as he passed. Grinning, Taron acknowledged every single one, and then he slipped quietly out the door and was gone.

Selyn yawned. Dawson put his arm around her and hugged her close. "I say we head for Artigos's cell and see if he's got someplace we can rest. You can't stay here, and neither can I."

Selyn nodded. Exhaustion was evident in every move she made. Even without a watch, Dawson was certain they'd been up for more than twenty-four hours straight. They'd finished their sandwiches long ago, and at this point, both of them were running on empty. He grabbed Selyn's hand and led her toward the doorway and the portal beyond.

Isra stood beside the opening with her arms folded across her chest. She glared at them, but she didn't say a word. Dawson glanced at the sword in his hand and silently asked the blade if the woman was a threat.

There was no response, even though they passed within a couple of feet of her. She continued staring at them, but she didn't speak. Dawson didn't say a word either. Ignoring Isra, he held Selyn's hand tightly as the two of them passed through the portal.

He still felt Isra's hatred long after they'd left the slaves' barracks behind them.

There were few guards about at this hour, whatever the hour was, thank goodness. Exhaustion had Dawson practically stumbling in his tracks as he and Selyn covered the distance between the women's barracks and the cavern in front of Artigos the Just's cell. Dawson let go of Selyn's hand and slipped around the entry, just far enough to observe the entire area.

Birk was seated at the guard's table. Dawson grabbed Selyn's hand and tugged her forward as Birk glanced up and frowned at them. "Is that crystal you carry as well, Dawson? Excellent." He patted his own sword, worn at his hip instead of across his back. It appeared to be steel.

"I thought your blade was crystal."

Birk grinned. "It is. Look." He drew his weapon. Crystal shimmered in the low light. He sheathed it once again, and a plain leather-covered pommel and a bit of steel blade showed above the scabbard. "The sentience appears to know that discretion is important for now."

Dawson glanced at Selyn. She yawned. "Don't ask me," she said, leaning against his shoulder. "I've spent my life in a hole in the ground. I know nothing." She yawned again.

Daws chuckled. "Birk, have you got any suggestions as to where we can catch a few hours' sleep? We're not going to be of any use to anyone without some rest."

Birk stood and nodded toward another ordinary door just down from the cell where Artigos waited. "Those quarters are empty and should be fully stocked. You can lock the door from inside so you'll feel safe. The guard relieving me later is one of us and aware of our prisoner's true identity. He's the only one I've shared details with at this point. So far, no one has recognized Artigos. We don't want anyone to know who he is, or who you two are, either. Not yet."

"How're the exorcisms going? Any problems so far?"

Birk shook his head as he opened one of the drawers and dug around a moment. "A couple of the guys are in sick bay with really bad headaches. I think it's like a hangover for the ones who've got a stubborn demon." He shoved some papers aside and mumbled a few curses before coming up with a key. "Your sword can probably open the door, but take this just in case. C'mon."

Dawson took the key, and he and Selyn followed Birk, but Daws was thinking of the guards. "Do you think they'll be okay?"

"I do. They understand they were possessed. I think they're more pissed off than anything." He rubbed the back of his neck and stared at the ground. "Pissed off and ashamed. We're supposed to be Lemuria's finest soldiers. Guards to the Council of Nine and all that. Finding out our every thought and act has been determined by the very creatures we fought so long ago . . ." He let out a huge breath. "It's hard to take, if you want the truth. We're still not certain how or if we'll ever regain our honor."

Selyn raised her head from Dawson's shoulder. "Working with us to put Artigos the Just back in power will go a long way toward redeeming all of us—our honor and our freedom. And, it will help those of us who have been slaves to avenge our mothers' terrible treatment."

Birk merely nodded as Dawson unlocked the door. "I'll come for you when the chancellor awakens." He gestured at Dawson's ruby sword. "Maybe you'll be able to drive demons out with yours, it being red and all."

"Maybe. Thanks, Birk."

The guard returned to his desk. Dawson opened the door and stepped into the quiet room with Selyn beside him. He had no idea what to expect, but when Selyn waved her hand over a fixture on the wall and the room lit up, he stood there like a complete idiot for what felt like forever.

Why did he expect something otherworldly? Maybe because he was in another world? He had to bite back a laugh, but it appeared that when he had fallen down that rabbit hole he'd landed in a really nice hotel.

There was a couch along one wall, a small table with chairs, and what appeared to be the Lemurian version of a refrigerator. There was even a kitchen sink that didn't look much different from the one in his home in Sedona.

A doorway led to another room. He was almost afraid to look, but there was a large bed in there. One bed. Big, but still one bed.

He didn't risk even glancing at Selyn. She'd gone straight through to what had to be the bathroom with her small pack slung over her shoulder. "I'm claiming the shower first," she said.

Then he did laugh. It was either that or cry.

Dawson left the bedroom to give Selyn some privacy and went back into the main room. He left his sword on the counter in the kitchen area. Curious, he checked the refrigerator. There were a couple of bottles that looked like small ceramic amphorae. When he pulled the stopper out of one, he smelled yeast and hops. Beer? He couldn't be that lucky, could he?

It was, and he was. He took the bottle with him and sat on the couch, slipped off his boots and socks and stretched his legs out. He sipped the brew which, while it smelled like beer, didn't taste remotely like anything he'd had before.

It didn't act like beer, either. He realized that when he awoke with the empty jug in his hand and his neck stiff from sleeping on the couch. No sound came from the bathroom, so he set the ceramic jug in the kitchen area and quietly walked through to the bedroom.

Selyn slept soundly, curled up on one side of the bed. Only the top of her head was visible beneath the soft blankets. He stopped and watched her for a moment, imagining what it would be like to sleep beside her, to hold her close in the middle of the night, but he'd already figured he'd make do with the couch. It was almost long enough.

Then she rolled over and blinked sleepily at him. "Aren't you coming to bed?" she asked.

Startled, he stepped back. *Come to bed? With Selyn?* "After my shower," he said. He took a deep breath. "In a few minutes."

"Good." Selyn flopped back to her stomach and tugged the blanket over her ears. "Be quiet, and don't wake me up. I'm exhausted."

Now that was more like what he'd expected. Grinning, Dawson went on into the bathroom. The shower was rather old-fashioned looking, but the water was hot and plentiful, and it felt good to wash the stink of the past day and a half off his body.

It felt even better to crawl into bed beside Selyn. He did it very quietly, and he didn't wake her. What surprised him most was how natural it felt to slide between cool sheets, to pull the soft blanket up over his shoulders and close his eyes.

Hovering on the edge of sleep, he drew in a deep breath and filled his lungs with Selyn's scent. Carefully, he slipped closer to her sleeping form and buried his nose in the sweet tangle of her long hair.

Sleep came more easily than he expected. Being immersed in her scent, her warmth, and the slow, even cadence of her breathing was a balm to his tattered senses. Knowing Selyn was so close, even though he couldn't touch her, was a comfort he'd never imagined.

But it was one he fully intended to experience as often as fate would allow.

Chapter Thirteen

Eddy's eyes flashed open. Breathing hard and fast as if she'd just run a mile, she darted out of a sound sleep with a terrible gut-deep sense of something wrong. Terribly wrong. She lay there beside Dax and sniffed the air. Okay . . . no reek of sulfur or sense of demonkind.

That was good. Next she catalogued the familiar morning sights and sounds in her childhood bedroom, and everything seemed the same. Of course, she'd slept alone here as a girl. There'd been no ex-demon lover beside her.

Not even in her wildest dreams.

Okay, so something she couldn't quite identify had awakened her, and it hadn't been Dax. With sleepy eyes barely open, she gazed slowly around her old room. Nothing had changed—all was still locked in the early shadows of a gray dawn.

She stretched full-length and arched her back, dismissing the weird sense of unease as a bad dream. She held the arch until her joints popped, but damn it felt good. Then she relaxed against the comfortable mattress. Thank goodness she'd been tall enough when she still lived at home to justify this king-size bed. Otherwise, she and Dax would never fit, and this was the only place they had to stay since her own little house had been thoroughly trashed.

She glanced at the man sleeping so soundly beside her. She'd take him over her house any day. Waging battle with the demon-possessed statue of General Humphries— horse, sword, and pigeon poop included—hadn't helped her already marginal Salvation Army décor. She didn't want to think about the damage done to the ceiling, walls, and carpeting—repairs were going to take a while.

Dax had been absolutely magnificent that night, shooting fire and ice from his fingertips while dealing with an onslaught of demonkind hell-bent on causing trouble. Unfortunately, fighting and defeating a full-sized horse and rider cast of solid bronze had made an unimaginable mess of her living room.

Life certainly hadn't been the same since. Eddy rolled her head on the pillow to get a better look at her man. He lay on his side with his back to her, his dark hair tousled and his broad shoulders bare above the down blanket they'd pulled over themselves during the chilly night.

She wondered if he might be interested in generating a little heat of their own this morning, but as that thought slipped into her mind, so did an unexpected sound—rain pounding against the roof and the wind whistling under the eaves of the house finally registered. The weather had definitely changed.

Eddy dragged her butt out of bed without disturbing Dax to see what the morning looked like. She went to the window and pulled back the shades.

Equal parts sleet and water whipped sideways, bolstered by a harsh wind that appeared to have snapped a few branches off her dad's trees. One long branch leaned against her bedroom window, though luckily it hadn't broken the glass.

That must have been what had awakened her.

Blinking at the gray day, Eddy tried to order her sleep-fogged brain around the consequences of a horrible winter-like storm in Evergreen, on a day when fair skies had been predicted.

Oh, shit. "Dax? Honey, wake up." She glanced over her shoulder and watched as Dax roused himself from sleep. The man was utterly gorgeous, and he was all hers, but she had a feeling this wasn't going to be one of those "hangin' out in bed making love for hours" kind of days.

He crawled out from under the covers and sauntered across the room, wearing nothing but a pair of black knit boxers that did more to emphasize his muscular, masculine body than to cover anything. When he leaned close, kissed the back of her neck, and nuzzled the sensitive spot behind her ear, she scrunched up her shoulders and giggled in spite of the weather.

His breath raised more shivers on her neck when he finally stopped long enough to whisper, "What's wrong?"

It took her a second to catch her breath. What that man could do! "This," she said, gesturing at the crappy weather outside. "It's supposed to be nice out today. Look at this! We can't get up the mountain to the portal. How the hell are we going to get Gaia and Artigos back to Lemuria?"

"But it's only a storm. We can walk through that."

She shook her head and wished he were right. "No can do. If we're getting sleet here, the weather on Shasta will be deadly. Too much snow for Dad's Jeep, winds too high and dangerous at the elevation where the portal is. I doubt we could drive to the vortex in Oregon, either, because weather this bad here means the interstate will most likely be closed by the storm."

Dax blinked. "There's no way at all into Lemuria? No other portals?"

She shook her head. "Nothing accessible. The portals are probably covered in snow by now. When it's blowing this hard down here, winds can be seventy miles an hour or worse up high. It's too dangerous."

Dax closed his eyes and turned away. Eddy stared out the window. Rain was beginning to turn to snow. The flakes were small and more like sleet, but that meant it would already be snowing heavily on the mountain. Groaning, she walked over to her old desk and flipped on her laptop.

The weather service and road reports didn't help her frame of mind. She read the stats and then turned around in her chair to look at Dax. "This storm blew out of nowhere. None of the weather models picked it up, but it's going to hang around at least through today and most of tomorrow. Interstate Five's already closed at the border, so the Oregon vortex is out, too." She shut the lid on the computer. "I think we're stuck here, unless we fly to Arizona and then drive to Sedona to use the portals there."

"Is that possible?" Dax was already dressed and buttoning his shirt. "Can we get an airplane to take us to Sedona?"

Eddy still had nothing on but her nightgown. She shivered in the chill air and glanced longingly at the warm bed. So much for snuggling with her guy. "I don't know how. You can't fly on a commercial airline without identification. You don't have an ID, and there's no way we can get anything for Gaia and Artigos. I don't know anyone with a private plane big enough to get four of us there, especially in weather like this."

Shivering harder now, Eddy wrapped her arms around herself and walked back to the window. "Can demons control the weather?" She glanced over her shoulder and caught Dax staring at her.

"I don't know," he said, thoughtfully. Then he raised his

head and flashed her a sexy grin. "But if they can, I imagine magic can change it back."

"Mari?" Eddy reached for her clothes.

"Mari," he said. "We have to get to Lemuria. Alton and Ginny are counting on us."

Alton awoke with the niggling suspicion that something was terribly wrong. He rolled over and snuggled close to Ginny. She slept soundly, so she wasn't the one worrying him, yet the feeling lingered. A bad dream? Possibly. Then he grinned, pushing the strange sense of unease out of his mind by recalling how he'd worn his lady out the night before. He propped himself up on one elbow and watched her for a moment longer, though what he really wanted was to wake her and make love to her once again.

Nine hells. The least he could do after last night was let her sleep in this morning.

Reluctantly, he slipped out from under the warm covers and headed to the back of his quarters for a quick shower. Even though the heated pool sounded a lot more inviting, he'd forgo that luxury for now. They had a busy day ahead. Plus, he'd quickly discovered bathing in his underground grotto wasn't nearly as much fun alone.

He showered quickly and grabbed one of his Lemurian robes rather than his Earth-styled clothing. Today would be spent in meetings as he worked to convince the rest of the council that he deserved to hold his father's seat as chancellor, at least until Artigos was able to take it back.

He still couldn't shake the uncomfortable feeling that something was wrong, even as he slipped on his familiar robe. Dressing as a Lemurian should make him more convincing in the chancellor's role, though adding the scabbard with HellFire across his back to any outfit certainly kept people from giving him as much trouble as they might otherwise.

His parents' presence would help, too. Dax and Eddy had promised to have them back by late today. Their brief contact when he'd slipped through the portal last night had sounded promising. As difficult as it was, he tried to imagine his father without the influence of demonkind.

Would Artigos accept Alton as his son once again?

One could only hope. That was really the least of his problems right now, with the fate of his entire world hanging on the events beginning to unfold. No one need know Artigos the Just survived. Not yet. Roland's short but positive report had certainly been encouraging, though Alton was a little concerned there'd not been anything else from the sergeant.

Maybe he needed to contact Roland and see if he knew anymore about the . . .

His eyes were drawn to Ginny. She sat up in bed and shoved her dark hair out of her eyes, looking so inviting with her tousled hair and the blanket barely covering her breasts, that Alton was tempted to remove his robe and crawl back in beside her.

"Good morning," she said. Then she yawned and frowned at him. "You realize Roland has to sleep at some point, don't you? He helped Taron all day yesterday, moving those crystal swords up to the level where the Forgotten Ones live. Wait until later to check on him."

"You're eavesdropping." Alton leaned over and kissed her.

"Shamelessly. If I didn't, you'd never let anyone get any sleep." Grumbling, she threw the blankets back and, completely naked, walked past him to the bathing room.

Alton groaned. It was so hard not to follow her. Ginny preferred long baths in the heated pool, and he really preferred bathing with her.

Nine hells. Not today. Sighing, he forced himself to look away from the path she'd taken to the bathing grotto. He stared at the exit portal instead. If he hurried, he could pick up some pastries in the great hall and have them back before Ginny even missed him.

Alton walked quickly to the portal and stepped through. Four armed guards stopped him just outside the doorway.

"No further, Chancellor."

The steel swords in his face were fairly convincing. He stopped, though he refused to step back. HellFire's deep, angry pulse vibrated through the scabbard on his back. Alton judiciously chose to ignore it, but he held his position.

The guards stepped back a pace.

Alton folded his arms across his chest and focused on the ranking guardsman. "Why are you here, corporal? Under what authority?"

The senior guard lowered his weapon. Alton had a feeling the man wasn't at all happy about his assignment. From what Roland had told him, most of the guards sided with Alton and hoped to see a new council seated.

At least this group was familiar to him. The guard sighed, confirming Alton's suspicions. "You've been placed under house arrest until further notice, sir. You were ordered restrained in house by a majority vote of the Council of Nine at a meeting called late last night."

Alton folded his arms across his chest. "Last night, eh? That's fast work for the council, especially when they're not supposed to meet without the chancellor present. Who was responsible for calling you up for this duty?"

"Council member Drago, sir. He had the signed document with the proper number of signatures. We have no other choice but to obey council law."

Alton nodded. "I understand, corporal, so I won't ask you to act against your orders. At least not at this time." He winked at the guard. The man blinked in surprise, but before he could question Alton's odd behavior, Alton had already turned around and slipped back through the portal.

So much for waking up uneasy. Next time he'd do well to pay heed to his instincts. He turned around and stared at the swirling portal.

Ginny was going to be so pissed. She'd truly taken on his crusade as her own.

What of Roland? He'd still not heard from the man. *Roland? You there?*

Nothing. No reply, no sense of the man at all. The sergeant couldn't have returned to the slave levels already—not after being away from duty for the past day. Where the nine hells could he be?

The thought flittered through Alton's mind, that the energy-powered bars in a Lemurian prison were capable of blocking telepathy.

Fighting the bite of panic, now, Alton sent out a call for Taron. If he was still below, Taron wouldn't hear him, but if the swords had all been delivered, Taron should be headed back to this level.

He tried again. Nothing. Alton glanced toward the guarded portal. If he could get to his father's office, he could at least access the portal to Red Rock Crossing and use his cell phone to call Dax and Eddy. If things had gone to hell, he didn't want them walking into a mess, but if there was still hope, he really needed his parents here to help him hold his position.

Although, there was no point in calling until he had some news. Right now, he had no idea what was going on, other than the fact that Drago and Maxl had obviously decided to make their move. How secure a move it was remained to be seen.

He stared at the portal for a moment. Then he went back

to the doorway and slipped through. Again, the guards met him with raised swords. "Sir, we . . ."

Alton held up his hand. "I know. I'm not planning to go anywhere. I have questions. Do you have any word of Roland of Kronus?"

The guard shifted uneasily and glanced at his companions. All four of these guards carried the traditional steel swords, so none of them were Roland's men, the three who carried crystal replicates of Roland's crystal blade.

He knew Darius, one of the three, was still in Evergreen with Mari the witch, but what of the other two?

Alton folded his arms across his chest. He didn't say a word, but his mere presence had all four guards shuffling uneasily. Finally, the one he'd addressed looked at Alton and said, "He's been arrested, sir. Early this morning, he and the other two who carry crystal were locked up."

Nodding, Alton realized he wasn't at all surprised. "What happened to their swords?"

The guard shook his head. "I don't know. I think they were left in their quarters. The men were taken before they would have risen for the day."

"Regarding this order for my arrest. Is my woman named as well?"

Again, the guard shook his head. "No, sir. The orders for house arrest are for you alone." He glanced at his companions and then turned his gaze to Alton. "I doubt they would even think of her, sir. The council members have little time for women." Now it was the guard who winked at Alton. "They still disbelieve stories of the women warriors in Lemuria's past."

Alton grinned. "Isn't that too bad? Especially when it's something that may come back to bite a few of our illustrious council members in their collective buttocks."

The other three guards had moved closer. Alton was

almost sure they stood a little straighter after listening to the conversation. He glanced both ways to be certain the corridor was clear. "You do realize that great change is afoot, that the risk to Lemuria grows by the moment?"

Obviously unhappy with the whole situation, the guard nodded. "I know, sir. But we're sworn to follow orders."

"I understand, and I'm not asking you to do anything at all treasonable, but please promise you will remember one very important thing."

The guard straightened and glanced at his companions before concentrating on Alton. "What is that, sir?"

"Remember you are sworn to uphold Lemuria's honor, not the dubious honor of the Council of Nine. The time may come, very soon, when the lives of our citizens and the very fabric of our civilization will be tested. Be certain you have chosen the right leader to follow."

The corporal met Alton's steady gaze. Then he slowly nodded his head. "Sergeant Roland of Kronus said as much. He is an honorable man as well as a good friend."

"Thank you." Alton nodded to each of the men and returned to his rooms. Ginny waited just inside the portal. Somehow she must have known something was wrong. She was dressed for battle in boots and jeans and her purple hoodie, with her hair tightly braided out of the way. Dark-Fire was strapped across her back.

"We've got a situation," he said. Then he sighed and held his arms wide.

Ginny slipped into his embrace and hugged him tightly. "What?"

"I'm under what you might call 'house arrest.'"

"You're what?" She leaned back and stared at him.

"You heard me. The majority on the council have effectively imprisoned me in my quarters. You, however, are not included." He grinned and kissed the surprise off her face.

She frowned. "I'm not? I don't understand."

"It appears our illustrious council members don't see you as a threat. You're just a woman, after all."

As realization dawned, Ginny's smile widened. "A woman with a crystal sword."

"And attitude." Alton laughed, but the laugher was short-lived. "I love you, Ginny, and I hate this, but I'm going to ask you to do a few things that are very dangerous. If my world's very survival weren't at risk, I'd never dream of it."

"It's our world." She pressed fingertips to his jaw. "You know I'll do anything for you. Or for Lemuria."

He nodded. "I know, which is why I'm almost afraid to ask. I couldn't survive if anything were to happen to you." He kissed her again. He couldn't *not* kiss her.

She kissed him back. Then she looped her hands over his shoulders and waited patiently.

He stared into her beautiful eyes—her golden tiger's eyes—and said, "Roland has been arrested. He's imprisoned in a level just beneath this one. We need to know what's going on with the Forgotten Ones, but the energized bars of the cells prevent telepathy."

Ginny nodded. "You want me to go see him. Will they let me in?"

"I think I can get one of the guards to take you. Their loyalty is with Lemuria, not with the council. Not even with me, for that matter, which is as it should be. We can't wait, though. I have a strong feeling that things are beginning to heat up."

"I know. I've been wondering about the demon king. Where is he? I can't imagine that I sent him back to Abyss for good."

Alton chuckled. "You did a damned good job of piss-ing him off, though. I don't think he's gone forever, either, but I believe our concern needs to be with Roland and the Forgotten Ones. Now that we know for certain that's my grandfather imprisoned below, we have to hang on until the women are ready with their crystal blades and their guards are no longer ruled by demonkind."

"When do you want me to go to Roland?"

Never. Nine hells, he hated for her to take such risks, but he knew of no other way. "As soon as you're ready. I'll talk to the guards, see if I can get one of them to lead you to him."

"Alton." She wrapped her fingers around his arm. "DarkFire will keep me safe."

"She'd better," he grumbled. "I'll do what I can from here. I need to reach Roland's wife, Chara, and let her know what's going on. I don't think Roland has shared any of this with her." He squeezed Ginny's shoulders. "He's never hesitated to do what he can for Lemuria. He's risked all for our world. Everything he is, all that he has."

Ginny leaned close and kissed him. "So have you, Alton. So have others. Sacrifice is often necessary for success."

"I know, but that doesn't mean I have to like it, or not fight like the nine hells to protect the ones I care for. And sacrifice had damned well better not include you. Be careful."

She slanted him a sly smile. "I have an idea. Follow me."

She slipped through the portal. Alton was right behind her. The guards blocked her way and then quickly lowered their swords.

Ginny stopped and smiled at each man. "Are you loyal to Lemuria? Are your hearts dedicated to saving your world from demonkind?"

The corporal glanced at his men and nodded to Ginny. "I can answer for all of us. We support Lemuria. Only Lemuria."

"I thought so. Draw your swords and hold them high." Ginny drew DarkFire. *I hope like hell this works.*

Me, too. Alton had no doubt. Even he sensed the energy pulsing in the dark sword.

Frowning, obviously confused, the four guards drew their swords and held the blades high.

"Press your blades to DarkFire." She lifted the amethyst blade and held it steady as four steel blades connected to crystal. DarkFire glowed and then flashed with a brilliant purple light. A dark flame raced the length of each steel blade.

Light flashed, energy pulsed from crystal to steel, brighter, hotter, until it exploded in a burst of lavender sparks.

There was a collective sigh as each of the four guardsmen lowered his blade—his crystal blade—and stared at the clear, blue light rippling along the faceted surface.

The corporal raised his head. "But how? Only the ruling class may . . ."

"Not anymore." Alton rested his hand on Ginny's shoulder. "Lemuria's ruling class has failed in its greatest obligation—to keep our world and our citizens safe. It is up to you, the ones who still hold Lemuria's best interests in your hearts, to carry crystal. Just as it will be up to you when there is a call to arms to fight demonkind, a call that may not come from the Council of Nine or even from me. Trust me that you will know it's the one you should heed. Remember, only crystal can vanquish demons. Be ready."

Ginny started to slip DarkFire into her sheath, but as the tip of the blade touched the scabbard, the sword spoke.

"Behold. Time grows short and the situation more dire. Guardsmen—your blades have the power to replicate others. Only those men whose loyalties lie with Lemuria can carry crystal. You will know the ones who wish you ill if steel remains steel."

The blade dimmed. Ginny sheathed her sword.

She folded her arms across her chest and gazed at the men. "You've heard DarkFire. You have the power to turn the steel blades of your fellow guardsmen to crystal. If their hearts are not true, if they're not willing to give all for Lemuria, their blades won't change. Now, though, I have to speak to Roland. Can one of you take me to him?"

The youngest of the group stepped forward. Carefully he sheathed his crystal sword. The blade subtly altered until it appeared as steel within the scabbard. He stared at it a moment, and then drew it again. It turned to crystal in his hand. He flashed a relieved grin at Ginny as he sheathed the blade once again. "My lady, I know where Roland and his men are being held. Your friend as well, Chancellor. The one called Taron."

"Thank you." She sighed and grabbed Alton's hand. "We wondered if Taron had been taken."

Alton glanced at Ginny. *If there's a way to free them, we'll have to find it, but for now, I hesitate to go against the council's direct order.*

Even if it's illegal?

Alton nodded. *Find out what you can. See where things stand below. I'll be here.*

Ginny glanced at the four guards, now armed with crystal. Their army was growing, one sword at a time. *I guess you will.* She turned and kissed him. *Be safe. Stay linked to my mind so you'll know what's up. I love you.*

And then she was gone, striding down the tunnel with the young guard leading the way.

Chapter Fourteen

Dawson awoke with the strange sense he was being watched. Slowly, cautiously, he opened his eyes—and looked directly into Selyn's blue-eyed gaze. She clutched the blanket against her chest and stared at him so seriously he almost laughed—yet even as he fought laughter, he wanted her more than he'd ever wanted a woman in his life.

"Good morning," he said.

She dropped the blanket, leaned down, and kissed him. Her naked breasts pressed against his bare chest, and he groaned against her mouth. He hadn't dared look at her when he'd crawled into bed. Hadn't wanted to know what she wore to sleep.

Now that he knew she slept in nothing more than her beautiful coppery skin, it was impossible not to want to see more, to touch more. He wrapped an arm around her and rolled Selyn to her back, but the blankets went with him and blocked the full contact of his body to hers.

It was probably just as well. He hadn't even considered the possibility of sleeping in the same bed, much less actually making love to her, and there'd been no need to carry his wallet on this trip into Lemuria—along with the condom he kept stashed inside.

She gazed up at him, wide-eyed as he hovered over her, and it suddenly hit him that he was probably scaring the crap out of her, looming over her like this. He leaned close and playfully rubbed his nose against hers. "Don't be frightened of me, Selyn." He kissed the end of her nose. "I'll never hurt you. I promise."

She blinked. Then she ran her tongue over her top lip, curled the tip, and brushed her bottom lip. He didn't even try to ignore the invitation she'd made, whether it was consciously done or not.

He leaned close and kissed her mouth this time, gently at first, sliding his lips over hers while silently cursing the blankets that kept their bodies separated. Selyn raised her hips, pressing as close to him as the bedding would allow. Dawson rested on his elbows and cupped her head in his hands. Her arms slipped around his back, and she hugged him close.

He held Selyn down with his greater weight, and the hard length of him was planted firmly between her legs. She squirmed and bucked beneath him. Not fighting him. No, she raised her knees on either side of his hips, clinging to Dawson, frantically rubbing against the promise that was bundled behind soft blankets. It was torture. Excruciating, amazing, blissful torture.

He tried to put himself in her place, tried to imagine what she might be thinking, what she was feeling. He knew, from things she'd said, she'd never been with a man. Selyn had spent her life apart from men, exposed only to the huge Lemurian guards who bullied the women with their cruel treatment. She probably didn't have any idea what her natural instincts were telling her body it wanted, what it needed.

She took sexual innocence to an entirely new level. Even though he hadn't been with a lot of women, Dawson figured he had to know more than Selyn with her total lack of experience.

And the one thing he was certain of was that she had no idea at all what she was asking for. Not a clue. It was going to kill him, but he had to stop this and stop it now. Knowing what was right didn't make it any easier—his body shook with need, and it took everything he had to fight his own instincts.

It was definitely going to kill him—he was absolutely positive he wouldn't survive—but he ended the kiss and the rubbing and the wonderful things his body was ordering him to do and, breathing hard, rolled away.

Selyn popped up on one arm and glared at him. It was impossible to concentrate on her flashing blue eyes with her bare breasts almost even with his lips.

"Why did you stop kissing me? Was I doing something wrong?" She frowned at him.

It probably didn't help his case one bit when he laughed. "Oh, Lordy, Selyn. No. You weren't doing anything wrong, but what you were doing was going to lead to a whole lot more, and I'm not prepared for that. Not at all."

"What?" She ran her fingers over his collarbone. He almost whimpered. "What aren't you prepared for?"

"Making love." He stroked her tangled hair. "You can't imagine how much I want to make love to you, but we can't. The risk of pregnancy is too high."

She stared at him for a long moment. Then she closed her eyes and nodded, took a deep breath, rolled away, and flopped down on her back. "Oh. Okay," she said. She stared at the ceiling. "Our women don't conceive easily, but I am proof that it can happen when least expected." Then she smiled ruefully at him. "But I hope you realize it is not very easy, this stopping when every instinct in your body wants to keep going."

He chuckled and dropped his arm across his eyes so he couldn't see her breasts. "Trust me. I realize it. Honest." He let out a huge gust of air. "No doubt in my mind."

This time, Selyn laughed with him. She ran a fingertip over his chest and made him shiver. "It's not just about making love, you know. I was hoping I would finally get to see you. My sisters and I talk about men, about what they might look like. How they're different from us."

He raised his arm off his face and stared at her. "You want to see me?" That he could do, though she might get to see a lot more than she expected. Just the thought of being naked in front of Selyn's curious eyes made him hard. Hell, breathing the same air, being in the same room—just thinking about her—made him hard. "I don't mind if you look."

He peeled the covers back to his waist. Selyn spun around and sat beside him with her legs crossed. He was almost relieved when the blankets twisted around her waist and covered her hips and thighs. She touched his chest and ran her fingers through the dark mat of hair that spread between his nipples.

"I've seen some of the guards without shirts, but they don't have hair like you do on their chests. Not so much." She stroked his dark pelt as if she were petting a kitten.

Dawson thought about sitting up, but decided against it. He was probably less threatening to her, lying on his side this way, propped up on one elbow.

Staring at her as if he could eat her alive.

She grabbed the blanket at his waist and looked at him.

"Go ahead. It's okay. I don't bite."

"I know that." Slowly, Selyn peeled the blanket down over his hip and thigh.

Her eyes got so big he chuckled. "We're definitely built differently."

"I can see that." She stared at him a moment. Then she reached out and touched him. His cock jerked. Her fingers tracing the length of him had to be the most erotic thing he'd ever felt in his life.

He sucked in a breath, and she paused. Her head shot up, and she stared at him with parted lips and a glazed expression in her eyes. Her fingers lingered on his full length, and he felt each fingertip like a brand burning into the flesh.

She'd leaned forward to touch him, and her bare breasts were mere inches from his lips, her nipples puckered into taut peaks. Dawson gave in to temptation, leaned close, and suckled one rosy tip into his mouth, laving the dark rosette with his tongue, and tugging just enough to bring a soft gasp to her lips.

She arched her back, forcing her nipple into his mouth. He licked and nibbled, suckling her deep, tugging hard. Her heart was pounding so hard he felt its pulse against his lips, and he knew she had to be wound tight as a spring.

He slid his hand over the soft swell of her belly and under the tangled blankets that covered her. She gasped when he parted the tight curls between her legs and slipped his fingertip between her swollen folds. Her hips bucked forward, and he pulled his hand back. The last thing he wanted to do was take her virginity with his fingers, but she whimpered until he cupped her mound in his palm and rubbed his hand slowly back and forth.

Her cries went short and sharp and desperate, and she clutched his forearm with both hands until her short nails dug into his skin. She was slick and wet, her labia swollen all hot and slippery beneath his fingers, and he wanted her with a desperation that was almost beyond his control.

After a moment, he sucked in a deep breath and hoped like hell he could hang on. He really didn't want to embarrass himself, but he was so close to the edge. He released her nipple with a light little "pop," and pulled his hand from between her legs.

Her breath hissed between her lips in short, sharp gasps, so he stretched up and kissed her. "Lie down, Selyn. There are things we can do that won't risk pregnancy. Things I can do for you to take away some of the tension. Will you let me?"

Nodding, she slowly pulled the blankets away from her waist, and lay down with her hands at her sides clutching the bedding. She watched Dawson like a cat watches a snake.

Daws rolled closer and knelt between her legs. For a moment he just looked his fill of her, lying there with her hair in black, ropey tangles around her shoulders, her left nipple shiny from his mouth. He stroked that damp tip with one finger, and then he circled its mate. "Remember when I said you were too pretty to eat, but that was what I wanted to do to you?"

"Yes." The word slipped out on a shuddering sigh.

"Let me show you what I meant."

Her entire body trembled. He leaned close and suckled her breast again. Her short, sharp, "Oh!" had him smiling around the nipple between his lips. He worried the right one and then the left. Then he kissed his way along her ribs. She giggled when he ran his tongue along her side, but by the time he reached the tuft of dark hair between her legs, she was panting, and her body shuddered with arousal.

He slipped his hands beneath her buttocks and lifted her. Sat back on his heels and took a moment to put her at ease with careful touches and an encouraging smile. Then he dipped his head and blew a soft puff of warm air against her damp petals.

Her body jerked in his hands, but her arousal was obvious in the glistening moisture sparkling in her curls and the way her body trembled and shivered beneath his touch. Her sweet, feminine scent had him mentally kicking himself for not bringing along at least a whole box of condoms. He lifted her long legs and hooked them over his shoulders, cupped her firm bottom once again, and ran his tongue slowly between her slick folds.

Her gasp was as much a cry of surprise as an invitation to do more of the same. He licked her again, tasting her honey, dipping his tongue deep and then circling the small bundle of nerves he'd already discovered was in exactly the same place on a Lemurian woman as on any woman from Earth.

She cried out, a long, keening note of pleasure as he loved her with his lips and tongue, with soft nibbles of his teeth. He wanted to drive deep with his fingers so he could feel her body ripple around him when she came, but once again he reminded himself Selyn was untouched and penetration might hurt. He wanted this first experience to be nothing but pleasure, even if it killed him.

Her hips bucked and writhed beneath his mouth. She clutched the bedding beside his knees, and he knew she was close by the sound of her cries and the rapid rush of her breathing. He suckled her, drawing her clitoris between his lips, using his tongue to lave and caress, to curl and lick softly between her sensitive folds. Suddenly her body went rigid in his grasp. She cried out, arched her spine, and tightened her thighs across his back. He tasted her release. The sound of her cries, the rush of her climax, almost took him over the top. He buried his face in her heat, licking, sucking, using his mouth to gently bring her down, and finally, when her body began to go pliant and soft, he lay her down on the bed.

When he sat back between her legs, Dawson couldn't quit grinning. The dazed expression on Selyn's face was the sexiest thing he'd ever seen in his life. Knowing he'd put that look of contentment there made him feel like cheering. He was hard as a post and his balls ached, but he knew he'd given Selyn an amazing climax—one that had her blinking owlishly with vague, unfocused eyes as she slowly returned to the present.

That alone was worth a little bit of frustration. Okay, a whole lot of frustration, but they'd have a chance before too long. He had to believe that. For now, though, he took satisfaction in knowing he'd given her an experience unlike anything she'd ever had before.

Selyn lay in the tumbled sheets, shivering and trembling, weak as a baby from the most powerful experience of her life. She'd heard about sexual orgasms and knew some of the women gave them to themselves or gave them to each other, but she'd never felt the need before. Never truly understood what her body was capable of feeling with the right touches, the right stimulation—the right man.

But what of Dawson? He lay beside her and stroked his hands over her belly and hip, but that man-part of his was still swollen and looked like it had to hurt. She knew he'd liked it when she touched him, just as she'd loved the way it felt when he touched her, even before he'd put his mouth on her.

She reached for him. His hand snaked out, and he grabbed her wrist firmly, stopping her.

"That's probably not a good idea," he said.

"Why?" She looked at her forearm, firmly locked in his

long fingers. "You touched me with your hands and your mouth. It felt wonderful. Why can't I touch . . ."

He laughed and shook his head. "Truth? I'll embarrass myself. I won't be able to last if you touch me. Hell, I'm having trouble maintaining just being close to you."

An almost palpable sense of power rushed through her. Selyn smiled and tugged her hand free of his grasp. "Good. Then it won't take us very long, will it?"

He blinked. It appeared Dawson Buck hadn't expected her to press the issue.

"Lie back." She gave his broad chest a gentle shove.

"And think of England?" He laughed, but he did as she said, and lay back against the pillow with his arms folded beneath his head.

Selyn straddled his long legs and studied the thick length of him that pointed almost to the ceiling. "I have no idea what that means, that 'think of England.' Some day you will explain. Now, though, you will have to tell me what you like. I need to know what will make you embarrass yourself."

He groaned, and she was almost sure he blushed. She wrapped her hands around his. . . . "What do you call this?" She squeezed him for emphasis.

He gasped. "You're killing me. You're doing this on purpose, right?"

"Of course I am. What is it called?" She ran her fingertip through a small bubble of white fluid that appeared at the tip.

"Oh, shit." He arched his hips, lifting her.

"Oh, shit?" She laughed. "I don't think that's right."

He groaned, rolled his head back, and closed his eyes. She continued to stroke him, slowly up and down. She cupped the sac that hung beneath and explored it with her fingertips, gently rolling the two hard little balls inside.

His legs trembled beneath her thighs, and his chest was heaving with each breath he took. His lips were drawn back, and if she hadn't known better, she'd have thought he was in terrible pain.

She remembered how it had felt when he put his mouth between her legs. Thought of those moments before her climax—how badly she'd needed. How much she'd wanted.

That must be how Daws was feeling now. Needy. Wanting her to finish this. She leaned over and wrapped her lips around the broad head of his parts and sucked, just the way he'd done to her breast, to those sensitive nerves between her legs.

She definitely got more than she expected. He cursed and cried out, his fingers tangled in her hair; his hips bucked hard, and suddenly her mouth was full of him. She wrapped her hands around the base to keep him from choking her, but she kept squeezing and sucking and licking. His cries were much as hers had been—incoherent and ruled by passion. She tasted his release—salty and a little bitter, but not at all unpleasant—and she held him in her mouth even when he wanted to pull away. Held him and licked and eased him down, just as he'd done for her.

When he was still and his member had gone soft, she finally set him free with a final lick and a kiss. His fingers slipped from her tangled hair, and his hands fell to his sides when she crawled along his body to lie beside him.

He turned and looked at her with what could only be wonder in his eyes. Selyn wanted to weep, to think that she and this man she was growing to care for so much, had shared something so personal, so intimate and unbelievably wonderful.

He leaned close and kissed her hard, and she wondered if that was the taste of herself on his lips, wondered if he tasted his release on hers. And then she realized he was grinning and so was she. "Now," she said, staring into those blue eyes of his and feeling powerful and feminine and much more sure of herself than she could ever remember, "are you going to tell me what you call that thing?"

They showered together, exploring each other's bodies with an ease Dawson really hadn't expected. Of course, he hadn't expected a lot of what had happened this morning, including Selyn's taking over in bed and leaving him cross-eyed and weak as a kitten.

He'd never had an experience like that. Not even close. He definitely wanted it again, and if it meant going all the way back to Sedona by himself, he was going to round up an entire crate of condoms.

He slipped on his jeans and boots while Selyn dressed in the scrubs she'd brought along, and wove her hair into a long braid. Neither of them knew what to expect today, but Daws wanted to be ready for anything.

"Are you hungry?" Selyn stepped out of the small kitchen area. "There's food here. Cereal and fruit. We need to break fast."

"I'm starving. Those sandwiches were gone a long time ago."

After a few minutes' preparation, Selyn handed him a bowl of hot cereal that reminded him of sweetened corn-meal. She'd sliced what looked like apples on top.

Tasted like apples, too. "Where do you get all your fresh foods?" He leaned against the counter and took another bite.

She shrugged. "I'm not really sure. I've heard we have traders who go out into other dimensions. Fruits and grains come from Earth, fish and some fowl from Atlantis. Some of the foods are manufactured here, though I'm not sure what they're made from. We don't farm or raise animals, yet we occasionally have chicken and even beef. Even those of us who are slaves have never gone hungry."

"This is good, and it's filling. Some day I really want to learn how this place functions. Like the light in here. When we went to sleep, it was dark, and yet we awoke to dim morning light that's brighter now, like daylight."

"The light comes from inside the rock. Most of the stone is crystalline and has a natural-looking glow that mimics sunlight on Earth. It's all set to a twenty-four hour clock, since that's what we had before Lemuria was destroyed. This light through the stone is all I'd ever known until I went to your home."

A soft knock had both of them turning toward the door. Dawson set his empty bowl down quietly, but Selyn put her hand on his arm before he could reach the door.

"Grab your sword," she said. "I'll see who it is."

He reached for his sword and jerked his hand to a stop just above the hilt. Instead of the bare blade he'd left on the table the night before, this morning it was enclosed in a red leather scabbard. Swallowing back a million questions, he unsheathed his sword and stood to one side. Selyn unlocked the door and swung it open just a crack. Then she flung it wide. "Good morning," she said, stepping aside as Birk and Artigos the Just slipped through the door. Selyn shut it firmly behind them.

Artigos immediately checked out Dawson's crystal blade. "Birk told me yours was a ruby. Good. Let's hope it will remove demons as effectively as DemonsBane."

Dawson swallowed. "It managed to create its own scabbard during the night. What's a demon after an accomplishment like that?" He laughed and glanced at Selyn. She held her sword in one hand, a red leather scabbard in the other, and a look of utter confusion on her face.

Grinning, Dawson turned back to Artigos. "How is that going, getting rid of the demons in the guards?"

"Very well. The trick will be convincing the women and men to work together. The soldiers in an army must have trust if they're to become a cohesive force."

"All but one of the women have crystal." Selyn was buckling her new scabbard on as she spoke. "Taron spent some time training them, though we all have much to learn. Unfortunately, there's one woman, a rather foul-tempered sort, who did not get a sword. She might be a problem."

"Any reason why she was skipped over?" Artigos glanced at Dawson, but Selyn answered.

"She tried to take a sword that hadn't acknowledged her and ended up with badly singed fingers. Then, when all the swords were handed out, the last one went to Dawson and not to Isra. I worry that she might be angry enough to give us away."

Silence stretched while Artigos seemed to ponder Selyn's information. Finally, he reached his decision. "She might, but for now we need to concentrate on removing the last of the demons from the few remaining guards. They're the only ones down here she could even go to. Plus, there are those six others, still possessed, who were called to work in the levels where the free folk live. They're a problem we'll deal with later."

Birk interrupted. "The last five men down here who still harbor demons are due to report in a few minutes. I'm going out to meet them. Lord Artigos, I'll contact you when I'm ready, but if the three of you show up with crystal, plus mine, we should be able to take care of the entire group at once."

He slipped quietly out of the room. Dawson shot a quick glance at Selyn. It was starting. He was going into his first mission in the battle against demonkind, and he was going with Selyn at his side and a sword in his hand. And a red leather scabbard strapped to his back. "What do you make of these?" He patted his scabbard.

Selyn checked the position of her sword across her back. "I'm learning not to question good fortune. I needed a crystal sword. I got one. My sword needed a sheath. There's one waiting when we awaken." She stepped close to Dawson and grabbed his hand. Her laughter gave way to the seriousness of the moment. "I needed a hero, and there you were."

How could she possibly see him as hero material? Dawson wanted to protest, but all he could think to do was lean close and kiss her. Then, glancing up, Dawson realized Artigos was studying him. "Sir?"

"I am still trying to figure out why a human would be here in Lemuria, fighting demons in a battle we may very well lose."

Dawson shook his head. He'd felt this war was every bit his as much as Lemuria's from the beginning. "From what I've been told, Lord Artigos, demonkind threatens all dimensions. If Lemuria falls, Earth will be next. Likewise, if Earth goes over to demon rule, Lemuria will follow, as will Eden and Atlantis. It's not just Lemuria's battle. It's one we all have a stake in, one that affects all our worlds."

Artigos looked almost weary when he nodded. For the first time, Dawson was aware of the man's age, the fact he'd been locked away for thousands of years.

As if he'd heard Dawson's thoughts, Artigos sighed. "I have been away from my world, from my people for much too long. I remember humans as a primitive, war-like people, yet you are obviously thoughtful and well-educated. Thank you for your commitment. And you as well, young Selyn. This battle is, for you, even more personal than for many." He raised his head. "Birk calls. Are you ready?"

Dawson glanced at Selyn. She leaned close and kissed him full on the mouth. "Now I am," she said.

Dawson noticed that Artigos was now grinning ear to ear as he led them out to meet the demon-possessed guards.

Selyn's first thought was that these guys were huge. Her second that she really didn't have a clue how to fight—her every step in the battle with Birk had been directed by Artigos's ruby sword. Still, she drew her clear crystal blade and stood between Dawson and Artigos, each man carrying a crimson blade that flashed with light the color of blood.

And, just like that, knowledge flooded her mind and body. How to grip the hilt, where to place her feet, how to feel as the battle began to unfold.

The guards immediately broke formation and drew their weapons, but it was obvious from the beginning they expected Birk to join them. When he sided with the prisoner and two strangers, the five stumbled back, confused and disoriented.

Birk drew his sword. What had appeared as steel within his sheath now glistened with blue light. "The five of you are known to be possessed by demonkind," he said. "Throw down your weapons so that we can remove the demons that rule your thoughts."

"Demons? There's no such thing in me." The guard turned and thrust, but his charge was toward Selyn, not his commander. She crossed blades with him, crystal to steel, and his arm twisted with the strength of her blow.

Artigos lunged forward, slapping at the man with the flat of his blade, but he missed. It was Dawson who got the hit, connecting with the man's chest while ducking to avoid a wild parry with steel.

The guard stiffened; his steel sword dropped from nerveless fingers, and he fell to his knees. The other four leapt back as a thick, oily mass oozed out of the man's chest. The sulfuric stench made Selyn's eyes water, but Artigos reached high with his ruby blade, and the demon burst into flames.

Dawson raised his blade, ready for the next attack. It came as the first guard toppled to the ground, unconscious. Dawson slapped his blade against one man before he had a chance to attack, while Artigos went for another. Selyn leapt to one side and reached for the demon mist escaping from Dawson's opponent.

Her sword seemed to swing under its own power. She caught the demon and destroyed it with a single well-aimed thrust. Artigos had his man down while Birk fought off the other two with his own crystal blade.

As soon as Dawson's man was down and out, Selyn shifted her stance and swung her blade through the mist escaping from the one Artigos had just downed. It flashed with blue sparks and left nothing behind but the stench.

Birk and Dawson engaged the final two guards. Where Birk used brute force to back his assailant across the cavern floor, Dawson's fight was one of finesse and skill. Selyn glanced at Artigos and saw that the man was standing and watching Dawson with a look of pure admiration on his face.

"Should we help them?" She shot Artigos a grin and got his answering smile in return.

"I've not seen footwork like that since I was a very young man. It's like watching a dancer."

Dawson parried and thrust, but the guard twisted away and Dawson's blade missed. "I could use some help, here."

Scrambling, Selyn caught up to the two as they fought

their way across the floor. "I'm here. Sorry," she said, ducking to miss the slash of steel just over her head. "Artigos and I were admiring your footwork."

Dawson slapped his blade against the man's back as he stumbled and turned. Selyn caught the escaping demon with her crystal, and it sparked and faded away in a cloud of smoke. As this demon died, Birk managed to corner the last of the guards. Artigos stepped in, forced the demon out with DemonsBane, and moved out of the way so that Birk could destroy the creature.

The five guards lay on the floor in various stages of consciousness. Only one, the first, was still entirely out of it. The others were slowly sitting up, shaking their heads, and gazing about with confused expressions and trembling hands.

Birk went to the one man who was still out. He shook the guardsman's shoulder and, when he opened his eyes, helped the man sit up. "Now do you believe?"

The guard nodded. Then he glanced at Selyn, realized she was one of the Forgotten Ones, and looked away. The other four had a similar reaction. They all huddled together on the floor, unsure now what was expected of them.

Birk sighed. "I imagine it's going to affect all of them this way, once we bring them together with the women." He looked at Selyn. "There's a lot of shame involved. I feel it. I know they feel it. We are the men who fathered all of the young women. One of us may be your father, Selyn."

He sighed and, like the others, glanced away. "We don't even know which ones are our daughters. Those were terrible times, and awful things happened. Somehow, we need to work past the shame the men feel, and the rightful anger harbored in the hearts of the Forgotten Ones. As impossible as it sounds, we need to learn to trust each other if we're going to form a cohesive fighting unit."

Selyn glanced at Dawson and then focused on Birk.

"Many of the women won't want to forgive. They're armed with crystal, though, and the swords seem to know we have to work together. It has to happen now, not later. Time may be running out."

Dawson wrapped an arm around her waist. "I'm worried that we haven't heard from either Taron or Roland. Not a single word since they returned to the upper levels, and Roland went back almost a full day before Taron. Something's wrong, but we have to get everyone working together here, or we won't be able to help them."

Selyn squeezed his hand. "Shouldn't we go above and find out what's happening?"

Artigos sheathed his ruby sword. "Not yet. Dawson is right. It's time to bring the women and the guards together." He glanced at the five men still sitting on the ground. Then he tilted his head, smiled at Selyn, and shrugged. "Then, all we have to do is convince them not to kill each other."

Chapter Fifteen

"So, Ragus of Kumer, do you understand what it means to carry crystal?" Ginny pushed the pace as they headed into the lower prison level, but try as she might, she'd not been able to get much out of the young guard who'd offered to show her the way.

"Yes, m'lady. It's a great honor." He kept his eyes forward, though she was certain he was just itching to pull his new crystal sword out and play with his unexpected treasure.

"But do you realize exactly what that honor signifies?"

He slowed just a bit and sent a quick glance in Ginny's direction. "I'm not quite sure what you're asking, m'lady."

"Let me tell you what it means to carry crystal. Listen carefully, Ragus of Kumer, because I don't know if you get it or not, and your life could depend on what you do and don't understand. It means your life, as you've always known it, is forfeit. Your life now belongs to the sentience within your blade. It may not speak to you yet, but it knows you. It watches you, and it will not allow you to do anything to harm Lemuria."

Obviously insulted, he stopped and glared at Ginny

with total disregard for the fact she was the one who'd made it possible for him to carry crystal in the first place.

"I am a Lemurian guardsman. I've sworn to protect Lemuria, m'lady. I would never harm my world."

He sounded so indignant that Ginny had to bite her cheek to keep from laughing. He seemed so young, though as a Lemurian, he could still be thousands of years older than she was. "I believe you, Ragus. Yet you follow orders that have been given to you and your men by a council member who is controlled by a demon."

He rubbed his forehead and frowned at her. "No. That can't be true. Drago has been a councilman since I was a child. He comes from a long line of loyal Lemurians."

"He is possessed by demonkind. Even Drago refuses to believe that a demon has become a parasite within his body, but the demon controls the way he thinks, the decisions he makes, the orders he gives. Think of that as you guard Alton, the one man here who is capable of protecting Lemuria from complete and total subjugation by Abyss."

She spun away and started walking. *Idiot.* How in the hell was she going to convince this dolt that Drago was the enemy?

Ragus trotted to catch up. "How do you know this to be true, m'lady? Please pardon my asking, but how do I know you're not lying to me?"

They'd reached the level where the prisoners were kept. A huge guard with long, black braids framing his face blocked the way. Ginny acknowledged him with a brief nod. Then she turned her back on him and gave her full attention to Ragus. The young guard stared at her almost insolently.

"Ya know, we really don't have time for this shit." She drew DarkFire—not to attack, but to show her blade to the young guard. "DarkFire, explain, please, how we know Drago is possessed."

The sword glowed a dark lavender. "Drago reeks of demonkind. The stench is unmistakable. He has been possessed since the great move from the Lemurian homeland."

Ginny noticed the guard at the gate had come to his feet. The big man moved closer. His attention was focused entirely on DarkFire. The sword glowed and spoke again. "Many of the Council of Nine are ruled by demonkind. The battle to save the soul of Lemuria draws nigh."

"That's the Crone's voice." As the prison guard stared at Ginny's glowing blade, a huge grin slowly split his face. "I'd heard she joined the spirit world, that she now lived in crystal." He raised his head and flashed his smile at Ginny. "I am of Daria's line. We disguised our name for many years following the purge of women warriors. Now I proudly call myself Grayl of Daria."

Ginny bowed her head to him. "You should be proud, Grayl of Daria. I am honored to bear Daria's spirit within DarkFire."

Grayl shot a stern glance at the young guard standing beside Ginny. "You've not brought this brave warrior to the cells as a prisoner, have you?"

Ragus shook his head. "No, sir. She wishes to speak with two of the prisoners, Roland of Kronus and Taron of Libernus."

The guard growled. "These good men should not be held behind bars. What laws have they broken?"

Ginny shook her head. "None that we know of, other than putting the fate of Lemuria first."

"I would free them if I could."

Ginny gently placed her hand on his forearm. "I believe you, Grayl of Daria. Do you swear to put Lemuria first, even if it means breaking a superior's order?"

Grayl's head jerked back, and his gaze flashed from Ragus to Ginny. She grinned. "This is not a hypothetical question. You will be asked to stand behind your oath."

He took a deep breath, stared into her eyes for a long moment, and then slowly nodded. "Aye, m'lady. I promise to serve Lemuria and not the politicians set on ruining it for their own gain. This I swear."

"Hold your sword high, Grayl of Daria."

Again he shot a look at Ragus, but he drew his steel sword and held it upright. Ginny touched DarkFire's tip to his blade, crystal to steel. Light flashed, a blast of purple burst from the tip, raced down the steel blade, and sparked in lavender lights around the guard's huge fist.

He stared at his right arm, and then raised his eyes to his blade. What had been steel was now a multifaceted blade of purest crystal. Wide-eyed, he turned to Ginny. "But . . . how?"

"We're building an army, one loyal soul at a time. Crystal will only form if your heart is true. Thank you, Grayl of Daria. Please take us to the prisoners. And keep your sword sheathed. It will appear as steel to any casual observer, but when the time is right, you will wield crystal against demonkind."

I see you've added another to our army. Alton's laughter slipped into Ginny's mind.

That I have. He's of Daria's line, and he holds the keys to the prison cells.

Excellent. We won't be able to communicate once you enter the cells, but don't break our friends free yet. I want to try proper channels first.

I was afraid you'd say that. Alton's laughter echoed in her thoughts. She missed him. She hoped it was merely their separation that had her feeling edgy and uncomfortable. She glanced about at gray walls and dark shadows.

Then the guard sheathed his sword and walked toward a heavy door set into the stone wall.

"Come, m'lady. This way."

With Ragus close behind, Ginny followed Grayl into the dark tunnel that led down into the prison.

Isra was not among the Forgotten Ones. Selyn called them, and each woman came, walking with a new confidence, wearing hand-stitched pants and tops, similar in style to Selyn's cotton scrubs. The garments were made from the robes they'd worn as slaves, cut now to clothe warriors carrying crystal. At each woman's hip was a crystal sword, sheathed not in the homemade fabric Selyn had expected, but instead in matching red leather scabbards.

Scabbards that had magically appeared, just as Selyn and Dawson's had, at some point during the night. That was the good news. The exciting news.

Isra's disappearance was something else. "What if she's given away our plans?" Selyn kept her eyes on the women gathered and waiting for instructions.

Dawson shrugged. "Who would she give them to? No one here. She'd have to leave the slaves' level. Has she ever gone above?"

"I don't know." Selyn's mind felt ready to burst with all the things that could go wrong. Isra had suddenly moved to the top of her list. "What if she goes to the guards?"

"What if she does?" Dawson merely shrugged. He didn't look the least bit concerned. "They're no longer possessed, and Artigos and Birk are speaking to them now. Relax, sweetheart. Everything will work. Are you ready?"

Relax? Right. Who was he kidding? She nodded and gazed at the army of women she'd known her entire life.

They faced a new world and unknown dangers. None of them, except for Selyn, had ever traveled beyond this level. Would all of them gather together, ever again?

And who would survive? They were going into battle. Much as their mothers had once fought to save their world—a world that then turned its back on the bravest of the brave—these courageous women now prepared to fight. What if their need for revenge was too great? What if they refused to help put Artigos the Just back into power?

So many questions. And no answers. Not a one.

She felt Dawson's strong hands at her waist. "Hang on," he said, and suddenly she was flying. Startled, Selyn almost lost her footing when he set her on the same table where she'd spread crystal swords just a few short hours ago.

She flashed him a quick smile of thanks. At least now she could see everyone. Then she turned and faced her sisters, the Forgotten Ones. Women who would be forgotten no more.

Holding both hands high, she called out to get their attention. "Thank you, all of you, for heeding my call. For heeding the call of our mothers. Already there are changes. We carry crystal, as our mothers before us. The machines have fallen silent, and our work in the mines has come to an end. Our lifetime of slavery is over!"

A cheer went up. She glanced from face to face, saw tears in the eyes of many, resolve on the faces of others, a flicker of fear on more than one. They had every right to fear. They faced an uncertain future, a totally unfamiliar world.

Slavery was familiar. Would they be accepted in the levels above? How would they manage, living among the free folk?

Selyn held tightly to her resolve. "You've all noticed the

guards are no longer watching us. There is a reason for that, a reason for so much of the evil that has ruled us for so long."

There was a bit of mumbling, the sound of feet shuffling, but without the constant roar of the mining machines, it still felt unnaturally quiet. She glanced at Dawson and absorbed his steady strength. With him behind her and a crystal sword in her hand, Selyn felt as if she could accomplish anything.

"Since the beginning, the wardens, these men who guard us, have been possessed by demons—lesser demons that insinuated themselves into the bodies, hearts, and minds of men who were, in the beginning, honorable soldiers. Before long, those demons controlled every thought, every action. It was demonkind directing our torment, leading the assaults against our mothers. Demons controlled the actions and caused the lack of morality in the men who fathered each of us."

Someone cursed; another woman spat. Selyn took a deep breath and carefully weighed her words. "Hear me now. We need to take another look at the animosity we have felt all our lives toward those men. They are victims. Just as we have been victimized by their cruelty, they have been victimized by the demons ruling their every thought and action for millennia."

"The bastards need to die."

Selyn didn't see who shouted the threat, but she noticed that most of the women before her nodded in agreement. "No," she said, raising her voice and making eye contact with as many of her sisters as she could. "The men don't need to die. The demons within them needed to die, and they have. Those same men want to fight beside us in this battle. They ask for our forgiveness. We need to give it to those who have been as sorely treated by demonkind as we have. They were nothing more than tools. We need to forgive them and fight with them, not against them. We have a common enemy, and we have got to fight together if we want to win, and we have to win if we want to survive."

The mumbling grew. Selyn glanced frantically at Dawson. What if she couldn't convince them?

"Draw your sword," Dawson said softly. "Let your blade speak."

"But it's not sentient," she whispered. "I don't think it can talk. I don't even know its name."

"Draw it. Hold it high."

His quiet confidence was actually sort of addictive. Selyn took a deep breath, nodded, and pulled her silent sword from the magical red sheath. As the blade slipped from the leather, Selyn thought of the way the scabbard had just appeared this morning, created out of nothing as far as she could tell.

If the sword could create its own scabbard, why couldn't it help her now? She was smiling as she grasped the hilt firmly in her hand and held the blade high. The crystal glowed, star bright and alive in her hand. The mumbling grew; the curses were more distinct. Her sword vibrated in her grasp, and Selyn clung tightly to the jeweled pommel. Holding the glowing blade high, she waited and hoped like the nine hells Dawson knew what he was talking about.

Dawson stood back with his arms folded across his chest and fought to keep the stupid grin off his face. He was so damned proud of her, the way she stood up there on the table, wearing his faded scrubs and Gaia's sandals, holding that beautiful sword over her head and facing her sisters as if she'd led armies all her life. What a natural!

Her blade glowed brighter, hotter. Then a burst of

sparks shot from the tip, looking for all the world like a cascade of shooting stars.

"Take heed."

Dawson knew she had them on the first words from the shimmering blade. As if every woman suddenly realized her own crystal sword had the same potential for sentience, the same living spirit inside, they surged forward, eyes wide, faces alive with excitement.

"Lemuria's true leader waits nearby with a small army of men. Your wardens, as you know them, yet they are changed men. No longer tools of demonkind, they have chosen to follow Artigos the Just. Most carry steel blades. Without crystal, they cannot prevail against demonkind. You must work with them to hold freedom for all Lemurians. Without your forgiveness, they cannot bear crystal. Their shame is too great."

The sword dimmed. Selyn stared at the blade for a moment, and then she slipped it back into her scabbard. "So," she said, her voice sounding weary beyond measure. "Power is in our hands. We must use it wisely. It's up to all of us. We must find it in our hearts to forgive the men who have treated us as the slaves we were for all these long years. One who is filled with shame cannot carry crystal. Only we have the power to lift that burden from their souls."

Nica stepped forward. She smiled at Dawson and then looked up at Selyn, standing above her on the table. "I'm not sure I have it in me to forgive, Selyn. I still bear scars from more than one beating. I would like to see these men first and judge for myself if they are worthy of forgiveness."

Selyn nodded and turned back to the rest of the women. "Are you willing to give them a chance?"

Mumbles and a few sharp retorts, more talking and a couple of brief arguments later, it was agreed. Selyn jumped down from the table. "What now? Do we just take them to Artigos?"

Dawson took her hand. "I think that's as good an idea as any. Don't you think it's time to find out just what kind of leader we've decided to back?"

It felt almost anticlimactic to grab up their small bags of belongings and walk away from the slave quarters and the mines, this dark piece of Lemuria where they'd been born, where they'd lived all their lives, where they'd watched their mothers die.

Where each of them, at one time or another, had faced some form of cruelty or ill treatment from the men who now waited nearby, hoping for their absolution.

Alton paced the small area inside his quarters, cursing under his breath. He'd changed out of that damned robe and wore his jeans and boots and a dark flannel shirt. With his hair braided back from his face, and his scabbard lashed across his back, he was ready for whatever came next. Screw the council and their frickin' robes, and screw this confinement.

He wanted to know where in the nine hells Ginny was. He'd lost touch with her when she entered the prison cells, as he knew he would, but that was hours ago, damn it, and the guards outside his door hadn't offered a bit of information.

Well, nine hells and then some. If they weren't going to offer, he'd go after it. He paused in front of the portal, thought for a good two seconds about whether or not this was going to piss them off, and then stepped through.

The corporal and his two remaining guards met him with crystal swords raised. "Nice blades," he said, pouring on the sarcasm. "Put your weapons away. Now." His growl must have been effective, because they complied immediately. He almost laughed, but damn it all, he was losing patience with this crap. "Any word from Ragus?"

"No, sir." Balti, their leader, carefully sheathed his crystal blade. "Not since they entered the cells. That was his last report."

"Okay. Then it's official. I'm worried. I've not heard from my woman. I don't like being out of contact with her this long, especially with things as unsettled as they are. Chancellor Artigos and my mother should have returned by now. At the very least, there should have been some contact from the members of the council regarding my arrest."

The three men looked at one another. "Doman. Check on Ragus. Make sure there's not a problem in the prison level."

The man saluted and took off at a quick trot. Alton watched him go. "Corporal Balti, can you reach Drago? Are you in contact with him?"

"No, sir. I've tried reaching him, but I believe he's gone through the veil."

"Into Earth's dimension?" A shiver raced along Alton's spine. Where else could Drago be headed, if not to Earth? But why?

Balti shook his head. "No, sir. He only goes as far as the vortex, stays for a while, and then returns. He always carries his sword with him."

"What color is the blade?" Alton tried to remember if he'd ever actually noticed Drago's sword, but he couldn't recall anything about it. All the council members owned crystal, they didn't always carry their swords, and none of their blades were sentient. At least as far as Alton knew, they weren't capable of communication with their owners. But what if . . .

Corporal Balti was scratching his balding head. "I've never noticed. He keeps it sheathed whenever he carries it, as do the other members of the council. None of them carry sentient blades. They're really just for show."

"I'm beginning to wonder." Alton reached out for Ginny once again. Nothing. Damn. That sense of unease he'd awakened with was growing stronger by the second. "Corporal, remember that pledge you made to Lemuria?"

The man nodded slowly.

"I may have to invoke your promise to fight for Lemuria sooner rather than later. Something is building, some change in our world. I sense it in my gut and . . ."

Crap. Why hadn't he just asked his damned sword? *HellFire? Tell me what's wrong. My senses are screaming right now, and not in a good way. Will you speak aloud? I want Balti to hear what you have to say.*

He reached over his shoulder and drew the blade free of the scabbard. Immediately, the crystal glowed, and Hell-Fire spoke.

"Demonkind grows more powerful. You must arm the citizens of Lemuria." The sword flashed. "Ginny and DarkFire have been taken. Find them in the cells below, imprisoned with Taron and Roland and his men. Beware the guardsmen who harbor demonkind."

"Nine hells." Alton stared at the blade. Then he shoved it inside the scabbard. "Okay, Balti. This has gone too far. While I'm stuck here in my quarters, Lemuria faces the risk of total annihilation. Make your decision, Corporal, and make it now. Who do you fight for?"

Corporal Balti snapped to attention. The men beside him did the same. "I gave my oath to fight for Lemuria. I'm with you, Chancellor. What do we do now?"

"We get Ginny, Roland, and the rest of them out of that

damned cell. Then we find out what in the nine hells Drago is doing in the vortex."

With Selyn at their head, the women marched into the cavern where Artigos the Just had been held prisoner since the great move from the dying world of Lemuria. All those long years, imprisoned with nothing more than his own thoughts and a few books to keep him sane, probably wondering if he'd ever again know freedom.

Selyn paused just inside the open area. Eighteen Lemurian guardsmen waited there. Eighteen men and one deposed world leader, waiting to see if the women warriors who had once been the wardens' slaves had it in their hearts to forgive, if those same women would honor the leadership of a man long thought dead.

Dawson stayed to the back of the group and scanned the area, looking for Isra. No one had seen her since the night before. He worried about what kind of damage she could cause, should she decide to take out her anger on her sisters.

He saw no sign of the woman. The walls glowed with their unusual inner light, but this was a place of prison cells and military quarters. There were no works of art, no golden columns, no crystalline formations to break the drabness of barren walls and smooth ceiling.

All attention focused on the very tall, whipcord-lean man wearing a plain white robe, standing at the head of a group of solemn guardsmen robed in blue. Artigos's long hair flowed to his waist, held away from his face with a single gold band around his forehead that appeared similar to the one holding Selyn's hair. In spite of the gray streaks amid the brown, he held himself with the bearing and confidence of a young man. A man in his prime, ready for anything.

The women arranged themselves in a half circle in front of the men. Their anger was a living, breathing presence in the room, but they held themselves in check. Now they stared not at Artigos, but at the guards in formation behind him.

Dawson caught Selyn's eye. She shrugged and turned her attention to Artigos.

"Lord Artigos, I bring you the Forgotten Ones, though I promise you, we are sworn to be forgotten no more. Our mothers were brave warriors who suffered much because of Lemurian politics and now, it appears, from demonkind as well. We carry crystal, we are strong, and we are courageous. Tell us why we should pledge our service, our very lives, to you. Convince us to put aside our need for revenge and fight beside the men who assaulted our mothers and abused all of us for so many years."

Artigos stepped forward, away from the men who were so recently under thrall to demonkind. He acknowledged Selyn with a courteous bow, folded his arms across his chest, and made eye contact with every woman there.

Dawson felt the man's resolve, but he also sensed his anger. Anger that these women had suffered, that his guards had suffered as well. When he spoke, it was with a powerful voice that commanded attention and sent shivers along Dawson's spine. He had no doubt he stood in the presence of a great leader. He hoped the women felt it as well.

"I cannot apologize for the wrong that was done to you, the evil you have lived with. Demonkind deserves no apology. Only death. Nothing else will serve, and nothing can undo the harm that has been done. We can only do our best to prevent more harm from occurring. The men behind me have spent untold millennia ruled by demons. Their lives have not been their own, just as your lives have not been yours to live as you choose."

He sighed and shook his head. "As your mothers' lives

were not theirs. I fear the war we Lemurians thought we had won so many years ago was nothing but a ruse to allow demons access into our civilization. They have infiltrated our leaders, our soldiers, the very fabric of our society, beginning when they first set into motion the destruction of our homeland.

"The decision is yours. You can fight us, crystal to steel, Lemurian against Lemurian, and exact your revenge against innocent men, or you can join with us to seek revenge against the demon horde that has caused so many deaths, so much misery to our entire civilization."

He looked across the gathering of women and smiled. "You are all so young, and yet you have the hearts and souls of women warriors who fought bravely. Even so, I imagine you know little of your past beyond this immediate history. I want to tell you about your people—what this battle is really about. It's a story very few souls even remember, as it was long before my time that Lemurians first settled on this world."

He glanced at Dawson and then turned and focused on the men behind him for a moment. "Sit down. All of you. Get comfortable. We have time for a bit of a history lesson. I want all of you to know exactly what you're fighting for."

Chapter Sixteen

Even when he'd been locked away from everyone and everything he knew, Artigos had not felt his age as he felt it now. Looking out over the sea of young and hopeful faces, he realized he was most likely the last living soul who remembered hearing the stories of Lemuria's beginnings from the mouths of those who'd actually lived them. He still recalled, as if it had been only days ago, listening as his grandparents described those terrifying times, and how they'd survived almost total annihilation of the original Lemurian civilization.

He could be the final link between those born on the home world, and those who had always called Earth—and now this Lemurian dimension within Earth's rocky crust—their home.

He knew, firsthand, where they had come from, and why they had fled a dying world long before their new home on Earth had been destroyed.

The story was written down and stored in the archives, but did anyone even care anymore? There were so few of them left. From the last numbers he'd heard, barely a thousand Lemurians survived—if this could be called survival, this sleepwalk through their empty, wasted lives in an artificially created world. At least he had an excuse for not working harder to keep his society vital and growing.

He'd been a prisoner, locked in a cell for well over ten thousand years, but the time for excuses was past.

He watched as the young women seated themselves on the stone floor and listened to the rustle of robes and scuffling of sandals as his soldiers took their ease behind him. He glanced at the human leaning against the cavern wall and once again felt drawn to him. Somehow that young man, a mere infant compared to everyone in this room, might very well be the single factor that could tip the scales and save the Lemurian people, their world, and all the other civilized worlds from the eternal damnation of demon rule.

How or why, he wasn't sure. The only thing Artigos could be certain of was the weight of too many lives hanging in the balance.

Worry solves nothing. It's time for action.

With that thought in mind, he turned so that he could see everyone and leaned his hip against the scarred desk the guards used for their reports. It was the only piece of furniture in the cavern—an old and much-used remnant from Earth. It, too, probably had stories to tell, but where to begin his?

Folding his arms across his chest, Artigos began at the beginning. "Long before there were humans Earth," he said, "when the planet was nothing more than a developing world teeming with primitive life, the world where Lemurians originated, the place they called home, was facing annihilation. Our sun was going nova, and we had no choice but to abandon our home, the place where our civilization began.

"Lemurians had been space travelers for many years,

and our technology was well advanced. I know that you must find that difficult to believe as you sit here on the stone floor of a cave in your rough garb and sandals, armed only with swords, but Lemurians of old once colonized other planets and regularly traveled among the stars. Unfortunately, the worlds we'd settled were in our same solar system, and they, too, faced destruction.

"Large ships for transporting our citizens beyond our solar system were prepared. Goods and people began moving aboard, until we had almost our entire population living on huge ships orbiting Lemuria, preparing to leave. Our scientists were hard at work, searching out worlds that could support us, but there weren't very many, and the distance was great.

"Very few planets looked promising. Our laws prevented us from moving to worlds that already had sentient populations, but a few were primitive enough, new enough, and without sentient species of their own; those we felt free to colonize. Coordinates were fed into the ships' computers, and we prepared for a diaspora beyond anything anyone had heard of before. An entire world— a long established, technologically advanced civilization— was moving en masse to another planet.

"Then the unthinkable happened. The sun exploded far ahead of the time our scientists had predicted. Instead of an orderly journey, the ships with their Lemurian cargo— the ones that were not destroyed in the initial explosion— were flung into space.

"We also believe they were flung through time, though we will never know for sure. Nor will we ever know how many of the hundreds of vessels survived. The ship my ancestors traveled on was damaged, but we made it to this world and landed on a lush continent in the midst of Earth's Pacific Ocean. It was difficult at first, but eventually the colonists thrived in their new world. We'd brought our technology with us, along with our sentient crystal swords. They were the one physical link with our home world, created out of the crystals that formed our planet, carrying the spirits of our long-departed warriors. We managed to save our swords, even though much of our advanced technology was eventually lost. Life here was too easy, and our people became lazy."

He smiled at the women who watched him so intently. "You have not had it so easy. You've struggled to survive; you've worked hard. You are more like our ancient ancestors than the spoiled free folk who run our world today. I imagine demons would not have found safe harbor within any of you."

He turned his attention to the men. Each one had opened himself to demonkind. Not consciously, but they'd not fought against the bastards, either. "You were young, brave soldiers, but most of you came of age at the end of the DemonWars. You were not tested in battle and had no idea how to fight the demons that raped your souls. Now you know. Demonkind will try again and again to gain access, but you cannot allow it. Fight them. With everything you are, you must fight them."

He caught Dawson Buck's eye, and nodded, sensing the young man's impatience. He was right to be concerned. Time was short, but Artigos needed to finish this tale. He had to explain how they had come to this point, to this pivotal battle, and somehow hope it was enough to convince the women he was a worthy leader.

The men would follow. Their confidence in themselves was badly shaken, and he offered them hope of redemption, if only to die in battle as heroes against demonkind. He certainly hoped to offer more than that, but it would depend on the women.

Everything depended on them. They carried crystal; the men did not. He'd tried using DemonsBane to change the steel blades the way Roland's sword had altered Birk's, but it hadn't worked. Some critical element was missing, and Artigos feared Selyn's crystal sword was right—DemonsBane had passed DarkFire's message on to him—that without the women's forgiveness, the men were incapable of bearing crystal. Their shame was too great.

He focused on his audience. "Eventually, many thousands of years later, when most of the original colonists were long gone, we discovered another advanced society on the far side of Earth. Though they called themselves Atlanteans, they were too similar to us for it to be mere coincidence. Amazingly, they had been here much, much longer than we had, which is when we realized our world's diaspora had taken some of our ships through time as well as space. The Atlanteans' technology was even more advanced than ours, but by then we had begun to lose much of what we had once had, while they had obviously continued to develop. They no longer remembered their off-world beginnings. Lemuria was legend, nothing more. But we knew they were our brothers." He laughed softly. "That is a tale for another time.

"For whatever reason, we had not been bothered by demonkind until shortly after making contact with Atlantis. Their world was rocked by massive upheavals, and they elected to encase themselves within a protective dimensional bubble that would allow them to continue as a civilization far beneath the sea. They exist there still, for all I know, living apart from all worlds, accessible only through the portals in the vortexes. As far as I know, they're unaware of the current demonic uprising, though their world is at risk, should Lemuria fall.

"I was the heir of the last king of Lemuria, a position

and title handed down from parent to eldest child. We had our share of queens who ruled. My grandmother was the last woman ruler. Her son, my father, took over leadership, and when he had tired of corporeal life, it was passed on to me.

"Because I was a young man, yet untried, when I took over the monarchy, I chose to lead as a king with a council of trusted advisors. I was king during the DemonWars, when we discovered that our crystal swords were the only weapon we had to effectively fight and kill demons. But after, when Lemuria was in constant upheaval with volcanic explosions and earthquakes, when our government was in turmoil with the forced move to a new world, I was taken prisoner. At the time, I had no idea my own son was behind the coup. Nor did I realize he was ruled by demonkind."

He shook his head and fought back a great welling of sadness, but he couldn't stop the tears from filling his eyes. "Demons have no concept of time. All these thousands of years while I have languished in a prison cell, they have worked to gain a foothold among our people. I believe demons were behind the destruction of Atlantis as well as our continent of Lemuria, and I know they are working even now to destroy this new home of ours, though this time they're doing it from within, by taking possession of the souls of our people.

"I have no idea how many of the so-called 'free folk' are actually slaves to demonkind, but I am certain, just as these guardsmen have been bound by evil, many of our council members and aristocrats are bound as well. The Lemurian population is small. There are barely more than a thousand of us remaining, but if demonkind ever completely controls Lemuria, they will have found that immutable, irreversible tipping point that will finally give them what they have worked toward all along—dominion over all worlds in all dimensions.

"Earth will fall. Eden, Atlantis . . ." He shook his head and wiped at the tears spilling down his cheeks. "All of us will become hosts to demonkind, and life as we know it will end for all time."

He focused on the women. "As slaves, your lives have been hell. What demons will do to our worlds will make your previous existence appear as paradise. My grandson is struggling to hold Lemurian society together, but he does not want to lead. I do, and I can. I am willing to fight this scourge, but I cannot do it without your support. Will you stand with me? Will you stand beside these men? Whether you want it or not, you carry their blood in your veins, as well as the blood of the warrior women."

He gazed at the faces watching him, and he spoke to each woman as if she, and only she, mattered. "You were born to be warriors, not slaves. Don't be slaves to your need for revenge. These men—these brave warriors—are ready to take up arms against our common enemy. Can you put aside your desire for revenge and focus that hatred on an enemy that will do anything possible to divide us? Even after the wrong done to you in the name of Lemuria, can you raise your swords in her defense? Not for yourselves. Not for me. For Lemuria!"

Selyn was the first one to her feet. She thrust her crystal sword into the air and shouted loud enough for her voice to echo from the cavern walls, "For Lemuria. Yes!"

One by one, and finally all together, the rest of the women, many with tears on their faces, leapt to their feet. The shout went up. The men were on their feet, with steel blades high and voices raised, and the echo of their shouted cries gave the women more power, more strength, until the stone chamber reverberated with their battle cry.

"Lemuria! Lemuria!"

Chills coursed along Artigos's spine. He felt the energy grow and intensify, a sacred trust these women and men had just given to him. He drew DemonsBane from his scabbard and held his sword high. Each of the women drew their crystal blades. The crystals flashed with brilliant bursts of blue and silver light. The cry of "Lemuria" grew louder, taking on a rhythm all its own until it became a song powerful enough to lead an army.

Then, without warning, with cries of "Lemuria" still echoing from the cavern walls, the women surged past Artigos with their blades drawn, and raced toward the men.

Artigos shot a fearful glance at Dawson Buck. What the nine hells was happening? Were they going to kill the men after all? But Dawson was smiling and holding his blade high. Crystal fire shot from the ruby tip and flashed in blood-red streaks across the ceiling. Artigos spun around, expecting carnage, but it wasn't that at all.

Not even close. Men and women stood in tight groups, swords held high, crystal blades caressing steel. Blue fire flashed, a blinding light that wiped away shadows until everything glowed.

Men, women, swords, all of them encased in cold, blue flames that flowed over arms, down bodies, across shoulders.

Artigos the Just sensed movement. Dawson stood beside him, just as awestruck, watching the power of crystal as it bathed the entire group of men and women, encasing them in light, and filling them with power.

Time stood still, and yet Artigos was aware of the sound of many hearts beating, the rush of blood through veins, the crisp spark of thoughts in so many minds. As if these disparate men and women were a single entity, a single life form, united at a cellular level by the power of crystal.

And he, the man known as Artigos the Just, was the

breath this form drew, the strength that lifted their arms, the mind that ruled their thoughts. An unexpected, compelling burst of power filled him and gave him hope.

Then, as if from another plane entirely, new voices intruded. First a whisper among the blades—whispers that became words—until he knew that the voices he heard were those of the spirits of the women warriors coming together, growing stronger, calling out to their daughters and their oppressors alike.

The whisper became a mighty shout as their many voices rose in battle song. *We are avenged,* they cried. *We are one people. Not wardens and slaves, not men and women, not adversaries. Now we are and forever, one people. We are Lemuria!*

Their passionate cry faded as the glow of many blades slowly dimmed. As raised swords lowered, men and women looked first at one another and saw their comrades for the coming battle, and then turned to their swords—crystal swords held by guards and former slaves alike. Swords with the sentience of the brave women who had gone before.

Birk was the first one to step apart from the crowd. The massive guard walked to Artigos and knelt at his feet with his blade pressed across his heart. "I pledge my sword and my heart to Lemuria, to her protector, Artigos the Just, and to our cause. All hail Artigos the Just. All hail Lemuria!"

Artigos stood tall as he tapped Birk's right and then left shoulder with DemonsBane. Birk rose, and Selyn took his place. Another man followed, and then a woman, until every single soldier—male and female alike—had pledged his or her loyalty to their leader and their land.

Soldiers. All of them. Not a single slave in the group.

When they were finished, Artigos clambered atop the desk so that he could see his army, all of them standing in formation now without regard to gender. Men beside the women they had mistreated; women next to men they'd sworn to kill.

Brought together by the spirits of warriors long gone, by the power of crystal.

"We march to the upper levels tomorrow. I've not heard from any of our comrades who went ahead, and can only assume the worst. I want you to eat well, and sleep." Then he grinned at the robed men lined up before him. "Philosophers fight in robes. Soldiers need pants to better maneuver. If any of you gentlemen know how to turn those robes into clothing such as the women are wearing, you may find yourself better able to fight." He sobered as he looked at them. "And if so, do it quickly. I think we will fight before too long. Rest well. We leave with first light."

Dawson held Selyn's hand as they walked away from the soldier's barracks. They'd eaten well, and the dynamics between the women and men had been fascinating. Everyone had been so tense at first. Then some of the women had offered to help the men turn their robes into pants. Before long, one of the men had approached a young woman and told her she looked exactly like his mother.

From there it had become a game, with the women trying to figure out which of the men might have fathered them. What could have been horribly uncomfortable had ended up with small groups of women and men cutting and sewing, and quiet discussions among others about who might or might not be related.

No one would ever know for sure. The men had little memory of that period, when they'd gone against all their natural instincts to protect women, and had abused them instead. Yet none could deny the powerful sense that those women warriors were there, in the same room, in the sentience of the swords.

Attending, and approving of the unexpected emotional connection between their daughters and their former guards.

"I didn't expect tonight." Selyn glanced at Dawson and then looked away. "I thought there would be a more lingering anger, a stronger need for revenge. We've talked of revenge all our lives. But those voices . . ." She shook her head. "Those were the voices of our mothers, the women warriors, and they're right." She sighed and leaned her head against Dawson's shoulder. "I once had so much anger against the wardens, but it's gone."

Dawson wrapped his arm around her shoulders. They were almost to the room they'd shared the night before. Anger and revenge were the last things on his mind.

"Maybe because you've found a new target for it," he said. "A common enemy. Something that pulls all of you together, rather than drives you apart. As Artigos said, you need to concentrate on fighting demonkind, not each other. The spirits of the women appear to agree."

"Are we truly ready for this?" Selyn rested her fingers on his chest. "I'm worried that we haven't heard from anyone. If they could have contacted us, both Roland and Taron would have done so. They know how important it is that we have news."

"That's why you and I are going on ahead. If we leave early enough, we should be able to get word back. Lord Artigos said he doesn't want us taking any risks, but if we can reach a level where you can contact Ginny or Alton, find out what the hell's going on, and get back below without getting caught . . ."

"Or worse?" She tilted one eyebrow.

He nodded. "Or worse. But I'm not going to think that

way. I can't, not if I want to have the courage to carry out Artigos's wishes. What I really wish is that I could go without you, but we need the information, and I don't do that telepathy thing you do."

She stretched up on her toes and kissed him. "Yeah, but there are other truly amazing things you can do. We don't have to leave until morning. That gives us a whole night. . . ."

He stood there like an idiot staring at her. She grabbed him by the hand and led him inside their room, but he didn't remember to breathe until she closed the door behind him. It was as if she'd shut the world, the war, and all of demonkind outside, leaving just the two of them. And, like she said, there was a whole night before they needed to return to reality.

"I need to bathe." Selyn let go of his hand and headed toward the bathroom. Then she paused in the doorway, glanced over her shoulder at him with a look that could melt ice and added, "Would you like to join me?"

If there'd been a prize for speed undressing, Dawson was positive he'd have won. But by the time he got into the small room where he'd showered the night before, there was no sign of Selyn. Then he noticed a narrow alcove he'd missed, and the sound of water beyond.

Slipping around a corner, Daws stumbled and had to hang on to a stone outcropping to keep from tumbling into the pool. If this was a typical Lemurian bathtub, he was giving up showers forever.

Selyn sat shoulders deep in a bubbling pool of dark water about six feet in diameter. It appeared to be cut from solid stone, so that the gray walls rose up around it on all sides. Hot water flowed in from a small waterfall on one side and trickled out through a hole on the other. Steam rose all around, and a soft, blue-green glow emanating from the walls cast strange shadows across the roiling surface.

"What's this? A hot tub?" He knelt beside the pool and dipped his hand in the steaming water.

Selyn tilted her head and frowned at him like he was a complete dolt. "Hot tub? We call it a bathing pool. We had one like it in the slave quarters, though it was much larger. Showers are for hurried bathing." She smiled, and he could have sworn she actually fluttered her long lashes at him. "Remember, we have all night."

"Oh, yeah." He slipped into the pool beside her. The warm water came to his waist—a perfect temperature for bathing. *Or other things.* Except he couldn't go there. At least, not beyond the amazing images crowding his mind. He found the ledge Selyn was sitting on and sat beside her.

She was sleek and warm where she leaned against him, all soft breasts and smooth skin. He slipped his arm up and over her back, tucking her close against his side where she fit perfectly—a wet, warm, and willing woman clinging to him. The water bubbled and steamed around them, and they had hours before they needed to slip into the upper levels and see what was happening among the free folk.

All night. Just the two of them. Dawson felt like screaming his stupidity to the world. They had all night, and no condoms.

Never, ever again was he leaving home without his pockets full of the damned things. He could have kicked himself, except it wouldn't help a bit. He told himself to accept the fact they weren't going to make love tonight, and relax. The warm water bubbled over his aching muscles, and Selyn was so close that at least the problems of demons and danger and a looming war melted away with the billowing steam.

Unfortunately, his raging libido remained, literally front and center—a painful reminder of his absurd lack of preparation. Selyn's fingers brushed his arm, and she gazed at him from pools of deepest blue. Dawson groaned and tightened his grasp around her. She surprised him by moving closer. Causing barely a ripple in the pool, she slipped willingly into his lap and straddled him.

Her puckered nipples brushed his chest. Her lips swept gently over his mouth. She was so close. Too close. Her feminine thatch of hair meshed with his dark tangle, and it would take just the slightest adjustment for him to slip inside her. Her heat surrounded him. She pressed her breasts closer against his chest, and her lips followed the line of his jaw. Her slim, muscular arms slipped around his neck; she tangled her fingers in his damp hair. It was too good, too much, too hard to resist.

He shouldn't risk this. She couldn't risk it, but still it took an act of will he wasn't sure he had, to wrap his fingers around her waist and lift her away. She laughed and tightened her arms around his neck, clinging like a burr.

"There's no need to push me away. Unless you've decided you don't want me." Her laughter raised shivers across his chest, and he was almost preternaturally aware of the taut points of her nipples teasing the hair that covered his pecs. Not want her? Who did she think she was kidding?

"I talked to Nica." She kissed his chin. "Her mother was a healer before she was a warrior." This time she planted a small kiss at the right corner of his mouth. "She taught Nica lots of her ways, including how to prevent babies."

No kisses this time. Instead, she leaned her forehead against Dawson's, and there was a sense of sadness in her voice. "It's not difficult for us, not when we prepare ahead of time. It's much harder for Lemurian women to conceive than it is to avoid conception, but because you worry, I'm being careful."

He was almost afraid to ask. "What do you mean? Just how are you . . . ?"

"Being careful?" She kissed him. A real one this time, a long, lingering kiss that spoke of sexual experience he knew she didn't have. Experience she was going to get if they both weren't careful. Whatever willpower he'd had was dissipating along with the steam rising above the surface of the pool.

"An herb," she said.

Her soft whisper against his mouth had him rising even higher, swelling even harder against her. "An herb?" Was that his voice?

"A simple herb in my meal tonight. Once a month is all it takes, until I want to try to conceive. Then I stop eating it and hope that somehow, at some point, we make a baby." She shook her head. "For most women, that never happens."

Her fingernails scraped the back of his neck, and his entire body trembled with need. He took a deep breath. Then he sucked in another and grabbed her hands from around his neck, held her arms down at her sides, and looked directly into those guileless blue eyes. Speaking very slowly and clearly, he said, "I need to be sure what I think you're saying. You ate an herb with your dinner tonight, and that's all it takes to keep you from getting pregnant?"

He almost laughed, but the sound he made was more of a croak. "I'm assuming that's including sex. . . . You're saying that you can have sexual relations and not conceive? As long as you've eaten this . . . whatever?"

She laughed, only Selyn's was full-throated and filled with joy. "Ah, Dawson. I wish you could see yourself right now. Yes, that's what I'm saying. But, knowing you, healer of small furry creatures and grown Lemurian women that you are, you want specifics."

She kissed him once again, and then, speaking as if she

were teaching sex education to a room filled with seventh graders, said, "Listen, carefully. I ate an herb known to our healers that will prevent implantation of the male sperm with the female's egg. It is one hundred percent effective in preventing pregnancy for Lemurian women. Is that information precise enough? I can't get pregnant if we make love. No matter how many times or what positions we are in, which means you have absolutely no excuse to avoid showing me what making love is like. Now do you understand?"

Oh, shit. Did he ever.

Chapter Seventeen

Selyn settled her bottom over Dawson's thighs and tried not to giggle, but it was so hard. Then she did laugh, but the laughter exploded into an unglamorous snort that morphed into uncontrollable giggles because it was definitely hard, that thing between his legs he'd identified by at least half a dozen silly names last night.

She tried to stop laughing and snorted again, which made the giggles even worse, but nine hells *he* was hard, and it was hard not to laugh, and he was poking her belly, not between her legs where she really wanted to feel all that perfectly hard length of him.

He raised one dark eyebrow. "Any reason you're laughing at me?" He sounded angry, but the twitch in his lips gave him away.

She sniffed and wiped her streaming eyes. Bit her lips and fought for control. Lost it entirely and doubled over, shoulders shaking, giggles making it almost impossible to breathe.

"I've certainly had unenthusiastic reactions from women, but yours takes unenthusiastic to an entirely new level."

His dry comment set her off all over again.

Finally, she took a deep breath. Then she took another and held it until she felt as if she had everything under control. "I'm sorry." She sniffed and had to clench her teeth to keep the giggles from breaking loose. "I guess I'm nervous and sometimes I laugh when I'm nervous, and then I thought how hard it was, only I was thinking how hard it was not to laugh, but then I realized how hard *that* is and . . . and . . ."

She slapped a hand over her mouth. His blue eyes twinkled. He didn't say a word. Instead he slipped his hand between their bellies, and his long fingers inched slowly between her legs.

Laughter was suddenly the last thing on Selyn's mind.

She moaned, thrust her hips forward and tilted her head back. His fingers slipped gently over that sensitive bit of her that he'd played so well last night. She whimpered. Then one finger slowly, gently worked inside her body. In, out, and in again. He added another, and the pressure was exquisite. Muscles rippled and pulsed—muscles she hadn't even known she had—and she caught his rhythm, sliding up and down his fingers, tilting her hips to find the perfect friction, amazed by what he could do to her with nothing more than his beautiful, long fingers.

The warm water lapped over her breasts and gave her body a buoyancy that turned everything dreamlike. The thick, hard ridge of his penis rubbed over her belly, but she didn't want him there. She wanted him inside, filling her, and she lifted herself away from his fingers, actually floating away from his slow but steady teasing.

"Now," she demanded, with a voice gone harsh from desire. "I want you inside me. Now."

He focused on her face, his blue eyes dark as midnight in the shadows, and he watched her while she shivered in his grasp. Watched her, she imagined, to be sure she knew what she was asking of him.

She did. She'd never wanted anything more. Not her freedom, not even her life. She'd not experienced life before now. It was her turn. Her time.

For whatever reason, he must have been satisfied she wasn't a complete idiot, because his hands grasped her hips, and he lifted her even as she lifted herself. She reached between them, grabbed the thick, hard length of him, and slowly, carefully settled herself down, taking him fully inside.

He was much bigger than she'd expected. Longer. Thicker. And hard. It might feel as if that part of him was covered in silk, but he was all steel and strength and hard, male muscle. Her channel burned as he stretched her. She felt her muscles rippling along his length, but her body adjusted. The burn slowly faded away, replaced by a pleasure so perfect, so utterly sublime, she knew she never would have believed had someone tried to describe it.

He filled her in more than just this physical sense. Though she'd not realized what was missing before now, Selyn finally felt complete. Emotions she'd never appreciated burst into life, feelings unfamiliar and yet so deeply embedded in her soul, she had no idea how she'd existed without them.

Dawson stretched her, and she clung to him, taking all of him, needing him inside her as much as she needed air to breathe and food to eat. Needing this fullness, this amazing connection, but not merely to another. No, specifically to Dawson Buck.

She'd never imagined needing a man—not like this. Her life had been as complete as a slave's life could be. Work in the mines; downtime with her sisters; the love she'd known from her mother so long ago.

This was completely different. Unexplainable, unimaginable.

Perfect.

Dawson's lips fastened over her nipple, and he suckled so hard she felt it between her legs. His hips kept up a simple rhythm—such simple physical acts to create such a complex tangle of physical sensations and emotions.

He moved inside her slowly, carefully, but Selyn wanted more. He was probably being careful because this was her first time. Nine hells, but she didn't want careful!

She planted her knees on the stone bench on either side of his thighs and took control. Rising and falling, tilting her hips to take him even deeper, to feel that delicious friction grow stronger, closer, she reached for something indescribable. Her breath burst out from between her parted lips in short, sharp gasps. Water splashed out of the pool and spread in ever-widening circles across the dark stone floor.

Dawson's eyes were closed, and his lips twisted in a rictus that could be either pain or pleasure. The cords on his neck were drawn taut—his entire body felt tight beneath Selyn's hands, straining, as hers was, against the climax hovering so close.

She didn't want to finish. Not yet. This felt too good to end it, but then she realized they could do it again, and again if they wished.

This wasn't an end, it was a beginning.

A beginning for her and for Dawson. The simplicity of it filled her mind, the joy and the absolute certainty of her feelings. Buoyed by unexpected love, she set herself free.

The first rippling contractions deep inside her body must have been the signal Dawson waited for. He thrust inside hard and fast, deeper still until the hard crown of his erection rode across the mouth of her womb.

She heard a loud, keening cry and barely recognized her own voice, that unfamiliar howl ripped from her chest as her body tightened and shivered and trembled in Dawson's powerful embrace.

She was still trembling, long moments later as they half lay, half floated in the pool. Dawson had slipped lower on the stone bench so that only his head remained above the water. Her chin rested on his shoulder and water lapped across her lips, but she made no effort to move.

What was the point? She couldn't have moved if she'd tried.

His lips caressed her brow. "You're not giggling anymore."

She groaned. "I think you've found the cure for my giggles."

"Good." He kissed her again. "No man wants to be laughed at. That's not the reaction we're looking for from a beautiful woman. Not at all."

She snorted and then choked it back. "I'll try to remember that."

"We should probably get out of the water."

She raised her head. "Why?"

"Gonna get all pruny."

She frowned. "What's that mean?" Some of the terms he used really didn't translate well at all.

He held up her hand and showed her the water-wrinkles on her fingertips. "That's pruny. Plums are fruit. When they're dried, they get all wrinkled, and they're called prunes. Your fingers are all wrinkled. Hence, pruny."

"But they're all wet. They're not dry at all."

"Exactly." He blew bubbles at the end of the word.

She held up her fingers and looked at them. "Huh?"

"Never mind."

Selyn wriggled her hips and felt him grow hard inside her once again. "I don't think you really want to get out yet."

He opened his eyes, though his lids looked heavy and slumberous. "There's out, like do we want to get out of the water, and then there's out . . . of you." Slowly, with a tilt of his hips, he lifted and thrust deep inside her. "I'd rather stay in." He emphasized his position with a quick kiss. "Though I don't mind pulling out again."

Wrapping his big hands around her waist, he lifted her just enough to slip himself almost free of her sheath. "As long as I can go back in," he whispered, plunging deep again.

Selyn shivered as she caught his achingly slow rhythm, taking every deep thrust with a tiny cry, and whimpering each time he withdrew.

Over, and over again.

A long time later, Selyn confirmed they were both really pruny when they finally dragged themselves out of the steaming, bubbling pool and into bed.

Eddy stared glumly at the ghostly image the streetlights cast through the steadily falling snow outside the window of Freedom and Spirit Schwartz's house. Trees sagged beneath their heavy load. A few branches had given way and lay broken and twisted in the yard. The narrow street outside the house was covered in an impassable layer of white.

Bumper slept in front of the woodstove that Freedom kept stocked with split pieces of oak. Gaia, Artigos, Freedom, Spirit, and Eddy's dad Ed were in the next room attempting to play a Lemurian card game Gaia had spent the afternoon trying—amid much laughter—to teach them.

They were having way too much fun. Artigos laughed, Ed cursed, and Freedom, feeling much stronger this afternoon as he recovered from back surgery, made some silly comment about Lemurians and their luck. Eddy turned and glared at the five older adults sitting at the kitchen table. They'd been in there for hours now, drinking cheap sangria and laughing, enjoying themselves as if all was right with the world. They were so damned happy she wanted to scream.

"How can they just sit in there and play cards like there's nothing going on and it's just a normal day? I don't get it." She flopped down on the couch next to Dax and glared at their reflection in the big picture window. "The whole world is going to hell in a handbasket, and they're in there playing games, acting like everything is fine."

Dax grabbed her hand. "Ah, Eddy. What would you like them to do? We're stuck here. There's nothing any of us can do for now, not until the storm ends. Mari's magic isn't enough to stop the snow; the roads are closed; airplanes aren't flying. . . . We just have to wait it out."

Damn. She hated when he was reasonable. "Aren't you worried about Ginny and Alton? They haven't contacted us since they went back into Lemuria. We should have heard something by now. If they were okay, they'd have access to the portals and could use their frickin' cell phones, if nothing else!"

Before Dax could answer, Mari flopped on the couch beside Eddy and sighed. "I'm with you, Eddy. I know worrying doesn't do anyone any good, but something is definitely wrong. Just look out the window. This isn't a normal storm. Evergreen never gets snow this heavy this early in the year. It's not even Halloween yet. The weather service can't explain it, and my magic doesn't affect it." Grumbling, she added, "I thought I was getting pretty good with weather."

Darius wandered in from the kitchen. The big Lemurian guard stood in front of the window and stared at the blowing snow. After a bit he turned away and folded his arms across his chest. "Mari? You've been concentrating so much on changing the weather. What about trying something different? What if you were to use your magic to transport us up the mountain? I don't know exactly what you're capable of, but . . ." He shrugged.

"Neither do I. Remember, I'm still pretty new at this." She stood up. "But I know who might have some answers. Mom? Got a minute?" She left the room in a swirl of her long skirts.

Grinning broadly, Eddy watched her go. "Mari's really embraced her inner witch, hasn't she? She always used to dress in button-down shirts and dark slacks, and wear her hair in a neat little twist at the back of her neck. I swear she was an investment banker in the sixth grade. Now look at her. Long blond hair, dangly earrings, a gauzy skirt, and a gypsy top with no bra . . ."

"I heard that!" Mari's indignant laughter had them all in stitches.

"I was complimenting you, Mari. I was just saying that you've set your inner witch free at last."

Mari stuck her head around the corner. "My inner what?"

Darius laughed. "Witch. Your inner witch is finally free. Now see if she can get us to the vortex."

Mari saluted and went back into the kitchen to talk to her mom. Bumper raised her head and growled. Darius reached for his sword, and Dax jumped to his feet. The lights dimmed, blinked, and went out.

"I was expecting that," Freedom said out of the dark

kitchen. His flashlight flickered on. "Spirit, where'd you leave the matches?"

"No problem, Dad. I'll get the candles." Mari moved through the dark room, pausing over candles and a couple of storm lanterns that flickered to life as she passed. "I knew this magic was good for something."

Eddy stared at Bumper. The dog had gone on alert before the lights went out. Now she stared at the front door. A low growl vibrated in ~~Bumper~~Willow's chest, and her ears were pointed forward. She focused so intently on the door, Eddy wondered if she heard someone.

Or some thing.

Willow? What's got Bumper so upset?

There's something outside. I'm not sure what. It's more a sense of wrong, not right, but I don't know what it is. See if DemonSlayer can tell.

With a quick glace at Dax, Eddy slipped her sword from the scabbard. The blade glowed and pulsed in the candlelight, shining brilliantly and throwing dark shadows against the walls. "DemonSlayer? Can you tell what has Bumper spooked?"

The sword flashed and Eddy heard the familiar voice of Selyn's mother in her mind. *Demonkind. Nearby. Searching, yet not finding. Wraiths. They're formless, not in avatars, yet there is more substance than normal. I sense them moving in small groups. Coming closer. Drawn by something that calls them.*

Eddy glanced at Dax. "Looks like we've got demons, guys. Not sure where, but they're getting close, and they're not using avatars. DemonSlayer says they're being drawn here."

Darius held a hand over his eyes to cut back on the reflection from the candlelight and stared out of the window. Snow swirled close against the glass. Finally he grunted and turned away. "I don't like this a bit. Can't see a thing out there. Do you think they've targeted Mari again? She no longer has the geode that called them before, but one of its crystals is going to be lodged in her heart forever."

Eddy shot a worried look in Mari's direction. "I don't know. I imagine they're drawn to all of us. We're the only ones who know of their existence."

"I agree." Dax stood by the front window and stared into the darkness. Candlelight reflected off the glass. Snowflakes swirled and danced outside. It would be nearly impossible to see these demons—they'd be nothing more than shadows within shadows on a dark night.

Artigos and Gaia led the others from the kitchen into the front room. "Does anyone know if my sword made the trip from Lemuria? I've not used it in many years, but if we're forced into a fight with demonkind, it's another blade for the good guys."

Eddy stood up. "Alton packed it, sir. He insisted we keep it near you. It's out in Dad's Jeep. No one's taken it out of the scabbard, but I'm sure it's okay. I'll go get it for you."

Alton's father had been quiet and withdrawn ever since Mari'd killed his demon. He'd clung to Gaia at first, but today his mind appeared to be working better, as if the man he once was hadn't been entirely lost.

And he was right. His blade was one more crystal sword they hadn't counted on. Eddy glanced at Dax. "It's wrapped in a blanket in the back of the Jeep. I'll go out and get it."

"Not by yourself, you're not." Dax reached for his coat and strapped his scabbard on over it. More relieved than she wanted to admit by Dax's offer, Eddy did the same. They both drew their blades, which glowed brilliantly against the shadows.

"Beats a flashlight." Eddy meant it as a joke, but her

heart pounded and shivers raced along her spine. The sense of something wrong was growing, especially with Bumper growling and staring at the front door as if she expected the demon king himself to barge through.

It took her a few seconds to work up the courage, but Eddy finally grabbed the doorknob, turned it, and slowly pulled the door open just a crack. She used her sword to cast enough light to look for demons. Snow swirled and drifted around the front porch, but all seemed quiet. She glanced over her shoulder at Dax, and they both stepped outside, using the glow from their blades to light the way.

"Hurry." Dax shut the door behind him, and then he went first, carefully walking down the icy front steps. He held his hand out for Eddy, and they waded through the drifts to the driveway where Ed had parked earlier today. There'd only been about six inches of snow on the ground, then.

Now snow buried the wheels past the hubcaps and covered the windshield. Dax stood beside the Jeep while Eddy sheathed DemonSlayer and then climbed into the vehicle. It took her a minute to get Artigos's crystal sword out of the hiding place in the back where she'd left it wrapped in a blanket.

Wind howled, and the snow was blowing sideways by the time Eddy crawled out of the Jeep and shut the door. Dax grabbed her arm and helped her as they struggled through what had suddenly become blizzard conditions between Ed's old Jeep and Spirit and Freedom's front door.

A banshee howl raised the tiny hairs on Eddy's spine. She clutched the sword under her arm and shot a quick glance at Dax. "Was that the wind?"

He shook his head. "I don't think so. Hurry."

The snow was so deep it reached their knees. They tried to follow the same trail they'd made from the house, but the wind practically blew them over, and stinging snow crystals burned wherever they found exposed skin. Eddy tucked herself behind Dax and hung on to his belt as he forced his way through what had become a complete whiteout.

With the electricity out, the neighborhood was black as pitch. None of the neighboring houses showed up at all. It was impossible to see Spirit and Freedom's house in these conditions. Even the brilliant glow from DemonFire barely cut through the darkness. The light reflected off the swirling ice crystals in a disorienting kaleidoscope of sparkling shapes and brilliant flashes, and the fierce wind had them squinting against the sharp bite of blowing ice. The footprints they'd made only moments before were already covered by blowing, drifting snow.

"DemonFire! Which way?" Wind whipped the words out of Dax's mouth, but his sword glowed brightly and pointed to the right of the direction they'd been heading. Dax and Eddy shifted their course, and within seconds they reached the front porch. The howl grew in volume, an angry screech of frustration and demonic wrath. Snow swirled up under the overhang, reaching with icy fingers as if it searched for them.

Eddy clutched the wrapped sword under her arm and drew DemonSlayer with her free hand. She turned away from the door, pointing her crystal blade and its brilliant beam of light toward the yard. Within the swirling snow, black wraiths swarmed overhead like huge vultures circling a carcass. Even though they were formless beneath her sword's light, Eddy knew exactly what had followed them to the house.

"Demons, Dax. Do you see them? They're all around us. Hurry."

He reached for the door and opened it just enough to grab Eddy and shove her inside. Artigos, Darius, and Ed waited in the foyer. Darius had his sword drawn, and he moved quickly to guard the door as Dax slipped through.

Once Dax was in, Darius shut the door and locked it. "I count at least a dozen on the front porch alone. Mari, forget the spells to move us to Lemuria. We need to concentrate on fighting demonkind. Now."

"Well, crap." Mari glanced wildly at her mother. "Grab the spell book, Mom. We need some good, fast, demon-killing spells."

Spirit headed for the bedroom where she'd left the book as Eddy carefully unwrapped the crystal sword.

"Your weapon, sir." She handed the sword to Artigos.

He took the scabbard with a quiet reverence, and merely held it in his hands. Then he raised his head. "My sword is not yet sentient. It's never spoken to me, never guided me, and I've not drawn it for well over ten thousand years. There was always an excuse. I believe now that part of me knew I'd been tainted by demonkind." He sighed and glanced at his wife. "I wasn't worthy of bearing crystal. Hopefully, my blade will forgive me."

He reached for the sword and wrapped his hand around the hilt. Then he lifted his head, stood proudly, and smiled at Gaia. "My beloved wife has forgiven me, and I have great hopes that our son will, as well. Here's hoping the crystal feels the same. I'd hate like the nine hells to see it shatter when I pull it from the scabbard."

Ed raised an eyebrow and grinned at Artigos. "That would definitely ruin the moment."

"Dad!" Eddy snorted and stared at her father. For whatever reason, the two men had hit it off from the beginning, and Ed's easy acceptance of Alton's father had quickly put Artigos at ease.

Ed grinned shamelessly, and even Artigos laughed.

"You're not kidding," he said. Then he slipped the blade out of the scabbard.

"It's yellow!" Eddy glanced at Darius. "Have you ever seen a yellow crystal sword before?"

Artigos frowned at the blade. "It was clear crystal when I was young. I wonder what the significance is." He turned it this way and that, and the blade glowed an incandescent yellow that was brighter than amber and gleamed with the brilliance of sunlight.

"I think it's citrine." Mari glanced up as her mother walked back into the room, spell book in hand. "Is that right?"

Spirit nodded. "Correct. Do you know the crystal's properties?"

"I do. It's one of my favorites." Mari smiled at Artigos. "It holds no negativity. It's a stone of optimism and self-discipline. I think it's supposed to lead to open-minded awareness and better communication."

"Mari's right." Spirit smiled that Earth Mother smile of hers as she leaned over to get a better look at the brilliant yellow facets. "I can't imagine a better crystal for you to carry as you begin your new life, Artigos. It negates narrow-mindedness and helps control anxiety." Gently she rested her fingers on his arm. "It's a happy stone, filled with goodness."

Then she glanced at the snow swirling just beyond the glass window and smiled sweetly. "There's nothing like attacking evil with a crystal sword full of goodness. I imagine it'll really piss off the little bastards."

Mari rolled her eyes. Freedom wrapped an arm around his wife's shoulders. "Let's hope so. You and Mari need to work on your spells. I'll help in any way I'm able. In case you hadn't noticed, dear, demons are massing just outside. It's going to be a long night."

A high-pitched screech echoed above the sound of the wind. Bumper leapt to her feet, barking like mad. Something thumped against the front door, and a subtle vibration passed through the floor. "What the hell was that?" Eddy drew DemonSlayer.

"That, I believe, was the sound of demons knocking," Dax said. He pulled DemonFire from his scabbard. "They want in."

Isra watched from the shadows as her sisters and their terrible guards sat around the gathering hall, chatting like old friends. Bastards. Bastards and traitors, every damned one of them. How could her sisters be so easily swayed by that bitch Selyn?

And that old guy. Artigos? She'd hidden nearby when he'd made that talk filled with lies about working together for the good of Lemuria. What had Lemuria ever done that was good for her? Not a damned thing, that's for sure.

She rubbed her palm against her robe. It still stung where the sword had burned her. For some reason it wasn't healing the way her injuries usually did. The raw and blistered flesh was a constant reminder that she wasn't good enough for one of their fancy crystal swords.

Well, let them try to stop her. She could find the way out, could find the portals that led to the levels where the free folk lived. All she had to do was get out of here and find a plain white robe. No one would know she was the daughter of a slave, but she knew things that someone in the halls above would love to find out—and she was more than willing to share.

Slaves carrying crystal? An exiled leader thinking of making a comeback? It all reeked of treason as far as Isra could tell.

She couldn't care less about the politics of Lemuria, but she damned well didn't want to see her pissy sisters and the no-good bastard guards coming out of this looking like heroes.

No. If anyone was going to look heroic, it would be Isra. Isra the slave. Isra the Forgotten One.

Forget that. They weren't ever going to forget Isra.

Chapter Eighteen

Alton groaned. Ginny placed a cool towel on his head and sat back on her heels, while Taron paced and Roland stared stoically at the bars of solid energy trapping them inside the cell.

"Can you hear me? Alton? C'mon, sweetheart. Wake up." She cast a worried glance at Taron, who just shook his head and stared at his unconscious friend.

"Bastards." Taron turned away. "We had no way to warn any of you. Six frickin' guards. That's all there are, but they're knocking us off, one by one. I feel like such an idiot."

Ginny shook her head. "Don't. We had no way of knowing." She glanced at Roland. "Even Roland didn't realize they were possessed. Their demons have been part of them for so long, they register to our blades as Lemurians, not demonkind. That's probably why they were selected to work on this level. No one would suspect them." She glanced at the glowing bars. "I'm worried about DarkFire. They wouldn't destroy our swords, would they?"

Taron shook his head and flopped down on one of the beds bolted into the wall. "How's he doing? Is he coming around yet?"

Ginny nodded. Alton's eyes flickered. The big guard
had come out of nowhere, hit Alton from behind, and
grabbed HellFire. She didn't know what he'd done with
Alton's sword, but at least he'd shoved Alton into the same
cell she'd been forced into with Taron and Roland.

The guard's companions had hustled the three men
who'd been with Alton on down the passage. She thought
they might be locked in another cell, but she had no way
of knowing. No way of contacting Dawson and Selyn, to
let them know their entire plan was currently facedown in
the toilet.

Alton blinked, his eyes opening and then slowly closing, as if the effort was more than he could bear.

"Alton? I know you're there. Wake up." She leaned
close and kissed him. His lips responded just enough to
tell her he was aware, so she kissed him again.

Taron had said they were a hard-headed bunch, that
Alton would be okay, but until she could ask him and get
an answer . . .

"Ginny?" This time he blinked faster. "What happened?
Where . . . ?"

He tried to sit up. She planted her hand against his chest
and held him down. "Not yet. Give yourself a minute. The
bastard hit you really hard."

"Who hit me?" He turned his head to one side and spotted Roland. "Shit. They've locked us up. Where's Balti? I
swear I'm going to kill that son of a . . ."

"No." Ginny helped him sit up, since he was obviously
almost back to normal. "Balti's locked up in another cell, I
think, along with Ragus, the guard who brought me down,
the ones who came with you, and even Grayl, the guy in
charge of the prison. There are six guards—they're wardens, actually, part of the force guarding Selyn and the
other women—and they're picking us off, one by one. We

can't use our minds to warn anyone because of the damned energy grid, and they've taken our swords."

"HellFire?" Alton reached for his scabbard.

"They took the scabbards and the swords." Taron helped Alton over to the bed so he could sit down. "I think the guards are afraid to touch them for fear of retribution. We're hoping our blades are okay, but there's no sense of them."

"Well, nine hells. That sucks." Alton rubbed the back of his head where sticky blood matted his blond hair. "What'd he hit me with? A hammer?"

Ginny sat beside him. "No. It looked like he used the flat of his steel blade. They want us alive, for some reason."

Alton cocked his head and stared at Roland. "Do you know any of these men?"

Roland shook his head. "No. I did my best to avoid the guards when I went below in the beginning. The last time I was down there, the six had already come to this level. Their uniforms are slightly different—a lighter shade of blue—but unless you were looking for clues, you'd never guess they weren't regular Lemurian guardsmen. I imagine this particular group was chosen for that reason—their demons are so well hidden within, our swords can't sense them."

Ginny clasped her hands and stared at her feet. "I think I know why they want us alive."

Alton merely gazed at her. Then he nodded. "They want to possess our bodies. They want us acting on behalf of demonkind, but if we're familiar, the people will accept our decisions. Demonkind will have achieved a bloodless takeover of an entire civilization." He glanced at the sticky blood on his fingertips and touched the back of his head again. "Well, almost bloodless. Nine hells but that hurts!"

"How could we ever think demons were mindless?"

Ginny felt like crying. "It's an f'ing brilliant plan, if you ask me."

Alton wrapped his fingers around her hand and squeezed. "Dax said he never knew of a government on Abyss. He had no idea there were leaders, and yet there's definite organization here. Even different kinds of demons. The one in my father is nothing like the demons in the wardens. Thousands of years worth of planning, a slow buildup of demonic infiltration into an established society. It all appears to be coming to a climax at once.

"I wish we knew what Artigos was doing."

Alton's remark reminded Ginny of how quickly time was passing, and how all of their plans were falling apart. "Artigos the Just or your dad, Alton? Which one?"

"I've essentially written off my father. I'm referring to my grandfather, Artigos the Just. I wonder if he's got the women working with the guards or if they're down there now, trying to kill each other." He leaned his head against the stone wall and shut his eyes. "Nine hells. Or, Ginny, as you would so eloquently put it, this has all turned into one giant clusterfuck."

"Not yet." Roland stood up and folded his arms across his massive chest. "Dawson and Selyn are still out there, and both of them are armed with crystal. Somehow, we need to contact them." He glared at the sizzling bars of energy that locked them and their thoughts inside the cell. "Unfortunately, I haven't figured out exactly how we're going to do that yet."

Dawson hadn't expected the way he'd feel after making love with Selyn for most of the night. He hadn't been ready for the overwhelming need to protect her, to keep her safe. But right now, as they climbed the stairs to the upper level and slipped through the occasional portal, he knew he'd rather be doing anything other than leading her into danger.

There was no doubt in his mind he'd gone and fallen in love. Even before they'd actually had sex last night, he'd fallen, but every touch, every caress, every kiss and cry and climax had merely cemented a feeling that was already so deeply entrenched in his soul it was never going away.

He knew it was impossible. She was immortal, a woman who would live until she chose death, until she turned her soul loose to exist beyond the veil. He was merely human, a mortal with the lifespan of an insect compared to Selyn's.

Yet wasn't everything he'd experienced in the past couple of weeks impossible? Hell, Aunt Fiona had to be laughing herself silly over the conundrum he'd gotten himself into. He could just hear her now, cackling and slapping her knee over little Daws, in love with a woman who couldn't possibly exist.

"Can it, Fiona," he mumbled.

"What?" Selyn stopped and turned around.

"Nothing," he said, but he grabbed her hand and kissed her, just the same. "I love you, Selyn. I wasn't going to say anything because it's not the right time or place, but I have to tell you how I feel. I love you. I know it's impossible, but . . ."

Her eyes had gone so big and blue he wondered if she was going to hit him, or run screaming, or some other weird thing, but then she merely smiled, leaned close, and kissed him. "Good," she said. "Because I love you, too, and I wasn't quite sure how to tell you."

"You do? Why not?" He reached for her but she backed away.

Smiling, she shook her head. "Think about it. You are

human with a wonderful lifetime of experiences. I'm a Lemurian slave. I've never been anywhere, done anything, experienced anything. Besides, I probably won't survive the coming battle." She glanced ruefully at the glowing sword in her hand. "I'm not meant to carry crystal, Dawson. I'm not an aristocrat, not one of the free folk. I'm really not worthy of crystal."

He stared at her and didn't know where to start. She stood on the step above him, absolutely regal in her cotton scrubs with the gold circlet holding her long, dark hair back from her face. The crystal blade glowed in her hand, her eyes shimmered in the flickering light, and she was so much more than she'd just described. So much better.

His throat tightened so badly he could hardly speak. "You'd damned well better survive, Selyn, because if you die, you'll be responsible for my death, too. You don't want that on your conscience. You are so far above the so-called Lemurian aristocrats that I won't even dignify your stupid remark with an answer. I love you, and you love me, and that's all that matters. That, and freeing this world from demonkind."

He heard the sound of her swallow. "Then I guess we'd better hurry," she whispered. "Demonkind doesn't wait."

He nodded. "Neither will Artigos the Just and his army. If we don't get moving, they'll pass us by."

She nodded and took his hand. They'd left long before the women warriors would even have risen, and Dawson knew they'd made good time. He recognized the way now and knew they were almost to the level where the free folk lived.

He wondered if Selyn hated that title as much as he did. Free folk meant there were those who were not free. At least that had finally changed, but what was that freedom going to give them? Would the women—once slaves—

find acceptance among the rest of Lemurian society, or would they forever be treated as a lower caste?

If it weren't for the risk to so many people and so many worlds, he'd just say to hell with them and let the demons have them. What a wasted society! Yes, it had turned out wonderful citizens like Roland and Taron and Alton, but they appeared to be the exception rather than the rule.

More of them were like Gaia, Alton's mother. She was a nice lady, but she'd known of the slaves and never said a word. He wondered how she'd managed to live with that knowledge for so many thousands of years. Of course, it was probably easy for her to ignore the plight of the women warriors—Gaia had lived up here in luxury while Selyn and the other women toiled below.

He could feel his blood pressure rising when Selyn stopped beside what he recognized as the final portal. "This will drop us into the main passageway near Alton's quarters," he said, recalling Ginny's description. "There's an alcove where we can hide while you try to contact Alton, Ginny, Taron, or Roland."

Selyn glanced around them and then whispered, "Okay. I can find it. Maybe you should wait here until I make contact. I'll be right back."

He grabbed her wrist as she turned around. "Not on your life. We go together, or not at all."

She looked at him for a long, silent moment. Then she nodded, just a short, sharp jerk of her head, grabbed his hand, and slipped through the portal. Dawson followed her out into a dark passageway and then took the lead. He tugged her toward a darker area that turned into a small cubby cut into the rock for storage.

She held her finger to his lips and closed her eyes. He knew she searched for their friends, so he stationed himself near the entry and listened for the sound of footsteps or voices.

It was still early, and the tunnels were quiet. Lights barely illuminated the way. He knew the lights would slowly brighten to mimic the rising sun and light the passages in a way akin to daylight within a couple hours.

Selyn touched his arm. "There's nothing. No sound of any of them. What do we do?"

"Let me try something." Dawson unsheathed his sword. Though the blade had not spoken, he hoped the sentience was alert within the ruby crystal. Concentrating on the blade, he softly asked, "Can you sense the presence of DarkFire or HellFire? The swords that belong to Ginny or Alton? Where are they?"

The blade pulsed ruby red, then dimmed. There was no voice, no other sense of life, and yet Dawson knew. He raised his head and stared at Selyn. "Did you get that, or was it my imagination?"

"Only if your imagination said they're locked up in cells on the level below us."

"Exactly. Let's go back and contact Artigos. He needs to know. Then we have to see if we can get them out."

Selyn nodded. Dawson checked the passageway, and the two of them raced back to the portal. Selyn slipped through with Dawson right behind her. It was much faster going down to a level where Selyn could connect with Artigos, but Dawson was still terribly aware of the passage of time, of the sense of danger growing all around.

Suddenly Selyn grabbed his arm and dragged him into a dark niche in the wall. Daws hadn't even heard the sound of soldiers, but they marched by seconds after he and Selyn had slipped out of the main passage. He watched as the three men passed. Their eyes stared straight ahead. One of them had what appeared to be fresh blood staining the front of his blue robe.

Dawson and Selyn waited for what felt like hours. Finally, Dawson checked the passage and dragged Selyn after him as he raced to the portal that would lead to the next set of stairs. They slipped through, heading to the level below where Selyn thought she'd be close enough to contact Artigos.

There was a powerful sense of events colliding, of too many things coming together at once, and they weren't coming together at all the way Dawson had hoped or expected. Hanging on to Selyn, he raced down the stairs and prayed for the impossible—that they'd have enough time to save their friends, stop the demons, and maybe even live to tell about it.

Isra heard the sound of footsteps and harsh breathing and she panicked. Which way to run? Then she spotted a dark niche along the wall and slipped inside. Her brown slave's robe blended perfectly with the gray stone, and she knew no one would see her unless they were actually looking for her.

She'd barely stepped into the darkness when that bitch Selyn and her human boyfriend raced past her, practically flying down the steps. Now where in the nine hells would they be going in such a rush?

She stuck her head out and watched until they were out of sight, but as tempted as she was to follow and find out what was going on, she was almost to the level where the free folk lived. She'd never been here before, but she was absolutely sure the actual civilization of Lemuria was merely one portal away.

As soon as Dawson and Selyn were out of hearing, Isra slipped out of her hiding place and started up the stairs once more. Her legs ached, and her nerves had her jumping at every sound, thank goodness. Otherwise she might have run right into Selyn, and that wouldn't do at all.

She reached the portal after a few hard minutes of climbing. Then she took a moment to look back down the stairs. Light faded into darkness, but that's exactly what she was leaving. Darkness and drudgery and not a single person who actually cared about her.

If anyone had thought she mattered, she would have had a crystal sword. But no, Isra didn't count. She'd never counted, but she would. After today, they'd all wish they'd been nicer to her. Every single one. She was leaving them behind and moving forward.

Nothing but good things awaited her. She was positive.

With a prayer to whatever gods heard the plea of slaves, she slipped through the portal into a wide, well-lit passage— directly into the midst of three Lemurian guards on patrol.

She recognized them immediately—and they knew her. They were part of the same group of guards who had watched over the Forgotten Ones for Isra's entire life, and one of them grabbed her before she had a chance to run. She grunted and twisted out of his grasp. The next guard grabbed for her robe, but she turned toward him, pushed at his chest, raised her knee, and planted it between his legs as hard as she could. He screamed and clutched for his crotch as Isra tore free, falling to her knees on the stone floor as the tension from his hold gave way.

She rolled, scrambling on her hands and knees out of the third man's reach, but the first guard had recovered. He jumped over his fallen comrade and wrapped his thick fingers in Isra's dark hair, jerking her to a stop.

He used her hair to drag her to her knees and then to her feet while she twisted and fought like a wild thing. The one she'd kneed rose slowly to his feet with a look on his face that spelled her death.

So be it. She had little to live for anyhow, though it didn't seem fair that Selyn ran free while she, Isra, would die here. The guard hauled back his fist. She had a moment to choose whether to face her death or shut her eyes.

Then the first guard blocked the other man's fist. "Wait," he said. "First let's find out why she's here."

"The bitch kneed me in the balls. She dies."

"After we find out why she's here." The guard holding her by the hair shook his fist. Isra grabbed his arm to take the pressure off her head and neck.

"I have important information for the Council of Nine," she said, praying these idiots would know who she was talking about.

"What kind of information?" The guard shook his arm again, shaking her like a rag doll.

Her feet kicked mere inches above the ground, and her arms ached from holding her weight off her hair. "Information for them alone," she gasped. "Turn me loose."

"I think not."

At least he lowered his arm so that her feet found the stone floor. She went from her tiptoes to full contact, breathing hard and fast. "Take me to the council. I have news of an insurrection in the slave quarters."

The three looked at each other, and the one who held her, who was obviously their leader, nodded. "Drago's still at the vortex, working on the portal. We'll take her there." He turned Isra loose and shoved her toward the one she'd kneed in the groin. "Bring her."

This one intended to hurt her. He wrapped his meaty fingers around her upper arm and tightened them in a painful grasp. "With pleasure," he said. Then he jerked so hard she was afraid he'd dislocated her shoulder, but he didn't let up on the pressure enough for her to find out. Biting back a cry of pain, Isra stumbled after the three men as they marched quickly along the passageway.

She had no idea where they were, what passages they followed. She'd hoped to see the fabled plaza with the walls of crystal and gold, but all she saw was gray stone and dirt floors. They moved quickly, following narrow passages that must have been designed for the guards to move separately from the free folk. She wasn't sure. Her shoulder hurt so badly she didn't really care.

But they'd pay. She had no doubt they'd pay for what they were doing to her. She had information this Drago would want. Information that would mean the end to her sisters' foolish dreams of freedom.

But were they so foolish? She'd had them too. Wasn't that why she'd run away, why she was putting up with the cruelty from the stupid guard? He jerked her arm hard, and she cried out. Then she bit back any further sound. She wasn't going to give him the satisfaction of making her cry.

They passed into a wider tunnel that was well lighted. A loud roar echoed off the walls and made the floor vibrate beneath her feet, but she had no idea what made the sound.

They rounded a corner, and she saw it—a solid wall of molten gold pouring from the ceiling and disappearing somehow into the ground. There was no sign of heat, no smoke from any fire, but the guards continued walking toward the wall as if they intended to walk through it.

They'd burn! Didn't they know that metal hot enough to flow would burn the flesh from their bones? She'd seen it in the mines, when there'd been an accident so many years ago, when one of the younger women had fallen.

She hadn't even had time to scream. The image of the girl's startled eyes and open mouth as she'd fallen into the cauldron of molten gold filled Isra's mind. Ignoring the pain in her shoulder she struggled, twisting and turning, pulling as hard as she could, but the guard merely laughed and kept walking.

He reached the wall of gold, and without a moment's hesitation, stepped into the flow. She knew she was going to die, knew it was all . . . all an illusion. They passed through as if it were nothing but a cool flow of air.

The guards were laughing. All of them laughing at her because she'd been ignorant of the truth. She held her head high and refused to look any of them in the eye. Still laughing, the bastard pulled her along the tunnel until they reached a larger cavern. A man wearing the flowing white robe of an aristocrat stood before the opposite wall.

He held what at first appeared to be a crystal sword, but then Isra realized the blade was black obsidian, which made no sense. Didn't a black blade mean the owner had died? Whatever, his was black, and he held it up at shoulder height with the tip pointed toward the wall of the cave. Energy poured from the blade, and a sense of evil surrounded the entire area.

The man turned and sneered at the guard in charge. "I told you not to disturb me. This is difficult work. Who is she?"

"Councilman Drago, she claims to have information of an insurrection among the slaves. We thought you should know."

The councilman cocked his head and stared at her as if she were a speck on an otherwise clean plate. "Let her go." He lowered his sword and sheathed it at his hip. "So, you have information for me? Why me? Why not Chancellor Alton, once of Artigos? Shouldn't you want to share your news with our revered leader?"

She shook her head. With a name like Alton of Artigos, he must be related to that old man. "No, sir. I think it's his father who's leading the insurrection. Or maybe his grand-father. He's an old man."

"What old man?" The councilman stalked across the cavern and grabbed her chin like she was a little kid. He pinched it hard between his fingers. "Look at me. What old man?"

It was hard to talk with him holding her this way, the bastard. "I don't know. He's an old man who's been imprisoned in the slave levels since before I was born. He's free now."

He turned loose of her chin and rubbed his own with a thoughtful expression on his face. "Artigos the Just has been detained since the great move. Given time, he could gain the citizens' trust once again." He glanced over his shoulder at the point on the wall where he'd been working. "We're too close. We can't let him screw this up, but I'm going to need a little more time to open the portal to Abyss."

To Abyss? He's opening a portal for demonkind?

His hand streaked forward before Isra could react. He grabbed her by the throat. "What else do you know of this insurrection, young lady? What of the guards? Were they overwhelmed by a group of women?" He laughed. "I find that a bit difficult to believe."

She shook her head, but her mind was spinning. He'd not cut off her air, though she knew he could crush her throat with very little effort. But did she want to tell him everything? If she did, what would she have left to bargain with?

And did she really want to help a man who was working with demonkind? She hadn't imagined anything so awful. Her mother had been a warrior who fought against the spawn of hell, yet this man wanted to help those evil creatures enter Lemuria?

Dear gods, what had she done?

He squeezed her throat tighter. Did it really matter?

"I'm waiting," he said. His fingers tightened even more around her throat. Gagging, struggling for air, Isra realized she very much wanted to survive.

"The guards joined the women." She could barely get the words past the constriction around her neck. He lifted her off her feet, holding her by the throat, and he glared at her with eyes that sparkled with madness. Madness and something more. Demonkind lurked behind his eyes. Was Drago possessed? Was everything Selyn said really true?

Isra clutched at Drago's arm with both hands, but he didn't seem to notice. A terrible, soul-deep sense of despair washed away all hope of survival. Isra was going to die. She'd taken her chance and she'd lost, but a last burst of anger kept her talking. At least she wouldn't die alone.

She barely managed to force the words out of her rapidly swelling throat. "They formed a single army. The old man . . . he leads," she gasped. "They're on their way here now, over one hundred strong, armed with . . ."

He cursed, flexed his arm, and threw her against the wall. Isra's head slammed into rock, and she slid bonelessly to the floor. Lights flashed behind her eyes. She felt herself fading, falling deeper into darkness. Still, even dying, she knew she had the last laugh.

The damned fool! What irony! He'd shut her up too quickly. She hadn't told him everything. He had no idea the women and the guards were all armed with crystal.

Blinking slowly, Isra tried to focus on her surroundings, but everything seemed to swirl and pulse in clouds of darkness. Was this death, this horrible icy chill that brushed over and around her skin?

She took a couple of deep breaths and planted her

hands on the rocky floor. Shoving with all her might, fighting the nausea that warred with the pain rocketing through her head, she finally managed to push herself up enough to lean against the rough wall of the cavern.

Everything spun and whirled, as if her body floated, and there was no particular sense of up or down. She fought a wave of nausea that almost pulled her under. If only things would hold still for a moment!

Light flashed and drew her blurred gaze. Blinking slowly, she forced herself to concentrate on the dark and eerie glow on the far side of the chamber. It pulsed with a powerful sense of anger, almost as if it lived. Squinting against the pain in her head and the sense she was still falling, she stared at the deep, red light.

Slowly, Isra brought it into focus. She blinked again, not quite believing what she saw with her own eyes.

Black figures oozed from the spinning center, sliding along the wall, gathering in roiling clouds of darkness on the floor beneath what could only be a portal to Abyss.

Drago had succeeded. The passage was open. Isra swallowed back a scream as one of the wraiths slid across the cavern floor, oozed over her leg, and floated around her body. Was it testing her? Trying to gain entrance to her soul?

"No!" She screamed at the thing, swung her hands, and tried to push it away. She merely succeeded in shoving her fingers through the mist. There was no substance to fight, nothing beyond the chill of death clinging to the demon wraith.

Scrambling awkwardly to her feet, Isra pressed her palms to the wall behind her. Moaning, she held herself upright with nothing more than the strength of her fear.

More wraiths poured through the passageway. The black cloud of demonkind grew, and the temperature around her dropped. She stared into the mass, terrified by the glimpses she caught of teeth and eyes, of long, sharp claws and scaled bodies.

Insubstantial as air and cold as ice, yet still they came, streaming into the cavern, filling it with their loathsome presence. Then the temperature dropped even more, and her breath hissed out from between her lips, visible as a white fog against the darkness.

A long-fingered hand slipped out of the portal. A scaled arm stretched out, then another arm and another, each with long, sharp talons that wrapped themselves around the stone edges of the portal, finding purchase on the rough-hewn rock. Four multi-jointed arms pulled something yet unseen forward, as if it aided its own birth from a dark and hideous womb.

It was mist, and yet not, this new creature entering the cavern. Isra trembled against the wall as slowly, carefully, the thing reformed amid the swirling mass of demon wraiths.

Reformed and stood upright, looking about with a visage that could only have come from Isra's worst night-mares. With one set of multi-jointed arms, it swept through the mass of demons, dividing them into three groups. Then, with a loud banshee cry, it sent one roiling mass of darkness toward another portal, a passage that swirled in shades of green. The second group shot out of the cavern and down a narrow tunnel that must lead to another portal.

At this point, Isra didn't care. She only knew she had to get back to Lemuria and warn someone—anyone. She'd never imagined anything so monstrous. Not this. Not de-monkind poised to attack her world. She watched, wide-eyed, as the rest of the evil creatures formed into the shape of a spear, hovered for a moment as if gathering strength, and then shot down the passage to Lemuria.

Horror-struck, Isra covered her mouth with her hand, holding back a scream of terror. She did not want to draw attention to herself. The huge demon remained. It stood, still as death, not five feet away from her—watching her.

Red light from the portal glowed dimly through its body, lighting the evil creature from within. For a long moment, the thing stared at her, almost as if it memorized her features.

Then it, too, turned into mist and followed the final group of demonkind to Lemuria.

Chapter Nineteen

Selyn clutched Dawson's hand so hard her nails dug into his flesh. "I've reached Artigos the Just," she said. "They're still a few levels below us, but moving fast. He said they're all ready to fight. We need to get back up there."

Dawson nodded. "I hope it's not too hard to find the prison cells. We have to free Alton and Ginny. With any luck, they'll know where Roland and Taron are." He glanced at the ruby sword in his hand. "It's not actually speaking, but somehow we're communicating. Hopefully our blades can lead us."

Selyn stuck her head through the portal for just a second. Then she was back. "Now," she said. "It's clear. Let's go." She stepped through the portal and raced up the flight of stairs.

Dawson ran behind her, though they paced themselves as best they could. In mere minutes they'd reached the level where the free folk lived. Dawson stepped through the portal with Selyn on his heels, expecting a quiet corridor and finding chaos.

Men and women in white robes raced along the passageway. Some were scratched and bleeding. All of them appeared terrified, panic-stricken, and out of control. Dawson grabbed one man by the arm and forced him to a halt.

"What's going on here? What's happening?"

The Lemurian didn't even notice that he spoke to a human. "Demonkind! Demons everywhere." Eyes wide, he struggled to break free of Dawson's grasp.

Dawson glanced at the sword strapped to the man's back. "Didn't you stay to fight? Why haven't you drawn your sword?"

The Lemurian looked at him as if he were absolutely nuts. "Fight demons? No. The soldiers will fight. I'm not a warrior."

"Then why do you carry crystal? Pull your blade, man. Defend your world!"

A woman screamed. Selyn grabbed Dawson's arm. "We have to hurry. Forget him."

Dawson shook his head. "We're going to need all the soldiers we can find, or demonkind will win. Draw your sword, damn you!"

Blinking wildly, the aristocrat drew his sword. The blade had no more glow than dark glass, and his arm trembled so badly he almost dropped the thing.

The crystal sparked a brilliant blue, and then it shattered. The man threw the useless pommel to the ground, ripped free of Dawson's grasp, and ran. Dawson stared at the tiny shards of glass littering the tunnel as a fresh wave of terrified Lemurians raced by. A soul had once resided in that blade. He wondered briefly what happened to the brave warrior who had been paired with a useless coward.

Then Selyn tugged his arm once again, and he followed her against the tide of Lemurians. He took the lead after a few steps. Dawson wasn't sure how he knew where to go, what turns to take, what portals to pass through, but somehow he led Selyn with unerring accuracy through the dark passages circumventing the main living areas of the free folk.

It had to be the sword. Without words, without any overt communication, it somehow led him through unfamiliar territory to a dark passage. A passage Dawson was certain led directly down to the prison cells.

He glanced toward Selyn. She nodded. "I think this is it. My sword isn't actually speaking, but how else could we have both known to come here?"

"Let's go." He started off along the main passage. Selyn grabbed his arm and pointed to another tunnel. "Wait. This is the way I have to go. I think the swords are this way."

"Go, then." He wrapped his fingers around the back of her neck and pulled her close, kissed her hard and fast. "Be careful, Selyn. I can't lose you. Not when I've finally found you."

She stared at him for a long moment, unblinking. "You too, Daws. I love you."

Then she spun away and raced along the passage, into the shadows and out of sight.

Dawson watched until she was gone. Then he tightened his grasp on his ruby sword and ran toward the flickering light reflecting off the walls at the end of the long, dark tunnel.

The cries and screams, the banshee howls, and the thick stench of sulfur faded into the background.

Eddy wiped the sweat off her forehead and glanced toward Artigos. They'd fought demonkind throughout the long night and the older man was breathing hard, leaning on his glimmering citrine sword, but he had a grin on his face that practically stretched ear to ear. Gaia was giving him hell about something, but she was fighting a smile as well, and if Eddy didn't know for a fact that the demons outside the door were massing for another attack, she'd have thought they were all having a gay old time.

"Here. I brought you some cold water."

She glanced up as Dax handed her the chilled glass, took it without a word, and drank deeply. She drained the glass and wiped her mouth with the back of her hand. "Thank you. How's Dad doing? I couldn't believe it when the damned creatures drew blood."

Dax sighed as he took the empty glass from her. "We've known from the beginning that demons are continuing to evolve. I think we need to be ready for anything at this point, but your dad is fine. Spirit has him bandaged." Even Dax's smile looked tired. "He's enjoying the attention. He and Freedom are in there bonding over their war wounds."

Eddy nodded, too tired to answer. At least Freedom's scratches were small. She'd been afraid he might hurt himself again, especially since he was finally recovering from the surgery that had brought Mari home in the first place.

Eddy lifted the curtain and glanced out the window. Mari stood outside in the fresh snow with her arms raised. She and Darius had surrounded the house with salt to slow the demons, and now she was casting a spell, one that would hopefully draw away the creatures' strength.

Darius stood beside her, sword at the ready. Black soot covered the snow from the many demons he'd already killed. Eddy, Dax, and Artigos had slaughtered hundreds more, both inside and out of the house, but there was a bit of a lull now, and, hopefully, time for Mari to use her developing magic to weaken the onslaught of demonkind.

Spirit stepped up beside Eddy and peered out the window. "So many of them. Is there no end? You've killed thousands."

Eddy slowly shook her head. "There must be a new

portal on the mountain, but damn! I hate this not knowing. That's the only explanation. I wish we knew what Alton and Ginny were doing. I can't understand why we haven't heard from anyone. I was sure Dawson would contact us by now."

She glanced at Spirit, and felt the anxiety pouring off of Mari's mom in waves. When Eddy and Mari had been little, Spirit's long hair had been a brilliant red. Now it hung in long, gray waves down her back.

She wondered if, now that Mari was a full-blown witch, Spirit's hair would finally turn snow-white from worry. She'd blamed the girls for every gray hair when they were teens.

She was still a beautiful woman, albeit—right now— a worried mother. Eddy couldn't blame her. Mari'd insisted on going outside in the storm with only Darius to protect her. Now she chanted something Eddy couldn't hear, standing like an ancient priestess with her arms raised to the gray predawn sky and her head thrown back, her blond hair cascading down her back. Snow swirled around her, clinging to her long-sleeved top and her flowing skirts. Light from a Coleman lantern turned the big flakes of snow into glittering gold and silver coins.

Darius lunged forward and slashed his blade through the falling snow, and another demon flickered and burst into flame. Mari didn't even flinch. Her arms stretched higher, and as Eddy watched, the snow appeared to part overhead and fall to either side of the witch and her Lemurian warrior.

It swirled about with dark forms all around. In spite of Mari's chant, the sense of evil grew stronger, the feeling that there was nothing to stop the tide of demons circling about the house. The salt appeared to be holding as a line of protection for now, but it felt like such a fragile barrier against the constant attack of demonkind.

Bumper trotted across the room, stood on her hind

legs, and looked out the window, growling, but Willow remained silent.

Artigos and Gaia joined Eddy, Dax, and Spirit at the window.

Artigos gave Spirit a quick hug. "She is truly a warrior, your daughter. Fearless and of strong will." When Spirit nodded, as if unable to speak, Artigos glanced at Eddy and added softly, "As is my son. I have much to atone for, when this is over. I pray to the gods he will forgive me."

Eddy glanced at Alton's father, a man she'd wanted to throttle just a few days ago. Much had changed in just a few hours. From a horrible and cruel man possessed by a demon, he'd awakened with the mind of a small and trusting child. He'd not stayed that way for long. His transformation had continued, until Eddy wondered if this was the man Gaia had fallen in love with. There was much of Alton in this version of the man they were getting to know without his demon.

He was proving himself to be charming and good-natured, with a sharp wit. He'd fought bravely with his citrine sword, and many demons had died. Though his face bore bloody scratches from talons and fangs, he'd not wanted to take the time to see to his wounds.

Eddy couldn't wait for Alton to meet this new and improved version of his father. She rested her fingers on his arm and smiled at him. "I imagine Alton will be more than willing to forgive, once we're back in Lemuria. Once demonkind is finally destroyed. He's going to be thrilled to have his real father back."

Light flickered outside. At first, Eddy thought the lantern had gone out.

Spirit screamed. Freedom and Ed raced in from the kitchen. Eddy and Dax lunged for the door with Artigos right behind.

Dax flung open the door, and the three of them ran into the storm with swords drawn. There was no sign of Mari.

"Where the hell did she go?" Eddy screamed at Dax over the banshee cries and wailing shrieks of demons.

"She's here. Quickly! Help us!" Darius's strained and breathless voice came from within a seething, shrieking cloud of demons.

Mari's chant was barely audible against the sound of demonkind. The only thing that marked her presence was the spark of flames from Darius's sword, and the stench of demons dying.

Calling on DemonSlayer, Eddy dove into the fight.

Alton stared at the energy flowing between them and freedom, and he wanted to rip the impenetrable bars of light right out of the walls. He glanced helplessly at Ginny, then toward Taron and Roland. "What if we concentrate our energy on the controls? Do you think, working together, we can shut this thing off?"

Ginny leapt to her feet. "We don't have to. There's Dawson!"

"Alton! Ginny? Thank goodness. We've been trying to find you guys. Shit." Daws skidded to a stop in front of their cell. "How do I shut this off?"

"Controls are there, just beside the opening." Alton gestured toward his right.

Dawson pulled a lever, and the bars disappeared. "What happened?"

Alton raced out of the open cell and headed down the passage. "Possessed guards from the slaves' level. C'mon. We've got more guys locked up." He flipped the lever holding Balti and the others inside the next cell. "Any idea where our swords are?"

"Selyn's gone after them. She headed down another passage. Follow me." Dawson took off running.

Alton grabbed Ginny's hand, and the others followed. He heard the distant sound of shrieks and demonic cries. "What the nine hells is going on up there?"

Dawson glanced back as he rounded a corner. "Demons have invaded Lemuria. I have no idea where they're coming from, but the people are retreating in panic. One guy drew his sword after I ordered him to fight, and the damned thing shattered. It's chaos up there."

"Dawson? Hurry. They're here."

Selyn's voice came from the end of the passage. Alton's longer stride took him past Dawson, and he was the first to reach Selyn. She was dragging the bundled swords out of a cabinet. The lock was melted, the door bent.

Her sword glowed brilliantly.

Alton and Ginny grabbed their swords. The others found theirs, going unerringly to the right ones. It appeared all of them were linked to their weapons, sentient or not.

"What now?" Dawson leaned close and gave Selyn a quick, possessive kiss.

Alton had no control over the grin he flashed at Ginny. It appeared their veterinarian had made excellent use of his time. "What of the women? And my grandfather?" Alton strapped on his scabbard and reached for HellFire.

Selyn answered. "They're almost here. They were only a couple of levels behind us, all armed with crystal. It appears the sentience within the swords has imparted battle knowledge to all of us." She grinned. "I actually know how to use this thing! Did you see what we did to that lock?"

"I did. Damn." Alton glanced down the long passage. "We need to shut that portal once again. I think one of the council members is opening it. Drago, most likely. Balti says he's been spending time in the vortex chamber."

Roland nodded in agreement as he checked his scabbard and sword. "Someone's opening it. I've not been able to keep the blasted thing closed, but I've never caught anyone down there working it."

Alton nodded. "We'll deal with the portal. You and your men see what you can do against the demons who've invaded. If you see men you're sure of, you might be able to turn their swords to crystal. Whatever it takes, we've got to win this one."

"Godspeed." Roland bowed his head in a subtle show of respect to Alton. Then he turned toward his men.

Balti, Ragus, and the other guards gathered before him. The big guard made eye contact with each one before turning back to Alton. "We go now, Chancellor, to fight demonkind. The gods' strength to all of us." He raised his sword high. "For Lemuria," he shouted.

His men joined in. "For Lemuria." Roland turned and winked at Alton, and then, running at full speed, he led his small band toward the distant cries coming from the direction of the great plaza.

Alton held Ginny's hand, but he addressed Selyn. "Can you reach Artigos? Has he gotten to this level yet?"

She shook her head. "No. I'm still trying. I give them about ten more minutes. It's not easy to move such a large group along those narrow passages."

"When he arrives, tell him we've been invaded, that some of the Lemurian guards are actually possessed. At least six of them at this level. Taron, I want you to shut down the portal. Your blade will know how. Ginny and I will go after Maxl and Drago. If it means their deaths, so be it. We cannot allow demonkind to prevail."

"Dawson!"

Selyn's scream echoed off the tunnel walls as the six possessed Lemurian guards raced into the room with their black swords drawn. Alton didn't have time to consider the meaning of the obsidian blades. He was too busy defending himself from their attack.

Ginny practically flew at the first of the men. Her blade clashed with his with the sound of breaking glass, and yet they remained whole. Sparks flew, and the stench of sulfur filled the small cavern.

Alton fought back an overwhelming need to rush to Ginny's aid. She was a warrior, a powerful fighter, and it was six to five—they were outnumbered and outsized, battling six huge, trained guardsmen. He'd be lucky to survive his own battle.

Taron engaged two of the men, slashing and stabbing, using his crystal as if it were the sharpest of steel blades. There was no hesitation in the sword that Alton could see, no turning away from drawing blood, and Taron buried his blade deep in the belly of the smaller of the two men he battled.

He barely managed to twist away in time before the second was on him again, but Alton was fighting for his life and couldn't see the final outcome.

He had to concentrate on his own footwork, his own fight. Had to trust that Ginny was able to hold her own, that Dawson and Selyn were capable of defending themselves. He heard Selyn scream, but he couldn't look. Heard Dawson's shout and then a curse, and Ginny's cry of triumph.

His own opponent drove him hard, backing him against the cavern wall, and still Alton fought on, with neither of them gaining the upper hand. Anger drove Alton, that this creature should defile his world, should threaten the peace all Lemurians held dear. He lunged forward, driving with his blade, slashing through the blue robe of the guardsman, burying his blade in the man's chest.

There was no hesitation this time. No sense that HellFire regretted taking a life or worried about a life force being used by the demons, and it dawned on Alton, as he felt the body fall from his blade, that these men were already dead.

That explained the black obsidian blades—he'd always thought a blade only turned black when its owner died. These men were already dead, their Lemurian souls long gone.

They were nothing more than avatars, animated by demonkind just as demons had animated the ceramic figurines on Earth.

Dawson had never, not in his wildest dreams, imagined that his training with a rapier in college would ever come in handy, but as he slashed and lunged and thrust with his ruby blade, he felt the moves coming back as if he'd never left his training in all the years since his studies at UC Davis.

He glanced at Selyn and had to force himself to look away. She was truly a warrior with her flashing eyes and her look of grim determination. She fought her opponent with grace and style, and it was obvious the man hadn't expected a woman of such beauty to show so much skill.

Taron shouted, and Dawson saw one of the big Lemurian's opponents go down. Demonic mist burst from the fallen guard, and Taron caught it with crystal. The second guard lunged forward, and Dawson lost them in his peripheral vision. Only Taron had faced two, and from what little he knew of the man, Dawson could already hear the tales he and Alton would be telling when this was over.

Dawson's opponent was growing desperate, thrusting awkwardly now, breathing hard, and going for the kill with more force than skill. Dawson eluded the man's blade as he spun on the balls of his feet and twisted away, first to the right, then to the left.

He suddenly realized he was actually grinning. He hadn't had this much fun in years, and he wanted to shout with the joy of the battle, the knowledge that he fought beside a woman he loved, that he fought for a world that had been nothing more than myth and legend.

He, Dawson Buck, small town veterinarian, was fighting demons with a magical sword in another dimension. Damn. Aunt Fiona would love this!

He parried a strong blow and went in for the kill just as Taron's final opponent went down. The huge guard Taron had fought was mortally wounded, but he managed a powerful kick as he fell, catching Dawson behind his left knee. The force of the blow buckled Dawson's leg. It folded beneath him just as his opponent slashed wildly at his chest.

Dawson felt the burn of the obsidian blade as it pierced his side, heard the scrape of obsidian against bone, and felt a rush of anger from his sword, that any demon should have harmed the one who wielded this blade.

Vaguely, he heard Selyn's scream and Alton's curse, but pain engulfed him and weakness drove him to his knees. His sword leapt from his nerveless fingers and impaled itself in the one who'd stabbed him.

Dawson stared, fascinated as his amazing ruby blade just flew out of his hand, all on its own, and avenged his death. For that was what it was, he realized. His death.

He gazed into the growing darkness and saw his Aunt Fiona smile.

* * *

The warmth woke her. Or maybe it was merely the lack of the icy chill that seemed to follow demonkind, but Isra opened her eyes once again, aware she was definitely alive.

But for how long? And, for what purpose? She should have died when Drago threw her against the wall. She should have died when she was surrounded by the icy stink of demons—or, at least, she should have lost her soul.

But she lay there—soul intact—on the dusty floor of the cavern, warmed by the energy vortex and the swirling lights from portals leading to Abyss and other worlds. Earth, maybe, and possibly Atlantis? She'd heard of those places, though she'd never seen any of them.

Nine hells, she'd barely seen her own. An entire life lived on one level of what her mother always called the new Lemuria. Exiled by birth, not by choice. Could she actually claim Lemuria as her own? And if so, would Lemuria ever claim her?

Just what *did* she owe Lemuria?

Anything? Or nothing at all?

But demonkind is invading, led by one who appears to be stronger than the other demons—stronger and smarter.

She had information that could help Artigos the Just and his army of Forgotten Ones and guardsmen. If she really wanted to help them. But what of Drago? He was Lemurian, yet he was helping demonkind. It made no sense.

Then she recalled the light of evil in his eyes, the madness lurking there, and Isra knew she had no choice. Her mother had fought for Lemuria. She'd given her life for Lemuria. Isra would not disgrace her mother's name.

Groaning with the effort of dragging herself to her feet, of planting her palms against the rough walls and finally standing only moderately upright, Isra glanced about, searching once more to see if there were demons here.

The vortex was empty, and she heard no sound. She was alone, utterly alone. But had she not been alone since her mother's death? Her sisters had long avoided her.

Or, had she avoided them? Blinking slowly, regaining her focus on the stone walls, Isra gained new focus on herself.

She saw herself afresh, and the vision was not a good one.

Damn, she was such a bitch! Foul-tempered and angry all the time. No wonder the others avoided her. It wasn't like she was the only Forgotten One slaving for the free folk. She and the others truly were sisters, if not of blood, then sisters through adversity, through hard labor and survival. She owed her sisters, if no one else. Owed them for putting up with her for so damned many years.

Even Selyn. She'd been so cruel to Selyn over the years, but only because Selyn was always hopeful things would get better. Isra had hated that sense of optimism that always seemed to color Selyn's aura with light and love. Hated the fact the others looked up to Selyn.

It wasn't Selyn's fault she was an optimist. Isra almost laughed at that foolish thought. As if optimism were a fault, not a blessing. Maybe, just maybe, she could try a little bit of that attitude out on herself.

Strength flowed throughout her body, energizing her bruised arms and aching shoulder. Easing the pounding ache in her head, and steadying her legs as she stood just a fraction straighter, just a little bit taller. She clenched her hands into fists and then straightened her fingers, aware of a newfound sense of power she'd not known before.

Power, finally, to do something good, something positive. She had to warn them. Somehow, she had to join her sisters in this fight against demonkind.

With or without a blasted crystal sword.

A small ache squeezed her heart as she thought of the crystal she'd hoped to wield. She hadn't deserved crystal. Not with that attitude that everyone owed her, that she had the right to take what she wanted, when she wanted. Someday, maybe, a crystal sword would be hers. Someday, should she prove herself worthy.

Isra shoved herself away from the wall, wobbling inelegantly for a moment before she regained her balance. Then, eyes focused on the portal that led to Lemuria, she stepped through the swirling light and into the tunnel beyond.

A flash of light brought her up short.

A blade lay in the pathway. Shimmering crystal, lying flat upon the ground. She stopped, transfixed by the glow that pulsed with life, that called to her. Then she glanced around, before and behind her, but there was no one else. Not another soul.

Holding her breath, Isra knelt beside the blade and slowly, cautiously, passed her hand over the shimmering crystal. Light flashed, and the damned thing practically leapt into her hand.

Her fingers tightened around the jeweled hilt, and the heft and balance were beyond perfect. For long moments she stared into the crystalline depths with the sense of somehow bonding to the entity existing within the blade. There were no words—not from the sword, and certainly not from her.

Standing again, she held the blade high, as if already sensing victory. More energy flowed into her body, along with a sense of wonder that finally, she had been found worthy of bearing crystal.

Swallowing back a sudden rush of tears, Isra took a deep and steadying breath. Then she grasped her sword and marched bravely through the shimmering veil of gold that had so terrified her mere hours ago.

Hadn't she sworn to be forgotten no more? Her crystal sword was proof she was a woman of value, proof she would be well-remembered by her peers. . . . This fight against demonkind had suddenly become very personal. Very personal indeed.

Chapter Twenty

Selyn planted her feet. Once again she parried her opponent's powerful thrust. Power rushed through her body, and she reveled in the sense of it, the knowledge that she and her blade were a single unit, fighting a foe who was larger and stronger, yet no more able—even with the added edge of demonic possession.

It was good. So damned good that she almost laughed at the bloodied guard before her. Grinning, she wondered what move to make that would irritate him even further before she vanquished him in battle.

She had no doubt she was going to win. She had right on her side. Right and Dawson Buck. She glanced his way, hoping to catch his eye as he fought not ten paces away.

And as she looked, everything slipped into slow motion.

Taron's blade practically eviscerated his opponent. The guard went down, flailing wildly. His leg shot out, catching Dawson behind the knee. As Dawson fell, his own opponent thrust wildly, scoring a perfect hit that buried his black sword deep in Dawson's left side.

He made not a sound. No, the scream Selyn heard was

her own. "No! Dawson, no!" Screaming again, Selyn pivoted out of reach of her opponent's strike. She grabbed the jeweled hilt of her sword in both hands and swung her blade, throwing every bit of the love she felt for her fallen man behind the powerful strike.

With sleek and sure intent, she easily beheaded the bastard she'd been fighting. Oblivious to the sounds of Taron taking out the demon she'd just freed, of Alton and Ginny finishing off the final guardsman, she ran to Dawson and knelt beside him. Carefully, she pulled the obsidian blade from the gaping wound in his side and tossed the damned thing away.

It shattered and turned to black dust, becoming nothing more than a stain upon the floor. Gently, Selyn took Dawson's blade from his lax fingers and lay it on the ground next to her own. Ruby red beside diamond bright.

The obsidian blade had pierced him deeply just beneath his heart, a wound much too deep for anyone—human or Lemurian—to survive. Blood welled from the gash in spite of the pressure she forced against his side.

Ginny knelt beside her and ripped off her purple hoodie. "Use this," she said, folding it into a thick pad. "Put more pressure on the wound. We've got to stop the bleeding." She glanced at Alton. "Is there a healer you can call? Anyone?"

Selyn glanced hopefully at Alton, but he stood there with tears in his eyes and HellFire's blood-soaked tip pointed at the ground, shaking his head. "No one. Not with the battle raging. There are probably many injured. Even if I could find one amid the chaos, a healer could not help him. I fear it's a mortal injury, one that would end even a Lemurian's life. Humans are so much more fragile than we." He sighed, closed his eyes a moment, and then took a deep breath. "I'm sorry, Selyn." His voice broke as he knelt beside them. "So gods-be-damned sorry."

With an almost preternatural calm, Selyn nodded. Alton was right. There was no point, no time, no way to save the man she loved. Already she knew it was too late. The flow of blood was slowing, not so much from the pressure she placed against his wound, but because his heart no longer beat, no longer forced blood through his arteries.

Screams and shouts from the great plaza echoed along the passageway, and it was obvious demons still poured into Lemuria. She heard a battle cry go up, and knew that Artigos the Just and his women warriors and armed wardens had arrived. She had no doubt the battle would be won. She had to believe they would win. There was no acceptable alternative.

But Dawson wouldn't live to celebrate their victory. It was too late for him. She stared at the red stain coating her fingers and knew his blood no longer flowed. No breath escaped his slightly parted lips.

His eyes were closed. Those beautiful blue eyes. She'd never see them again, never feel the joy in their sparkle, the heat in his heavy-lidded gaze.

Never again. She brushed her fingers over the soft beard that covered his jaw, and thought of the way it felt against her breasts, her belly . . . her thighs.

Never again. Would he remember her, wherever his soul finally found rest? Did Lemurians and humans share the same afterlife? She had to believe they did.

She could accept nothing else.

Slowly, she traced the line of his jaw, the curve of his lips. *How odd,* she thought. *He has a smile on his face.*

What had he been thinking at the moment his soul passed over? What did he see as he entered the afterlife? Old friends? Family? Would he wait for her there?

How long could one be expected to await an immortal?

How long must she wait, before choosing to make that final leap herself? She wanted to join him. She had to. There was nothing left for her here. Nothing at all.

"Ginny?" Alton rose to his feet, moving like a very old man. "Do you wish to stay with Selyn and Daws? Taron has to close the portal to Abyss and I have to fight. The battle rages, and every sword will be needed."

Selyn raised her head, and her voice was strong and steady. She'd not wept for Dawson. Not yet. His loss wasn't real at this point. Her grief was so far beyond imagining, she'd not truly reacted to his death, still could not accept an end to the man she loved. "Your sword will be needed as well, Ginny. I'll stay with him. Please. Don't waste this brave man's death. He would not want that."

Ginny nodded in agreement. Her face glistened with tears, but she carried about her a look of resolve that could not be ignored. "His death is not wasted, Selyn. Never think that. We'll be back as soon as we can." She brushed a thick lock of Dawson's dark hair back from his face. "He's a hero. He didn't ask for this fight, but he's never once turned away from it. Nor from us." She leaned over and gently kissed his forehead.

"You're a damned good man, Dawson Buck. A brave warrior and a true friend, and the only man I know who'd ever think of hunting demons with a vacuum cleaner." She made a sound halfway between a laugh and a sob, and brushed her arm across her eyes.

"We have to go." Alton held out his hand. Ginny took it. Taron offered a brief salute, and then, within moments, Selyn was alone with Dawson, listening to the sounds of battle and the harsh rasp of her own ragged breath.

She clasped his hand and knew the warmth would

quickly leave him, which made her want to hold him tighter, to wrap his body with hers and keep him warm.

To think she'd found love, only to lose it so quickly. Selyn ran her fingers through the thick, dark hair curling around his face and wasn't quite sure how she should feel. Grief was too simple a word to describe the sense of loss, the emptiness and utter devastation that seemed to have taken over her mind, her body . . . her soul.

He was gone. There was nothing left for her. No reason to fight on, no desire to continue. She'd finally discovered love, barely tasted the joy to be had with a man who had seen her as someone other than a slave. He'd thought she was a woman of worth, of value.

Without him, did she still have value? It was impossible to know. She folded her legs and sat beside him, watching the still perfection of his face, remembering the way he'd kissed her and held her, the way he'd laughed with her. Dawson had taught her the joy to be had between a man and a woman in love.

At least she had that to hold on to. To help her remember.

"Take his blade and lay it across his chest, ruby crystal to living flesh."

"What?" Selyn's head whipped around. She searched for the source of that voice speaking so clearly in her ear. A flash of blue light caught her eye, and she glanced at her sword. It glowed, pulsing with life.

"Quickly, before life flees. Lay his sword across his chest. Now."

With shaking hands, Selyn ripped Dawson's shirt open. Buttons scattered and fabric tore as she parted the fabric over his bloodied chest. Then she quickly placed the ruby sword across his body, so that the blade rested over his heart.

The moment the blade touched Dawson, red fire flashed. Light poured from the ruby facets, filling the small cavern, enclosing Dawson in a crimson explosion of cold fire and brilliant, shimmering shafts of light. Selyn tried to watch, but the glow was blinding. She covered her streaming eyes with her arm and turned away.

Long moments later, the light dimmed. Selyn slowly turned around. Breathless, unbelieving, she looked into Dawson's dark blue eyes. He blinked slowly, as if coming awake from a long and restful sleep.

When he finally focused on her face, it was as if she snapped out of a trance. "You live! Dawson, you live!"

Blinking, obviously confused, he struggled to sit up. Selyn didn't take her eyes off his face, but she grabbed his sword from his chest, set it beside her own once again, and then wrapped her arms around him. "You were dead. I saw you die, but you're alive!" The tears flowed now as she held him tightly, sobbing, kissing his throat, his lips, his perfectly healed body.

"I saw Aunt Fiona." He frowned as if he tried to recall what had just passed. "She said it wasn't my time, that I had to come back." He glanced at his left side, and Selyn knew it was the place where the blade had slipped between his ribs, through his lungs. There was no mark. Nothing but smooth, healthy flesh and a smear of dried blood.

Holy shit! Where . . . ?

She'd never heard his thoughts before, yet suddenly they were as clear in her mind as if he'd spoken aloud. She almost laughed, listening to his thoughts as he glanced around.

Damn it all. Where's my sword? Shit, I hope I didn't break it.

Selyn shook her head, but she couldn't bring herself to turn him loose. *No, my love,* she said, answering him telepathically. *It wasn't your Aunt Fiona who sent you back,*

*and your sword is here. Beside you. Your blade saved you.
It's right . . .*

He gazed at her in shock. "I hear you. In my head. But
how?"

She kissed the shock right off his face. "That's what I'm
trying to tell you. Your blade saved your life. Maybe that
changed things in you. I don't know for sure, but you're
alive!"

She clasped her own sword and looked at it with
wonder. "And mine spoke to me. She told me to place your
sword across your chest, and I did. And you came back."

Her blade glowed and pulsed with life. "I am called
StarFire, Selyn of Elda's line. We will do well together."

"StarFire?" Selyn barely whispered the name, and yet
she felt the connection, the sense that this blade was more
than a mere weapon. Much more.

Dawson stared at the swords with a look of utter bemusement on his face. Selyn glanced at the floor beside
him. A crystal blade glowed and shimmered just like hers.
There was no trace of red within its crystalline facets, yet
she knew immediately it was Dawson's. "Here," she said,
pointing. "There's your sword."

He shook his head, obviously confused. "But it can't
be. My blade is red. Ruby red." Even so, he reached for it,
wrapped his fingers around the jeweled pommel, and lifted
the weapon. "It feels right. I don't understand. What happened?"

"I am DemonsDeath. I was not prepared to lose you,
Dawson Buck. It was not your time to leave us."

"Holy shit." Clutching the blade, his head snapped
up, and he stared at Selyn. "The damned thing really is
alive. How?" he asked, addressing his blade. "I was dead,
wasn't I?"

The sword glowed and pulsed with life and light. "Very

close. I sacrificed chromium, the element that gave me color, to bring life back to you. You have a greater purpose, Dawson Buck. It was necessary to recall your spirit. You will live long and fight many battles beside your woman."

As if those words snapped him out of whatever dream he'd been trapped in, Dawson scrambled to his feet. He tossed aside his ripped shirt so that he stood there with his chest bare and his worn jeans riding low on his hips. Drying blood covered his side and soaked one leg of his pants, but he was whole and strong and ready to fight.

Selyn gazed up at him, loving him more than she'd ever imagined possible.

A series of cries rang along the passageway. The sound of warriors engaging in battle, of women screaming and demons wailing those eerie, terrifying banshee howls. Dawson grabbed Selyn's hand. "None of this makes sense. Right now, I feel as if I must be dreaming, trapped in some alternate universe where nothing is as it seems, but damn it all, Selyn, as long as you're with me, it's all good."

He wrapped one arm around her shoulders and pulled her close, kissing her hard and fast. When he ended the kiss, he pulled back just enough to look into her eyes. His eyes absolutely glowed, and the smile on his face was one of pure joy.

"We'll figure it out later," he said. "But right now, we've got a war to win."

Selyn linked her fingers in his. "I love you," she said, and for some odd reason she felt like laughing.

"I love you, too. Now move!" He took off, tugging Selyn behind him. She stretched her legs and caught up, and together they raced along the passage, away from the empty prison cells, into the midst of hell.

* * *

Artigos the Just paused at the final portal, the one leading into the levels where the free folk lived—the one that would put him, once again, among his people.

And yet he'd never once set foot in this new Lemuria. Had no real idea what Lemurians were like anymore, how they functioned as a society, who their chosen leaders were, what their politics were like. All he knew were the bits and pieces of information he'd stolen from people's minds over the years. Mere snips of what Lemuria was like in this modern era.

Would they even remember him? His son had led Lemurian citizens ever since the great move from a dying continent—led them with a mind ruled by demonkind.

Artigos knew many in the Council of Nine must be compromised as well, and, if what Selyn and Dawson had reported was true, his grandson, the one he'd hoped would support his claim for leadership, was currently imprisoned in a jail cell, along with those who'd sworn their allegiance to the man.

Unless, of course, Dawson and Selyn had succeeded in freeing them. So much depended on luck.

Luck, and skill, and the power of crystal.

He glanced behind him, at the men and women standing ready to fight—willing to lay down their lives for an old man whose time might have already passed. Their amazing loyalty alone should give him the strength to move forward.

'Twas not luck that gave them the courage to stand behind a once-proud king. No, it was loyalty to Lemuria and the magic of crystal that empowered this small but magnificent army.

With that thought in mind, Artigos the Just stepped through the portal and left his thousands of years of imprisonment and exile behind him.

Stepped away from his lost life, into unimaginable chaos.

Men and women running in blind fear crowded past. Many were bleeding, covered in deep scratches and bites. Screams rose all about them, and the stench of demonkind was thick within the halls and tunnels of this strange, underground world.

Light overhead reminded him of the sky he'd not seen for thousands of years, and yet the light was false, manufactured by technology he'd heard was long forgotten by the people who still made use of it.

Wisps of black sped by, pursuing the Lemurians who'd just passed. Artigos caught the hint of talons and sharp fangs before the wraiths disappeared down the long passage. The stench of sulfur remained, a foul stink he'd never forget.

Demonkind. But how? There were demon wraiths here, inside Lemuria? He'd expected to fight against possessed Lemurian guards and possibly members of the Council of Nine, but demons flying free, aggressively attacking Lemurian citizens? Demons obviously capable of inflicting injuries while in wraith form?

That hadn't been part of his plan!

He turned as his army spilled through the portal. Men and women took their places, lining up along the tunnel. For now, the panic-stricken flow of Lemurians had ceased, though screams and shouts echoed in the distance.

Artigos stood tall and gazed at the anxious faces of the men and women before him. "I have no idea what scourge we face, but there are demons herein. Go forth and fight bravely. Not for me, not for any ruler, not for any political party or ideology. No. We fight for our world, for our people, for Lemuria!"

He raised his sword high, as did each of his soldiers.

The shout rose, loud and clear from many voices, from former slaves and the formerly possessed.

"For Lemuria!"

Light flashed from the shimmering tips of blades joined, and then shot along the tunnel, a brilliant arrow of energy flying in the direction of the sounds of battle.

Artigos watched the light, tracked its direction, and gave a mighty shout. Then, raising his sword, he led his army down the trail set by crystal.

Eddy leapt into the thick mass of demonkind with her blade flashing and snow falling all around. She was careful of Mari—the most amazing, magical Mari—standing tall within the mass of wraiths, still chanting her spell. Blood ran down her arms from long, deep scratches, and her face was marked as well, but Darius fought beside his woman like a man possessed, and he protected her as best he could.

With Artigos, Dax and Eddy helping, they managed to clear a space for Mari, but the wraiths kept coming and the snow kept falling, and Eddy couldn't help but wonder how long they could hold out.

This wasn't the way it was supposed to happen! She and Dax were supposed to take Artigos and Gaia and join the fight in Lemuria, but here they fought on Earth's soil, and the demons continued to arrive in an unending, unrelenting stream.

Were Ginny and Alton all right? And what of Dawson and Selyn? There were others as well, Roland and his men—brave men who worked within Lemuria, fighting not only demonkind but their own government, their own leaders. Did Alton still hold the chancellor's position? Did Artigos the Just truly survive?

She'd not asked the prior chancellor Artigos about his father. Not yet, though that question could not be put off forever.

Neither could her attention to the fight! Sharp talons raked her arm. Eddy ducked away from a demon with more form than most. She caught a quick glance of teeth and eyes and a long, forked tail before the foul creature shrieked and disappeared into the falling snow.

"Dax? What's going on? They seem to be gaining strength, not growing weaker." She glanced his way. He ducked beneath a pair of demons, but still managed a shrug.

"I don't know." Frustration leant an edge to his voice as he slashed DemonFire through that foul, oily mist, leaving a trail of flames and sparks behind. "Mari's spell is supposed to slow them down, not make them more vicious."

What the hell was going wrong? Eddy felt the emotional tug of her sword. *DemonSlayer?* she asked. *How can we help Mari?*

Her blade's familiar voice whispered in her mind. *She needs the power of crystal. Touch your blades to her body, your hands to her flesh as well. Share with her of your life force. Empower her to tap into that great well of strength that lies within your world.*

Hookay . . . that wasn't quite what she'd expected. Eddy reached high for a demon, caught it with her blade, and watched with grim satisfaction as it shattered and scattered into foul smelling sparks. In the lull between attacks, she passed on what her blade had told her must be done.

"DemonSlayer says Mari needs more power, from us and from our swords. Touch your blades to her shoulders, your hands to her body. Share what you can to strengthen her spell."

No one questioned her instructions. Eddy pressed the

flat of her blade to Mari's back and rested her hand upon her friend's shoulder. Artigos, Dax, and Darius did the same, connecting Mari to their human and Lemurian life force as well as to the power of crystal.

Mari shuddered, as if she'd been jolted by a powerful shock, but her voice never faltered.

"Demon's spawn in dark of night,
I charge you—lose your will to fight.
Be thou afraid. All, rush to flee!
Return to Abyss. So mote it be."

Again and again she repeated her spell, a simple rhyme that was merely a framework to hold the magic she was still learning to control. But now, with the power of crystal, with the strength of her companions' life force, there was a ring to her voice that hadn't been there before.

Now, as she chanted the simple words, the dark wraiths milled about. They seemed confused, as if unsure of their goal. Mari stood tall and unwavering, though she'd held her arms aloft now, had spoken her spell continuously, for over an hour.

Eddy felt the drain on her energy and knew she fed into Mari's. It was the strangest feeling, as if something were being sucked out, and yet at the same time, that power was being replaced. DemonSlayer? Was her sword finding the balance that allowed her to give without giving up, to share of herself without depleting her own reserves?

"Mari?" Darius sheathed his sword and pulled Mari into his arms. She stumbled into his embrace, but he caught her as her legs gave out.

Eddy blinked and looked around, aware the snow had stopped falling, that the sky was actually growing lighter as the cloud cover thinned. How long had they stood out here in the freezing cold?

And why wasn't she freezing? Had Mari's spell kept them warm as well? "Are they gone? I don't see any demons." She sheathed DemonSlayer, noting that the light of her blade had dulled. She looked up at Dax. He blinked as if he were just waking up from a long sleep. Artigos leaned on his yellow sword, and his breath came in deep pulls that left a frosty cloud in front of him.

Darius brushed Mari's hair back from her face. "You did it, my love. You ran the bastards off." He leaned close and kissed her.

Mari shook her head. "Barely." Her voice cracked, as if she fought tears. "I couldn't have done it without all of you, your energy . . . life force, whatever it was you shared with me. Thank you. But they're not gone for good. They're growing much stronger." She held up her arm and stared at the blood running from her wrist to her elbow.

Eddy noticed that all of them were covered with numerous small cuts and bites. What looked like insubstantial smoke had enough solid form to inflict injuries. All of them were bleeding.

Spirit opened the door and stepped out onto the porch. Bumper raced past her and sniffed the ground, her tail wagging full speed. "I've got coffee on and a late breakfast cooking," Spirit said. "Come in, clean up. Get some food and some rest. You were all absolutely amazing."

She hugged Mari. "I'm so proud of you! Even covered in scratches you look powerful. Sweetheart, you are truly a skilled and powerful witch." Spirit chuckled and wrapped an arm around her daughter's waist. "My daughter the witch. I never dreamed this would come to pass."

Laughing, Mari grabbed Darius's hand, and they headed inside with Dax and BumperWillow following.

Artigos brought up the rear, but he'd not spoken since they'd joined the battle and seemed unusually quiet.

Eddy stopped him at the door. "Are you okay?"

He raised his head and stared at her out of eyes clouded with grief. "I've brought this on, haven't I? How can I ever forgive myself, much less ask my people to forgive me?" He stared down at the yellow crystal sword grasped tightly in his hand. "Will my son ever forgive me? My father?"

Eddy gazed at the man who had literally condemned an entire world by his actions, and yet it was difficult to lay all the blame on his shoulders. After a moment, she focused on his sword—a sword that had served him well throughout the long night.

"Crystal won't serve a warrior it doesn't respect. If your blade feels your heart is true, isn't that what matters? And won't your people, the ones you love, accept that?"

Artigos raised his head and frowned. "It has served me well, but it has not yet spoken to me. I have much to prove before my blade feels I am worthy."

Eddy smiled and linked arms with him. "Then I guess you just need to keep doing your best, don't you agree? You're certainly not going to prove anything by wallowing in self-recrimination. Or, by missing one of Freedom's really good breakfasts."

She tugged, opened the door, and they entered the house that way, linked arm in arm. The sun was breaking through the clouds behind them, casting its light over the snow-covered peak of Mount Shasta. Eddy glanced over her shoulder as Artigos shut the door, and wondered how they could get to the nearest portal and find their way to Lemuria.

How in the hell were they going to stop this blasted invasion that kept expanding in numbers as well as strength?

The feeling that Alton and Ginny needed their help

grew stronger by the minute. The sense that everything depended upon the battle she knew must be underway, deep inside the mountain in Lemuria.

Eddy wandered into the big, bright kitchen and glanced up as Dax handed her a cup of steaming coffee. Her dad grabbed the remote and turned on the small TV sitting on the counter near the table, slipping through channels in search of local news. Finally he found a familiar station.

They all gathered at the big kitchen table while Freedom brought platters of eggs and fried potatoes, bacon and sausage, and hot cornbread right from the oven.

The plates were passed and food consumed, but everyone's attention remained focused on the news. After a few minutes, Eddy frowned at her father. "Nothing. No reports of strange happenings, possessed creatures or wandering statues, nothing. Are the demons coming here, focusing on this house and nowhere else? What's going on?"

"I think it's my fault."

"Mari? Why you?" Gaia reached across the table and covered Mari's hand. "You're making spells to weaken them, not call them. Why would you think such a thing?"

Mari glanced at Darius.

He leaned over, kissed her softly, and sighed, but he was nodding his head in agreement. "Last week," he said, "when Mari chased off the demons that were invading her mom's shop and attacking Leland, Matthias, and me, a ruby geode exploded in the midst of her spell. We didn't realize until then that something about the ruby crystals in the geode had been calling the demons to the shop. We don't know why they were attracted to it. When the geode exploded, one of the crystals lodged in Mari's heart. It's still there." He covered Mari's hand with his. "The crystal in her heart gives her immortality, but it might also be giving off a signal, one that attracts demons to her."

Mari gave Eddy a rueful smile. "Sort of a good news, bad news thing. The good news is I'm immortal. The bad is the fact that demons are drawn to me, no matter where I am or what I'm doing. Because of that magical crystal, I've become a magnet for them, a veritable lodestone for demonkind. If they're at all near, they're going to come looking for me, first."

Chapter Twenty-One

"Dawson? Nine hells, man, I never thought I'd see you again! I thought you were dead!" Alton thrust his sword through a mass of approaching demons, but he flashed a speculative glance at Daws. "What happened?"

Dawson held up his sword. "My sword brought me back." He tightened his grasp on Selyn's hand. "My sword and Selyn. What's going on?"

"Chaos," Ginny said. She took a deep breath. "Absolute chaos."

Dawson focused on a group of familiar faces. Roland and his band were protecting a small pack of Lemurians huddling in shocked silence beside the dais at the head of the plaza. All about them, the ground was littered with sparkling bits of crystal. "What's happened to their swords?"

"Shattered. They're cowards, all," Alton said. He swung his blade again and more sparks flew. "They finally drew their swords when they realized there weren't enough of us with crystal to protect them, but their blades shattered."

He paused, thrust his blade through another stinking demon. "The problem is, the citizens don't trust us. Drago's been speaking out, rallying them against us, telling them we're possessed by demonkind. He's got the idiots convinced I was the one to open the portal to Abyss and allow the wraiths entry."

"Bastard." Dawson glanced about the huge plaza, but saw only a few dozen Lemurians. "Where is everyone?"

"Hiding in their quarters," Taron said. "They scattered quickly, once demons broke through. At least, so far, anyway, there's no sign of the demon king. Alton said he's the one who seems best able to get the others organized."

Shouts and the clash of steel erupted from a passage behind them. Alton glanced at Ginny and raised his sword. "Do you think it's him?"

Dawson frowned. "Who? The demon king?" He glanced at Selyn.

"No," she said. "His grandfather. Come."

The five of them slipped into the passage in time to see Artigos the Just with his army of former slaves and once-possessed guards engaging in battle with a squadron of Lemurian guardsmen. Steel clashed with crystal, but the Lemurian guardsmen were vastly outnumbered.

"Enough!" Alton leapt to the top of a table and raised his sword. "As Chancellor pro tem and head of the Council of Nine, I demand you lay down your arms."

The soldiers pulled apart, but no one disarmed. They did, however, stop fighting and turn their attention to Alton. Alton pointed to his grandfather, a man he barely remembered. "Do you not recognize the true leader of Lemuria? You raise your swords against Artigos the Just, who has been held prisoner these long years since the great move."

Some among the guardsmen seemed to recognize their former leader. Dawson could hear them mumbling among themselves, but he had no idea what they said. Finally, one of the men stepped forward and bowed, showing Alton the proper courtesy due his position.

"We know not these men, Chancellor, dressed in their strange uniforms. They are, and yet are not, of the Lemurian guard. They are guardsmen who bear crystal, and yet we are not so armed. And who are the women? They're not the women warriors of legend, and yet they bear crystal as well."

He folded his arms across his chest, pointedly turning his back on the rest of the men and women, focusing his attention on Alton.

And Alton focused on the soldier. He'd stated his questions clearly, without malice, but the man had to be confused. Who in the hell was the enemy?

"These are the daughters of the warrior women. The guardsmen were their wardens, holding them enslaved for all these years, but the men were possessed, each of them ruled by demonkind until my grandfather, Artigos the Just, freed them."

Alton glanced at his grandfather and then looked down at his friends. Dawson flashed him a wink. *Going good so far,* he said, using his newfound telepathy. *No one's trying to kill anyone else.*

For now. Alton held his sword high. "Demonkind is invading Lemuria. The only way to stop them is with crystal." He faced the soldiers carrying steel and spoke quickly, his voice urgent, his expression one of firm resolve. "Swear allegiance to our world, to Lemuria, and you shall carry crystal as well. Drago is possessed by demonkind, as was my father. We can only prevail against this evil scourge if we work together. Not for me, not for Artigos the Just. For Lemuria."

Before anyone could answer, a sudden chill swept over them. Dawson grabbed Selyn's hand and pulled her out of the way. A seething cloud of demons shot from the great plaza, heading directly at the soldiers in a whirlwind of sulfuric stench.

Those armed with steel ran for cover. The Forgotten Ones and their guards leapt into battle. The air filled with the stink of demons and their terrible banshee screams, with the cries of warriors fighting strong and true.

Dawson whirled out of the reach of a huge demon, one he'd not seen before. It had shape and form, and rather than attack, it hovered just before him, its multi-jointed arms tipped with deadly talons and its shimmering scales reflecting the ambient light in the broad passage.

This was no formless wraith, yet when Dawson thrust his sword through the creature, it merely screamed a shout of triumph and lunged forward.

Daws rolled out of the way, barely ahead of the slashing talons.

Alton's shout rang in his ears as he scrambled to his feet. "The demon king! Ginny, we need you."

Ginny raced toward them, holding DarkFire high. The massive demon turned and shrieked, growing in size until it towered over even the tallest of the Lemurians. Ginny looked like a child, standing before the huge creature, but she was fearless in her attack.

Alton stood beside her, with Dawson and Selyn on either side, but the demon backed away, shrieked again, and suddenly collapsed in upon itself, formed a tiny tornado of pure, dark energy, and flashed back toward the great plaza.

Absolute silence followed in its wake. Silence punctuated by the sound of heavy breathing and the soft murmurs of warriors.

Alton took a deep breath, glanced at Dawson, and nodded. Then he turned to face the assembled group. Those armed with steel had rejoined them, but their expressions had gone from confident and self-assured to humble.

It was impossible to deny the power in Artigos the Just's army, standing here in a room filled with the sulfuric stench and blackened soot of dead demons.

Alton looked to that group of warriors first. "Are you willing to share the power of your crystal blades with men who truly are not your enemies?"

There was no hesitation at all. Those bearing crystal— men and women alike—walked forward, joining the men carrying steel. Holding crystal to steel, they quickly repli- cated each of the crystal swords. As light flashed and crystal flared to life, Dawson watched the expression on Alton's face turn to one of hope.

Their army had just grown considerably.

Artigos the Just walked through the crowd of warriors and stood beside the table where Alton once more held court. "You've done well, grandson. I'm proud of the man you've become."

The shimmer in Alton's eyes matched the glow of his sword.

Selyn squeezed Dawson's hand. *It's been a long time coming,* she said. *Ginny's told me of his father's cruelty.*

But his father has been possessed by demonkind, Dawson said. *There may be resolution there, as well.* He leaned close and kissed Selyn, but the moment was bit- tersweet. He knew all about resolution. He'd never found it with his own father. No, but he'd found something even more powerful, more important with the woman holding tightly to his hand.

He'd found love.

* * *

Isra heard the sound of fighting long before she reached what must be the great plaza. She saw huddled groups of unarmed Lemurian men, and many soldiers bearing crystal. Her sisters fought in a number of areas, battling the black wraiths she'd first seen at the portal.

But where was that big one? The one that had paused and practically taunted her with his strength and fierce power?

A scream caught her attention. Nica! Little Nica fought alone, swinging her crystal sword against a swirling mass of darkness. Isra raced across the open area. How in the hell did one fight demons? She'd only had this crystal blade for a few short minutes.

And yet, she knew exactly what to do. Thrusting the tip into the stinking, shrieking mass, she felt a huge pulse of power and blinked at the shower of sparks as demons exploded at the barest touch of crystal.

"Isra!" Nica shot her a huge grin. "We couldn't find you anywhere, and you've got crystal! I'm so glad you're alive. I was worried. Thank you." She took a deep gulp of air, and then another. "There are so many." She held up her scratched and bloodied arm. "Don't let them get close. They may look like mist, but they've got sharp teeth and claws. I got separated from the others. Stay with me, please?"

Isra nodded. Nica showed no animosity toward her at all, even after a lifetime of cruelty and harassment? Amazing. "Of course I'll fight with you, but I must find Selyn or Artigos. Either one. I have terrible news and must warn them."

Nica grabbed her hand. "This way. I saw Alton, Artigos's grandson. He's the one you need to tell."

Fighting raged around them. Her sisters and the guards,

fighting together, battling an endless army of demons. For the most part, it appeared the Lemurian aristocrats had either gone into hiding or cowered in corners, terrified of both the Forgotten Ones and the demons.

Cowards, all. Once again, Isra wondered why she bothered, but then she remembered—this fight wasn't for those foolish free folk. This was for her world.

For Lemuria. She turned to Nica. "Alton?"

"Yes. There. The one with blond hair who fights beside Taron." Nica pointed toward the two men and the tall, dark woman who fought between them. Their swords flashed and demons died, and yet, for each that died, two others took its place.

Isra had to speak to him now. She knew where all these creatures were coming from. Somehow, he had to close the portal. Isra raised her hand, hoping to gain his attention, but a sudden chill stopped her before she could call his name.

She turned, and found herself looking into the eyes of that same, huge, hideous demon. He stood not six feet away, watching her as he'd studied her before, in the chamber where the portals pulsed and swirled. Caught in his diabolical stare, she could neither move nor scream.

His lips parted in a parody of a grin, and, as Isra stood, frozen in place, he flexed very solid looking talons and slowly walked toward her.

Selyn heard what could only be Nica's scream. She turned loose of Dawson's hand and raced toward the sound. "Dawson! He's here." The demon king had materialized not a hundred yards from where they'd seen him last, only now he stalked Isra.

Isra with crystal? But how?

And Nica! Little Nica protecting the one who had

tormented her for most of her life. So many questions, but the time for answers would have to wait.

Nica swung her sword, but the crystal passed through the demon king's body without visible effect. The massive beast turned and swung two of his huge arms, batting Nica away as if she were nothing more than a small irritant.

"Nica!" Isra pivoted out of the demon king's reach.

Nica cried out, hit the ground hard, and lay silent. The demon turned on Isra once again, but she stood her ground. Dawson raced past Selyn and stood beside Isra with his sword drawn. Selyn went to Nica. Slowly she knelt beside her friend.

Nica's head was bloodied, but her eyes were open. Long scratches ran across her neck and shoulder. "I'm okay," she said. "Help Isra. She has important news for Chancellor Alton."

"Take care, my friend." Selyn helped prop Nica against the wall, away from the fighting. Then she grabbed up her sword once more. Dawson and Isra slashed at the demon king, but all they seemed to do was infuriate the beast. Their crystal had no obvious effect. Was Ginny's DarkFire the only sword capable of harming the creature?

Selyn lunged, driving her blade deep into what she hoped was the demon king's heart—if he had one, and if it resided in his chest. He twisted away, shrieking now as three blades pierced him, cutting and slashing without visible damage.

There was no blood, no sign of cuts or tears. His scales remained in place, his body whole. He was mist and yet not. Substantial enough to reflect light from his reptilian scales, solid enough for his knife-like talons to leave deep cuts where they met his opponents' living flesh—and disgusting enough for the stinking saliva from his gaping mouth and yellowed fangs to turn the ground beneath their feet foul and slippery.

Solid, yet not entirely—light showed through his huge body, and the shadows of movement, when Isra or Dawson lunged with a blade, seemed to dance within his frame. He fought them now, turning and swirling, reaching out with his four arms to slash and cut, kicking with his huge, clawed feet. Still, Selyn felt as if he merely toyed with them, as if he tested their skill and laughed at their inability to best him, even with crystal.

Until Ginny joined the fight. Charging in with DarkFire glowing that unbelievable shade of purple, she headed straight for the demon king. His massive head whipped around, and he shrieked. Movement within the great plaza halted as everyone, demon and Lemurian alike, turned in the direction of that unholy noise.

Before Ginny could swing her blade, the creature lost all form, turned into a black tornado of seething mist, and disappeared down a dark tunnel, away from the battle.

Demonkind throughout the entire area screeched and rose into the air, swirling and pulsing in thick, oily masses of mist. Then with an ear-splitting shriek that seemed to come from all directions at once, they coalesced into a single massive spear of darkness and sped after the demon king.

Alton threw an arm around Ginny's shoulders and kissed her. Dawson drew Selyn into an embrace, and they all stood there, blowing, gasping for breath, staring in the direction the demon king and his minions had gone.

The few aristocrats still cowering in dark corners were the first to head toward Alton, followed by the warriors who'd fought and killed so many of the demons. Artigos the Just stayed toward the back of the plaza with many of his army around him.

Drago, it appeared, had been among those hiding. He leapt to the dais and pointed at Alton. "Arrest him. He is in league with demonkind. Did you see what happened? He allowed that thing to escape. It's headed straight for the living quarters where our people hide from this terrible invasion. No one will be safe."

Alton glanced at Ginny, and the anger boiled off of him in waves. She reached for him, but he shrugged her off and marched across the open plaza. When he reached the dais where Drago stood, he took the steps two at a time as if he intended to physically attack the councilman. Ginny was right on Alton's heels, with Taron, Dawson, and Selyn following close behind.

Alton reached the same level as Drago and towered over the man. "Put a lid on it, Drago. Now." He turned to the gathering crowd and glared at his people—people who had cowered in fear when demons attacked. Men whose swords had shattered rather than allow cowards to wield them. "Those of you who believe Drago's lies are fools. Every gods-be-damned one of you. Fools and cowards, all."

No one spoke, but eyes shifted from Alton to Drago, and the mood grew ugly. Alton dismissed them with a curse and glared at Drago. "A test, Drago. Draw your sword. Show them that the blade is black as sin."

Drago took a step back as Alton turned once again to the crowd, now watching him intently. "Crystal turns black when the one who wields it has died. The Drago who once inhabited this body died long ago. You see the man, but he's nothing more than demonkind—possessed for so many years, almost nothing but the demon survives."

Drago took another step back. Then he seemed to catch himself. "Lies, Alton. Nothing but lies!"

"I think not." Alton glanced at Ginny and then focused once more on the Lemurians watching this drama play out in front of them. "Let DarkFire prove the truth of my words. My mate's blade is capable of forcing demonkind from even the darkest heart. Dawson? Taron? Hold Drago so that Ginny can show these good people what the councilman really is."

Before Drago could flee, Dawson made eye contact with Taron, and the two men acted as one. They grabbed for Drago and caught his arms. He struggled, fighting against their control, but the two of them held him so tightly restrained he couldn't break free.

Ginny stepped up and drew her blade. Drago's eyes went wide, but she didn't hesitate. Instead, she touched the tip of her blade to his chest, just over his heart. The dark crystal glowed, just as it had in this same plaza mere days ago when the people had witnessed DarkFire's power for the first time.

Drago screamed, but it was a banshee cry, not the sound of a man. His body jerked in Taron and Dawson's grasp . . . and then a thick, oily mass began to seep out of him.

There were gasps and cries throughout the vast plaza as those in the front pushed back, away from the dais, and the ones in back surged forward for a better view. Selyn looked out over the crowd and realized that people were coming in from the various passages, though not from the direction the demon king had taken.

She wondered where he'd gone, if there were people yet in danger. Now, though, both male and female Lemurians filled the great plaza as Ginny forced more and more darkness from Drago.

He seemed to shrink, like a child's toy balloon deflating. At first he struggled, but as more and more of the demon was drawn forth, his struggles lessened. Finally, he hung limp and diminished in Dawson and Taron's grasp, but a thick, oily substance floated in the air just above his head.

Ginny thrust at the mass with DarkFire, but the wraith shot out of reach, just ahead of her blade. Someone in the crowd screamed. Ginny cursed and lunged again, but the mist spun in an ever tightening circle and then shot down the passage, following the direction the demon king had gone.

"Shit." Ginny stared at her sword and shook her head. "I didn't expect it to move so quickly. How's Drago?"

Dawson grabbed a fistful of Drago's hair and raised the man's head, but he was limp and barely breathing. Alton glanced at the crowd. "Can we get a healer up here? It appears the demon's force may have been all that kept him alive."

"You were right. That explains the black sword." Taron adjusted his grip on Drago's arm.

An older man moved through those standing closest to the dais, climbed the stairs, and went straight to Drago. At the same time, there was a commotion toward the back side of the plaza, a shout and angry cursing.

Roland and Birk moved toward the dais. Roland had a tight grip on one man, while Birk grasped the arms of two more. A third Lemurian guard came from another part of the crowd, marching yet another man ahead of him.

"Thank you, gentlemen." Alton pointed to the guards and their prisoners. "These members of the Council of Nine have ruled Lemuria since the great move from our dying continent. None of us knew, at the time, that they had been possessed by demonkind, their every thought controlled, their will that of a Lemurian no longer."

He folded his arms across his chest and gazed out over the plaza that was now filled with Lemuria's citizens. "You will hear the full story as soon as we can take the time to explain it all to you, but I can tell this to you now—we will remove the influence of demonkind from our leaders and from any of our citizens who have been infected with this scourge. My father is being treated even now. He's with a healer in Earth's dimension."

At the mention of Earth, a mumbling rose among the people. Alton raised his hand. "Do not fear that which you do not understand." He pointed to Ginny and Dawson. "Without these humans—humans who now carry crystal—demonkind would rule our world. Your lives would be forfeit. I charge you to treat them with honor."

Selyn glanced at the council members held captive before the dais. Each of them had a crystal sword carefully sheathed, yet even from here she could tell the blades were black. A chill crossed over her spine. The demon king was still free and demonkind still wandered the halls of Lemuria. This battle was far from won.

·Ginny stepped down from the dais and led the guards and their captives to a point out of view of the crowd where she could safely remove the demons, but a familiar voice drew Selyn's attention once again.

"Selyn! I really have to speak to the chancellor."

"Isra?" She leaned down and held out her hand. "Come. Let me help you. It's too crowded for you to get to the stairs."

Isra's hand tightened around hers. As Selyn tugged, Isra jumped and landed lightly beside her. "I have news he must hear," she whispered. Then Isra looked over her shoulder at the huge crowd of free folk. More people than she and Selyn had ever seen in their lives.

For a moment, Selyn wondered if she had the right to interfere with the chancellor's speech. Then she sensed the power of StarFire and knew she had every right. She stepped up and tapped Alton's shoulder. "Isra says she has important news for the chancellor."

He flashed her a cheeky grin. "That would still be me." And, without a moment's hesitation, he turned his full attention on the two Forgotten Ones.

Isra glanced quickly at Selyn and then swallowed with an audible gulp. "Sir," she said. Then she took a deep breath, and the words spilled out. "I freely admit I came to this level to do harm, but I was captured by guards possessed by demonkind. They took me through a magical wall of molten gold and thence along a passage that led to a chamber filled with portals. That man"—she pointed at Drago—"was using his black sword to open a portal. It's a massive doorway that swirls in colors of darkest red and stinks of demonic presence."

Alton's hand snapped up to stop her speech. "Taron," he said. "Dawson, you need to listen to this." He turned back to Isra. "I'm sorry. I want my men to hear your message."

With Dawson and Taron on either side of the chancellor, Isra continued. "Drago completed the portal, and demons began pouring through. Thousands of them, filling the chamber with a solid wall of stinking mist. Then that large one crawled through the portal." She stopped and took another deep breath.

Selyn reached for Isra's hand and squeezed it tight. Never in her wildest dreams had Selyn imagined feeling pride in Isra, her most unfriendly sister, but now Selyn stood tall and proud beside one who had always wished her harm.

Isra's fingers tightened in Selyn's. "When the demon king finally crawled out of the portal, he divided the demons into three separate groups. One group went down a passageway to the left and disappeared. Another went through a gateway I didn't know—it was off to the right and had a well-traveled path before it. The third group invaded Lemuria."

Dawson and Alton exchanged glances. Alton nodded. "I agree. They've gone to Earth. The passage she mentions to the left takes them to Sedona; the other portal will drop them onto the flank of Mount Shasta." He shook his head. "We've not heard from Eddy and Dax for much too long. Taron, I want you to close the portal from Abyss if you can, but also try to contact our friends in Evergreen. Darius should be the strongest communicator. I need to know if they're all right, if my father lives."

Taron nodded and clasped Alton's shoulder. "Alton, I am so sorry. I was caught in the battle. I never got to the portal. I'll go now. Be careful. The demon king is here, and his army is growing. Plus, he'll have gained strength from the one that possessed Drago."

"I know." Alton pulled Taron into a quick embrace. "It's okay, my friend. There is nothing to forgive. Go quickly." Then he turned to Selyn and Isra. "Thank you, Isra. I hope you've lost your desire to do harm to Lemuria, as I have a feeling we'll be able to use one with your fortitude when it comes time to rebuild this world." He smiled at her, and then he sighed, as if the weight of his world were growing too heavy for any one man's shoulders to bear.

He gazed out across the vast crowd and then smiled and raised his arms to draw the attention of his people once again. "As my mother explained when I took over my hereditary seat as chancellor of the council, it was to be a temporary position. I want to introduce you to the rightful leader who should have held this seat all along. It is with great honor that I give you my grandfather, Artigos

the Just, once king, now the rightful chancellor of the
Council of Nine."

Gasps rose from many. The crowd parted, and Artigos
the Just, followed by his army of former slaves and once-
possessed guards, strode across the great plaza with his
ruby blade held high.

Selyn fought back tears of pride as her sisters, some of
them bloodied, all of them smiling, followed their leader,
each of them carrying crystal and walking with more pride
than any of the free folk could ever hope to understand.

Chapter Twenty-Two

The crowds had long ago dispersed; the plaza was empty of all but a few guards remaining on duty. Others had been sent to search below, to look for evidence of demonkind, though so far there'd been no sign of the foul creatures.

They were still somewhere within Lemuria, but where?

Dawson held tightly to Selyn's hand as they gathered around a large table, all of them eating in the dining area normally reserved for the members of the Council of Nine. Though the battle was far from won, it was a time of celebration. A small one, but a celebration all the same.

At least enough of the older citizens of Lemuria had remembered a time when Artigos ruled, before the great move from their world in the sun. They associated his leadership with more than the DemonWars—when they heard Artigos the Just speak, it took them back to a time when they'd lived a totally different existence, outside beneath blue skies, free of the fear of demonkind. Free, as well, from the restrictions that had slowly tightened around them—restrictions that denied them the open discourse they'd been so proud of for so long.

They'd led the cheers when he ascended the dais. They'd been the ones to nod in agreement as he painted his picture of the Lemuria to come. There'd been no question as to whether or not his rule would be accepted. Dawson had the feeling he wouldn't have been able to abdicate, even if he'd wanted to.

It was obvious his people loved him, and just as obvious that he was a born leader. He'd glossed over his son's part in locking him away and stealing the chancellor's seat. Had praised his grandson for picking up the mantle of leadership during their prior chancellor's sudden "illness."

He'd introduced the Forgotten Ones as women of honor to be treated as the saviors they promised to be, and he'd held up the members of the Lemurian Guard, each man carrying his crystal sword, as equals in every way to the aristocracy. Fighting side by side with the Forgotten Ones, who were forever now to be called *Paladins* of Lemuria, they would hold strong against the threat of demonkind.

Artigos had promised that somehow he would find a way to return Lemurians to, if not the same life they'd had before, at least a life filled with challenge, one that would reawaken the ancient spark of adventure and expectation that had long been buried here in this well-appointed grave they called the new Lemuria.

Man was not meant to live beneath the ground, he said. Lemurians were not meant to exist within caves and tunnels like so many trolls. He'd called on those among them who still had a grasp of the ancient technologies that had once brought them to this world so many eons ago, that had helped to create the new Lemuria within a separate dimension.

Called on them to find a way to create a world in sunlight, separate and yet part of life above ground. He admitted that it could not be done overnight, that it was not going to be easy; but he charged all his people to look toward a future where, once again, they could walk proudly as people of the light, not huddle in darkened caverns, arguing philosophical points that had no bearing on anyone or anything.

And then, with a final call to action, he explained that he was instituting changes that would begin immediately—that women would once again have a voice in their political structure; that the five seats on the board so recently held by demon-possessed men would now go to either women or members of the Lemurian Guard or the working class. All people of all levels of society would have a voice in the new order. Lemuria had once been a democracy. He, Artigos the Just, who was a king by inheritance, would rule, instead, as their new chancellor, both member and head of an entirely new Council of Nine—with all nine of them acting as true representatives to all Lemurians.

It had been a lot to swallow, and with the Lemurian penchant for philosophical discourse, Dawson imagined many, many years of discussion would ensue before all of the new chancellor's visions came to pass. He hoped to be a part of it, to see this world prosper once again, in the manner in which Artigos described.

But for now, he wanted nothing more than food, and sleep, and time alone with Selyn. So much had happened today, and he was far from absorbing even a fraction of the changes in his life.

Thank goodness for Selyn. She anchored him in a way he'd never expected. Holding on to her made all of this more real. Now his once mundane life was what seemed like the fantasy.

As impossible as these past hours had been.

He'd died today. He'd been dead enough to see his Aunt

Fiona, and then he'd been reborn. His sword had saved him, and it had spoken to him, though only that one time.

Of course, he'd not asked it any questions, either.

Like if that "live long and fight many battles" Demons-Death had promised him meant he'd gained immortality. Was he now a fitting consort for Selyn, and not someone who would, as far as she was concerned, be gone in the blink of an eye?

Of course, all of this might make more sense if he wasn't teetering on the edge of absolute exhaustion. Daws rubbed his eyes and wondered how embarrassing it would be if his head just sort of dropped into his plate.

Definitely uncool in front of all these brave warriors—the ones who had risked all for their world. Those who would continue to risk all until Lemuria was safe from the threat of demonkind.

He blinked owlishly. Good Lord in heaven, he was one of them, wasn't he? Who'd have ever thought . . . well, crap.

Dawson Buck, demon fighter!

Laughing out loud was probably inappropriate, too.

Artigos the Just ruled with a natural grace from the head of the table, but they'd all spent the past half hour eating without much conversation. Dawson couldn't recall the last meal he'd eaten, or how long it had been since he'd slept, but he still felt high, both energized and exhausted from the events of the preceding hours.

The moment he allowed himself to relax, he was probably going to crash, and crash hard. That image of his face in his plate flashed through his mind again.

Then Artigos rose to his feet, tapping a golden fork against his crystal goblet to get everyone's attention. He looked at Alton first, and then his gaze seemed to pass over and light upon every one of them at the big table.

"There are no words powerful enough to relay my

feelings," he said. "My gratitude . . . my absolute pride in all of you. My grandson Alton, Ginny, Roland, Taron . . ."

He smiled at Taron. "Thank you, young man, for closing the portal from Abyss today. I know you fear 'tis but a temporary repair, but it appears to have slowed access from Abyss to Lemuria for now, and for that we are all grateful."

He shook his head slowly, side to side. "So many of you have risked all today. Selyn. Dawson Buck. All of the Forgotten Ones . . ." He chuckled. "Excuse me, *Paladins* of Lemuria, their wardens, brave men all, who showed themselves to be strong and honorable warriors . . ." His voice broke as he continued. "I am honored to have such brave, powerful, true . . ." He cleared his throat and a shuddering breath gave weight to his words. ". . . such good, decent people on my side."

He looked around the crowded table, at the three remaining council members—the only ones who'd remained free of the demons' taint—then at Nica and Isra, Birk and Grayl, and his eyes sparkled with unshed tears. "This battle is far from over. The demon king and many of his minions remain within the walls of Lemuria, but we will flush him out tomorrow, after we've rested. Guards have been set with orders to warn of any sign of demonkind. Unless they raise the alarm, I don't expect to see any of you before dawning."

He glanced at Alton with a very tired smile on his face. "Is that what they still call it here, in this tomb we've existed in for so many millennia? Dawning?"

Alton grinned and slowly nodded his head. "Yes, grandfather. It's still called dawning, though few, if any, of our citizens recall what a real dawn looks like."

Artigos nodded and looked away. Dawson thought of

inviting him to Sedona when all of this was over. Artigos would like it there, with its vast open spaces and colorful mountains—and its blue, blue sky with the sun shining overhead.

For now, though, all of them needed sleep. Isra and Nica were the first to rise. They left, accompanied by the Lemurian guards who'd joined the gathering here with Artigos. They'd be heading toward the barracks where they'd bunk in quarters that had been quickly divided to allow a place for the women, separate from the men.

Women would forevermore make up part of the Lemurian Guard.

Roland was right behind them. He'd spent much time away from his wife, and Chara wanted him home. Dawson grinned as he returned Roland's jaunty wave. The loyal, hard-working guard deserved a night off.

They all did, and yet demonkind was a bigger threat at this point than it had been at any time before. The demon king was hiding somewhere in Lemuria, undetected even by crystal. They'd searched after the battle, but there'd been no sign of him.

More men searched even now, deep within the levels beneath the ones where the free folk lived. *Free folk.* . . . They were all free folk now, weren't they? He wondered if it had really sunk in for Selyn.

"Are you ready?" Selyn stood up and tugged Dawson's hand. He nodded. They followed Alton and Ginny as they showed them where Alton's quarters were, where he and Selyn planned to spend the night. Ginny and Alton were staying in Gaia's rooms, and Artigos the Just was moving into Alton's father's quarters.

Everything was temporary, and yet Dawson felt a sense

of homecoming. At first it surprised him, until he realized that home for him was wherever Selyn decided to stay.

They paused before the portal to Alton's place, and Ginny drew her sword.

The blade pulsed with a gentle lavender glow and then went still. "Looks clear," Ginny said. "No sign of demonkind." She yawned. "See you guys in the morning." Then she sheathed DarkFire and followed Alton along the passage.

Holding tightly to Selyn's hand, Dawson slipped through the portal into the apartment. It was clean and quiet; the refrigerator stocked; the bed freshly made. After a moment of searching, they discovered the bathing pool in the back.

Memories of the last time he'd bathed with Selyn flooded Dawson's mind, but he quickly controlled his wayward thoughts.

At least, he tried to, and he figured he was doing a pretty good job until Selyn grabbed his hand and dragged him toward the steamy room with the sound of flowing water and the softly glowing walls.

She quietly undressed, tossing her torn and ragged scrubs into a pile on the floor. Dawson slipped out of his boots and the worn jeans still caked with dried blood. He kicked his clothes to one side and slid into the steaming water beside Selyn.

She groaned, floated close, and lay her head against his shoulder. "I ache in places I didn't know could hurt," she said. Her eyes were closed, her lips softly parted. The soft curves of her full breasts, barely visible beneath the steamy surface, teased him unmercifully.

He rubbed his cheek against her dark hair, overwhelmed by feelings of tenderness for his brave warrior woman. "Poor baby." He said it lightly, but he was only partially teasing. "You're covered with cuts and bruises and scratches. Soaking should help." He tilted his head and kissed a long, red mark that ran over her shoulder.

"My injuries are nothing." She turned and stared gravely at him, cupping his cheek in the palm of her hand. "You died today, Dawson. I saw you die and felt a part of myself die as well. Then I watched you return to life. I still can't believe what happened." She paused and took a deep breath. "I don't want to think about what could have happened. I didn't cry. I couldn't. My grief was too great. I was afraid if I started, I would never be able to stop."

Her soft words tugged painfully at his heart. He didn't want to think what it would have been like if Selyn had been the one to fall. So easily it could have been her, not him, and it could happen still. They'd not yet won this battle. Not by a long shot.

Selyn raised her head. Her sorrowful gaze, tear-filled eyes, and parted lips were more than he could deny. Daws kissed her, gently at first, not intending more than this most basic connection, but Selyn wrapped her arms around his neck and shifted, half floating, until she straddled him. Then she locked her knees against his hips and kissed him back.

All thoughts of sleep, of drying off and crawling into bed for a good night's rest, deserted him with the first taste of her lips. The tip of her tongue brushed his; her full breasts pressed tightly against his chest. He pulled her closer, wrapped his arms around her waist, and held Selyn so that she could never be free of him.

Not ever.

When she rose up on her knees and then lowered herself, slowly and carefully taking him deep inside, Daws groaned with the purity of their joining, with the sense that he might never have had the chance to touch Selyn like this again, might never again have known the utter bliss of making love to her.

Slowly she moved her hips back and forth over him, finding her own rhythm, one she shared with Dawson. A rhythm as strong and steady as a beating heart, as powerful as forever, until the two of them were loving to a beat that was theirs and theirs alone.

He thought he could do this forever, this slow and easy rock and sway, but then he felt her body quicken and tighten around him. He opened his eyes to watch her climax, to see the almost painful twist to her lips, the tightly closed eyes, and the flair to her perfect nostrils as she drew in a long, sighing breath.

The visual was more than he could take. That, and the tight, rhythmic clenching of her inner muscles finally pulled him off the edge. He leapt with his heart wide open, with the shock of sensation coiling from the base of his spine down the full length of his erection.

Pumping his hips, his body moving now of its own volition, Dawson thrust hard and fast. Selyn's satisfied whimpers and his own sigh of completion played counterpoint to the final clenching spasms of climax that left both of them limp and half asleep in the steaming pool.

Long moments later, Selyn raised her head from his shoulder and looked at him out of sleepy blue eyes. "We're both turning pruny."

He chuckled, bouncing her against his chest. "I know. But getting out of the pool means getting out of you, and I'm not ready to end that connection. Not yet."

She kissed his chin, and still had the energy for a cheeky grin. "Both of us need sleep. I don't want to drown in Alton's bathing pool. That would be so rude, don't you agree? We are his guests, after all."

It was impossible to deny logic like that.

A few minutes later, Dawson tucked Selyn into bed beside him. It was late, but they still had time for a few hours of rest, unless the demon king chose to attack again tonight.

For now, though, he fought sleep, even as his body cried out for it. He hated to miss a moment of Selyn lying naked and warm beside him, her damp hair neatly braided, her fingers resting on his chest, just above his heart, the soft puffs of air from her parted lips tickling his throat.

He wanted to hang on to this moment in time. Hang on to the warmth of her body close to his, the peace of the night, and the hope that they would have more moments just like this, again and again in the years to come.

But, just in case that wasn't to be, in case life, as it so often did, kicked his ass once again, he knew he would always remember tonight.

Darius was already at the kitchen table, coffee in hand, when Eddy and Dax finally dragged themselves out of bed. No one else appeared to be up yet, but Eddy poured a cup for herself and fixed one for Dax before joining Darius at the big kitchen table.

She stared at the steam rising from her mug for what felt like a long time. Then she took a sip and sighed. "Ahhh . . . perfect. Darius, I'd never guess you're new at making coffee. This is ambrosia . . . and strong enough to melt the tines on a fork. Just the way I love it." She took another sip. "Where's Mari?"

It was Darius's turn to sigh. "She sleeps, still. It's been almost 'round the clock. Yesterday's battle took much from her. I fear today will be even more difficult."

"Why's that?" Dax leaned against the counter, but he paused with his cup halfway to his lips. "What's going on?"

Darius shook his head and his frustration was obvious. "Taron contacted me after Mari's battle, shortly after everyone here had finally gone to bed. All hell has broken loose in Lemuria. Alton and Ginny and many of the others were captured and imprisoned, but Dawson and Selyn managed to free them. Artigos the Just has formed his army of Forgotten Ones and their wardens, who, it appears, were all possessed by demonkind. The demons are gone from the wardens now without damage to the men, but the council members were not as lucky. It looks as if their demons were more deeply entrenched. They were all that kept them alive. Maxl and Drago are dead, along with one other. Two barely survived, but their minds appear to be gone."

Artigos and Gaia wandered into the kitchen, followed by Freedom, Spirit, and Ed. BumperWillow trotted along behind with her tail wagging. Eddy glared jealously at the dog. She appeared to be the only one who'd gotten enough sleep.

Artigos nodded to Darius. "We heard most of what you said, Darius. What else has happened?"

"Your father has assumed leadership of Lemuria."

Artigos nodded his head again. "As it should be. I was so terribly wrong. He never should have been deposed, and I'll back his rule a hundred percent."

Gaia reached for his hand, and Artigos took it. "Good changes, my love. They're all good. What else, Darius?"

"Five of your council members were possessed. Drago appears to have been their leader, and he's the one who's been opening the portal between Abyss and the vortex chamber. At least that's one mystery explained. We were going nuts, trying to figure out why we couldn't keep the damned thing closed. Roland would close the portal, only to find it open again the next day. Even with guards set, it was being reopened. We had no idea the guards were also possessed. It appears demonkind had been taking over Lemuria for thousands of years, one person at a time."

"They're subtle, I'll grant them that." Artigos took the chair next to Eddy. "I never suspected I wasn't making my own decisions. There was no sense of anything changing."

"Even when you left my quarters? When you left our marriage bed?" Gaia stood behind him with her fingers clasping his shoulders. "You didn't think there was anything wrong with that?"

Artigos bowed his head, shaking it in slow denial. "No. I felt that all my decisions were made for the good of Lemuria. Leaving you became a sacrifice I made for our world. I'm sorry." He bent back, looked over his shoulder, and shot her a cheeky grin. "Will you let me move back?"

"I don't know." She tilted her chin, but there was a definite twinkle in her eyes. "Maybe if you grovel."

"I like that." Spirit stood by the stove where she'd set water to boil for tea. "Groveling is always good. Remember that, Darius."

"I'll do that." Darius glanced out the window, but he didn't smile at Spirit's teasing jab. "Anyway, the demon king reappeared. . . ."

"Shit." Eddy slapped a hand over her mouth. "Sorry, but I had hoped he was going to stay gone a little longer. What else?"

"He's somewhere inside Lemuria with at least a few hundred more demons. He was also seen sending demons here and to the portal leading to Sedona. Do we have anyone in Sedona we can call, to see if there are problems?"

"Yep." Eddy glanced at Ed. "Ginny's cousin Markus lives there. Dad, do we have a phone number? Ginny said she told Markus that she and Alton were secret agents fighting demons or something like that, so Markus is supposed to keep an eye out for anything strange. If we can get a phone number, we can check with him."

"Okay," Darius said. "What about the demons sent here?"

Dax went to stand by the window, but Eddy could feel his worry. How many more might be coming to Evergreen?

"I think those are probably the ones we fought yesterday," Dax said. "The time frame sound's about right."

Eddy nodded. "There were definitely thousands. That's the most I've ever seen together at any one time, and they kept coming for what felt like forever. But what of the ones in Lemuria?"

"That's the problem." Darius stretched his big arms high overhead, and groaned. All of them were sore and tired from the battle that had lasted through much of the previous day. "The bulk of the demons headed for Lemuria, and while a lot of the devils were killed in yesterday's battle, Taron said more were coming through the portal even as he was closing it. He killed what he could, but those that escaped all headed directly into Lemuria. Our guys are going to be facing the demon king and what sounds like a full-scale army, defending Lemuria on Lemurian ground."

Dax turned away from the window. "How can we get there? The roads here are impassable. There's no way we can get to the portal up on the mountain or the one in Oregon. The snow will be over our heads. We've got to figure a way into Lemuria, or the battle could well be lost."

Darius folded his arms across his broad chest. Eddy thought he looked decidedly unhappy about something. "Okay, Darius. You look like you've got a bee up your butt. What's up?"

"A bee where?" He frowned.

Eddy snorted her coffee. "Sorry. Guess that's another

one of those things that doesn't translate well. What I meant was, what's got you so upset? Why are you frowning like that?"

Mari walked into the kitchen with a big grin on her face. "He's grumpy because he doesn't like my idea for getting us all into Lemuria." She went straight to Darius and planted a big kiss on his mouth. "But he'll get over it, won't you, sweetie?"

He glowered at Mari, but Eddy noticed he also got up, grabbed a fresh cup, and poured coffee for her.

"I don't know that I want to get over it," he said, glancing over his shoulder, "but this is your department, not mine."

"Right." Mari leaned against the counter next to Darius. "We've run out of options. We need to get to Lemuria, but the snow's too deep. There's another storm due later today." She folded her arms over her chest and grinned. "But, I think I can spell us to the vortex."

"A spell?" Mari's mother raised her head and tapped her fingers against her chin. "I know we discussed it, but do you think your power is strong enough?"

Mari nodded and took a sip of her coffee. "I do. I felt it growing earlier, as tired as I was. It was especially strong when everyone gathered around with their swords and their hands on me." She gazed at all of them, smiling with absolute confidence. "I felt the power of the crystal separately from your life force, but it really charged me. I think if Darius shares his visual of the chamber where the portals are, I can transport all of us directly into the area."

"Now that would be pretty darned excit . . ."

"No, Dad." Mari laughed. "You are not going to Lemuria while still recovering from surgery. I'm talking about Artigos, Eddy, Dax, Darius, and me." She turned to Gaia. "I know you want to be with Artigos. When it's safe, okay?"

Gaia nodded in agreement, but she clung to her husband's arm.

BumperWillow barked.

"No, Bumper. You need to stay here, too, and make certain there aren't any demons around. If you sense any, let Mom know so she can take care of them."

"And how do you expect me to do that?" Spirit cast a glance in Freedom's direction. "I've never fought demons before."

"Time to start, Mom. I tried a simple spell yesterday on one that was trying to get in after we'd come inside. I must have missed him earlier, but all I did was imagine the thing going back to Abyss. Keep that thought in your head and say, 'Demon spawn, be gone.' I don't think it actually kills them, but it does send them away."

Spirit laughed and threw her arms around Mari for a quick hug. "Ya know, for a girl who denied her powers of witchcraft for the first thirty-three of her thirty-three years, you've certainly figured things out in the past, oh . . . week?"

Mari's smile slipped. "It's amazing, isn't it? It was just a week ago I fully realized I was a witch. I can't believe I was in denial my whole life."

Freedom chuckled at that. "You always were a stubborn little thing, but Mom and I are proud of you, sweetheart. Darius, don't worry about Mari. She'd never do anything she wasn't certain was going to work, and she'll never harm anyone."

Darius stared directly at Mari. "She may never harm another, but Mari knowingly sacrificed her life for me and my companions. That was unacceptable."

"Quit complaining, sweetie." She kissed the frown right off of Darius's face. "I'm perfectly healthy, and it all worked out just fine. Trust me. I really do know how to get us to the portal. But not until we've had breakfast. I've discovered that using magic really makes me hungry."

Are you sure you don't want me to come? Bumper-Willow sat at Eddy's feet and stared at her with all the hope that a blond, brown-eyed, curly-haired pit bull/poodle-cross mutt could muster. *I can find demons even better than DemonSlayer.*

Eddy stared down at the hopeful face and caved. "Mari, do you think you could add BumperWillow to that spell? She's even better at finding demons than our swords, and if demons are hiding somewhere in Lemuria, I'd trust Bumper's nose over anything or anyone else."

"If Dax or Darius is holding her, no problem. But first, food." Mari gave her father the same kind of hopeful look Bumper'd just given Eddy. Somehow it seemed entirely apropos.

Darius carried the coffee pot to the table and refilled everyone's cups while Freedom started cooking. Snow was beginning to fall once again, and the morning was all but gone.

Eddy gazed out the window in the direction of Mount Shasta and the energy portals. All was lost behind a heavy wall of white, but somewhere, deep within the mountain, she wondered if the battle raged once again; if Alton and Ginny were okay; if Dawson Buck and Selyn had figured out just how attracted they were to each other.

Now that could prove interesting. She'd sensed Dawson's interest from the very first day, but they faced the same problem Alton and Ginny had once faced— a mortal and an immortal had a hard time with a long-term relationship.

Then she glanced at Dax and smiled. Caught Mari's raised eyebrows, and wondered if she'd been listening in. She, Mari, and Ginny, all perfectly normal, mortal, human women, now paired with immortal men and facing lives that could go on forever.

Who said Dawson and Selyn didn't have a chance? She found it hard to believe in the possibility of anything being impossible. Not anymore.

Chapter Twenty-Three

The wind was picking up, and fat snowflakes whirled all about by the time they gathered in the backyard beneath the old gazebo. Dax eyed the ancient structure and shot a questioning glance at Eddy. She bit back a grin. *It's perfectly safe. I really don't think it's going to collapse.*

There's a lot of snow on the roof.

It will be fine. Relax.

At least she hoped it would. She hoped a lot would be fine, including this first-time magical spell of Mari's. Dax had a tight grip on Bumper with both arms, while Eddy held on to the belt loop at the middle of his back with her right hand and linked arms with Artigos on her left. Darius was on Dax's right, hanging on to Eddy's hand and Dax's belt loop with his left hand, and clasping his right arm tightly around Mari's waist. Artigos hugged Mari from the other side.

They'd decided that hanging on to each other in a tight huddle was more important than holding their swords against Mari while she cast the spell, though first they'd had her hold each of the blades to draw what power she could.

Spirit, Freedom, Gaia, and Ed waited inside the house,

watching nervously through the back window. Mari'd been concerned about their being caught up in her spell, something none of them wanted. Well, none except Freedom who was terribly disappointed that his beloved daughter had told him he couldn't go with them to Lemuria.

He'd insisted that it was, after all, something he'd dreamed of for years, but Mari held firm. Now she glanced at her mother and grinned, but when she faced forward, her smile was gone. "Okay," she said, and it was easy for Eddy to picture the professional investment banker behind that solemn voice. "I've never done this, but there's no reason it shouldn't work."

Eddy snickered. "If that's supposed to inspire confidence, Mari, you need to work on your spiel."

"Yeah. Right." She smiled brightly. "Okay. Improved version. Darius has given me a great visual of the chamber inside the energy portal, and we will all arrive together, safely, without any problems." She let out a quick breath. "But just in case we land outside, we're all dressed warmly, right? Eddy? Is that coat of mine going to be enough?"

Eddy nodded. "I'm fine. But let's hurry. I've got a terrible feeling they really need us."

Mari nodded. "Me, too. Not about the spell, about Lemuria, and I've never even been there."

"There's a first time for everything." Darius kissed her cheek. "You can do this. We all can."

Mari took a deep breath, let it out, and looked at each of them. "I know." Then she began to chant.

"The battle calls. Our comrades wait.
Transport all six to Lemuria's gate.
Artigos. Dax. Eddy. Darius. BumperWillow and me.
Send us now. So mote it be."

Nothing happened. She glanced around, blinking as if surprised they'd not moved. "Okay. Let's give this one more . . ."

Before she could repeat her spell, light flashed, and Eddy felt that weird sensation of weightlessness that happens just before a rollercoaster makes its downward run.

Light swirled, darkness and then color and darkness again. And, as if she'd jumped off a bottom step, Eddy's feet hit the ground. "Oh. My. God! Mari, you did it!" She glanced around at the familiar portals. "You really spelled us here. Fantastic!"

Dax set BumperWillow on the ground, and the dog raced across the small chamber, barking and growling. Artigos stumbled and then righted himself. Darius held Mari in a tight embrace, holding her up. She trembled from head to foot and looked as if her legs were ready to fold.

But she was smiling. "I did, didn't I? So this is what an energy vortex looks like, eh?" She glanced around. Then she jumped when Dax and Artigos both drew their swords. "What's wrong?"

"The portal's open again." Dax slashed through a dark wraith, and it burst into blue sparks and stinking smoke. "Who the hell . . . Darius, can you close this thing?"

"I can, but it's a big portal, and it could take a while. Dax, you, Eddy, and Artigos. Go and see what you can do to help Alton. I'll close the portal. I bet the demon king had something to do with this." He glanced at Mari and smiled broadly as she mumbled her spell, pointed at a demon, and watched it disappear in a cloud of sulfuric smoke. "Mari can take care of the demons while I work on the portal. We'll meet up with you inside."

"BumperWillow! C'mon." Eddy snapped her fingers, and the dog immediately trotted along behind her as she drew her sword and followed Dax and Artigos through the portal to Lemuria. Down the passageway and through the flowing wall of gold, and then along the broad, brightly lit tunnel toward the great plaza.

The eerie yet now familiar sound of banshee cries echoed off the walls. Shouts and curses, and an overwhelming sense of dread radiated from the direction they traveled.

Dax broke into a run.

Eddy glanced at Bumper to make sure she was following and caught up to Artigos and Dax. Three abreast, with BumperWillow now leading the way, they turned the final corner and burst into the great plaza.

Demons were everywhere! Swirling in masses of black mist, charging the soldiers, and dying against their crystal blades, their numbers seemed unending.

Dax was immediately drawn into battle, with Alton's father standing at his back. Their swords flashed, and demons died, but more came to take their place. "I'm going to find Ginny," Eddy shouted. "I want them to know we're here."

Dax nodded and swung his sword. Eddy slipped past groups of combatants and raced toward the dais. A flash of dark light pinpointed Ginny's location.

Ginny stood beside a man wielding a ruby sword who could only be Artigos the Just. He reminded Eddy of Alton, but he fought as if he were merely another soldier in this terrible fight, not the returned ruler of an entire civilization. The stench of sulfur was almost suffocating as demons died, as more rushed in to take their place.

"Ginny! We're here. Darius and Mari are working on the portal. It was open again."

"Hey, Eddy!" Ginny ducked as a demon flew overhead. "Taron was afraid his fix wouldn't hold. He said Drago had made a huge gateway, bigger than any he'd seen. Who'd you bring?"

"Me, Dax, Artigos, Darius, and Mari. Oh," she laughed as BumperWillow barked, "and Bumper. She's good at finding demonkind."

"No need to search." Ginny thrust her blade into a mass of dark, oily mist that took on form and shape in Dark-Fire's lavender light, and died in a mass of sharp fangs and deadly talons. "They're everywhere. The demon king is here somewhere, but he's staying clear of DarkFire. Mine seems to be the only blade that will harm him."

"Good to know." Eddy thrust DemonSlayer into another mass of demonkind. She might not see them as clearly as Ginny could in the dark glow of her amethyst blade, but they died in just as satisfactory a manner. "How are Selyn and Dawson?"

Ginny laughed. "Wait until you see! Dawson's got a sword. It's already saved his life. He pulled a Dax and died on us, but he's back and better than ever—maybe even immortal. I think he and Selyn are a definite pair."

"I hoped as much. That's great. Not that he died, but . . ." Eddy ducked as another group of demons whistled by overhead. A soldier she didn't recognize, one bearing crystal, stopped their attack with a single thrust.

There'd definitely been a few changes while she'd been trapped in Evergreen. She spun around, dodged another black wraith, and called out, "Ginny! I almost forgot. Tell Alton his father is fine. The demon inside him is gone, and his father is here fighting. He plans to support Artigos the Just and make a public apology to all Lemuria."

"Eddy! You're here!" Selyn called out from the dais. She stood atop the platform with her sword in her hand and Dawson by her side. "And Bumper, too!"

Ducking down as a demon whizzed by, she jumped

from the dais and raced to Eddy, dodging small groups of soldiers and armed women fighting. "I'm so glad you're here!" She hugged Eddy and then waved at Dawson. "It's so weird this morning. The demons are all over the place, but they're not able to show themselves like they did yesterday. They're not able to injure anyone, either. We were all scratched and bloody after fighting them before, but now it's like batting down harmless insects."

Dawson joined them. Eddy noticed the easy way he looped an arm over Selyn's shoulders, the natural slide of her body against his. "Selyn's right," he said, glancing all around. "I know there are literally thousands of them here, as if they've been pouring through the portal for most of the night, but they don't appear to be as solid as they were yesterday. They're practically throwing themselves at our swords."

"What about the demon king?" Dax draped his arm around Eddy and glanced over the crowd. Though the air reeked of sulfur, the masses of flying, attacking demons appeared to be falling off dramatically.

"Haven't seen him today." Dawson glanced over his shoulder. "Ginny drove him off last night. Maybe she's scared him away."

"Don't count on it." Ginny and Alton joined them. "I've got a bad feeling about things. This morning has been much too easy."

Roland strode across the open plaza. "No sign of the bastard, Alton. I've heard back from my men. They've checked as far as the third level beneath the prison, and there's no sign or scent of demonkind."

"There's no sign he's gone, either." A huge guard joined their group. He bowed his head toward Eddy. "Birk, m'lady. I was one of the wardens guarding the Forgotten Ones."

Before Eddy could respond, Selyn punched him almost

playfully on the arm. "Paladins, Birk. We're not forgotten any longer."

He nodded. "I stand corrected. As we are no longer possessed. But I'm uncomfortable with the disappearance of the demon king. He did not strike me as an entity willing to give up so easily."

Eddy glanced up and felt a shiver race along her spine. Mari and Darius were entering the plaza, walking hand in hand toward their small group, and she thought of Mari with that damned crystal in her heart, the one that attracted demons. She hoped it wasn't a mistake for her to come here.

Dax squeezed her hand, and she knew he'd picked up on her worries. "She'll be okay," he said. "We'll all stick close."

Selyn turned and waved at someone on the far side of the plaza. "I see Isra and Nica. I want you to meet them, Eddy. They're friends of mine." She kissed Dawson's cheek. "Be right back." Then she turned away and trotted toward the two women.

Reluctantly, Dawson watched her go with an uncomfortable and unaccountable sense of dread, but he held back the words of caution he wanted to shout, fully aware Selyn would hate his overprotective nature. He had to get over this constant need to guard her. Selyn was a warrior in her own right—powerful and strong and so beautiful she made him ache.

His hovering over her would be the last thing she wanted. She was reveling in her newfound freedom, enjoying the first time in her very long life when she could make her own decisions, choose her own future.

He still couldn't believe she'd chosen him. Wouldn't believe it—not yet. It was still too new, too wonderful.

Just as Selyn was too wonderful. She looked like a dark-haired angel in her beautiful white robe. A lot better than he did, dressed like Lemuria's finest, that was certain.

They'd both ended up wearing traditional white Lemurian robes this morning. He really felt like a dork, but there was no way Selyn could don her torn and blood-stained scrubs, and his jeans had been covered with the blood from his mortal wound.

Just thinking of that made his blood run cold.

He guessed running around Lemuria like a white-robed monk was better than dead, and that's exactly where he should be right now. Instead, he was alive and in love, and carrying a crystal sword that had already said it wanted him around.

A far cry from his life as a small-town vet in Sedona, Arizona, that was for sure. No, this was definitely a change, and one he still had trouble believing.

Selyn had reached Nica and Isra. The three women hugged, and Dawson was reminded of their deep commitment to one another. He'd discovered he actually liked Isra, something he'd not expected, but she'd made an amazing transformation over the past couple of days.

He had to believe it was finally holding crystal that had given the woman the sense of worth she'd obviously lacked. He understood that. He was a guy who'd always thought of himself as a nerd. Yet standing here with a crystal sword in his hand had a way of changing a man's self-image.

A soft breeze blew past. The tiny hairs at the nape of his neck stood on end. He glanced all about, looking for the source of his discomfort. There was nothing to see, nothing that accounted for the growing, almost overwhelming sense of dread.

No demons flew through the air. The sulfuric stench was almost gone, and small groups of people—soldiers and citizens alike—stood about talking.

BumperWillow growled, a long, low rumble that definitely had its beginnings deep in her chest. "What is it, Willow?"

The dog continued staring straight ahead. Dawson caught Dax's eye. "Do you feel anything?"

Dax shook his head.

BumperWillow growled again. *Bumper senses demonkind,* Willow said. *Neither here nor there, but all around. Growing stronger, more distinct by the second.* Then the dog yipped. She took off running, reached the steps to the dais, and bounded up, scrambling to the top taking two stairs at a time.

Standing atop the dais, the dog had a better view of the vast plaza. Her ears were perked forward, her tail held stiffly upright, but she seemed confused by her inability to pinpoint the source of the sense of demonkind.

Selyn raised her head and caught Dawson's eye. He waved to her. The air felt thick, as if it sucked at him as he started in her direction. Something was here, some horrible evil, powerful enough that voices were falling silent and everyone in the huge chamber was nervously glancing about.

His sense of unease exploded. Dawson drew his sword and raced toward Selyn. Her crystal was still sheathed, but she'd started trotting across the plaza, heading directly to him. He knew he'd feel better once he could hold her, know she was safe in his arms.

A low howl filled his head—a howl that rose to a terrible, ear-splitting crescendo. Dawson stretched his legs and ran full out, but it felt as if he raced through glue. Everything slipped into slow motion, and yet there was a clarity to his vision he'd never experienced before.

Selyn ran toward him with her arms spread wide, reaching out for him. Her eyes flashed with fear, her hair, falling free today and held back with nothing more than the simple gold band around her forehead, flowed behind her like so much black silk.

The faces of the people he passed morphed from curiosity to fear. A dark shadow flowed over all of them and enveloped everything within the plaza. Darkness and fear and the suffocating stench of demonkind.

Crying out for Selyn, her name echoing in his ears, Dawson reached for his woman.

And then everything sped up. Moving like a whirlwind of darkness, the demon king swept down between Dawson and Selyn. Solid and fully formed, the king reached for her with his many-jointed arms, grabbed her up in his disgusting embrace, and spun high overhead with Selyn clasped to his chest, spinning higher and higher, to the very top of the domed ceiling.

Selyn screamed. Dawson heard his name on her lips, felt her terror, and he leapt, reaching high with his sword for that foul creature as it stole Selyn away.

Swirling, twirling with the force of a tornado, with the roar of a freight train and a wind that shrieked throughout the huge plaza, the demon king carried Selyn higher, faster, farther.

And then, with a loud *pop!* they disappeared.

Dawson didn't remember falling to his knees, had no idea how long he knelt there, staring at the ceiling overhead, hearing the echo of Selyn's scream as the demon king bore her away.

"Shit." Alton grabbed Dawson's left arm, Dax took hold of his right, and they hauled him to his feet. Still cursing, Alton grabbed Dawson by both shoulders and shook him. "Out of it, man. There's no time to waste. We have to find her, now. We need you with us."

Dawson blinked and stared into those emerald green eyes, but all he could see was the fear on Selyn's face as that creature took her. "Where?" He shook his head. "Where in the hell could he have taken her? Not to Abyss. He wouldn't dare take her. . . ."

"No." Dax turned Dawson's arm loose. "He knows she can't survive in Abyss. The air's too foul for Lemurians or humans to breathe." He stared at Dawson with eyes full of pain—full of guilt. "Daws, I'm so sorry. He's not going to go far. He wants me. Wants this body, I think. At least the life force within. The demon king *is* me. That was my form when I was demonkind. My body. I fear he's using Selyn as a lure to draw me close."

Dawson had never, not once in his life, known such anger or such a devastating sense of loss. Not when his mother died, not when he'd lost his Aunt Fiona, not even when he'd felt his own life slipping away.

With an almost fatalistic determination, he pulled his sword from his scabbard. Dax and Alton backed away, and he was sure they thought he'd cracked. No, he was nowhere near losing it. There was something steadying about anger like his. Something about it that anchored him and gave everything around him a clarity he'd not expected.

Dawson raised his blade and watched the light shimmer over its many diamond-bright facets. "Find her, Demons-Death. Tell me where the demon king has taken Selyn."

A flash of brilliant blue shot from the blade, light so bright he would have covered his eyes had he not been afraid he might miss something.

Instead of blinding him, the light seemed to make everything even clearer. Power pulsed from the crystalline blade, through the jeweled hilt and along his arm, until he felt the power of crystal deep in his heart.

"Follow the small one." The light pulsed, and suddenly Bumper was bathed in its brilliant glow. "Follow the small one in the form of the beast. She and her animal host will lead us to StarFire, and hence, to Selyn. But we must hurry. Go now, while our woman yet lives."

Selyn sensed the demon king was near, but she kept her eyes tightly closed. At least she wasn't bound, and from the weight in the scabbard on her back, she still had StarFire.

That was good. What was bad was the fact there was no sense of anyone else around—at least not anyone she wanted to contact. The demon felt like a black smear in her mind—unclean and evil—and she did her best to block him.

She lay there a while longer, muscles aching from the awkward position she'd been dumped in on the floor, before sending out another mental quest. Again, she came up blank. No sense of Dawson or Ginny, not of Alton or Eddy. No one.

Only the foul sense of the demon king, the knowledge that he watched her. That he wanted her. She repressed a shiver, forced down the gorge that rose in her throat, the visceral experience of his disgusting needs flowing over her like so much filth.

Dawson! Where are you?

The stench of sulfur grew stronger. She heard the scuff of heavy feet moving over the ground, shivered as the temperature dropped precipitously, and knew the creature stood over her, that he watched her.

There was nothing wraith-like about him now. His scales were sharp, and they'd cut her hands when he carried her away. His body had felt solid—rock hard, cold, and reptilian. The creature's foul breath made her want to vomit, and as he drew closer to her, she felt his disgusting need.

Sensed his physical reaction to her feminine form, his

glee that she was here, that she was his, that she was the lure he'd needed to draw what he truly wanted.

She willed her body not to react. Willed herself not to scream, though the terror rose in her like bile, gagging her in silent agony.

She'd been a slave for thousands of years. Had endured beatings and harassment and all sorts of terrible things. She could endure this. She would endure this. For the first time in her long life, she had something to live for. Someone to love, who loved her in return.

Whatever happened, she would survive. She had to. No matter what this creature might do to her. No matter what, Selyn fully intended to live.

Down! He's taken her down, into the depths of the mountain! BumperWillow barked once and raced across the plaza, heading for the nearest portal.

Dawson was right on her heels, running as fast as he could with the damned robe swirling around his legs. He had no idea who followed him, who chose to stay behind. He had DemonsDeath in his right hand and Bumper-Willow in his sights and her thoughts in his head.

They'd find Selyn. They had to.

He'd likely gained immortality, but life meant nothing without Selyn. The dog leapt through the first portal with Dawson right behind. He heard feet pounding the stairs behind him as he followed BumperWillow down to another level, but almost lost her when she disappeared through a portal just beyond the stairs.

Then her curly blond head poked out through the swirling light and she barked, one sharp yip that caught him in mid-stride. He turned to go through the portal and almost collided with Alton and Ginny. Eddy and Dax were right behind them, followed by Mari and Darius.

He had a veritable army with him! There was no way to express his gratitude. No time. He jumped through the portal and took off after the dog. Willow's voice was in his head, urging him on, telling him to hurry, that they must go deeper yet, farther into the mountain, away from everything familiar.

Or was it? Within minutes they'd reached the level where Selyn had been enslaved for so long. The machines were silent, now, the hallways empty. It was like running through a ghost town filled with the spirits of the lost women from the DemonWars.

Now, even their children were gone. Many of the spirited women had found new life as the sentience within crystal swords, but what of those who hadn't? What of the ones who'd not given birth? Who had no daughters to carry on, no crystal swords to give them a new chance at life. Where were their spirits?

Maybe they were still here. Maybe they'd be able to help. He had no idea, but Dawson called out to them, begged them to help him find Selyn. *She's Elda's daughter,* he said. *Elda, now DemonSlayer, was your friend. Help us save her daughter!*

BumperWillow barked again and disappeared through another portal. Dawson vaguely recalled this same path. He'd followed it the day they'd gone in search of Taron. Was that where the bastard demon king had taken Selyn? To the crystal caves so far beneath the levels where the free folk lived?

It had to be. Something in crystal drew demonkind, even as it killed them. "I think I know where he's taken her!" Dawson skidded around a corner, right behind the dog. "The caverns where Taron replicated the swords. The crystal caverns. I bet he's got her there."

"I've not been this deep before," Alton said. "Damn! We should have brought Taron. He knows the way."

Dawson flashed him a grin. For the first time he felt hopeful. "So do I," he said. "So do I."

Chapter Twenty-Four

StarFire? Can you help me? What should I do? Selyn hadn't moved, but she knew the demon squatted beside her. Knew by the stench of his body and his foul breath. She'd managed not to shudder when he ran one talon down the front of her robe, parting the fabric so that it gaped open, exposing her breasts.

No, she'd kept her eyes closed and her body as still as death. She would not scream. She refused to show him fear. For now, he thought her unconscious, but for how long?

Help comes.

StarFire's soft words gave her courage. She bit back a moan. *Dawson!* It had to be Daws. Would he get here soon enough? What did this thing want with her? It was massive— at least three times the size it had been yesterday.

The way the demons behaved today finally made sense.

Somehow the demon king had stolen their life force. He'd drawn it off of the thousands of demons swarming Lemuria, and he'd taken it into himself. That had to be how he'd gained so much size and strength. How he'd managed to pick her up and take her away. But why had he chosen her? What could he possibly want with a slave?

No. Not a slave. A Paladin. A guardian of Lemuria—a powerful warrior, armed with crystal. She had to keep reminding herself, she was a woman of value now. A woman of worth.

A woman loved by a wonderful man who was coming, even now, to save her.

She sensed the change in the air currents at the same moment the demon king let out a furious shriek, leapt to his feet, and spun away from her. Finally, Selyn risked opening her eyes. Light shimmered all around—a thousand lights reflecting from the walls and ceiling.

The crystal cave! She was in the cave where Taron had replicated her sword and the swords for all the other women. Carefully, without moving at all, she glanced around, trying to find where her captor had gone. She spotted the ruby altar, saw a few primitive candles burning in the same sconces where Taron had set glow sticks.

It didn't take many to light a chamber made of diamonds.

A dog barked.

The demon king shrieked again, but his voice came from the far side of the cavern. Selyn leapt to her feet and drew StarFire.

"Selyn! Selyn, where are you?"

"Here, Dawson! I'm over here!"

Dawson stood at the entrance to the cavern. She saw the shadows of others behind him—Ginny and Alton. Two she'd not met before, who she deduced must be Mari, and Darius, Dax, Eddy—and Bumper, who raced across the chamber at full tilt so intent on reaching Selyn that she ran much too close to the demon king.

The beast reached for the dog but she yipped and scrambled out of his way, tumbling head over heels in her rush to get to Selyn. Selyn knelt and hugged the wriggling, quivering dog, getting more than her share of wet, sloppy kisses.

She heard Dawson curse. Hugging Bumper to hold her still, Selyn looked up as Dawson, Dax, and Eddy attacked the demon king.

She shoved her fist against her mouth to keep from screaming as Dawson lunged for the beast, thrusting hard and fast with DemonsDeath, drawing some kind of thick, dark blood with the crystal blade. Dax and Eddy moved in on one side, Alton and Ginny on the other, all of them slashing and stabbing as the demon king howled and reached out with his four, long, multi-jointed arms.

Dawson pivoted away from the creature's talons and raced toward Selyn, grabbed her in his arms, and held on as if he'd never let her go. She felt him shudder, sensed the fear and the anger he'd been holding inside, and she kissed him. Held his face in her hands and kissed him hard.

"Dear God, I thought I'd lost you." He trembled from head to foot.

She held on to him even tighter. "Never," she said. "No matter what, I will always find my way back to you."

"Are you all right?" He tipped her chin up with his fingertip and kissed her once again.

"I am. C'mon. We have to end this. Now."

Dawson nodded, but he kissed her once more, grabbed her hand, and they ran across the cavern, closer to the battle.

"Dax. Look!" Eddy used her sword to point at the dark puddle gathering in the dirt wherever the demon king stepped. "It's bleeding from the wound Daws left, just like the gargoyle—it's real now, not merely a wraith."

"If it can bleed, it can die!" Dax lunged at the demon king and slashed rather than thrust. The unexpected move caught the beast off guard, and DemonFire cut through one of his multi-jointed arms as if it were made of butter.

The limb fell to the ground, twitching and grasping, as

if it was trying to crawl away. The demon screamed and slashed at Dax, but Dax had already pivoted and spun out of reach.

Eddy cursed and jumped out of reach as the demon shifted direction, pivoted on one leg and went straight for her. Dax leapt between them, cutting and stabbing with his crystal blade, but two of the demon's three remaining arms snaked out and snagged his shirt with long, curved talons.

Dax cursed, but he couldn't pull free. Alton and Ginny closed in from one side, Darius and Eddy from the other. Dawson and Selyn split up, each moving to opposite sides of the demon.

Selyn stalked the demon, with StarFire in her hand and Bumper on her heels. Mari stood to one side, chanting some sort of spell with her arms held high.

Dawson watched the witch for mere seconds when something clicked. He shouted to her, "Mari, call on the spirits." He slashed at the demon's legs, but the creature danced away, spinning out of reach with unexpected speed and agility. The demon king still hung on to Dax with two of his arms, like a child holding a rag doll.

"The spirits, Mari," Dawson repeated. "Artigos's sword mentioned waiting for rebirth in Mother Crystal. He meant this cave. The warrior's spirits are here. Call the spirits of the warrior women. They're here. I can feel them."

Mari nodded, and her voice rang out until the crystal walls of the cavern vibrated. The demon tried to spin faster, as if to take Dax away, but something seemed to hold him back. Alton buried his blade in the demon king's back, and Ginny attacked with DarkFire. Flames shot from her blade whenever she connected with the beast, but instead of weakening, he seemed to grow stronger.

"Damn you!" Eddy drove forward with her blade and

slashed at the demon's legs. "He's stealing Dax's life force. We've got to stop him!"

The demon king clutched Dax against his chest, but Dax no longer struggled. Instead, he hung there, limp and lifeless.

"No!" Selyn charged the demon king at the same time that Eddy leapt to the top of the ruby altar and from there to the creature's back. Clinging to his shoulders, she swung DemonSlayer across his throat and began to saw at the thick, corded muscle guarded by heavy scales.

Ginny stabbed frantically, burying DarkFire in his side and legs. Sparks flashed and blood flowed, but it was hard to attack without risking Dax.

Dax, who dangled helplessly in the demon king's grasp.

Mari's chant created an absurd, almost musical backdrop to the life and death battle, but her voice never wavered. Instead, she seemed to grow stronger. Light flashed all around, as if the crystals embedded in the cavern walls had come to life; they pulsed in time with her spell.

The room grew brighter; the pulse of life took on sound, and the beat of many hearts filled the chamber. White wraiths spilled out of the walls, bursting forth from the crystals, swirling through and over the demon king, filling the small space between the hideous creature and Dax's body. Wherever one touched, the demon burst into boils and burned flesh, until it howled in agony, yet the white wraiths covered Dax with a protective blanket that held him apart from the demon.

Screeching, the demon king shook hard enough to dislodge Eddy. She fell to the ground with DemonSlayer clutched in her hand, rolled out of the way, and rose shakily to her feet.

The wraiths continued their graceful attack, floating over

and around the demon king, slowly but surely destroying his skin and scales with nothing but their gentle touch.

Howling and wailing, he tried to spin but somehow the wraiths controlled the beast and held him to this spot. Finally, shrieking and bleeding, the demon king dropped Dax and backed away with BumperWillow snapping at his bleeding legs.

The dog avoided the blood and the gore. Selyn realized why when the demon shook its head and a drop of dark blood splashed on her arm. Her skin sizzled as if from an acid burn.

Mari's chant continued, growing stronger, louder, and the sense of power within the crystal cavern grew. The white wraiths circled the demon king, spinning faster and faster until he was lost in a swirling blanket of glowing white light. Then, with a final, ear-splitting scream, the demon seemed to collapse in upon itself. It disappeared in a flash of light and disgustingly familiar sulfuric stench.

The white wraiths floated away, hovered for a moment overhead, and then settled on Dax where he lay immobile on the hard ground. Eddy knelt beside him, holding his hand, weeping softly.

Selyn broke free of Dawson's grasp and ran to Eddy. "We need to use our blades. They'll share their life force with him. I know they will. That's how we saved Dawson."

Eddy didn't hesitate. She grabbed her sword and placed it over Dax's heart. Dawson and the others pulled theirs, and all of them lay the blades across Dax. The white wraiths continued to hover, covering him with a sense of life and hope impossible to ignore.

Long moments later, his eyes fluttered and then opened. Selyn reached for Dawson's hand and held on tightly as Dax slowly regained consciousness. Finally, he smiled at Eddy. "I bet you're getting really tired of this, aren't you?"

He reached for her, and she tumbled into his arms, crying and laughing at the same time.

Selyn finally looked away from the two and glanced about. The white wraiths were gone. "Where are they?" She gazed in Mari's direction. "The spirits of the warrior women. Did you see them? Where did they go?"

Mari waved her hands. "Into the crystal walls. They must be part of this cavern. Maybe that's why Taron was sent here to replicate the swords—because the spirits that bring them to life live here."

Dax slowly sat up with Eddy's help. He still looked weak, but his color was returning. "They kept me alive. They were sharing their life force with me, even as the demon king was siphoning mine away." He shook his head. "Such a feeling of goodness, as if they were everything the demon king isn't."

He looked at Ginny. "Is it dead this time? I saw you nail him with DarkFire."

She shook her head. "No. I think he'd already drawn too much power—from the other demons during the night, and from you just now. He's gone, but I have a feeling he'll be back."

"How can we kill him?" Mari wrapped her arms around Darius and leaned against his side. "What will destroy him for good? This fight will go on until he's dead and gone."

Eddy stood up and held out a hand to Dax. When he took it, she tugged him to his feet. "I think it's going to take everything we have, a combination of magic and crystal." She glanced around them at the crystal walls. "And maybe even the spirits of long-dead women warriors. I wish we knew for sure." She turned to Dax. "You okay to head back?"

"I am," he said. "Thank you. All of you. And Selyn, I'm so sorry for what happened to you."

"Sorry? Why should you be sorry?" Selyn looked at Dax and finally just shook her head and laughed. "It's not your fault, Dax. I'm okay. I think, after this, I can survive anything. I'm a lot tougher than I ever realized, and it's because of all of you."

BumperWillow barked. "And you, too, Bumper. And Willow." She grabbed Dawson's hand. His warm fingers wrapped around hers and she squeezed his in return. Definitely stronger than she'd ever dreamed.

Dawson held on to Selyn's hand all the way back to the main levels of Lemuria. He wasn't about to let her go for anything. Not yet. Her abduction was too recent, the fear he'd felt when that monster stole her away still a knife to his heart.

All he could think of was taking her back to Alton's quarters and making love in that perfect pool, but the minute they reached the main plaza, he figured that was one dream that was going to have to be put on hold.

Artigos the Just and Artigos the younger called out to them as they slipped through the portal. Taron stood right behind the two leaders with his arms folded over his chest. His expression was impossible to read.

Alton stepped forward. "The demon king was badly wounded, but we don't think he's dead. He's probably escaped back to Abyss. I'm sorry that we failed."

His grandfather stepped forward and wrapped his arms around Alton. "You've not failed. You've returned Selyn safely and brought your comrades back unharmed. That was your goal, wasn't it?"

Alton glanced at all of them and slowly nodded. "I guess you're right, Grandfather." He turned to his father and held out his hand. "I hope you'll forgive me for the actions I ordered against you."

His father grabbed Alton's hand and pulled him into

a warm embrace. "You saved my life, son. I will be forever grateful that you had the courage of your beliefs . . ." His voice broke, and he took an audible breath, but he didn't release his son. ". . . that you were willing to risk all for Lemuria. I couldn't be more proud. Your mother feels the same."

Alton pulled back. "Have you spoken with her?"

"I have. Taron and I went through the portal, and I contacted her. The snow is still much too deep to traverse, so we'll need Mari's magic to get back to Evergreen, but for now she is safe with Spirit, Freedom, and Ed. They've seen no sign of demonkind since we left Evergreen."

"What about Markus?" Ginny glanced at Eddy. "Eddy, didn't you just say your dad was going to try to reach him?"

Artigos sighed. "Markus hasn't answered his phone, but Ed said that wasn't all that unusual. They're going to keep trying, and we'll make contact again tomorrow. Now that you're back, though, we need to discuss our future plans for Lemuria. There's an army to organize, a new government under your grandfather's rule, new members of the Council of Nine to choose. . . ."

He grabbed Alton's arm and turned away, obviously intent on going straight to work on everything that could be done now. Dawson glanced at Selyn. She winked, grabbed his hand, and tugged him toward a small portal he'd not noticed before.

Without drawing anyone's attention, the two of them slipped through the portal, into one of the narrow passages generally used by the Lemurian guards.

It was also a wonderful shortcut to Alton's quarters. Laughing at their escape, Dawson let Selyn tug him along the passage and through another portal into the private rooms.

"Do you think they know where we are?" Selyn kissed

his chin, but her fingers were busy tugging at the ties holding the neck of his robe closed.

"Do you think they care?" Dawson grabbed the sides of her robe and pulled it over her head. She was entirely nude beneath the soft folds. "If I'd known before what Lemurians wore under these things, I might not have insisted on giving you my old scrubs."

Selyn giggled, still tugging at the ties she'd managed to tangle into a knot. Dawson leaned close and rubbed his beard over the sensitive tips of her nipples.

"That's not fair." She gasped when he turned his head and nibbled with his teeth.

"I think it is." He sucked the entire nipple between his lips, tugging until Selyn rose up on her toes, but when he released the pressure, she spun out of his way and grabbed his robe, tugging it over his head without untying it.

"Ouch! I've gotten used to keeping both ears, thank you."

Laughing, she pulled harder until the fabric finally came free. They'd managed to work their way down the passage to the bathing room as they undressed. Dawson kicked off his boots and grabbed Selyn up in his arms.

Then, slowly, and with many dips and kisses, he lowered her into the water. Steam rose all around, and Selyn was slippery as an eel, but he held her tight against his chest and kept her there as he sat on a ledge beneath the water's surface. It bubbled all around them, washing away the stench of demonkind, soothing and removing fear and loss. Cleansing them in a way that renewed Dawson, that energized Selyn.

Holding her against him, Daws felt the tension seeping out of his bones. He allowed his muscles to relax, let the events of the day fade away with the wisps of steam floating on the surface of the water.

His life had changed, but so had Selyn's. Dawson had the strange feeling that they were merely in the midst of a chapter of a much larger story, that the events leading to this moment in time were nothing more than bullet points on a much longer list.

He'd never imagined finding love. Not like this. Never dreamed he'd find himself playing the part of a warrior, a member of an elite group charged with saving an entire civilization from demonkind, but he was.

Selyn nuzzled beneath his chin and kissed him softly. "I love you, Dawson Buck. No matter what comes, no matter where our lives lead, I swear I will always love you. Forever."

He returned her kiss, opening his thoughts to her, sharing everything that filled his heart. "Always is a damned long time. Are you sure about that?"

"Oh, yeah." She snuggled close, slick and warm and perfectly aligned to take him deep inside. Sighing as he filled her, she tightened her grasp around his neck, rested her forehead close to his. Kissed him. Then she kissed him again.

"I'm sure," she said, nuzzling the soft beard covering his jaw. "I just hope forever's long enough."

Be sure not to miss

WOLF TALES 12,

the final book in Kate Douglas's sizzling series!
An Aphrodisia trade paperback on sale July 2011.

Turn the page for a special preview. . . .

Montana, early August

He paused, raised his muzzle to the dark sky, and sniffed the subtle currents on the night air. The scent was there—faint, but still calling to him, even as the silent night, the gentle breeze, the resinous scent of pine and fir called.

His eyes narrowed, and his ears pricked forward. Using all his senses—those of the wolf, those of the man within, and those amazing Chanku senses—he tested the world around him.

This was where he belonged, in this wild, unforgiving place. This was home—the only home he wanted. The only place where he could truly be free.

But, what good was freedom without his mate? What was the point? She didn't run with him tonight. She hadn't run with him for much too long.

A low whine sounded from the thick tangle of willows. Cautiously he sniffed the air again. The scent was stronger. Not his mate. No, but someone every bit as important. Someone he sought here in the forest, in the ripe hours balanced on the knife's edge between darkness and dawning. Those perfect hours, when all about him slept.

Even the skitter of mice in the long grass, the squeak of bats overhead, the soft hoot of owls . . . even those sounds had faded away as all the woodland creatures went off to sleep, to hide, to mate . . . to celebrate another night of life before the rising of the sun.

But he was awake, and so was this other, the one who was his friend, his brother, his closest male companion. The one he loved above all other men. The one who called to him now.

"Anton? Over here."

Anton Cheval slowly turned in the direction of the soft call and blinked as Stefan Aragat rose to two feet. Despite the darkness, Anton saw his smile. Thank the Goddess for a man who smiled, even when all about them seemed so . . . what? How could it be, that he felt so dissatisfied?

Life was good. All was well, and yet . . .

Shifting, standing as a man beside his lover, Anton chuckled. "You couldn't sleep, either?"

Stefan shook his head, ran long fingers through dark hair threaded with silver, and sighed dramatically. "Teething is the bane of parenthood." His familiar dry sense of humor eased some of the odd tension stringing Anton tight as a bow.

"I did my fatherly duty," Stef said, placing his right hand over his heart. "I spelled Xandi the first half of the night, but it's her turn. She's on kid duty now, praise the Goddess!"

Anton flashed him an understanding grin as he stepped over the low-growing willows. "Lucia was fussing, too. I waited until she fell asleep. Unfortunately, Keisha was nursing her when they both drifted off. There wasn't much room left in the bed."

"There was always plenty of room for four adults." Stefan laughed and hooked his arm around Anton's neck. "How is it a single woman and a three-month-old can take up the entire bed?"

Silence stretched between them for a long count as Anton thought about the statement Stefan had made in jest. "So much has changed," he said, unsure if it was a good or bad thing. He leaned into Stef's casual embrace and stared toward the east, searching for the coming dawn. Was that a faint glow between the trees? No. Not yet. He glanced at Stef. "It's all good, I think, all these changes, but . . ."

Stefan's amber eyes twinkled. "But you're dissatisfied. I can feel it. What's wrong, my friend? Everything is as it should be. The pack is growing with so many new babies. We've gone a full five years without an attack, a kidnapping, an assault of any kind against any one of us. . . ."

"Not since the assassination attempt." Anton shoved his tangled hair back from his eyes, remembering. Those hectic months following the attempt on the president's life had ended with lengthy prison sentences meted out to their worst enemies. There were still plenty of bad guys out there, but at least none were focused on controlling or destroying Chanku.

Their secret was still safe. With Nick and Beth Barden continuing as private security for the First Family—at least until the president's second term ended—they certainly had powerful friends in high places.

"So, what's the problem? It's not like you to go searching for trouble." Stefan planted both hands on Anton's shoulders and stared solemnly at him. There was no teasing now, no sense of humor. Merely concern. Loving concern.

Feeling a little foolish, Anton slowly shook his head. "I don't know." He shrugged. "Maybe things are too good, too settled. I have a strong sense of change in the air, as if something is going to happen. No reason for it. We're all healthy; our children are growing." He smiled. "Our numbers are growing, that's for sure. I never once imagined myself as a husband, much less a father of four."

"You're not the only one. At least I think Xandi's happy with our three. I hope."

Anton raised an eyebrow. "I believe Ariel counts as two."

"That's sort of what Xandi and I think. She's made Alex look like the world's easiest baby." Stefan chuckled. "So why the dissatisfaction? Our once cozy foursome of known Chanku now numbers fifty-six, a number that will be growing quickly with Liana, Jazzy, Tala, and Daci expecting. No one's tried to kill us in the past five years." He raised one expressive eyebrow. "In case you're wondering, that's a good thing. You've completed purchase of over half a million acres adjoining this property, and the economy has the bank accounts smiling. Anton, my friend, only you could find something wrong with so much that's good."

Again Anton shrugged. He wished the sense of foreboding would leave him, but he'd learned to listen to his premonitions. Still, he hated to worry Stefan. He wasn't about to let Keisha in on his fears, either, not until or unless they actually proved valid.

"You know me," he said, feeling just a little bit foolish. "I'm never happy unless I'm worried about something." He laughed. "I imagine it has to do with control issues. If I can't identify it, I can't be in charge."

Stefan chuckled, but he kept his comments to himself. That alone got him a raised eyebrow from Anton, but he disliked a sense of something waiting when he didn't know what to expect. "It's odd. Nothing I can put a finger on, but I have the strangest sense that things are about to change. I can't explain it, but I'm afraid to ignore it."

Stefan leaned his forehead against Anton's. "Aren't you the one who told me change is good?"

Keisha stood in the doorway and smiled at Anton. They'd run as wolves and grabbed quick showers. The baby was sleeping, the older kids watching a movie, and they were alone. For now. He waited impatiently in their bed as she leaned against the door frame and stretched one arm overhead, brushing her free hand down over her thigh, parting the shimmering fabric to display one long, dark, sleek leg.

Immediately his body hardened, and he was ready for her as he was always ready, wanting her with a need that was almost painful in its intensity.

Then she blew it.

Keisha managed to hold the seductive pose for a good five seconds before bursting into giggles. "Sex queens are us. C'mon, Anton. You're supposed to be impressed. Not bad for forty-two, eh, big guy?"

"Not even bad for twenty-five." Stefan grabbed Keisha from behind and whispered, "Happy birthday, Keish!" She squealed with surprise and laughter as he planted a sloppy, wet kiss on the back of her neck. His mate, Xandi, slipped past them and flopped down on the bed beside Anton.

"Happy birthday, sweetie." Xandi held up a bottle of chilled wine.

"What's this?" Keisha glanced over her shoulder at Stef's twinkling eyes and then sauntered across the floor to the bed. "Where are your kids?"

"With yours." Laughing, Xandi punched Anton lightly on the shoulder. "You didn't tell her, did you? I'm impressed! You actually kept our secret. We got Jazzy and Mei to watch the babies while Oliver and Logan take the big kids to the new Disney movie and then out for ice cream."

"After which," Stefan added, sounding awfully smug for a guy who hadn't made any of the arrangements himself, "they are camping out in the backyard in a tent. We will, of course, owe them child care for the next twenty years."

Keisha glanced at Anton. "You knew this and didn't tell me? How'd you ever manage that?"

He shrugged, almost embarrassed to admit how much he wanted this time for all of them—how much he wanted Keisha to understand how he'd missed this. As he spoke, he opened his mind to her, showed her how much he loved her, how much he needed this night where all of them could step back to what they'd once had. "I wanted it to be a surprise, and I didn't want you fretting over details." He reached for her hands, took both of them in his, and gently squeezed. "It's been a long time since we all got together without rug rats underfoot. I've missed time with you. With all of us together."

The interlude in the forest with Stefan had reminded him of what they'd so easily taken for granted for so many years. Maybe this was all that was missing. Time as adults. He could only hope. Keisha's smile spread so wide he thought he'd burst with the sense of having chosen correctly, at least as far as birthday gifts went.

"It has been too long. And I'm not wasting a second." She slipped the silky fabric over her shoulders and let it fall to the floor in a puddle of teal blue silk. In spite of her bravado, he sensed her worry, that her body might not be quite as firm after her fourth child, that the others might not find her as appealing.

"You're wrong, you know." The words slipped out before he even considered the fact he'd invaded her private thoughts. "You're more beautiful now than ever before."

She blinked rapidly, and he hoped he hadn't made her cry. That wasn't what he had wanted at all. Then she slid across the smooth sheets, reached Anton first, and kissed him soundly. Before he could deepen the kiss further, she turned and gave Stefan a quick kiss, but she saved the last for Xandi.

He savored her joy in this long, deep kiss with the woman she loved. Heard her thoughts, open to all of them now. It had been much too long since they'd kissed one another with passion in mind. Too long since they had been together without either having a baby slung on one hip.

He noticed Xandi had braided her hair—dozens of tiny braids falling in auburn perfection, each one tipped with a colored glass or wooden bead, and it reminded him of an earlier time, when they'd all been new to this now familiar reality, new to the world of Chanku.

The memories were fresh in Keisha's eyes as she lifted a handful of Xandi's braids in her palm. They clattered softly, beads bouncing off one another, sparking old and treasured memories that she shared with both men.

Arousing, sensual memories with graphic images filled all their thoughts, images so clear they were almost tactile.

"Remember our first time?" she asked, and while she spoke directly to Xandi, the words were obviously meant for both Anton and Stefan as well. "Remember when I was so damned scared, so afraid to be touched, and you made love to me? Your hair was braided, just like this." She ran her fingers through the tiny braids. "I remember thinking those beads felt like dozens of tiny fingers trailing across my skin. When you swept your hair across my breasts, I almost came, just from that alone. It was such an amazing time. The first time, ever in my entire life, that I had sex with a woman, that I climaxed with a woman. That experience took away so much of my fear."

"Do I remember? Are you kidding? You spanked me!" Xandi laughed. "How could I forget that? You tied me to the bed and spanked my butt, and you got me so turned on I was practically screaming." Muttering in mock outrage, she added, "Telling me I had to address you as the alpha bitch. You wouldn't let me come for the longest time."

"Yeah, but when I did, I did you right." Keisha wrapped her fingers around the back of Xandi's neck and pulled her close for another kiss.

Anton tapped her shoulder. "Whoa, ladies. Wait a minute. I want more details. Did you ever tell us about tying Xandi to the bed? Why don't I recall that part of the story?" He glanced over his shoulder at Stefan. "Why is it, with these two, you and I are always the ones in restraints?"

Stefan shook his head. "I'm not sure, but don't you think we need to do something about that terribly unfair and sexist dynamic?"

Anton nodded. "I do." He glanced again at Stefan, carefully keeping his mind shuttered and his thoughts hidden from Keisha. He knew she was still wondering about those shielded thoughts when he pounced. She'd barely let out a shriek when he flattened her to the bed, holding her down with the weight of his body.

Anton awoke in darkness. Body sated, mind moderately relaxed, he lay in the tangle of arms and legs and ran a silent inventory of what body parts belonged to which of his lovers.

Xandi's arms were wrapped around his lower legs, and Keisha's cheek rested on his thigh. That had to be Stefan's head on his belly—he recognized the stubble from a day's growth of beard. Anton lay quietly, thinking of the night past, of the joy they'd all taken in this very special time with one another.

Still, the restlessness remained. He couldn't attribute the subtle sense of something undone, of change looming, to anything in particular. He'd wondered if he might be frustrated by the changes in their lives with so many children— Keisha certainly hadn't planned on twins, but Gabe and Mac were identical, and that single egg had split all on its own. Lucia had come along when Keisha had suddenly realized her boys were no longer babies, that Lily—already an old soul—was growing up faster than she'd expected.

Anton hoped she no longer felt guilty about her unplanned pregnancy with Lucia. She'd released an egg without actually discussing it with him, thank goodness. Lucia was already proving to be a treasure, one they might not have had if he'd allowed his practical nature to interfere with Keisha's powerful need to mother.

Still, four children meant so little time alone together.

So little time like this past evening, making love. Playing grown-up games as if they had all the time in the world.

Keisha stretched and shifted her position until she lay alongside him. She ran her fingers through his tangled hair. *Thank you for last night. This feels so good, just lying here without anyone depending on us. Without anyone needing anything.*

It does. He nuzzled his cheek against her breasts, now swollen with milk, and sighed. She'd need to leave soon and feed Lucia. He'd heard her get up once during the night, but already it was time again.

Something troubles you, my love. What is it? Everything is so good right now. What can possibly be worrying you?

Her question interrupted his convoluted thoughts, but for some reason, knowing Keisha worried helped him focus his concerns, and it came to him, then. So clearly he couldn't believe he'd not realized before what was wrong with their lives. What they were all missing.

Don't laugh when I tell you. It's the fact that everything is so good. He rolled his head to one side and smiled sheepishly at her. *I worry that we've grown complacent, that we've adjusted so completely to our lives as Chanku that we've settled into a routine. Routines frighten me. Complacency is dangerous.*

Stefan rolled slowly to a sitting position. "Sorry," he said, stretching. "I was eavesdropping without shame."

Xandi sat up and leaned against the headboard. "Sweetheart, your middle name is shameless. So what's this about complacency, and why are we all awake? It's barely dawn."

Anton sat up and crossed his legs. He pulled Keisha into his lap and grinned at Stef and Xandi. All of them awake and sitting on the big, rumpled bed, hair in disarray, bodies damp from sweat and hours of sex. It reminded him of those first early months before Lily and Alex were born, when they'd made love every night, when all of this had been so fresh and new.

"Stef and I talked about this a while back," he said. "The fact we're all healthy, the children are healthy. We've gone five years now without an attack or any threats to our safety. Our lives are as close to perfect as I'd ever imagined, but this perfection reminds me that we've forgotten something important."

He wrapped his fingers around Keisha's hand and squeezed. "What if I hadn't found you? What if Stef hadn't rescued Xandi, or Oliver hadn't found Adam walking along that road? If Mik and AJ hadn't stopped in that little bar in New Mexico and saved Tala, or Baylor hadn't gone in search of the wolf girl and ended up with Manda? Stef? Remember how we used to argue about coincidence versus fate? I still believe in fate, but I think we need to help it along, not wait complacently for fate to happen to us. I've been thinking of all the others, the Chanku out there who don't know who or what they are. The desperation in their lives. The unfulfilled destinies of people just like us, who don't know they're like us. Who haven't got a clue what their lives could be."

Stefan grabbed Xandi's hand and lifted her fingers to his lips for a quick kiss. "I would have no life without Alexandria Olanet as my mate, as my wife. None at all." He turned to her and rested his palms on her shoulders, touched his forehead to hers. "Anton's right. We've grown much too comfortable; our lives are fairly well cocooned. But how do we find them? It's not like we can run an ad or spike the water supply with Tibetan grasses."

"No." Anton chuckled. "Though I hadn't thought of the water supply angle. I'm actually thinking more along the lines of talking to Liana, maybe even reaching out to Eve. As an ex-goddess, Liana might be able to help. As our current goddess, Eve could possibly steer us in the right direction."

He raised his head. "All the packs are planning to come for the birth of Adam and Liana's baby next month. Let's see if anyone's got any ideas. We can't be the only ones." He shook his head and tightened his grasp around Keisha's waist. "There are others out there. They have no idea who or what they are. We have to find them."

Keisha squeezed Anton's hand, and he stared into her beautiful amber eyes. They were filled with tears—tears that sparkled on her dark lashes.

"I agree with you, my love. I know we should be look-ing, but it makes me afraid, too." She sighed. One of those errant tears ran down her cheek and trembled against her lips. With a brusque swipe of her fingers, she wiped it away. "I'm sorry, but I keep thinking of that old saying, something about borrowing trouble." She shook her head. "Why do I have a horrible feeling that's exactly what you might be doing?"

A shiver raced over Anton's spine. Without a word, he tightened his hold on Keisha and held her even closer.

Books by Bestselling Author
Fern Michaels

___The Jury	0-8217-7878-1	$6.99US/$9.99CAN
___Sweet Revenge	0-8217-7879-X	$6.99US/$9.99CAN
___Lethal Justice	0-8217-7880-3	$6.99US/$9.99CAN
___Free Fall	0-8217-7881-1	$6.99US/$9.99CAN
___Fool Me Once	0-8217-8071-9	$7.99US/$10.99CAN
___Vegas Rich	0-8217-8112-X	$7.99US/$10.99CAN
___Hide and Seek	1-4201-0184-6	$6.99US/$9.99CAN
___Hokus Pokus	1-4201-0185-4	$6.99US/$9.99CAN
___Fast Track	1-4201-0186-2	$6.99US/$9.99CAN
___Collateral Damage	1-4201-0187-0	$6.99US/$9.99CAN
___Final Justice	1-4201-0188-9	$6.99US/$9.99CAN
___Up Close and Personal	0-8217-7956-7	$7.99US/$9.99CAN
___Under the Radar	1-4201-0683-X	$6.99US/$9.99CAN
___Razor Sharp	1-4201-0684-8	$7.99US/$10.99CAN
___Yesterday	1-4201-1494-8	$5.99US/$6.99CAN
___Vanishing Act	1-4201-0685-6	$7.99US/$10.99CAN
___Sara's Song	1-4201-1493-X	$5.99US/$6.99CAN
___Deadly Deals	1-4201-0686-4	$7.99US/$10.99CAN
___Game Over	1-4201-0687-2	$7.99US/$10.99CAN
___Sins of Omission	1-4201-1153-1	$7.99US/$10.99CAN
___Sins of the Flesh	1-4201-1154-X	$7.99US/$10.99CAN
___Cross Roads	1-4201-1192-2	$7.99US/$10.99CAN

Available Wherever Books Are Sold!
Check out our website at www.kensingtonbooks.com

Romantic Suspense from
Lisa Jackson

See How She Dies	0-8217-7605-3	$6.99US/$9.99CAN
Final Scream	0-8217-7712-2	$7.99US/$10.99CAN
Wishes	0-8217-6309-1	$5.99US/$7.99CAN
Whispers	0-8217-7603-7	$6.99US/$9.99CAN
Twice Kissed	0-8217-6038-6	$5.99US/$7.99CAN
Unspoken	0-8217-6402-0	$6.50US/$8.50CAN
If She Only Knew	0-8217-6708-9	$6.50US/$8.50CAN
Hot Blooded	0-8217-6841-7	$6.99US/$9.99CAN
Cold Blooded	0-8217-6934-0	$6.99US/$9.99CAN
The Night Before	0-8217-6936-7	$6.99US/$9.99CAN
The Morning After	0-8217-7295-3	$6.99US/$9.99CAN
Deep Freeze	0-8217-7296-1	$7.99US/$10.99CAN
Fatal Burn	0-8217-7577-4	$7.99US/$10.99CAN
Shiver	0-8217-7578-2	$7.99US/$10.99CAN
Most Likely to Die	0-8217-7576-6	$7.99US/$10.99CAN
Absolute Fear	0-8217-7936-2	$7.99US/$9.49CAN
Almost Dead	0-8217-7579-0	$7.99US/$10.99CAN
Lost Souls	0-8217-7938-9	$7.99US/$10.99CAN
Left to Die	1-4201-0276-1	$7.99US/$10.99CAN
Wicked Game	1-4201-0338-5	$7.99US/$9.99CAN
Malice	0-8217-7940-0	$7.99US/$9.49CAN

Available Wherever Books Are Sold!
Visit our website at **www.kensingtonbooks.com**

Thrilling Suspense from
Beverly Barton

Available Wherever Books Are Sold!

Visit our website at **www.kensingtonbooks.com**